I0720001

DAVID WILLIAM PEARCE

THE OBJECT OF OUR DESIRE

A MONK BUTTMAN MYSTERY

Black Rose Writing | Texas

©2024 by David William Pearce
All rights reserved. No part of this book may be reproduced, stored in a retrieval system or transmitted in any form or by any means without the prior written permission of the publishers, except by a reviewer who may quote brief passages in a review to be printed in a newspaper, magazine or journal.

The author grants the final approval for this literary material.

First printing

This is a work of fiction. Names, characters, businesses, places, events, and incidents are either the products of the author's imagination or used in a fictitious manner. Any resemblance to actual persons, living or dead, or actual events is purely coincidental.

ISBN: 978-1-68513-378-8
LIBRARY OF CONGRESS CONTROL NUMBER: 2023948137
PUBLISHED BY BLACK ROSE WRITING
www.blackrosewriting.com

Printed in the United States of America
Suggested Retail Price (SRP) $24.95

The Object of Our Desire is printed in Chapparal Pro

*As a planet-friendly publisher, Black Rose Writing does its best to eliminate unnecessary waste to reduce paper usage and energy costs, while never compromising the reading experience. As a result, the final word count vs. page count may not meet common expectations.

By David William Pearce

MONK BUTTMAN MYSTERY SERIES

Where Fools Dare to Tread
A Twinkle in the Eyes of God
Too Many Women, Too Little Time
In the Service of Others
The Fist Inside the Glove

Available from Black Rose Writing

PRAISE FOR

The Object of
Our Desire

"An irreverent, offbeat crime thriller featuring a memorable protagonist and a quirky cast of gangsters."

–Best Thrillers

"Highly recommended to any fans of humor mysteries with a complex cast."

–Sublime Book Review

"...a well-crafted, enjoyable and intriguing mystery..."

–IndieReader

The Object of Our Desire

1

Sterling's wife sat in the chair across from the door.

I sat on the bed.

It was early evening and the room was darkening, save for a thin shaft of light passing through a break in the window curtain splitting the room in two.

Neither of us said anything.

We were waiting for Sterling, my half-brother.

Felicia sat stone-faced. She had called a month earlier. Sterling was spending more time away from her and the kids. She was worried. Moses, my father, was worried too. He had alluded on several occasions to Sterling's increasingly odd behavior. Now Sterling was disappearing for longer than usual. I didn't ask what that meant.

"Moses told me you could help," Felicia explained.

The stories of my running around looking for people had come full circle. Now, I was looking after my own. I tried dumping it in my brother Isaac's lap, but he was taking full advantage of his part in the Manaforte affair and claimed he didn't have time.

"I'll see what I can find," I told Felicia.

What the detective I hired found led us to this building and this small apartment at the edge of Berkeley.

The bright shaft of light methodically crossed the small room before defusing and turning the room a dusty red. Outside the door, we heard voices, muted at first, then growing in volume and clarity.

Sterling's voice echoed in the outer hall. "Show it to me."

"You can't wait till we're inside?" Another voice asked.

"No, I want to see it now..."

A loud thump reverberated through the room as they hit the other side of the door. The voices produced only grunts and moans and the sounds of two people pushing and sliding against one another.

The door burst open with Sterling and the woman intertwined. The erection was visible under the woman's dress. They made it nearly to me before realizing they were not alone. The woman let go of Sterling and moved towards the door.

Felicia stood up. "Sterling!"

I did as well.

Sterling stared at us, uncomprehending, his eyes darting between his wife and the woman at the door. "No. Don't go," he said to her.

I went around Sterling, heading him off. "You have things to discuss with your wife. I'll make sure your friend makes it home."

The woman backed into the door. Fear colored her eyes as she tried to make sense of the situation. To me, it seemed straightforward enough.

Sterling stepped towards the woman and me. "Please don't go—"

"Sterling," Felicia shouted.

"You can't make me," he shouted back.

"And you can't run away from this," I said.

Sterling glared at me. His eyes shifted to the woman at the door. Tears began to form, and he tried to speak. Nothing came out. He put his hands to his face and began weeping, filling the small room with his sobs.

Felicia remained stone-faced. "Sit down, Sterling." She directed him to the bed before looking at me. "Would you please leave us alone?"

I nodded and opened the door. "Come with me," I said to the woman.

We left to the sounds of a grown man crying.

The woman hesitated once I closed the door. "Where do you expect me to go? This is where I live," she sputtered as she followed me down the stairs to the building's entry.

"There's a place to eat across the street. I'm hungry."

"You expect me to just go with you? Who the fuck are you?" she demanded.

I smiled at that. "You can take off if you like. I'm not holding you. But if this is where you live and... Well, I guess you can call the cops." I looked up at the stairs. "I don't know how long they'll be in there and I'm hungry. If you're interested, you can join me. If you're not, you're not."

I opened the building's entry door. We stepped out into the crowd of people coming and going along the sidewalk.

I looked at the woman. She was a light-skinned black woman, a few inches shorter than me, heels and all, with dark hair that she wore loose, so it fell on her shoulders. Her eyes were a soft brown highlighted with blue mascara. The erection was gone.

"My name is Monk. Sterling is my brother." I noted the confusion on her face. "You asked who the fuck I was."

The confused look morphed into a more knowing one. "Yes, I did."

We stood on the sidewalk. People walked by, occasionally glancing at the woman beside me.

"What's your name?" I asked, though from the investigator's report I already had a name.

"Aisha."

I pointed to the restaurant across the street. "Well?"

Aisha looked at me, then the restaurant, before following me across the street. Once inside, we were taken to a table in the back. Aisha kept her head down. I took the chair that allowed me a view of the entrance and the people around us. The incident in Michigan continued to haunt me even though nearly a year had passed, but that's what you get when you don't pay attention, when you let your guard down. I thought of Josef. What would he think? I should ask him when I got back.

Aisha fiddled with her purse, her shoulders hunched, like she was trying to be smaller, less noticeable. I ordered a whiskey, Aisha a daiquiri.

"Is this what you do, Monk, spy on people?" she asked.

"Apparently."

Aisha grimaced at that. "You think this is funny?"

"Do you?"

Our drinks arrived. I ordered the split pea soup and a salad with bleu cheese. Aisha ordered a veggie burger with sweet potato fries. It was a perfectly ordinary meal between a spy and his brother's lover. Little was said.

Midway through the meal, I spied Sterling and Felicia leaving Aisha's building. Sterling had his hands in his pockets and his head down. Felicia, walking in front of Sterling, her expression still tight and angry, stared straight ahead.

"You can go home now," I told my dining partner. "They've left."

Aisha turned around, craning her neck. Sterling and Felicia were out of sight.

"Any reason I should stay?" She gathered her purse.

"No."

She got up and weaved her way through the tables until she was free of us.

I finished eating and paid the bill. It had been a long day and there was still the drive back to LA.

Aisha stood in the doorway of her building as I left.

2

"Gamps!"

Zachary Montaigne, born Zachary Bohrman before being adopted by Fidel Montaigne, and whose biological father was a mystery, was not a happy camper. He stood before me, his arms crossed, and his demeanor stern. For a five-year-old, he had become quite demanding.

Agnes, my devoted wife, was standing in the kitchen smiling. Lizzy, standing just behind Agnes, was smiling too. Lizzy was Zach's little sister. Jacob, their brother, and the newest member of the Montaigne family, was the reason Zach and Lizzy were here. Unlike Zach and Lizzy, Jacob was not consistently sleeping through the night, though he was more than seven months old. Their mother, Rebekah, my perpetually pregnant daughter, was exhausted. Consequently, Agnes and I were on kid patrol.

"Is there a problem?" I inquired of my petulant grandson.

"You promised," he said in a crisp, tight tone.

"Promised what?"

"It's big pool day, Gamps! You promised."

"Did I?" I was certain I hadn't.

"Yes, you did!" He was certain I had.

"Didn't we just go to the beach yesterday?" I looked at Agnes, who continued to smile at me and the stern Zachary Montaigne.

"That was yesterday, Gamps."

"Are you sure?"

"Gamps!" I noted the exasperation in his voice. My baiting of the stern five-year-old was having its intended effect.

I peered at my amused wife. "What do you think, my love?"

"Well, you did promise," she said, which brought a smug look of satisfaction to Zach.

"See," he harrumphed.

"Was I drunk?" I asked. Agnes shook her head no. "Is there any way I can weasel out of this?" Agnes again shook her head no. I had one last card up my sleeve. "This is a plot, isn't it?" I was certain it was.

"Let's go, Buttman," she said, still smiling.

I sighed as Zachary Montaigne stood there in triumph.

· · · · ·

Southern California, and Beverly Hills in particular, can be quite nice when you have no real problems, certainly where money is concerned, and today was no exception. The sun was in no more of a hurry than I was as it drifted lazily across the sky. While Zach and Lizzy made use of the infinity pool Judith Delashay had installed at the beautiful house she left me after she died, I sat in the shade with a cool glass of ice tea and the latest financial report left by my chief of staff, or whatever her title was this week, Natalya Constantinescu. She had thoughtfully dropped it off at the house the day before while I was at the beach avoiding her. It's not that I had any reason to avoid her personally—she was a rather droll young woman with a sharp wit—it's just that I had no interest in all the doings of Sunshine Holdings LLC.

Agnes chided me for my ambivalence. "You do this every time," she said. "Just read it."

"Why don't you read it?"

"How much will you pay me, Mr. Big Bucks?"

"How much am I paying you now?" I smirked.

"Not enough." She lifted her sunglasses just enough for me to get the message. "And be very careful with the next smartassed remark you make."

"Or what?"

"Or I may not be so understanding in the future, that's what."

"Sounds like an empty threat," I said mockingly.

Agnes Duquesne laughed. "What's your point?"

"Exactly." I gave a quick thought to mentioning that Monika Danalek was back on the prowl, but I'd been warned and decided to save that little tidbit for another time. I knew better than to poke the bear too many times.

Lizzy and Zach spent the afternoon splashing and annoying each other while Agnes napped, and I, more or less, went over the reports. Apparently, there would be enough money for the next day and many thousands after that. Even after giving a sizeable chunk of it to the endowment in my dead brother's name; the brother after whom my newest grandson was named, there was still a boatload of money left.

It all seemed rather pointless.

The phone rang as I was wallowing in my own particular brand of self-pity over having far more money and responsibility than I, or anyone else I knew, should have.

It was my attorney, Taylor Lagenfelder.

"Yes?" I answered.

"The FBI would like to talk to you, Mr. Buttman," she informed me.

"Would they?"

"They would. And to answer your next question, it has to do with some of your recent activities with a certain Russian oligarch. They would like both you and Agnes to be present. Any objections?" I noted the seriousness in her voice.

"Not that I can think of. Where would they like to have this talk?"

"Here at the office, if it's convenient."

"Alright. Let me know when. Should I say thanks?" I asked.

"Perhaps. It might be advisable that we have a brief meeting prior to," she added. "Should I alert Mr. Durant?"

"Perhaps."

"I'll let him know. Goodbye, Mr. Buttman."

"Goodbye."

Agnes was eyeing me as I put the phone down. "Trouble?"

"The FBI wants to talk to us," I told her.

"Again?" was all she said.

"That was off the record."

Having the phone in my hand, I rang up my daughter to determine whether Agnes and I would have to entertain the grandkids further. I knew the answer, but preferred a verbal confirmation.

"I know it's a lot to ask, but Fidel's exhausted after three straight nights working, and Jacob has finally pooped out. You guys wouldn't mind taking care of them till tomorrow?" she asked in a rather pleading voice.

I looked at Agnes, who shrugged and smiled. "We don't mind. Get some sleep."

"Thanks," she said, and I was left with another languid evening to contemplate here in my rich man's paradise.

No one seemed to mind.

I ordered pizza from Tomassa's because I liked to spoil my beautiful wife and it turns out the kids liked it too. "You know they're only going to expect this the more we do it," I chided Agnes instead of myself.

Agnes grinned while chewing a big bite. "You love it as much as I do, Buttman," she said after swallowing.

"Yeah, Gamps." Zach added his two cents.

"Uh-huh," I answered.

At dinner, Lizzy was busy picking her slice apart. She had developed the bizarre habit of eating her food only after first disassembling it. It was disconcerting early on as she seemed to be rather finicky, but once disassembled, she would then finish her meal. I watched her carefully remove the pepperoni, the sausage, and the cheese, which she ate individually. She left the crust for last.

"Don't you think it would be better together, Lizzy?" I had to ask.

She regarded me with a puzzled look. "No," she said, after giving it a moment.

Both Agnes and Zach thought that was funny.

After dinner I read them a children's version of a story about a crazy guy chasing a whale to the detriment of everyone around him. They thought he was crazy, too. They were then shuffled off to bed.

"It's beautiful tonight, isn't it, Monk?" Agnes was sitting close to me on the divan by the pool, a glass of wine in her hand.

"It is, much like you, my love." I leaned in and kissed Agnes' cabernet flavored lips.

Agnes scooted closer. "Does that mean someone's in the mood?"

I moved my lips to her ear and her neck, brushing away the hair. "I believe it does."

"Then I think we should move this party to the bedroom," she said, before kissing me more passionately.

Who was I to say no?

.   .   .   .   .

I woke the next morning to find Agnes running her fingers along my ear. "Morning, Sunshine. Did you get some sleep?"

"I did."

"I had a really good time last night. I hope you won't make me wait so long till next time," she said. Her hand made its way to my thigh and was slowly caressing it.

"Me neither," I assured her.

"Are you busy now?" she cooed. We both noted the erection as she continued to run her hand along my thigh.

"Can I use the bathroom real quick?" Sadly, nature was calling.

"So long as you come back quickly."

"I can do that," I assured her.

Round two was as pleasant as the first. I had no good reason for avoiding sex, other than I wasn't actually avoiding it. It simply didn't seem very important anymore. But that wasn't it, either. It was something I hadn't expected, something I'd run into that hurt more than I wanted to admit. Mostly, it was that goddamned business with Sterling and Aisha.

It fucked me up, no pun intended.

Much as I tried, I couldn't forget it.

Couldn't forget Orestra Blakely's murder.

3

It was late morning, and I was at the office.

"There's a woman here to see you, Mr. Monk." Natalya was standing by the fancy desk in the fancy office I rarely used at the headquarters of the Jacob Bohrman Veterans Service Foundation. It also was home to Sunshine Holdings LLC.

I had come in for no other reason than I felt duty-bound to stop by periodically. That way, Natalya wouldn't become too great a megalomaniac in my absence. "Anyone I know?"

A smirk crossed her delightful face. "You tell me, Mr. Monk." Natalya, due to her history with the repulsive Big Mike Kovalenko, was well acquainted with the seamier side of life, and had an attuned sense of when people were playing a role. Evidently, this woman waiting was.

"Then you should send her in," I said.

Aisha Diamond walked in, eyeing both me and Natalya. It had been three months since I'd received the aggrieved call from Felicia that led to the apartment in Berkeley and Sterling's transgendered lover. She was dressed in a flowing sleeveless blouse of washed-out purples and whites atop lavender slacks. Her hair was cut in a long bob with its own lavender streaks. Natalya smiled before closing the door. I motioned for Aisha to sit down.

"What brings you to my door?" I asked as she slowly took her seat.

"What do you think?"

"I try not to. Saves me from foolish assumptions." My assumption was something to do with Sterling. I wasn't convinced he was staying away from her as he had promised Felicia.

Aisha Diamond sat there staring both at me and the view behind me that looked to the west and the shimmering Pacific.

"It's quite a view, isn't it?" I turned to the sunny California day on the other side of the glass.

"You have quite a life here, Mr. Buttman."

"I try not to complain. What can I do for you, Ms. Diamond?"

"I want you to tell Sterling that I'm ok, that I'll be ok, and he doesn't need to worry about me," she said while continuing to admire the Pacific.

"Has he been asking after you?"

Aisha tightened her eyes and curled her lips. "Yes. And before you inquire further, I know he's supposed to forget about me, but love is a powerful emotion, Mr. Buttman..." She smiled at that. "You probably think that's wrong, don't you?" Her eyes had grown tighter still.

"No, and before you assume, this isn't about what I think. I would have preferred to have had nothing to do with it. I didn't consider it my business then, and I don't consider it my business now. It was his decision," I said, knowing that wasn't true.

"And it's better for him to be with his normal family than with someone like me, right?" Her voice had grown tighter, too.

"How would I know? And besides, it's not my fight. Sterling's not a child, though he sometimes acts like one. If it was that important and he had the courage to leave his family, he would have. Maybe for him it isn't love so much as exciting or exotic." I didn't actually know.

"Did he say that?"

"Not directly," I lied.

Aisha laughed, but it too was tight. "So, I'm just an exotic fuck to you, Mr. Buttman."

"I wouldn't know."

Aisha Diamond stood. She took a tissue from her purse and dabbed at her eyes, which had grown shiny and wet. "You'll see he gets the message?"

"I will."

I got up and showed her to the door. Natalya and I watched her leave the office.

Natalya followed me back into my fancy office. "Who's your friend, Mr. Monk?"

"Why do you ask, Natalya?" My chief of staff was grinning at me. "It's not what you think. Remember when I had to go up north three months ago?"

"You go up north many times," she said, continuing to grin.

"I suppose I do, but this was me alone..." I shook my head at her smarmy grin. "It was the thing with Sterling."

"Oh," she said.

"Yes. Don't you have something to do?"

"I like to stay busy, Mr. Monk, you know that." The grin seemed to be permanent.

"Yes. How is Xavier these days?" I hadn't heard from Xavier Dunkle II since we'd returned from Michigan eight months before.

The grin slipped away. "I don't know. Maybe he's found someone new? Would you like me to call him?"

Xavier's gone? "Yes, see if you can raise him," I said.

"Ok."

The rest of the afternoon was a familiar ritual of Natalya bringing in reports, papers to sign, and peppering me with questions concerning the future. Isaac Bohrman, our erstwhile frontman, and my younger brother, was due back in town in a couple of days. Natalya decided it was time for a proper meeting once he was back. She would also arrange for our moneyman, Carson Macklgrew, to join us.

"Sounds like a plan," I said. It was time for me to head back to Agnes and West Covina.

"Don't forget about the gala on Saturday, Mr. Monk." Gala? Natalya noticed my befuddlement. "At Ms. DuBare's gallery," she said. Ah, yes, Ms. Brigitte DuBare, Natalya Constantinescu's mentor.

"How is our delightful Ms. DuBare?"

"Delightful," my chief of staff assured me. Everyone's delightful today.

Will I be seeing you on Saturday?" I asked.

She frowned at that. "Of course, Mr. Monk. And don't forget Agnes, she's invited too." More reminders; was I really that bad?

"Yes, dear."

Natalya laughed at that.

· · · · ·

Agnes and the grandkids were in the backyard making noise and merriment.

"Let me guess," I said to no one in particular, "someone isn't sleeping, causing others not to sleep, causing us to spend our time watching the kids."

"What's this *us* business, Buttman?" Agnes snarked.

I laughed at that. "My apologies, beautiful."

Zach and Lizzy took two seconds to see who was talking before returning to their own interests. Zach was in the dinky pool I forced upon him because I'm mean and wouldn't let him live in the pool at the big house or in the ocean. Lizzy was playing with the dollhouse I bought for her at the garage sale down the street.

"You're worth how many millions and you buy her something used?" Agnes said, trying to get my goat when I bought it.

"It's perfectly serviceable and toys need to be loved by new generations of kids. Didn't you hear the cowboy in that toy movie? Besides, Lizzy seems perfectly happy with what she has, an attitude you might try embracing." I was trying to get hers.

My devoted wife laughed. "You're a jerk, Buttman."

"I prefer delightful," I said.

"I'm sure you do, and to answer your question, yes, Rebekah asked if we could give her a break. Apparently, Jacob isn't sleeping through the night, and with Fidel on night patrol with his film company, she's out of gas."

"I'm not surprised. But I'd like to point out that I did mention to my baby-happy daughter that more kids don't necessarily translate into more fun." I sat down in the lawn chair next to Agnes.

"Yes, it's true. No one listens to poor know-it-all Monk," Agnes chided.

"I only do it for their benefit," I said, knowingly.

"And yet they continue to ignore you. How terrible." At least she was smiling.

"It's my cross to bear," I admitted.

Zach, bored, decided it was time to splash his sister. Lizzy, frowning, picked up the dollhouse and took it to the other side of the yard. Zach scooped up a pail of water and gave every indication he was ready to douse Lizzy for big laughs. Agnes cleared her throat loudly. Zach looked at me.

"I wouldn't do that, little dude, unless you want to spend the rest of the afternoon in a timeout," I said.

The little dude frowned and poured the water back into the pool. Lizzy stuck her tongue out at her brother.

The afternoon came and went. I cooked a portable dinner because Agnes felt we should feed Rebekah along with ourselves and the grandkids.

"I'm not finding this to be the good life I assumed my millions would provide," I whined.

"We could always order a pizza, or, Mr. Moneybags, you could hire a chef to cook for us, since you like to work yourself into a huff whenever I suggest we order pizza." Agnes was on a roll.

"Yeah, Gamps!" Zach shouted from his chair. He was in a timeout for hassling his sister.

"Quiet, Zach!" Lizzy shouted, added her two cents.

Zach frowned at us.

"Alright, now that everyone has had their say, let's load up the war wagon and head on out." I put the chicken in a container.

Agnes, who was in charge of the sides, brought over the picnic basket, and we filled it with our delectable dinner. Five minutes later, we were entering the home of my stressed-out daughter who lived down the street.

"We're here to save you from yourself," I told her.

"Not in the mood, Dad."

"That's not what I heard." I pointed at the two kids at my feet and the one in her arms.

"Monk!" Agnes acted shocked.

"Then here, Mr. Know-it-all!" Rebekah held the fussy Jacob just under my nose. Jacob squirmed and pinched his face.

"Fine." I handed the basket to Agnes and took Jacob in my arms. He was a little more than six months old, and looked nothing like the late Jacob Bohrman, his namesake. On the plus side, he was gaining weight and plumping out. He had bright blue eyes than shone like the stars, wispy blond hair, and a miserable attitude. He didn't like anybody but me.

I took incredible delight in that.

Rebekah frowned and furrowed her exhausted brow as Jacob immediately calmed down. Within minutes, he was fast asleep.

"It's a gift," I said, humbly, but not really.

"It's because you're so delightful, Buttman." Agnes kissed my forehead.

I retired to the couch as Agnes and Rebekah organized the dinner table, the highchairs, and the food. Once the food was doled out, I carefully moved from the couch to the table. Jacob blissfully slept through dinner as Rebekah continued to frown.

"Maybe I should just give him to you," she snorted.

"No can do, Becks. Besides, you of all people should know that this is all part of God's great plan." I winked for effect, which made Zach and Lizzy laugh.

"Don't encourage them, Dad!"

"I don't know what you're talking about," I said mischievously. "So why isn't Fidel at home helping? I thought he hired three new people and they would be doing all these crumby night shoots?"

"He did, but he said he needs to get them up to speed, so he's been working extra hours," she groused.

"And miss all this fun? Such dedication!"

Agnes smacked me for that. "Be nice, Buttman!" she demanded.

"Yeah, Dad!"

"Yeah, Gamps!" Mr. Timeout had to have his say.

"You're already on double secret probation, little dude," I cautioned him. "I'd hate to have to ban you from the big pool for a month. Know what I'm saying?"

"That's not fair," he grumbled, before he stuck out his tongue.

"Life's not fair," I said.

"Looks who talking," Agnes laughed.

"That's beside the point. Anyway, I'm not the best example."

"You got that right," Rebekah snorted.

"Careful," I warned her. "Might wake the baby." I smiled broadly at her.

"Then it's best if you take your know-it-all ass back to the couch!" she said, pointing in the couch's direction.

"Fine. We don't need you jerks, anyway." I nuzzled the sleeping Jacob. "Right, little dude number two?"

Rebekah continued pointing. I shrugged and returned to the couch. The dinner and the softly breathing Jacob quickly put me to sleep. The others must have gone downstairs because Jacob and I were alone when he woke me. My watch indicated three hours had passed. I got up and warmed the baby bottle I took out of the fridge. Jacob watched in rapt attention. I cradled him in my lap and fed him the bottle.

"I don't think you should hassle your mother so much. Remember, it's not a good idea to push a gag too far, know what I mean?" I touched the tip of his nose as he sucked on the bottle. His eyes continued watching my finger as I continued to touch his nose. "She's not as much fun when she's cranky."

"Very nice."

I turned to see Rebekah standing off to my left. "I'm doing what I can to help, my dear."

She came over and sat in the chair next to me. I was at the small table in the kitchen. "He really likes you," she said as Jacob finished his bottle and I set him on my shoulder to burp him. "That's the first time I've seen him finish his bottle. He doesn't even do that for Fidel."

"Is that true, Jake?" I grinned at him. Jake burped and spilled a small portion of his formula on the front of his bib. I wiped his cute, plump face. "Finally, someone who truly gets me." I kissed his forehead, which made him smile.

"And you only had to wait forty-seven years," she smirked.

"Good things come to those who wait."

"Uh-huh." She didn't seem convinced.

"Be thankful I have this unbelievable talent, otherwise you might never get any sleep." I smiled at Jacob, who was watching his mother and me. "Isn't that right, little dude number two?"

Rebekah shook her head. "I don't know that I like you calling the boys 'little dudes.'"

"No?"

"No. You're hardly a surfer dude with the suits and all."

"So, you're thinking I should start wearing long shorts and tees and grow out my hair?" I said with my best surfer dude 'tude.

"I don't know why I bother talking to you?" she sighed. I could tell she was stifling a smile.

"No?"

She lost it and smiled. "No."

That made me smile.

4

The gala at the DuBare Gallery was, as I found all of these events Natalya dragged me to, tedious. After the usual introductions and niceties, she dutifully led Agnes and me across the gallery, explaining the art and adding her critical analysis. I had almost lost the will to live when I noticed Xavier Dunkle II in the corner of the room. He waved me over.

"Cover for me," I said to a less than happy Agnes.

"Not too long, Mr. Monk," admonished Natalya, though with a smile which she passed along to the skulking Xavier.

"Well, well," I said, "if it isn't our recluse. What brings you out into the sun?"

Dunkle frowned. "You had Natalya badger me; you know that!"

I laughed as I took him in. I hadn't seen him since he warned me of the coming storm that Ashley Carmichael had unwittingly unleashed, or so Dunkle believed. He was convinced his uncle Seymour had been "taken out" by the killer Aaron Alan Sobeski at the urging of Delton Manaforte, the billionaire longing for a more organized and logical world order. Xavier's face was haggard and his shoulders slumped, but other than that, he looked quite good, having apparently spent his idle time exercising and eating right.

"I was merely concerned for your welfare," I assured him.

"Uh-huh." His eyes darted through the rambling crowd.

"Are they after you?" I took in the crowd.

"You never know."

I laughed at that. "Really? This bunch?"

Dunkle scrunched his forehead.

I noticed a familiar figure sashay into an adjoining room. She was still as gorgeous as I remembered her. I looked back at Dunkle.

"You think this is all over, don't you?" He asked.

"Why shouldn't I?"

His eyes continued to focus on mine. "Because it's not finished. They're all still out there," he said.

"And?"

"And that means we need to be careful."

"Of what?"

"Of ending up dead." He was one nervous dude.

"There's no benefit to bumping us all off. Besides, in the grand scheme of things, I'm still just a nobody. Even with all the money Judith dumped in my lap, I'm nowhere near the top of America's, much less the world's, wealthiest. Don't let all the conspiracy talk get to you."

Xavier Dunkle shook his head. "It's because you're a nobody that bumping you off, or me for that matter, wouldn't raise an eyebrow or any genuine concern. Who gives a fuck about any of us anymore?"

I sighed. "Who gave a fuck about us to begin with? That's where all this foolishness started. Our presumed importance," I said. He continued to frown. "Seriously, have you had any threats made against you?"

After a moment he said, "No."

"Do you have any toughs here to protect you from a public assassination?" I spread my hands out towards the crowd deeply disinterested in our little problems.

He tilted his head to the side towards a tall, thick, unsmiling man about twenty feet from us.

I smiled at the unsmiling man. "Good for you," I said, turning back to Dunkle. "I'm not worried, and I don't think you should be either. Besides, if these people are as connected as you think, there's nothing we can do outside of hiding in a bunker. Is that what you want?" He just stared at me. "Enjoy your life, Xavier, it's short enough as it is." I put my arm around his shoulder. "Where are you hiding? Up north?" Dunkle had a nice inconspicuous house in Gallinas.

"Yes. I got the whole property set up so no one can come close without me knowing about it," he said.

"And Natalya?" Xavier Dunkle had, since he first laid eyes on her, a mad crush for Natalya Constantinescu.

"Other than when she called me, I haven't spoken to her since before she went on her trip." He turned his head in her direction. "I don't want anything to happen to her," he said as we stood in our corner.

"Why would anything happen to her?"

Xavier shook his head again. "Do you even know where she went while she was on vacation?"

"I don't, as a general rule, insert myself into her affairs. We both like it that way." I was tired of hiding in the corner and Agnes and Natalya were motioning for us to join them.

Xavier continued to frown, but the conversation, such as it was, ended as we neared my wife and chief of staff. Small talk ensued as Natalya graciously directed us to the imperious Ms. DuBare. She inquired about our health and our obsessions, mainly I think, to needle the phobic Mr. Dunkle, who was not nearly as attentive to the delightful Ms. Constantinescu as he had been in the past. Ms. DuBare, like Agnes, had reservations about the older Xavier being infatuated with the younger Natalya, much to Natalya's consternation. But, I think, both had become, reluctantly, accepting that Xavier's feelings for Natalya were genuine and that the balance of power between them was squarely in Natalya's court.

"We've missed you and your many astute observations, Mr. Dunkle," Ms. DuBare said with the sharp eye of one who knows well fools like Dunkle and yours truly. "The art world is lessened by your absence."

"My apologies. I've been, unfortunately, preoccupied by more mundane affairs, and I do miss these showings of yours. I hope to be less of a disappointment in the future." Xavier Dunkle II offered a sly smile, which made me laugh.

"Finally, the more interesting Mr. Dunkle shows himself," I said.

"You two are quite the pair," Ms. DuBare noted, while raising her eyebrows at Dunkle and me.

"As long as we don't end up like Rosencrantz and Guildenstern, eh dude?" It seemed appropriate, given our earlier conversation.

"Droll," Xavier replied.

"I don't get it," Agnes said.

"Hopefully, neither will we," I added, laughing.

"Are you two through?" Ms. DuBare, quite aware of my reference, was not amused.

"Yes ma'am," I said sheepishly.

"Good. This is an art gallery, not a comedy club," she continued. "Did you get a chance to review the proposal I sent you regarding next year's budget?"

I didn't have the slightest idea if I had. I turned to my chief of staff, who had her head cocked just enough to support the look of supreme confidence that she was way ahead of me on this. "Have we, Ms. Constantinescu?" It was all I had.

"Jesus, Monk," it was Dunkle's turn to laugh. "Even in my hibernation, I had time to review Ms. DuBare's proposals."

"Yes, Mr. Monk, the proposal was reviewed, and you signed it two days ago when your lady friend called on you. Remember?" The devious side of Natalya Constantinescu was showing, and I didn't care for it much.

"There you go," I said to Ms. DuBare, "it's in the mail."

Ms. DuBare could only smile and shake her head.

"Who's this lady friend, Buttman?" Agnes had her arms crossed and her well-practiced pout on.

"Yeah, Buttman," Xavier exclaimed melodramatically, "who's the babe?"

I glared at Natalya, who found this all very amusing. "I would hardly call her my lady friend. It was Sterling's lover. She stopped by to tell me to tell Sterling she was ok and to not come after her. That's all it was."

Agnes quickly went from pouting to curious. "Really? Do you think Felicia knows?"

"I don't even want to think about it," I said.

"What if it comes up? We're supposed to go up there next weekend," she huffed.

"What? We were just up there," I whined.

Agnes groaned. "That was two months ago, Buttman. Should I be reviewing these proposals?"

I looked between the agitated Agnes and the smirking Natalya. "I don't want to think about any of it."

Both shook their heads and followed Ms. DuBare, trailed by Dunkle, into the next room. I held back, noting a scent that made my knees weak. Monika Danalek eased up next to me, her breasts brushing against the sleeve of my jacket. She took hold of my hand as she came to my side. "You look very gentlemanly, Monk. I like that."

"My dear Monika, you are as beautiful as ever," I told her, trying desperately not to picture her as I last remembered when I went to her apartment.

"How kind of you to notice."

It wasn't hard to notice. From the sheen of the bluish black hair flowing to her shoulders, the curve of her cheeks, her mischievous gray eyes and pouting full lips, her fine breasts exposed just enough to entice, and her voluptuous hips and thighs, it was a wonder I could stand up. She pressed herself close to me, her mouth next to my ear.

"I suppose you're still attached to your Agnes? Or are you available to come visit me?" She sucked on my earlobe just in case I wasn't getting the point. The raging hard-on made the point succinct.

"I'm still attached and in this very moment grateful that I am," I said, as I turned to face those deceptive gray eyes.

She brought the hand she was holding up, so it brushed against her breasts. "Grateful? Really?"

I don't think she believed me. "Yes, very much so."

"And why is that, Mr. Buttman? You don't find me desirable anymore?" Her breath was warm and her lips were close to mine.

"Because I don't think I could make it to the door before I had to have you, and in front of all these important people. Think of the scandal." I kissed the hand that was holding mine. Her other hand brushed my erection.

"That doesn't mean you can't come visit me…" She pulled me back towards the corner where Xavier had been hiding.

"I thought you were spoken for these days…"

"That was merely a fling." She brushed her thigh against mine.

I put my lips to hers and kissed her with all the passion I could muster. They were sweet and moist. She smiled when I pulled back. "If I were unattached, I wouldn't let you go until my heart exploded," I said as I noticed I was breathing fast, too fast. "But I like my life too much to give it up, even for so delectable a woman as you."

"Why don't I believe you?" She was breathing fast, too.

"Because you like adventure, and what's more fun than fucking someone else's man?"

"You think you know me, don't you Monk?" Monika Danalek pushed her hips into mine.

"Just enough to be mindful," I said as I kissed her again.

"Mr. Monk." A voice I recognized was calling me.

I smiled at the beautiful woman in front of me. "My apologies, but I have to go."

Monika peered over my shoulder at Natalya. "You know where to find me when you change your mind, Mr. Monk."

"I do, Ms. Monika. Till then." I kissed her and left, trying to walk in a way that didn't draw attention to my still stiff cock. "Damn woman," I said, under my breath.

Natalya was shaking her head as I drew a tissue from my coat pocket and wiped my lips. "Should I worry, Mr. Monk?"

"Probably, but it's not what you think," I said.

"No?"

"No. I was simply having a little fun with the delightful Ms. Danalek." I grinned at my chief of staff. "It's kind of interesting being on the other side of the hunt. Anyway, I'm not, assuming you care, fooling around or even entertaining the idea of fooling around with her. However, let's keep this between us for the time being. I don't need Agnes freaking out over Monika Danalek."

"So long as you don't, Mr. Monk," she admonished.

"Exactly, so keep those beautiful ears of yours open in case people start talking."

"Don't lie to me, Mr. Monk," she said in as serious a tone as I could remember.

I put my arm around her and kissed the side of her head. "I won't," I assured her. She smiled at me, but I recognized the darkness in her eyes. I knew it would keep me in line. That and I didn't really want to get into a relationship with Monika Danalek. I had plenty on my plate already. For some reason, that brought Xavier's words into my head. "Where did you go on your vacation?"

Surprisingly, the darkness in Natalya's eyes grew. "I went to Thailand."

"Really? What'd you do there?"

"I had some things I had to take care of," she said in a cold, sharp voice. It reminded me of the blowup she had at Big Mike Kovalenko, of her standing over him screaming.

"Should I ask?"

"It's done. That's all I want to say, ok?" She was shaking.

I kissed her head again. "Ok."

We regrouped with Agnes and Xavier in the main gallery. Ms. DuBare was off being imperious to another group of well-heeled know-nothings.

"Where have you been?" Agnes was growing tired of the scene.

"Sorry. There was a painting. I just stood there looking at it," I lied.

"Uh-huh. Did it lead you to any great epiphany?" Her scowl was quite lovely.

I leaned in so my mouth was close to her ear. "It gave me ideas, my love," I whispered.

She perked up. "What kind of ideas?"

"The kind that make me want to take you down to that big Mercedes you made me buy; the one with the dark tinted windows, and make you squeal with delight. Any interest?" I kissed her earlobe for effect.

"Maybe," she cooed.

"Excellent, because I'm already primed." I reached down and patted her beautiful behind.

"Got to be more interesting that this," she said, patting mine.

"That's the spirit."

We said goodbye to Natalya and Xavier and thanked Ms. DuBare for another wonderful showing. I noticed Natalya smiling at me, and Xavier wondering what was going on.

Soon we were in the big Mercedes that Agnes had talked me into buying, replacing the Mercedes Judith left me, even though there was nothing wrong with it. The back seat was large and soft and perfect for inappropriate sex. The window tint would keep any looky-loos away. Agnes was taken aback by the ferocity of my lust, but once we got going, she was all in, telling me how exciting this was as I frantically pulled at her clothes and mine.

"What brought that on?" she asked later as we sat there panting and reaching for our underwear.

"I saw you were bored and tired and I couldn't help myself," I said as I began assembling my clothes.

Agnes started laughing. "You are such a fucking liar, Monk."

"You don't believe me?"

"No, I don't, but I *was* bored and tired," she said while still laughing. "At least that part was true." She kissed me as she pulled up her panties. "I saw your friend *Mon-i-ka*. I don't suppose that had anything to do with this outburst of affection, did it?"

"I'm shocked you would think that!" I tried desperately not to smile.

"Uh-huh." She pinched my exposed leg, causing me to flinch. "I don't care if she turns you on so long as I'm the one you're fucking. Got that?"

"Yes, dear."

Seemed reasonable.

5

Two days later, I was back at the office, mumbling incoherently, reacquainting myself with what I had signed the week before, and waiting for Isaac Bohrman, my half-brother and point man for our lobbying efforts around the country. Natalya smirked as she handed me the proposal Ms. DuBare had prepared and I had signed.

"Shouldn't you be more deferential," I complained.

"Oh, but I'm very respectful of you, Mr. Monk." She grinned and returned to her desk.

I didn't believe her for a minute.

It didn't help that on the desk was the signed proposal I couldn't remember then, but that I clearly remembered now. "This can't be a good sign," I mumbled to myself. The next hour was another mind-numbing walk through the various documents that needed my attention, attention I had no interest in providing.

I was hungry; it was nearly twelve-thirty, and my legs were stiff. I wandered into Natalya's office. She peered up at me and raised her eyebrows.

"Interested in lunch?" I asked.

She shook her head. "Sorry, Mr. Monk, I'm joining my friends this afternoon."

"Will you be here when Isaac shows up?"

"No, you're on your own. I hope that's ok?" She cocked her head slightly and grinned.

"So long as I don't have to hear about how I screwed things up in your absence, Ms. Natalya?" I grinned back.

"I would never do that, Mr. Monk," she lied.

"Good to know," I said.

Natalya got up and straightened her desk before collecting her handbag. I watched as she sashayed towards the door, mostly for my benefit. "Bye, Mr. Monk."

"Bye."

She waved and closed the door.

I didn't make it to my office before the door Natalya had just closed was opened and a light knock on its glass surface was heard. I turned to find a statuesque black woman in a light gray striped suit looking at me.

"Mr. Buttman?"

"Last time I checked," I said.

The woman approached me and held out her hand. "My name is Orestra Blakely. I'd like to ask you a few questions, if I may?" She had piercing black eyes and a firm handshake.

"Concerning?" I watched as she sized me up. I stepped back so the whole of Monk Buttman might be discerned.

"Aisha Diamond," she said.

"And if I have no interest in questions concerning Aisha Diamond?" I was curious.

"I don't plan on holding a gun to your head, Mr. Buttman." A slight smile found her lips.

"I'm pleased to hear that." A slight smile found mine. "I'm hungry, Ms. Blakely, and have some time to kill before others have questions for me. You may join me for lunch, if you're so inclined. If not, then we'll have to find another time to talk."

"I might be so inclined."

I motioned to the door. "After you."

A block down the street was a bistro with a dive bar vibe: low lights, wood tables, and the collected detritus of ancient times, specifically the 1960s. The bar itself was a long stretch of distressed wood behind which was a meandering list of craft beers and whiskies along with three bartenders, all young, two with scraggly beards and drawn back hair, and the third with black lipstick and eyeliner. A young woman with a rose tattoo snaking from her right ear down into her shirt led us to a table in the back. I didn't know whether to smile at the tattoo or not. Given its connection, at least for me, to Desiree Marshan, I thought the better of it.

I pondered my tablemate. Ms. Blakely's dark brown hair, which she wore in short tight curls, shone in the diffused light from the street. She had strong features and a quiet face. We looked over the menu and ordered. Having been dragged here a number of times by Natalya, I knew what I liked and ordered an avocado club and a salad. Ms. Blakely chose the Poke bowl, and we both ordered the stout.

"Why the interest in Aisha Diamond?" I asked after the beers had been brought to the table.

"I'm looking for Ms. Diamond."

"Why come to me?"

"I understand she came to your office last week and that you previously had her under surveillance," she said.

"How would you know that?" The answer was surely Sterling. Didn't Aisha Diamond tell me to tell him to back off?

Ms. Blakely shifted in her chair. "I'm afraid that's confidential."

"To whom?"

"Same answer, Mr. Buttman." The server brought our order. Blakely cocked her head as I looked down at mine. "You don't strike me as the vegetarian type."

"True, but I've been advised that it's good for me to try new things, and my chief of staff likes this place and frowns when I eat another of God's creatures. Of course, she a bit of a sneak, and is probably having a steak as we speak." Blakely smiled at that. "What's your game? Investigator? Detective? If you're a cop, you have to own up, correct?"

"Assuming I'm not a corrupt cop, yes," she said.

"Assuming."

"I'm a private investigator. I have a client who would like to speak to Ms. Diamond. I apologize that I can't at this time name my client, but I would appreciate whatever information you are willing to provide."

"Have you always been a private investigator?" I liked asking questions, even if there was no point to them.

Blakely shook her head, aware of my tactic. "No, I started in security, first in the Army and then here in LA after I got out. A few years ago, after I transitioned, I went into the investigative services."

"Interesting. I have a friend whose story is very similar to yours. You know a man named Mr. Jones?"

Ms. Blakely's face darkened. "I know Mr. Jones. I used to work with him."

"You were with him in Iraq?"

She played with her food. "I don't think there's any need to go into that, Mr. Buttman. That I know Mr. Jones is enough."

"My apologies." I took a bite of the avocado club. Despite my initial misgivings the first time Natalya brought me here to try something new, the sandwich was very good, which is why I continued to order it. "As to Ms. Diamond, I don't know where she is. Our conversation, such as it was, was short and to the point. She simply wanted me to relay a message to a family member."

"Which family member?"

I thought of Sterling, head down, following Felicia out of Aisha's building in Berkeley. "Since I haven't had a chance yet to speak to him, let's say it's my turn for confidentiality."

"Fair enough. Do you anticipate speaking to this family member soon?"

"It's possible," I said, though it wasn't something I wasn't looking forward to.

Ms. Blakely reached into her clutch and produced a card. "I'd appreciate it if you'd let me know if your family member might be willing to talk to me after you do."

"I'll do that." I took the card and put it in my pocket.

She took a drink and stared at me for a while. "You don't have a problem dealing with a black transwoman, do you?"

"Why should you be any more of a problem than all the other women I have to deal with?" I said.

"A lot of people don't like it."

"Yeah, I've come to understand that."

"Do you understand it?"

I finished my glass of beer. "It's not important that I understand."

The server took our dishes, and I paid the bill. I shook hands with Ms. Blakely and watched her walk away.

·   ·   ·   ·   ·

Isaac was waiting in my office. He was standing by the large window looking west to the Pacific. The buildings of LA proper peppered the sightlines to the soft blue water in the distance. It was a hazy day and the mixture of smog and ocean mist obscuring the view lent a surreal image as if a painting. He retreated to a chair when he saw me coming in.

Isaac Bohrman was the middle child of the three boys my father Moses had with Meredith, his common-law wife. Sterling, the oldest, worked the business side of the farm's growing concern in the production of varietal grapes for the local wineries around Ukiah. Jacob, the youngest, had been a Marine and his death two years past continued to haunt Moses. Isaac, the assured attractive and peripatetic middle brother, having wasted several years in Africa with his former wife, was now hustling for the foundation I set up after Jacob's death with Judith Delashay's blood money.

"How's DC these days?" I asked.

"It's the earnest conniving bullshit pit it's always been," he said.

"I imagine so. Are you and Jontaveus still popular?"

He laughed at that.

Seven months earlier, he and Jontaveus Montgomery, having joined the venture capitalist Delton Manaforte in DC to meet the president, were inadvertent heroes when an "unhinged" Secret Service agent attacked the president. They tackled the man before he could do any real damage. For a short while, they were in demand as the country buzzed at the possibility of assassination. This occurred at the same time Aaron Alan Sobeski was trying to kill me and Agnes in Michigan.

"There's still a lot of chatter, but most of it is hushed off-the-record stuff. Fortunately for me and Jon, the noise has died down and we can get back to business. But it's always one of the first things to come up when we meet someone," he said. "As a means to getting a foot in the door, it's been very effective."

"I'll bet. Jones tells me Jontaveus is making the most of it."

Isaac smiled. "The guy's an operator, I'll give him that. But making contacts is the bread and butter of this business; who you know matters. So, he's working his ass off meeting people and making himself known. I admire him; he's quick and smart. I think it's good that he's on our side."

I wasn't so sure, not with Manaforte lurking behind Montgomery. "I suppose it is," I said.

"Yes..." A glint in Isaac's eyes made me think he, too, was aware of the possibilities, good and bad, with Jontaveus Montgomery.

He reached for a binder he had set on the desk and opened it, passing a handful of papers to me.

Just what I wanted, more stuff to read and go over.

"Here are my reports. Got a chance to talk to quite a few people in DC, staffers mostly, but quite a few representatives and senators, too, about getting those with less than honorable discharges access to healthcare. I also picked up some donations and pledges; nothing huge, but every little bit helps, right?"

I smiled and nodded.

The room was quiet as I listlessly flipped through the papers. I'd have Natalya and Carson Macklgrew go through them; they liked this sort of minutia. I didn't. Isaac sat in his chair, staring at the hazy world outside the big picture window. I put the papers back in the binder.

"Looks good to me," I said.

"Thanks. I assume formal congratulations will come after Ms. Constantinescu and Mr. Macklgrew approve," he said, smiling.

"You catch on quick, Mr. Bohrman."

He returned his gaze to me. "We have to go to the farm this weekend. Don't we?"

"So Agnes tells me." It was nice that I was no longer the sole dissenter on these trips up north.

"Mom sent me a text. Moses wants us boys to talk. She thinks he's finally ready..." He turned back to the world outside. "What do you think?" He continued before I could answer. "I know it's bad form, but I'm tired of hearing about Jacob and how fucked up it was, and on and on. We need to let it go. He's not coming back; it is what it is." He looked at me, a pained expression on his face. "It's not that I don't miss him, I do, but all this sorrow and depression, I don't like it. And it makes me not want to go back. Know what I mean?"

I laughed. "More than you'll ever know, but I don't think it's just about Jacob. There's been issues with Sterling, and Moses, obviously. Agnes talked with Meri and she seems to think that maybe Moses is ready to move on... I hope so, but I don't know."

"Yeah."

"I will say I'm no more enthusiastic about it than you are, and I really don't want to take care of this Sterling thing, or listen to another lecture on how we've failed everybody by leaving."

Isaac smiled. "What's going on with Sterling? I asked Mom, but she said it was a personal thing between him and Felicia."

I sat back in my chair.

"He was cheating on her with a transwoman in Berkeley," I said. I watched his eyes grow wider as he processed that. I knew that Meri was aware of it, and maybe Moses, but Sterling wasn't going to discuss it, and neither was Felicia. "This is between you and me, understand?" He nodded. "Felicia asked me to look into Sterling's disappearances. I think Meri sent her my way because of my sordid past. Anyway, I had an agency track him, and Felicia and I confronted him in Berkeley with his lover. As far as I know, he's been staying away." I kept Aisha Diamond and Orestra Blakely out of it.

"Wow. I didn't know he was into that. I mean no offense to trans people..."

I smiled at his squeamishness. "We're all into our own things." I thought of all the things I'd gotten into recently, like the threesomes with Agnes and MaryAnn. Who was I to talk?

"Yeah," he said.

The room was quiet again.

"Anything else?" I asked. I was ready to head out.

"Nothing that can't wait," he said, though it was evident in his distant eyes that he was still processing the idea of his brother sleeping with a transwoman and no doubt had more questions.

I looked at my watch. There was time for a drink. I got up and went to the bar opposite the desk and the window overlooking the city. "Care for a drink?"

"Sure," he said, mostly to himself.

I poured expensive whiskey into two expensive glasses and handed him one. I returned to my chair, put the bottle on the desk, and watched my younger brother drink and think.

"What do you think it's like?" he asked after finishing the whiskey in his glass.

"Don't know. It's not something I was ever into. I'm not terribly adventurous in some ways. I assume by your question that you haven't either." I took another sip of my drink.

He filled his glass. "No, it's never come up. Well, that's not entirely true. A guy in DC asked me if I wanted to try something different, but it didn't sound appealing, so we went our separate ways." He took another drink. "You've never been propositioned?"

"Not by a transwoman." In truth, I only knew one: Dahlia Leonard. "I've had a few men proposition me, but... I wasn't interested."

"What if you can't tell? I mean some of them look just like women," he said. For all his fooling around, there were gaps in Isaac Bohrman's sexual experiences.

"I don't know. It's a world I don't inhabit, and with everything I've got going on, I'm happy to have Agnes and leave it at that. It makes my life very simple and saves me from what I might do if I ever did come into contact with a transwoman I might be attracted to."

"Yeah." He drained his second glass of expensive whiskey. He added a little more whiskey to the glass. "I'm probably going to need a ride home."

"Probably."

"Mind if I go with you this weekend? I don't want to go alone."

"Sure."

I know just how you feel, Mr. Bohrman.

6

After dropping Isaac off at his apartment, I made the delightful drive across town to the hamlet of West Covina, and a rather harried looking Agnes Duquesne. She was holding Jacob Montaigne, who was crying. She handed him to me.

"Alright Buttman, work your magic!"

I took Jacob in my arms and kissed his forehead. He calmed down, and after a minute or two, rested his head against my shoulder and closed his eyes.

Agnes shook her head. "It's not normal."

"What in the world is, my love?"

"Babies are supposed to love their mothers first and foremost, Monk. It's universal law," she harrumphed.

"Yes, dear." I leaned over and kissed my wife.

"You smell like whiskey."

"Expensive whiskey," I said, "and it was only a glass. Isaac had a lot more, so there."

"Uh-huh. Is the other Bohrman brother aware that he has a date at the farm this weekend?" Agnes pretended to be angry at my, and Isaac's, reticence at going to the farm and dealing with the unhappy Moses. She liked to keep us organized.

"He is aware and is coming with us. So why is Jacob here? I thought this was our day off?" I looked down at the sleeping baby.

Agnes frowned. "Because Becky needed a break from Mr. Grumpypants here and wanted to spend a little time with her other children."

"Well, I done warned her bout pumping out them children. Perhaps this'll learn her," I said in my best hick drawl.

Agnes continued to frown. "It's a good thing I love you Sunshine, because sometimes you're a real ass."

"Yes, dear."

We spent the evening in the quiet of the backyard. Agnes ordered a pizza, rationalizing that if I had to cook, Jacob would once again start bawling, and he needed his sleep. I chose not to argue the point. I fed him when he woke up. After dinner, he smiled as I teased him before falling back to sleep. Agnes shook her head repeatedly.

"It's not normal," she again said.

Jacob spent the night with us. We had a spare bassinette, and, to the delight of Agnes, and the consternation of Rebekah when I told her, he slept through the night.

"It's not normal," Rebekah complained, though having had a full night's sleep, she seemed in better spirits.

"What is?" I said to no one in particular.

I handed Jacob to his mother. Neither seemed thrilled. I had to go, having promised to meet Mr. Jones at the Manifesto after returning Jacob to his family.

"You sure you don't want to take him with you?" my daughter asked. Jacob was already beginning to fuss.

Zach wandered in and stood by his mother. "Can I go too, Gamps?"

"It would just be us dudes," I said. "You'd have to behave and not run around."

"Can I play the drums?" Mikal had foolishly taught him a little rhythm on a Cajon and since then he was eager to keep pounding on it.

"Maybe." Zach grinned. He knew that was code for yes.

"I'll get you his bag," Rebekah said, as she handed Jacob back to me. "What's Agnes up to today?"

"She and MaryAnn have plans." I assumed they didn't involve me.

Rebekah methodically loaded the baby bag with formula and diapers, wipes and bibs, and a spare change of clothes. Zach and I sat quietly watching, though Zach was getting antsy. He wanted to get going, but knew not to whine. He'd reached the age where he was expected to toe the line as far as his behavior was concerned. While his mother was no longer a conservative Christian, she was still a conservative woman and had little patience for children acting up.

Rebekah was not amused when I'd bring up the fact that she was no better at Zach's age than he was. "Uh-huh," was her usual response to my jibes.

"Here you go," she said, handing me the bag.

"Thanks," I said, immediately handing it to Zach, who groaned.

"It's too heavy, Gamps," he whined.

"Welcome to the good life," I told him.

·　　·　　·　　·　　·

The Manifesto was its usual beehive of activity. What had started out as something of a pipedream for Orville Riley, aka Mr. Jones, and Mikal Thorvaldsen, musician, and former lover of Joanie Whalen, had become everything they dreamed of and more. The studios, classrooms, and stages were always busy and bookings stretched into the distant future. Every week there were concerts and shows, from earnest kids developing their chops to seasoned LA professionals playing the music they wished they got paid to play. Even Carson Macklgrew, who was not thrilled with the idea of my wasting many of Judith's millions on this almost certain money pit, was mildly surprised that it was, mostly, pulling its own weight. Anna, Agnes' daughter, was in charge of the food court, and we found her at her "Truck." The food court was set up like a series of food trucks to give it a cool vibe.

Zach saw her first. "Anna!" he cried, running towards her. She smiled and waved. Zach wrapped his arms around her as she bent down.

"Here for more bongo lessons?" she asked him.

"Yep!"

"Where's Mikal?" It was my turn for questions.

Anna let go of Zach, smiled faintly, and cocked her head towards the hallway leading to the smaller, more intimate stage affectionately known as the Closet. "He's in there practicing with Joanie."

Joanie?

She must have noted the surprise on my face. "Yes, Joanie. She's been coming down here quite a bit lately. You didn't notice?"

"No." Although I did note that Anna's tone was just like her mother's when my ignorance was showing. "Are you suggesting something is going on between them?"

"I don't have to suggest," she said. "And before you inquire, no, it doesn't bother me." Anna smiled as she said this.

"Because?" At one time, she and Mikal were sort of an item, though neither would admit it. It drove Agnes crazy, both because she thought Mikal was too old for Anna, and because they would never admit to her that something was going on.

"I'm seeing someone, that's why."

"Anyone I know?"

"Jerome," she said.

"The sax player?" He was the only Jerome I knew, part of a big band outfit that played every other Wednesday.

"Yep. He's also an attorney specializing in patent law, or something like that. You can ask him. We've been going out for a while so I'm thinking of introducing him to mom, maybe next week. And yes, you can tell her."

"She'll be bouncing off the walls," I cautioned her.

"I wouldn't expect anything less." She looked down at Zach, who was starting to fidget. "Are you hungry, Zach?" Zach nodded enthusiastically. Anna looked at Jacob, who was awake and staring at her. "Is he still partial to just you, Monk?"

"Yep. If I didn't know better, I'd say he was doing this just to piss off his mother." I turned to Jacob. "Isn't that right, little dude number two?"

Jacob grinned.

Zach pulled on my pants. "I'm little dude number one, right, Gamps?"

"That you are," I agreed.

Anna led us to a table and waved to Pluto, the guy running her truck. Pluto, whose birth name was Arnold, was a long-haired guy with tattoos, an easy smile, and a laid-back demeanor. He kept his hair in a man bun, which was covered by a hairnet. At one time, he was a student at UCLA studying dentistry before falling in with film students. He studied that for a while, felt the industry was too stifling, somehow found his way here, struck up a conversation with Anna, and was now running her truck while she kept the rest of the food court humming along. With all the activity in the house, the trucks kept busy. Anna's thing was making sure the fare was interesting, fresh, and varied.

"The usual, Zach?" she asked.

"Yep," he bellowed.

Pluto, who was standing by, nodded. "A superdog special coming up. For you, Mr. Monk?"

I sighed. Foolishly, I'd brought Natalya here, who called me that, and Pluto, charmed, had used it ever since. "The chicken salad," I said.

"Got it," and off he went.

Anna sat down and watched as I got out the formula and bib in preparation for the fidgeting Jacob. He, too, was hungry. "Mind if I feed him?"

"Not at all." I handed Jacob to her.

He squealed with trepidation. At the microwave by the condiments, I nuked a cup of water and immersed the bottle to warm it. Zach and I watched to see if Jacob would pull his usual stunt of thrashing around. To our surprised he took to Anna as he had taken to me. Zach looked at me and I at him. We both laughed at that.

"What?" Anna asked.

"Jacob's not very fond of women," I said.

"Really? He seems very sweet to me." She ran her finger along his nose. He shook his head and cooed. I handed her the bottle. Pluto brought our food and stayed for a moment to watch Anna feed Jacob. She smiled at him, which made him smile, which made me and Zach laugh again.

Mr. Jones, who had just come in, asked, "What's so funny?"

"Jacob's found a woman he likes," I said.

"Bout time," said the always loquacious Mr. Jones. He ordered a crab salad and watched us watch Anna and Jacob as he picked at his plate. "So, this is what passes for entertainment now, huh, Buttman?"

"So it would appear, my friend. What's new with you?"

"The usual, I suppose." He moved the half-eaten plate in front of him to the side and rested his elbows on the table. He looked tired.

Anna wiped Jacob's mouth and placed the bib and him along the back of her shoulder in order to burp him. He obliged without too much spillage. Jacob smiled after the last burp, pleased with himself. Anna cradled him and wiped his mouth one last time before removing the bib. She looked at me and then at Jones, who was lost in his own little world.

"I have to get back to work," she said, handing me little dude number two. "I'm sure I'll see you soon."

"Thanks," I said. She headed back to her truck.

Little dude number one, who had been remarkably well behaved, decided enough was enough. "I wanna play the drums, Gamps."

That pulled Mr. Jones out of his stupor. "What?"

"Then we better find Mikal," I said, smiling at Jones. "Won't take long." He merely grunted. Pluto came over and took the empty plates.

They were, as Anna had said, in the Closet, sitting very close and talking in hushed tones. If it hadn't been for the ruckus of the impatient five-year-old, I doubt they would have noticed us.

"Mikal," Zach hollered.

Both looked up; Mikal amused, and Joanie plainly embarrassed. I tried to remember a time when her cheeks were that flushed. None came to mind.

"Zach. Is it time for some drum lessons?" he asked.

"Yep."

"I see you brought Monk and Mr. Jones with you." Mikal rose and offered his hand, which Jones and I shook.

I had a big grin on my face, mostly for the benefit of Joanie Whalen, wife of Brian. "He did," I said. "Anna told us we could find you here. I hope you don't mind?"

Joanie furrowed her brow as she stared at me. The room was quiet, other than Zach bouncing around. "I should get going," she said, grabbing my tie and pulling me and Jacob towards the door. "Thanks for reviewing the charts with me, Mikal. I'll see you at the show on Friday." I looked back to see both Mikal and Jones grinning.

I took my tie out of Joanie's hand. "Careful, my neck's finally feeling better. I want to keep it that way." Memories of eight excruciating weeks wearing a neck brace suddenly came to mind.

"It's not what you think."

"No?"

Her cheeks flushed again. "Ok, so maybe it is, but if it is, I don't need you telling me you said so, got that?"

I laughed. "I'm not the guy you have to square it with, honey."

"Be nice."

"No."

"I do have to go," she said, stammering.

"What, no kiss goodbye?" I moved closer, certain she would smack me.

Instead, she took my face in her hands and kissed me for longer than was necessary. Her lips were as I remembered, soft and inviting. After lightly pulling my bottom lip with her teeth, she stepped back. "Be nice for a change, Monk. Please?" Her eyes were wet and her hands were shaking.

I smiled, kissed her softly, and said, "No."

She tried to smile and walked away. Behind me I could hear the instructor teaching the student a pattern on the Cajon. I turned to find Jones standing behind me.

"I can't do drums today. Let's go someplace quiet," he said.

I ran my finger along Jacob's head. His eyelids were struggling to stay open. "Yeah, and Jacob needs a nap."

I signaled to Mikal that we'd be out by the food court. He nodded.

Instead of the food court, we went outside. For once, it wasn't stiflingly hot. There was a pleasant breeze, and the temperature had dropped into the mid-seventies, perfect for two middle-aged men in suits and a sleeping baby. There were benches and tables, but no people. I thought that strange.

"You're unusually quiet," I said after we found two seats just out of the sun.

Mr. Jones stared at the building across the street. "Got a lot on my mind, that's all."

"Anything I can do?" I looked over my sunglasses.

"I doubt it, unless you can keep kids from being kids," he said.

"Marcus or Ella?" They were his kids, both still in school. Ella was at UCLA and Marcus at LA City College.

"Both. Marcus can't seem to get his shit together and Ella's been more interested in protests than finishing her degree. Coretta's all worked up... I got too much shit going on at work..." He sat back and rubbed his forehead.

"Sounds like you need a vacation."

"I ain't got time for that," he said. "What's your rich ass been up to lately?"

"The usual, though I met a woman who says she used to know you, used to work for you, but I think it didn't end well." I watched him turn my way, slowly.

"Name?"

"Orestra Blakely," I said.

Orville Riley shook his head, and his mouth grew tight. "I don't know anybody by that name."

I knew he was lying.

7

I thought about pressing the issue, but Jones was in no mood for my brand of intimate banter. Instead, we went back in the Manifesto and wandered till we came across a rehearsal room where a group of musicians were working through a series of charts. The music was pure 50s jazz. Piano, drums, upright bass, sax, and trumpet bringing Miles, Mingus, and the better-known Monk back to life. We asked if we could hang out and listen and got the ok. I don't think any of the musicians were out of their twenties. Jones didn't cheer up, but he did relax, at one point closing his eyes.

Jacob liked it too. He'd open his eyes periodically, stretch, look at me, the musicians, and go back to sleep.

We listened for forty minutes before Mikal found us.

"I should get going," Jones said, and we walked him to the door.

Zach was in the food court eating ice cream. I thought about asking Mikal what was going on with Joanie, but again, thought better of it. I knew she'd be calling soon enough. As Zach was finished, the three of us said goodbye and went home.

•　•　•　•　•

The merry mother was waiting.

"You guys were gone a long time," she said. Lizzy came up behind her mother and frowned at Zach, who was making faces at her.

"Doesn't look like Lizzy missed us." I patted her head as she came and stood by me. Zach stuck out his tongue and ran off to his room.

"I missed *you*, Gamps, not Zach," she said emphatically.

I smiled at that. "Yeah, sometimes he a jerk."

"Just like Gamps, eh?" Rebekah chided.

"I like to pass along my best traits," I said. "And," I handed Jacob to her, "the boy here does like women. Anna held him and fed him and he didn't fuss once. How's that?"

"Yeah, yeah, yeah," she answered. "Maybe now he'll be nicer to me."

"Maybe." I wasn't so sure.

I left them where I found them and made my way down the block to Agnes and our little place in the California sun.

Agnes and MaryAnn were in the backyard, sitting under the shade provided by the neighbor's tree, drinking wine. They both smiled and waved me over. MaryAnn was wearing an off-white blouse and blue stretch pants. Her hair, chestnut and straight, rolled down along her shoulders. As was her style, the color of her lips, a shiny blue that complimented her pants, matched the color around her eyes. Agnes was wearing a floral summer dress, white with flowers of red, yellow, and orange. Her dirty blond hair was piled upon her head, and her makeup, what there was of it, was basically lipstick of a washed-out red, and rather delightful false eyelashes, which she batted at me.

She knew I had a thing for them.

Neither were wearing bras.

"Our Mr. Sunshine has returned in all his sartorial splendor," MaryAnn announced. She thought Mr. Sunshine was cute.

"I do look nice, don't I?" I was wearing a favorite gray suit with a pink shirt and a white tie from my collection of previously owned outerwear from the 50s and 60s. "What have you two been up to this fine day?"

"Drinking and talking," Agnes informed me.

"Sounds delightful. May I join you?" They nodded, nearly in unison. I sat down in one of the empty chairs beside them.

Our relationship, that of MaryAnn, Agnes, and I, had changed considerably since the evening when Agnes decided that the threesome MaryAnn had suggested was worth a try. Before that, MaryAnn was simply Agnes' friend from long before I met her, and I was Agnes' husband. Now it was more complicated. Fucking your wife's best friend while she's there can't help but do that. For reasons I didn't quite get, Agnes was ok with our occasional get togethers. I was less ok with it. It wasn't the sex so much, it's hard to say no when two attractive women are enthusiastic about getting naked with you.

Some things never change.

It was something else, something I couldn't quite articulate. And it was at times like this, when they'd been together, drinking and talking, that my concern kicked in. It didn't happen often, but we'd done it more than once, and I'd become mindful of finding them as I found them now, smiling, dressed up, and primed by a fair amount of alcohol.

I felt like the proverbial rabbit thrown to the foxes.

"Why don't you get yourself a drink?" My dear Agnes said. She liked me to be comfortable. I obliged and returned with a rum and Coke.

"Are either of you hungry?" I asked. Both smiled.

"We had a little something," MaryAnn replied. "You?"

"I had a little something." They continued smiling at me. I also noticed that the buttons on MaryAnn's blouse had loosened while I was getting my drink. "Any interest in going inside?" Might as well get the ball rolling.

"What'd you have in mind, Mr. Sunshine?" MaryAnn loosened another button as Agnes got up and bent down beside her. I watched Agnes' hands reach around and caress MaryAnn's breasts.

"As the writers say; show, don't tell." I got up and held out my elbows. "Ladies?"

Each took an elbow, and we headed into the house.

The props had already been set out on the bed.

MaryAnn liked the idea of S&M, but wasn't interested in pain or being bound tight. She liked the sensation of being controlled, of being told what to do, which she encouraged, no matter how lascivious. Silk ties and masks were her kind of thing and she loved anticipation, as if we were all part of an erotic romance novel.

We had a big bed with posts and we covered her eyes and I gently held her arms above her head as Agnes tied them to the bed's posts. We slowly began undoing her blouse and removing her pants and underwear, kissing her along the way. I've never seen a woman orgasm so fast, as we, as Agnes liked to say, pleasured our guest.

We followed that with what sex toys had been laid out, and everybody took a turn being the center of attention. Both Agnes and MaryAnn reveled in explicit directions, and they had their way with me. I didn't mind, but I did have to figure out ways to not come early, which wasn't easy.

After our first get together, MaryAnn gave me a book on controlling one's orgasm. "Here, you should read this," she said with a wink.

I did.

I also got used to them watching and participating, in their own ways, while I was fucking the other. Agnes liked using her fingers, while MaryAnn preferred using her mouth. Both enjoyed giving and receiving, and both would come up with ridiculous "encounters" for us to act out.

It wasn't a bad way to spend an evening.

•　　•　　•　　•　　•

The two of them sat at the table watching me cook a late dinner. Threesomes make you hungry. Neither had much on other than shirts and underwear. I fed them salmon, asparagus, and wine.

After that, we went back to bed. MaryAnn spent the night, which was unusual, but we had plenty of room. If it weren't for the fact that they both snored, it might have been perfect. In the morning, I made breakfast, and we said goodbye to our guest. MaryAnn kissed me at the door and I noticed a tear fall from her eye.

"Thanks, Mr. Sunshine." She kissed Agnes and left.

Agnes put her arm around me. "Thanks, Mr. Sunshine."

"Sure." I closed the door. "Why was MaryAnn crying?" I asked.

"She's just happy," Agnes said. "And maybe a little sad."

We went into the kitchen and sat down. "Should I ask?"

Agnes shook her head. "Sometimes I wonder if you notice anything at all."

"What do you mean?" Apparently, I should be connecting the dots.

"She gets lonely, Monk."

"I thought she had lots of men friends? You told me that."

Agnes glared at me. "I had a lot of men friends too." She let that sink in. "MaryAnn hasn't had a decent boyfriend in a long time. She's tried being nonchalant about it, using dating websites and all that, but these guys weren't very good to her. So, she's been on her own for a while."

"Ok, so we're her diversion. Is that why you don't mind us getting together?"

"Kind of." She played with the wedding ring on her finger. "You know how I worry sometimes," she looked at me and smiled. "But now that we've been together a few times, I think it's ok if—"

"Seems to me you think it's more than just ok," I said smiling.

"Don't interrupt." Agnes frowned, which made me smile even more. "Fine, I like it and maybe I don't feel so threatened when you're fucking her like I thought I would, but it's not that…"

"What is it then?" I was enjoying her discomfort.

Her eyes tightened. "I don't want you smirking or laughing when I tell you this, ok?"

I stifled my smile. "I'll be good."

Her attention returned to her wedding ring. "You may not believe this, but sometimes it's hard to be alone—"

"I'm well aware of what it's like to be alone."

"Monk!"

I shifted in my chair. "Sorry."

Agnes took a deep breath. "You know that MaryAnn likes sex and sometimes, as we *both* know, that can get you into bad situations. So, when she asked if maybe we could get together, even though I wasn't wild about the idea, I said ok. I mean I did sleep with her a few times, and I've slept with you plenty, so I figured it'd be ok that one time since I know what you're both like in the sack." A slight grin crossed her lips.

"That doesn't sound silly to me," I said.

"That's not the silly part."

"No?"

"No. The silly part is I don't mind sharing you every once in a while, even though I said I worried you might like MaryAnn better. I don't mind because it makes MaryAnn feel good, and yeah, I know how that sounds, but I care about her and I don't like it when some jerk fucks her over."

"Just this jerk," I said. I couldn't help myself.

"Yeah." She smiled broadly before growing more serious. "Not that I'm saying this is going to keep happening, but a woman likes to be, you know, treated a certain way and I know you can be fun to be with, and you make her happy, and yes, I know that makes me something of a hypocrite. But I'm ok with that, and, let's be honest, you don't seem to mind."

"I don't mind," I said.

Agnes shrugged her shoulders. "I'd rather she come here for sex than have a miserable experience with some scumbag who won't take the time to find out what she likes, or who mistreats her, or any of that. And..." She looked at me with wet eyes, "I think it kind of makes her sad that she has to come to us for love or sex or whatever..."

"It is nice to have someone special," I said, stating the obvious.

"Yeah."

We sat there smiling at one another.

I remembered there was still coffee, so I poured us both a cup. The morning sun was streaming through the kitchen window. We sat there soaking in the light and warmth. The birds were chirping in the backyard.

"Anna has a boyfriend," I said, out of the blue.

"What?" Agnes sat up, nearly spilling her coffee.

"Your daughter, Anna, has a boyfriend," I repeated. "She said she'd bring him around sometime." I smiled at her perplexed expression.

"Why didn't you tell me?" Perplexed turned to the obvious as I cocked my head towards the bedroom. "Oh yeah, that." I raised my eyebrows and nodded. "So, what'd she say? Did she say who it is?"

"Guy named Jerome. Plays the sax," I said, knowing she'd jump the gun.

"Sax player?" I watched her frown.

"Yeah, plays in that big band we saw a couple of weeks ago, remember?"

More frowning. "You know I don't."

"Maybe you'll remember when she brings him around," I said.

"He's not old, is he?" she grumbled.

I laughed, almost spilling my coffee. "No. He's probably a little older, but a bit younger than Mikal, and that's a good thing because apparently, Joanie is seeing Mikal again."

Agnes' eyes went from tight to wide. "Wait a minute. Isn't she married to that guy who helped you screw over those geezers at your old bungalow?" She laughed at that.

I did not. "I did not screw over the geezers, but yes, she's married to the guy whose company bought the Moonlight Arms from me."

"Maybe they'll have a threesome?" That made Agnes laugh even harder, which made me laugh.

"I'll suggest it when she calls."

"So long as you don't join in," she said, cackling.

"Uh-huh. Are you done?"

She grabbed her sides; tears were running down her face. "Yes," she cried, which only made her laugh more. I waited for her to fall out of her chair. "I'm ok," she said after a few failed attempts to stop laughing. Finally, she calmed down. "Did Anna say when she was bringing this...what was his name again?"

"Jerome." I was still smiling.

"Oh yeah, Jerome. Did she say when they were coming over?"

"No."

Agnes sat back in her chair, clearly exhausted from her laughing jag. "Anything else interesting I should know about?"

"I got a visit from another black transwoman. Investigator, looking for Aisha Diamond." I took a drink of coffee.

She stared at me for a moment. "You're kidding, right?"

"No, but it should make for a fun talk this weekend, eh?"

"Yeah."

She didn't suggest I have a threesome with the two transwomen.

8

The weekend came quickly, and we gathered ourselves for the fun and games sure to happen at the old man's farm up near Ukiah. The only surprise was Jontaveus Montgomery hopping out of Isaac's car.

"You don't mind if Jon comes along?" Isaac asked, as if at this point, I'd say no.

Jontaveus had an amused expression on his face. "Sorry for not asking sooner, but I only learned of it yesterday, and I've been curious about the whole commune thing. And when Isaac offered, I thought, why not?"

I looked at Agnes, who shrugged. "Well, I don't mind, and I can't think of why anyone else would, so sure, come along and witness the joys of communal life."

I popped the trunk on the Dodge, an emerald green 1968 Dart GT convertible with a white interior that had recently been returned to me after being repaired. Two goons on motorcycles had trashed the paint and exterior after our ill-fated visit to Ashleigh Carmichael's desert compound months before. Bernie's shop had restored it to its restomod glory, and I was once again ensconced in a classic from the past.

We piled the bags in the spacious trunk.

"Wow, nice car," Jon enthused.

"Yes, it is, and—"

"I get to take a turn driving, right, Buttman?" My delightful wife nudged me.

I eyed the three of them. "I suppose that, within reason, anyone who wants to drive, assuming a valid driver's license, can take a turn," I said.

Agnes took the keys. "Becky and the gang are waiting. Let's motor."

Jon and Isaac got in the back, and I joined the ace driver and hellion Agnes up front. I said a silent prayer as Agnes hit the gas and headed up the street.

It was a pleasant experience outside of Agnes driving too fast and the occasional snarls of too many cars packed onto too few lanes. Everyone took a turn behind the wheel. As was our custom, we stopped at In-And-Out for lunch. Rebekah, tight eyed and scowling, handed Jacob the grump to me before getting back in their car, and I held him for the rest of the trip to the farm.

Moses and Meredith were there to greet us as we pulled in.

Moses, his hair and beard grown out, wearing a pair of jeans and a *Fuck Power* tee shirt, had returned to the more acerbic style I remembered from my youth, when he'd rail against the entrenched national pathologies needlessly killing young people and their enthusiasms.

"Nice," I said, tapping his shirt as we embraced.

"Don't be a wise-guy, Sunshine," he said, somewhat facetiously.

"Right back at you, dude."

He smiled at that, and the baby in my arms. "I see that Jacob is still a problem child."

Jacob looked at me and his great-grandfather before yawning. "Aren't we all?" I said, as I passed the baby to his mother. Rebekah's scowl returned as she and Fidel left with the rest of their brood.

Isaac introduced Jontaveus to Moses and Meri, and we all went into their little house.

"And what do you do, Mr. Montgomery?" Moses asked as we stood in the living room staring at one another.

"I'm an agitator, Mr. Bohrman—"

"I prefer Moses, young man." Moses grinned at his use of the phrase "young man."

"Moses." Jontaveus Montgomery passed along his own grin, which Moses appeared to appreciate.

"We'll have to discuss how agitation has changed since I was a radical raging against the machine."

"I look forward to it," Jontaveus assured him.

With that out of the way, we went to our rooms to unpack before meeting again in the great room adjacent to the communal kitchen, which was just beyond their back door. Dinner was not far off. Agnes and Meri excused themselves, while Moses and Isaac were ready to give Jontaveus a quick tour.

"Are you joining us, Mr. Buttman?" Moses was in good form this evening.

"No," I said, "I'll join you later. I promised to look up Emily. I assume she's around."

"Check the garden," he said.

Indeed, Emily was in her garden. She smiled upon seeing me and came over and gave me a hug.

"How's life?" I asked.

"It's ok," she shrugged, holding on tight, pressing her face against my chest.

Emily was no longer the headstrong child I'd met some five years before. Instead, she was well on her way to what was once called womanhood. A foot taller than she was at ten, she was also somewhat gangly with long fingers that went along with her lean arms and legs. It was obvious she would not be small like Calista, her mother, but at fifteen, she had not filled out as she would at twenty.

She had also turned into something of a mope.

I was blamed for this, having exposed her to the enticing spectacle of wealthy LA living. "So, what's up, Miss Emily? The communal life got you down?" I remembered when I was here at fifteen and how much it got to me.

Emily sighed. "I don't mind the farm. It's just..." For whatever reason, she didn't expand on that.

She let go of me and we sat at the corner of her herb garden, the one she'd been tending for as long as I'd known her. She still kept it clean and organized, and the herbs were doing well. Emily stared at the hills in the distance with her hands cradling her chin.

"Care to share?" I figured I'd give it one more shot.

"Why? It's not going to change anything. Mom won't let me leave and dad isn't an option either. I told you they had another kid, right?"

"Yes, you did." She had, in fact, mentioned it many times.

"And there's our baby…" Her chin seemed to sink further into her hands.

Her father lived in Philly, with his wife and three kids, and with baby Jasper on the scene, Emily now had four half siblings. It was one of the many things the two of us bonded over: half brothers and sisters, broken nuclear families, and an uneasy relationship with the farm and our parents. I was also something of a surrogate father, which Calista didn't care for, though of late and with her son Jasper's arrival, she was less angry about it. Calista's wife, Andrea, found it all quite amusing.

"I'm sure something will come up," I assured her, though I didn't know what.

We sat in the quiet of the late afternoon, killing time, both of us wanting to be some place else. I thought about the house in Michigan, and how it might be nice to go back and visit. The house was part of the estate Judith had left me, and my one time there was interrupted by felonious characters and murder. I don't know what Emily was thinking about. Our quiet was broken up by Moses leading Isaac and Jontaveus on their tour of the farm.

Emily popped right up upon seeing Mr. Montgomery.

"This is Emily," I said. I, too, stood, though it took me a little longer to get up.

Emily immediately stuck out her hand, which Jontaveus took with a smile. "It's nice to meet you, Emily."

"Me, too," she said, smiling in kind.

"Time for dinner," Moses informed us. We got in line and followed him to the communal dining hall.

. . . . .

As expected, Jontaveus Montgomery and Isaac were the focus and of great interest at dinner. I, fortunately, was no longer particularly interesting. Except, that is, for my part in the lack of interest Jacob Montaigne had in his mother, Rebekah.

"It's not natural," I said with a grin. Jacob was sleeping, nestled in my arm under my right shoulder.

"Very funny. But you don't have to deal with this every day," Rebekah pouted.

"I'm sure he'll grow out of it," Meredith assured her. "Sterling was much the same when he was that age."

Ah yes, Sterling. "Is he going to be here this weekend?" I asked.

Meredith shook her head. "I don't think so. He and Felicia and the kids haven't been around much since...well, they've been busy." She leaned towards me. "Why, is there something I should know, Monk?"

"Not that I know of. I was just curious." With everyone at the table, I saw no reason to blurt out that I needed to talk to him. The situation was uncomfortable enough. Better to hassle my daughter, but that passed as the conversation between Jontaveus, Isaac, and Moses grew more animated.

Some of that had to do with Isaac playing the imp.

"I'm just saying that changing the system is a bit of a pipe dream, that's all. Better to fight from within, get what you can," he smirked, knowing it bugged the old man. "The idea of us all massing in the streets to take down the man is just so much spectacle. Sound and fury and all that. Flash and bang."

"And you, Jon? Do you share such a jaundiced and pessimistic take on change?" Moses asked.

Jontaveus smiled at Isaac, knowing he'd been set up. "To a point, but I do think you have to agitate for change. It won't just happen. Good intentions are just that, intentions. I believe you've got to find a crack in the surface and exploit it. Get people excited and active. But as much as hard work and pressure have their place, we've found in working together that," he gestured towards the smirking Isaac, "if you don't have any connection with those in positions of power, it's tough to get people to listen to you. And the ugly truth in this country is if you're poor or unrepresented, you're basically invisible. That's why I think you have to hold your nose and play to power."

"Power corrupts, plain and simple," Moses grumbled. "We said a lot of the same things back when I was your age, and look where that got us. We're still in the same prison, swinging the same broken hammers at the same broken rocks, while the same smarmy bastards profit from it."

"And you call me a pessimist," I said.

"I thought you said you were an absurdist. Besides, with all your money, you're part of the problem now," he harrumphed.

"Thanks." Jacob opened his eyes and smiled at me. I looked over at Rebekah, who rolled her eyes. "I'll be sure to take it up when us bastard autocrats get together."

"Aren't we just as much a part of the system here as anyone else?" Isaac was in the mood to irritate. "Isn't wine as bourgeoisie as it gets?"

"The difference is we're not profiteers, and wine has existed long before class distinction," Franco Mackinaw said. He and his brother Brewster started the commune with Moses. "And as much as we'd all like to hear this old argument drone on and on, I say we open another bottle and toast to the fact that we're still here doing our own thing, even if it's not quite what we envisioned fifty-years ago."

"Amen," I added.

The conversation thus redirected, and the wine flowing, the rest of dinner was pleasant if less charged. Emily peppered Jontaveus with questions about his life, while Andrea peppered Isaac with questions about DC and what the hell happened to him and Jontaveus at the White House.

"It was one of those spur-of-the-moment things. We were standing in line waiting to shake the president's hand, when one of the Secret Service guys came at the president. I noticed he had something in his hand and I impulsively stepped in front of him," Isaac said, shrugging his shoulders.

"And you, Jon?" Emily's eyes were wide and bright.

"I grabbed the guy's hand and held on for dear life."

Isaac laughed. "The next we knew, there were what seemed like ten guys on top of us—"

"And that was that!" Jontaveus added. "Well, that and all the interviews later with the Secret Service, FBI, DOJ."

"Wow," said Emily.

"Was he really going to kill the president?" Andrea asked. After the attack, there were rumors going around that the whole thing was staged for the president's benefit. "Seems to me if a rogue Secret Service agent really wanted to off the president, he'd just shoot him at close range!" Andrea didn't care for the president.

"Seemed real enough to me," Jontaveus said. "I mean, I don't know how we would know if it was some kind of stunt, but that seems kinda out there, don't you think?"

Andrea curled her nose. "I wouldn't put it past that guy, to be honest."

"Yeah," I said, "maybe you two were dupes in something much bigger."

"Like what, baby man?" Agnes smiled and tipped her glass in my direction.

"Like maybe it wasn't a stunt by the president, but was a message by certain interests that they could get to him whenever they wanted." I looked down at Jacob. His eyes were open. "Isn't that right, little dude number two?"

Rebekah frowned. "Dad!"

"I'm little dude number one," Zach said to whomever was interested. Laughter erupted at the table. Triumphant, he crossed his arms and stuck his tongue out at Lizzy, who ignored him.

"Don't encourage him, Dad." My daughter seemed in a mood.

"Oh, lighten up or I'll give your son back to you."

"I'll take him," Meredith offered.

I reluctantly passed him to her. Jacob pinched his face, but didn't whine.

·   ·   ·   ·   ·

After dinner, I helped clean up alongside Emily.

"I didn't see your mom at dinner." I handed her the plates as I washed them.

"Jasper's sick," she said, drying and stacking them. "Andrea took her some dinner."

"I see."

Emily stopped stacking the plates and leaned against the counter. She played with her hands and fiddled with the buttons on her dress. "I want to go with you to Los Angeles."

I turned to my erstwhile plate dryer. "I don't think your mother would go for that. What about your schoolwork?"

"She's got Jasper now, and she's got Andrea. She can live without me for a while. I can study there. I'm tired of being here. I want to leave..." Emily lifted her head and stared into my eyes. "Like you did."

"I left under trying conditions," I said.

The pupils of her eyes tightened. "I know the story."

"And?"

"And I don't think that would have mattered. Sooner or later, you would have left. You and Rebekah and Lilith."

I handed her a plate and smiled at the mention of Astral, or, as everyone else on the planet called her, Lilith. "Probably, but that's neither here nor there. It won't justify your leaving." I looked into the sink. Five more plates. "And even though Jasper takes up a lot of your mother's time, babies are like that, you know," I tilted my head just because, "I'm sure she'd miss you, as would everyone else here."

"Everyone else will be just fine if I'm not here for a while." She took the plate in my hand and dried it.

"What would you do in LA? There's more to life than hanging out by the pool and keeping Zach from pestering Lizzy." I gave Emily the last plate and wiped down the sink.

"I can do lots of things—"

"You can do lots of things here." I rolled down my sleeves and pulled my tie from between the third and fourth buttons on my shirt.

A wounded look filled her eyes. "You don't want me either, do you?"

"I didn't say that. What you can do won't matter unless your mother gives her ok, and don't ever tell me I don't want you!" I reached for her and she came and put her arms around me. I hugged her and kissed her forehead. "You will always matter to me, Emily. Always."

"I still want to leave," she cried.

"I know."

Agnes and Andrea were standing by the door when I lifted my head.

9

The next morning brought more good times. I had forgotten Moses wanted a meeting with the boys. I was dreading having to face Emily's mother, Calista, and foolishly contemplated hiding in bed.

"Rise and shine, Mr. Sunshine," my delightful wife bellowed. "Moses wants you up and ready by ten."

"What for?" I pulled the covers over my head.

Agnes had been up for hours, working in the kitchen, as was her wont here in commune-ville. "Your brotherly meeting, what else?" She laughed when I groaned. "I don't think you're getting out of it, Sunshine"

"Damn."

She pulled back the cover and kissed me. "I still love you."

"Yeah, but you have issues," I grumbled.

"Look who's talking." She left me where she found me.

After finding the inner strength to get out of bed, I clothed myself and ambled to the dining hall. Agnes handed me a plate of eggs, bacon, potatoes, and scones.

"Don't expect this every day, Buttman," she said.

"I try to keep my expectations low, beautiful. Thanks."

She slapped me on the ass. "They're waiting."

Isaac, Jontaveus, Moses, and Meredith were at the far end of the hall. Moses waved me over. I sat next to Jon, across from the Bohrman clan.

"Do you always get up this late?" Moses had a self-satisfying smirk on his face.

"When I feel the need, yes," I said.

"Be nice, Moses," chided Meredith.

"Shouldn't Sterling be here?" I raised my eyebrows while taking a mouthful of breakfast.

"He should, but he had other things to do. Besides, I've already talked to him about this." Moses turned to Mr. Montgomery. "Jon, would you give us a minute?"

"Certainly. I promised Andrea I'd check out her print shop," he said, rising from the bench we were sitting on.

"It's that way," Isaac pointed, "in the old bunkhouse."

Jontaveus said, "Thanks," and left us.

"What's on your mind?" I asked.

Moses shifted in his seat, and his eyes went between me, Isaac, and his hands. It had been a tough few years for the old man after Jacob died, and it didn't help that none of his boys were here with him on the farm. We'd had several interventions as he sunk into depression and then became a little too enthusiastic when dope was legalized. Lately, though, he seemed to find some space to clear his head, as he used to say.

"As you know, I'm getting on in years and I have to consider what to do with my—" Meredith gently elbowed Moses in the side. "Sorry, our stake here in the farm. I had hoped that it would go to you boys, and I've harangued you enough about it, but it seems pretty clear you have no interest in being a part of our life here." He took a deep breath and interlocked his fingers. "Much as I'd hoped differently, I think we're going to leave our share of the farm to the people here."

I looked at Isaac. "Well, that might be one way to go, but it's possible we may change our minds, or that the grandkids or the great-grandkids might want a piece of the action." I stared at Moses and then Meredith. "I know you really wanted us boys to stay, and even I'm surprised we all left, but—"

"But?" His eyes bored in on me as they had so many times before. The only difference was the gray in his bushy eyebrows.

I smiled and lowered my eyes. I hadn't thought about having no connection to the place other than memories. "But we'd have to have a bigger talk about this, with Agnes and Becky and Fidel. Let them know; see how they feel about it."

Meredith patted Isaac on the leg. "What do you think? You've been quiet for the most part."

"I don't know. I like being out in the world," he said. "I find it exciting. That doesn't mean I'd never want to come back, but I think maybe that's for the best. The people here are dedicated to making this work, and while I like coming around, right now I don't see myself living here."

"What did Sterling say?" I asked. It was odd not to have him here for this.

Moses' eyes softened and watered. "Sterling didn't say much when we told him. I..."

Meredith took his hand. "We're worried about Sterling. And Felicia. They're still struggling because of—" She looked at Isaac.

"Monk told me about Sterling," he said.

"He said he wasn't going to talk about it right now." Moses held Meredith's hand between his. "We didn't expect any of this. We always thought you boys would, I don't know, travel down a similar path; more like ours." A tear rolled down his cheek into his beard. "But that's not how it's turned out. I'm trying to be more cleared headed about who you boys are, not who I wanted you to be."

"That doesn't mean the farm isn't still a part of us," I told them.

Moses shook his head. "I think you're just saying that. Would you be here if it weren't for Agnes? I think she loves this place far more than you."

"Agnes sees it much differently than I do. There's no weight on her here. It's not the same for us." I gestured towards Isaac. "We grew up here, and I see much of it through that lens, and some of what happened to me here, I can't shake. But," I needed to take a deep breath, "I will say that Agnes and Rebekah and Emily have made me look at this place a little harder, a little more introspectively. I don't feel like I did when I first came back to California and wanted nothing more than to hide in LA. There is a part of me that has come back and enjoys being here." I wiped away the tears running down my cheeks. "And I like that Zach and Lizzy and Jake have a chance to spend time here."

There was quiet in the big room.

Meredith put her other hand on Moses.' "Do you know what's going on with Sterling, Monk?"

"Only a little. I was hoping to see him, talk to him, but... I guess that'll have to wait," I said.

"Felicia told us you helped her, but she didn't go into any detail, and it was obvious she didn't want to talk about it. Is it bad?" Moses asked.

I looked at the two of them. "I don't know anything other than Sterling had a lover in Berkeley. I assume they're dealing with it in their own way."

Meredith had her own question. "What kind of lover?"

"What do you mean?" I glanced at Isaac, who looked away.

"I guess it doesn't matter, does it? It is what it is, and there's not much we can do, anyway." Meredith let go of Moses' hands and wiped her eyes with her apron.

I checked my watch. I was supposed to go picnicking with my brood. "Let me talk with Agnes, and we can get together later and discuss what we want to do going forward."

"And I was going to take Jon into town. Show him the joys of small-town northern Cali," Isaac said as he got up.

We gave each other hugs, and I said it would be all right even if I didn't know that.

•   •   •   •   •

On the way to our picnic site, we made a quick detour to the two cemeteries to visit Jacob, James, and Esmeralda. As I stood there trying to remember their faces, I wondered what had become of Miguel. We had promised to get together, but it never happened. Just a note saying he had an opportunity in South America. Bolivia, I think, that he couldn't pass up. I hoped he was still alive.

I saved Moses' words for after we had eaten.

Agnes and Rebekah were not happy about my possibly giving up a stake in the farm.

"I didn't say I was giving anything up," I protested.

Agnes glared at me. "You better not, Monk Buttman!"

I was mildly surprised at how quickly Agnes got worked up over this.

"The kids love this place, Dad." Rebekah gestured towards Zach and Lizzy, who weren't paying attention.

"I did make that point, Becks."

Fidel put his arm around his peeved wife and looked at the land rolling around us. "It is a nice place. Quiet. The kids get to run around and learn about farm life and animals."

"Yeah, Dad."

"Take it up with Grandpa Mo. I told him we needed to get everyone together to talk about this. So put the pitchforks down and pass me a piece of Agnes' ever delightful apple pie. Besides, it's not like we couldn't come here. It just means we would have no stake in the affairs of the farm." I don't think that helped.

"You grew up here, Monk." Agnes reluctantly handed the pie to me.

"Sunshine did," I said. "Do you lay claim to where you grew up?"

"It's not the same and you know it," she grumbled.

"It's a nice day. There's no reason to spoil it. We'll talk with Moses and Meri before we head home. Ok?"

They grumbled some more before cleaning up.

We let the kids run between the rows of grapes. Agnes held my hand as we walked behind. I couldn't help but wonder if it was time to keep or let go of this place. I thought of all those moments Moses put dirt in my hand.

"This is who we are," he would say.

I didn't think much of it even when I tilled my own land all those years ago in Virginia. I didn't miss that land. Why should I miss this land? It wasn't ours to begin with. It belonged to something longer and older than a lifetime, a clan, or any family. The native tribes that lived on this land for generations knew that. We were only custodians for the time we were here. Beyond that, we were simply stories and myths.

"I like it here, Monk." Agnes stopped us and put my arm around her shoulder.

"I picked up on that," I said. "It's not as if we're being kicked out. Moses is thinking out loud, that's all. He does that sometimes. Don't let it get to you."

"I guess."

I turned her head to face mine. "What are you worried about?"

"What's our connection here after Moses and Meri are gone, Monk? What would we be? Shouldn't one of us or all of us be a part of it? Moses doesn't see this as a job. It's his life!"

"I'm well aware of that, beautiful." I kissed her. "It'll be all right."

"You know you say that whether it's true or not." It was a day for staring into each other eyes.

I laughed as I took in her beautiful face. "Sometimes."

•   •   •   •   •

I had a glass of wine and was sitting in the courtyard, turning my phone over in my hand. The picture on the screen, taken by Agnes, of me, Zach, and Lizzy at the beach, stared back at me. I ran my thumb along the faces before swiping up. The phone feature listed a series of names. I scrolled till I reached Sterling's. I hesitated before tapping it. A song began to sing.

Then a voice.

"Yes?" Sterling's voice.

"It's Monk. I have a message for you."

"What kind of message?"

"From Aisha Diamond," I said.

Quiet.

"And?" he asked.

"She's ok and you don't have to worry about her."

More quiet.

"Thanks," he said and hung up.

I returned the phone to my coat pocket. Brewster Mackinaw sat down next to me with a bottle in his hand. I held out my glass, and he refilled it.

"Word getting out?" I asked him.

He laughed and filled his glass. "It was meant to," he said.

"I imagine so. Has he been throwing this around for a while?"

"He has." We enjoyed our wine. "We oldsters are feeling death's slightly cooling hand on our shoulders. Moses especially, and that inevitably leads him to you boys."

"He gets it from *his* old man," I said. "If he meant to set the bees a buzzing, then he got his wish. Agnes and Becky are all kinds of worried. Even Fidel."

"Even Fidel?" Brew shook his head and took another sip of wine.

"Yep."

"And the answer, Sunshine?" Brewster Mackinaw put his burly arm around my shoulder and pulled me close, as he did for years when I was a kid.

"I don't know, but something tells me no more dallying. Which is too bad, because I like dallying," I said.

"That you do, my boy, that you do."

"Might be time to dither."

Brew squeezed my shoulder. "I wouldn't push it."

There was a voice. "Ahem."

We looked up to see Agnes, Andrea, Emily, Calista, and Rebekah. Emily was holding a grumpy Jacob Montaigne.

"Ladies," I said.

"We had a talk, Mr. Monk, and it's ok if I come and stay with you and Agnes for the summer," Emily told me as Jacob squirmed.

I turned to Calista, who was holding Jasper. "You agreed to that?"

Calista turned to Emily. "Yes. She's been whining and moping and if this will help, then yes, she can go. I can't stand the moodiness anymore."

"You know we don't live at the big house—"

"She knows that, Monk," Agnes said. "I'm going to have her help me with my quilting, she going to help Becky with the kids, and..." She gestured to Andrea.

"And, in talking with Isaac and Jon, I thought it would be a good thing for her to see how the world works. Maybe she could spend some time working for the foundation," Andrea added.

"Maybe." I could hear Brew chuckling in my ear.

"See, it all comes together, Monk," he said.

"And your schoolwork?" I asked.

"She has a series of courses she has to finish. Right, Em?" Calista nudged her daughter.

"Yes," Emily mumbled.

"All right, Monk, let's get this nonsense about our not having any stake in the farm over with," Agnes demanded. "Moses is waiting."

"I'm not finished with my wine." I was certain that would save me.

"Let's go, Buttman!" she bellowed. Apparently not.

Brewster Mackinaw laughed and helped me up.

The malcontent, Moses Bohrman, was sitting in his accustomed spot at the head of the dining table. His eyes followed the phalanx of five women and two men as we approached him. Meredith joined us from the kitchen. Fidel and Rebekah brought in Zach and Lizzy. Other folks here at the farm came in as well.

Rebekah, with Zach in one hand and Lizzy in the other, stood in front of her grandfather. Agnes stood right behind her. Meredith stood on the other side. Isaac and Jontaveus stood beside her.

"Grandpa Mo," Rebekah started, "maybe we can't be here as much as we'd like, but we feel this is our home as much as it is yours, and we don't want you thinking we won't carry on for you." She lifted Zach up to his great-grandfather. "Tell Grampa Mo what I told you, Zachary."

Zach took Moses' hand and put the dirt he had in his hand in Moses.' "This is us, Grampa Mo."

"That's right Grampa Mo," Lizzy added.

Grandpa Mo started crying and hugged Zach and Lizzy. He turned to me. "And you, Sunshine?"

"I'm right there with them, Moses Bohrman," I said.

"Isaac?" Moses held the dirt out.

"I just washed my hands," he said with a smile.

"Thank god for the kids," the old man said.

I kissed the side of Agnes' head. "I told you it would be all right."

Agnes leaned into me. "You had nothing to do with it, Buttman. It was Becky."

"Whatever works, beautiful."

10

She came in just after Emily and Natalya left.

It had been a relatively quiet couple of weeks. Emily had settled into routine and found her groove as it were. She helped us take care of the kids when Rebekah asked. She helped Agnes sort through her new life as a quilter. Agnes, no longer gainfully employed by JD Financial, and having found no particularly compelling interest online, decided that, like Leslie, her new Virginia friend married to my old Virginia friend Carleton, she would take to the needle and thread. We had two spare bedrooms, so one was converted into a sewing room.

Agnes was no longer bored.

The same could not be said of Emily.

She knew the basics, such is life on a commune, but had no real interest in sewing. Her interest was found in the likes of one Natalya Constantinescu, who to Emily seemed worldly and incredibly cosmopolitan. Natalya was bemused and a little standoffish at first, but warmed to Emily, mainly because they shared a number of common interests, or perhaps it's more accurate to say that Emily found Natalya's sense of style, fashion, and outlook interesting and wanted the same.

Because of that, both Emily and I were spending more time at the office.

Natalya let Emily help her help me. That's how she put it.

"It's good to have help, no, Mr. Monk?" she asked just because.

"I suppose it is," I answered just because.

Today they had a lunch date with Natalya's friends, and I was about to head to the big house. It was pool day for the irascible

Zachary Bohrman, who, though ignorant of the days of the week, seemed to instinctually know that Wednesday was the day he was allowed to swim in Judith's big, beautiful pool.

Orestra Blakely met me at the door.

"Have a minute, Mr. Buttman?"

"A few," I said, "but not too many. I have places to be."

Ms. Blakely followed me into my office. I watched her sit down before I did. She was wearing a pinstriped business suit with a white blouse. A thin silver chain with an outlined silver heart was around her neck. Crossing the heart were two hands joined in the middle, holding a deep blue Sapphire.

"Interesting necklace," I said.

She put her hand to it and smiled. "Family heirloom. My grandfather gave it to my grandmother."

"Very nice. What can I do for you, Ms. Blakely?"

"Did you get in touch with your family member about Aisha Diamond?"

"You're still looking for her?"

"Interested in," she said.

"I see." Ms. Blakely stared at me with a look I'd describe as conversational: She watches, not intently, but continually to keep one's focus on her. I was half-tempted to play coy, but that wouldn't get us anywhere, and I had concerns over what Sterling was up to with Aisha Diamond. "I relayed a message over the phone. I anticipated speaking to him, but because of this issue with Ms. Diamond, he didn't join us."

"This was your brother, Sterling Bohrman, correct?"

"You tell me, Ms. Blakely. I think at this point we have to decide where we stand with one another. To me, you're looking for information about my family, information that has already caused a great deal of hurt and anger to people I care about. The idea that I should openly and without thought blather on about them strikes me as imprudent." I found myself thirsty and reached to the small refrigerator tucked into the credenza behind me. "Would you care for a bottle of water?"

"Thank you." I handed her a bottle. "I understand your position, Mr. Buttman, or should I call you Monk?"

"Either works," I said.

"Beyond her relationship with your brother, what do you know about Ms. Diamond?"

"Only where she lives, or lived. I don't know if she still has the apartment in Berkeley."

"She's moved," Blakely said with a slight grin. "Do you have any idea how or where they met? The circumstances; any of that?"

"No. I didn't feel the need to know. I wasn't happy I'd been enlisted to find Sterling in the first place. And once it was determined where he was hiding out, I told his wife and left it to them to sort out." I took a long slow drink of the water. It made me think of the cool inviting waters of the pool.

"Do you think they're still getting together? Your brother and Ms. Diamond?" Blakely was methodically tapping on the bottle cap.

"I wouldn't put it past them," I admitted.

Ms. Blakely cracked a wide smile and opened her bottle of cool, clean water. "The question, then, is what I know and what I'm investigating, is it not?"

"I originally assumed you were working for Sterling to try to find her, but now..."

"Now?"

It was my turn to smile. "Now I'm not so sure," I said.

"I am not working for your brother, Sterling Bohrman, Mr. Buttman."

"Is that an inference that you might be working for another brother or another Bohrman family member?" I tried to picture Isaac or Moses hiring a private dick. Didn't work. Maybe Isaac.

"I can assure you that I'm not working for any member of your family that I know of," she said.

"Ok, so where does that put us, Ms. Blakely?"

"Call me Orestra, Monk."

"All right, Orestra, where does that put us?"

Orestra Blakely leaned towards me and put the bottle on the desk in front of her. "First, I'd like to ask you a few questions."

I leaned forward. "Shoot."

"What do you think of black transwomen?" she asked.

"If I'm honest, I don't think of them at all. No offense," I said. "Why?"

"Because being black, female, and trans puts us at the bottom of people's priorities, whether in our own communities, or with our families. And certainly not white America's. We're on our own, Monk."

"Ok, I get that because of who I am, black transwomen aren't going to be on my radar—"

"Unless..." she picked up her water bottle and took a drink.

I didn't need to think long. "Unless that's what turns me on," I said.

Orestra Blakely smiled. "We all like to feel needed and loved, wouldn't you say, Monk?"

I returned the smile. "Yes, I would say that."

"And let's say that you're intrigued, Monk. Maybe something inside you longs for something different, exotic. Something, I assume, a straight white married man might be interested in, but it's scary territory if your only avenues to someone like me are online or on the street. Even in this day and age, people are mindful of who they are and what can happen when they give in to their passions."

I finished my water while keeping my eyes on my visitor. "Okay, let's set aside the fact that I have no interest sexually in black transwomen. But if I did, how would I go about it so it wouldn't destroy my privileged-white-straight-married world, while still allowing me to indulge in my sexual desires and impulses?" I put the empty bottle on the desk and leaned back. "Is that your interest in Aisha Diamond, and I would think, by extension, my brother Sterling? What you're describing probably fits him to a tee."

"It does, doesn't it?" she said.

"Tell me, do you know Aisha Diamond personally, Orestra?"

Orestra nodded and raised her left eyebrow. "I know Aisha through a LBGTQ group. We meet periodically to support each other and let off steam. It's not easy being who we are. But I've only talked to her briefly here and there, so I don't know as much as I'd like."

"Like how she and Sterling met?"

"Like how she and your brother met," she agreed. "But I'm not the right person for what I need to do…"

"What sort of person do you need?" I asked, knowing full well.

"I need a man, Monk." She smiled and tilted her head my way. "I need someone like you—"

"Because?"

"Because you're a rich white straight man who, by all outward appearances, is devoted to his family." Orestra Blakely finished her water and handed me the bottle.

I set it next to mine.

"So, you need a man who, by all outward appearances, looks like me. The next question, though I have an idea where this is going, is why me? Which raises other questions such as why me, in that you don't know me, and how do you know you can trust me? Or that I'd have any interest in helping you, assuming I have any idea what it is you're asking of me."

"I agree. This might seem a little out there, but I can connect the dots, Monk. First, I'll admit that I've done some digging on you and know you've had some experiences that make you a reasonably good fit—"

I laughed. "That's the best description of me yet."

"Do you often interrupt women when they're speaking, Monk?" Ms. Blakely scrunched her forehead.

"My apologies, please continue."

Orestra shifted in her chair. "Do you remember a woman named Dahlia Leonard?"

"Yes, I remember her. You asked her about me?" I hadn't seen or spoken to Dahlia Leonard since I dropped her off at her friend's apartment the day Jones and I discovered Desiree Marshan and the others murdered in South Laguna.

"She said you were a decent guy in a way that intimated you helped her out of quite a jam."

"All right, I'm a decent guy. And I'm rich and white and all that, which begs the question of why I should help you, and what it is you think I can help you with? I don't need more money and I've lived through all the trouble I can stand."

"I understand that, Monk, just as I understand you'll probably turn me down, but people like me disappear, and it's hard to get the authorities interested if we're missing, or overly interested if we're killed." She stood up. "I think we can change some of that if you're willing to help me. I've still got some work to do before you can help me, but for now, I'm asking that you keep an open mind and consider assisting me if you can."

"As someone who might have a thing for a nice black transwoman?" I stood up.

"Yes."

"I'll think it over, Orestra." I put out my hand. She took it. "I assume I'll be hearing from you. We can talk about it then." I reached in the top drawer of the desk and took out one of the personal cards Natalya had made up.

"Seems fair," she said, as I handed the card to her. I noticed the tattoo on her wrist: vines and yellow roses. "I'll be in touch. Goodbye, Monk."

"Goodbye."

I walked her to the door.

•   •   •   •   •

It was a quiet evening, minus the splashing and running and my admonishments to be careful. Natalya dropped off Emily and she quickly donned her bathing suit and joined the festivities. Agnes couldn't wait to dump fussy little dude number two in my lap.

"Here!" she harrumphed.

I put on my swimsuit and amused young Jake in the shallow end. I tried to focus on the moment, but my mind kept replaying the conversation with Orestra Blakely over and over.

I didn't need to get into any of that.

And what of Sterling? What kind of mess was he in?

Agnes sat next to me as I absentmindedly let Jake slap the water with his hands.

"Earth to Monk. Earth to Monk, come in Monk." She thoughtfully poked me in the ribs. "You're really out there this afternoon," she said, after I turned towards her. "Anything I should know about. You're not fooling around or thinking about it, are you?"

She grinned when I glared at her. "Good lord no," I said. "One time. One time, and that was years ago, and—"

"And I knew all about it! Yes, I know the story. Someone's a little sensitive on the subject, aren't they?"

"I wonder what Monika's doing this evening," I said, to be a jerk.

Agnes frowned. "Be nice."

"Right back at you, beautiful."

"All right, if you're not cheating on me with *Mon-i-ka*, then what's with the thousand-mile stare? A mumble for a hello when you come home late, no kisses—you're way behind on your kisses, Buttman— and then you zone out. I know you, Sunshine. What's up?" Agnes pinched her lips to make sure I knew she was serious.

I leaned in and kissed her.

"Gamps!" Zach no longer cared for our public displays of affection.

"Want to get out of the pool, little dude?" I shouted.

"No," he huffed.

"Then quiet."

Emily and Lizzy laughed as he tried to splash me and Jake, before storming off to the other side of the pool. Jake laughed, too.

"Kid's getting a little uppity," I said. "Must get it from his father."

"Because it certainly doesn't come from the Bohrman side of the family," Agnes laughed.

"Exactly." It was at that moment that Jacob grew still and tightened his face. I lifted him from the water and watched his face relax. He smiled at me. "Looks like someone had his afternoon bowel movement." I got up. "If you're still curious, join me at the changing table," I said to Agnes.

She followed me over.

"So, what going on?" her face alight as it was when we were getting ourselves into trouble the previous summer.

"Do you remember when I said I got a visit from an investigator before we went up north?" I carefully removed Jake's dirty swim diaper.

"Vaguely."

"She was looking for Aisha Diamond, Sterling's girlfriend. Wanted to know if I'd spoken to him about her. I said I gave him a message."

"What message?" I hadn't said anything to Agnes about this when we were up there.

"Aisha told me to tell Sterling that she was ok, and he didn't have to worry about her. I had some questions for him, but he didn't show, and hung up before I could ask when I called. Then today, Ms. Orestra Blakely returns, still interested. Anyway, I guess it got me thinking this and that and, unfortunately, caused me to be remiss in my kissing obligations. My apologies." I cleaned up the odiferous Jacob Montaigne and rediapered him.

Agnes was now deep in thought. "You think maybe Sterling and his girlfriend are still at it?"

"I wouldn't be surprised, but I got the feeling something bigger is in play. Ms. Blakely intimated there's a way that more connected, more established, or privileged types, like yours truly, can get busy with people outside the strict male-female paradigm should that be where their libidos take them," I said.

Agnes frowned. "English, Buttman."

"If I want to fuck a black trans chick, there's a better way for a rich guy like me to make that happen than looking for it online or down on Hollywood Boulevard. Clear enough?" I winked at her.

"Uh-huh. And do you have a desire to fuck a black trans chick, rich guy?" She winked back.

I laughed. "Fortunately, I have all the sex I can handle with you, and occasionally with you and MaryAnn. That ought to be enough for any man, eh?"

"Uh-huh. You know you didn't answer the question?" she had her hands on her hips.

"Didn't I?"

"No."

I reached over with my free hand and pulled her in around the waist. "You're really sexy when you do that, you know?" I leaned in and kissed her.

"I know." She kissed me back.

Zach groaned.

11

It's not good to be an easy touch. I tell myself that. It doesn't help.

What was supposed to be an uneventful day turned out to be anything but. It began with the decision to avoid the onerous plodding need for education; this was Emily not having any interest in completing her coursework and being in league with a sneaky five-year-old itching for more time in God's blue waters.

Emily protested when I brought up the not so inconvenient fact that she blew off her studies the day before to hang out with Natalya. She also was substituting Mr. Monk for Mr. Sunshine, which I didn't mind. "I can study at the beach, Mr. Monk!"

"Uh-huh."

"I will, I promise," she said in a huff.

"I don't know that you should try that with me." I glanced over at Agnes, who was well aware of my habit of making promises merely to postpone the inevitable.

"I'll make sure she gets her work done, Monk." My dear Agnes being helpful.

"Then it's on your head, beautiful, when Calista finds out about our little delinquent here," I said, wiping my hands of the whole affair.

"I'm not a delinquent! Just a little behind is all," Emily equivocated.

"Uh-huh." I pointed to the door to indicate my surrender.

Zach let out a whoop and bolted for the garage.

It was a pleasant day; most are around here for those of us with no real concerns. The beach was crowded, but not terribly, and I had a chance to sport the new Hawaiian shirt Agnes had given me at

Christmas. Apparently, even she had tired of my habit of wearing suits all the time.

"Geez, Buttman, relax," she would say.

Generally, I said "No," but relented in this instance. It was a good-looking shirt.

"You look nice for a change." She adjusted the collar.

"I always look nice," I countered.

She curled her lips. "You know what I mean."

"Sometimes I wonder if I do, beautiful."

"Uh-huh."

Having found a suitable spot and pitched the umbrella, we gooped up the kids and sent them on their way. Emily was put in charge of Zach and Lizzy while I had Jacob patrol. Agnes felt it was best if she caught some rays.

"I need the vitamin-D," she said as she stretched out on the beach blanket.

"Uh-huh." I nuzzled Jacob's ear. "We know the truth, don't we, Jake?" He didn't answer, but I didn't expect him to. Agnes ignored me.

Emily came to get Jake a short time later. "We're building a sand castle and need his help," she said.

"Uh-huh." I handed him to her.

I sat watching. A hand tapped my shoulder, and I turned to find an older man is a dark suit standing next to me.

"I'd like a minute of your time, Mr. Buttman."

"About what?"

The man forced a half-smile. "Sobeski."

I looked over at my snoring wife and then the kids not far in the distance. Emily seemed to have things under control. "Sure"

"Leave the phone," he said. I placed it under Agnes' blanket. "We'll take a short walk."

The man was as non-descript as an older gentleman could be. He was neither fat nor thin, stood roughly five-foot eight, had graying hair, a thin nose hosting dark-framed glasses, a square jaw, and strode in a straightforward, methodical manner. Made me wish I had worn a suit.

"And who might you be, if I may be so bold?" I asked, while staying in stride.

He said, "You can call me Fairfax."

"And how does the name Sobeski fit in, Mr. Fairfax?"

"Just Fairfax will do." We reached a fairly deserted stretch of the beach with only a few surf bums coming and going, their minds more on the tide than the two of us. "It fits in with the interests of those concerned with his whereabouts."

"And what makes you think I know?"

"Little bird," he said. "More to the point is whether you're being disingenuous, Mr. Buttman. It has its own quality when used appropriately, but not so much if the end result is mischief for its own sake. Sobeski has gone missing and your name popped up. I'm asking around."

"Have you asked Delton Manaforte? He might know more than I. As a matter of fact, the last time I heard the name was in his company," Which was true, though Sobeski was dead by then.

"Mr. Manaforte has decided to withdraw from public functions of late. You were aware of his connection to the late Ashley Carmichael?"

"Yes."

"And Mr. Dunkle?"

"I know Xavier met Mr. Carmichael. And I assume he knows Manaforte. If he met Sobeski, he didn't mention it."

"He's been rather squeamish about being in public as well." Fairfax watched as two seagulls were fighting over a bag of chips, no doubt pilfered from an unsuspecting beachgoer.

"He has," I said. "He worries for his safety going forward."

"And you?"

"I think he'll be ok." We watched the seagulls for a moment more. "Why the interest in Sobeski? If he can't be found, isn't that a good thing?"

A faint turn of the lips was as close as Fairfax came to a smile. "To some, yes. To others with whom he had business, the answer is no."

"And you think I fit into this?"

"I know you do. I also know there's more to it, but for now, you should be aware that this matter is not settled. Thanks for the moment, Mr. Buttman. If we need to talk more, I'll know where to find you."

"I imagine so. Goodbye."

Agnes was still snoring when I returned. I wandered over to where the kids were building their sand castle and sat beside them, watching.

"Want to help, Mr. Sunshine?" Emily had reverted to form.

"No, I'll just watch," I said.

It wasn't a great sand castle and had no need to be, as Zach was soon to Godzilla it in all the maniacal zest a kid his age could muster. Lizzy joined in, as did Emily, after handing Jacob to me. Having sufficiently destroyed the castle, they pronounced themselves hungry and in urgent need of food.

"I want a hotdog," Zach demanded.

I patted his head and said, "No."

Lizzy laughed and Emily said, "I told you so." Zach pouted.

We woke Agnes with a lot of unnecessary noise and had lunch. After lunch, Agnes took the kids along the water's edge, Jacob took his nap, and an aggrieved Emily did her homework.

"I hope you're happy," she grumbled.

"I'm not unhappy," I assured her.

I tried to take my own nap, but was interrupted by my miserable phone. Ms. Constantinescu called to let me know I'd received a peculiar package. I was surprised as we got lots of packages, mostly solicitous, and she didn't call to tell me of them.

"It's just a key," she said.

"What do you mean?"

"It's just a key in a big box. There's nothing else in it."

"The return address?"

"Only that it's from here in LA. Post office box," she said. "What do you want me to do with it?"

"Drop it off at the big house, if you would."

"Ok, Mr. Monk."

I closed my eyes, hoping I would forget about it. I did, but it wasn't due to a nice nap. The phone buzzed a second time. Joanie. I groaned, which caused Emily to look over at me. "Just heartburn," I said.

"Can you stop by the Manifesto tomorrow?" Joanie asked.

"Why?"

"You know why. It's kinda important," she added.

"I'll bet." I heard her groan and felt better. "I'll let you know tomorrow."

More groaning. "Fine."

I said goodbye.

Emily did her own groaning for an hour before I relented and let her join the others. By four, they were tiring and Jacob was done with his nap. It was time to go back to the house in the hills.

"You'll have time to finish your homework," I helpfully said to Emily, smiling as she heaved a heavy sigh.

"You're a jerk, Mr. Sunshine," she whined.

The rest of the clan thought it was pretty funny.

Natalya arrived around six, said hello to the grump Emily, and handed the box to me. It was ten by eight by six inches in size. Had no postage on it. The return address was in the same writing as the office address.

"Who dropped this off?" I asked, puzzled.

"A woman," Natalya said. "I have to go, Mr. Monk."

"Sure."

In the box was the key. On the key, was stamped, 267. As Natalya had said, nothing else was in the box. No note, instructions, receipt, nothing. A box and a key. My phone dinged, alerting me to a text. I didn't recognize the number. *have to talk to you tomorrow important manifesto 2 OB*

I texted back: *ok.*

Rebekah and Fidel sauntered in at seven, looking refreshed after two days without the kids. We had dinner and watched kiddie movies out by the pool.

·   ·   ·   ·   ·

The morning had been consumed with kids and grandkids and getting them fed and out the door. Emily and Zach fussed more than Jacob, who was content to annoy his mother.

"What are you up to today, Sunshine?"

"Meetings, my love. I'm suddenly in demand," I told my suspicious wife.

"Anyone I know?" She arched her eyebrows and crossed her arms.

I did the same to annoy her. "Yes, and no. Joanie wants to talk about what's up with her and Mikal, and, I think, Orestra Blakely wants to talk, too."

"You think? And who's this Orestra?"

I rolled my eyes. "I think, because I don't know, but she's the only OB that comes to mind." I smiled at the blank look on Agnes' face. "She's the detective looking for Sterling's lover. Remember?"

"Oh," she said after a moment. "Do you need me to assist you?" She grinned at that.

"No, I can handle it." I assumed.

I texted Joanie: *I'll see you at one.*

·   ·   ·   ·   ·

I arrived at the Manifesto a little after one in the afternoon.

Joanie pointed at her watch, as I was a little late.

I shrugged. "You're not the only woman in my life, you know."

"Yeah, yeah, yeah. For once, can we focus on my problems?" She had her arms crossed, which reminded me of Agnes. I probably shouldn't mention that. They didn't care for one another.

I laughed. "Don't we always?" She didn't care for that. "Can I get you some coffee or a rich sugary version?"

"A Caramel Macchiato, if you don't mind," she said.

"When do I ever mind?"

"Just go!" She pointed towards the barista at the coffee bar.

I set the coffees on the table. "So, what's new, other than you're cheating on your husband?"

Joanie frowned as she picked up her drink. "Who says I'm cheating, Buttman?"

"My apologies." I picked up mine while keeping an eye on her face. Joanie had a few ticks I'd noticed over the years that telegraphed when she was being less than honest: Touching her cheek more than usual, looking away, and she blinked a lot. She was doing all three. "So, what are your problems, my dear, if it's not you and Mikal getting busy?"

"You know, you suggested my coming down here and singing again—"

"Yes, I did. If I remember correctly, at the time you were conflicted and lonely in your new life as a married woman," I said before taking a drink of my black coffee.

"Uh-huh. I don't think I said lonely and conflicted," she huffed.

"My apologies. Please continue." I was sure she'd crack soon.

She took a long slow sip of her drink while keeping her eyes on me. "All right, maybe something is going on, but don't call it 'getting busy'."

"Why not?"

"Because it makes it sound like a casual hookup, which it's not! And... Mikal and I have a history, as you well know—"

"Do I?" 1,2,3...

"Monk!"

I laughed. "Sorry. I'll be good."

"Uh-huh." Her eyes glistened as she blinked. "Can't you be nice anymore?"

I handed her a new napkin to dab her eyes as her napkin had residue from her sugary drink on it. "I can, but it frustrates me, because I knew it would come to this. You should have stayed with Mikal, but no, you had to run off and do this thing with Brian. Are you happy with the guy?" I didn't let her answer. "Seems unlikely, since you're here. And I'm not blind. I can see how you look at Mikal, how you're constantly touching him and smiling and laughing."

Joanie wiped her eyes and slumped down in her chair.

"Does Brian know you're sleeping with Mikal?" I asked. She shrugged. "What does that mean?"

"Brian has his own life, which keeps him busy. We don't talk much about what I'm doing. I'm mean, he knows I'm down here singing; he did come listen, if you remember?"

"I remember that it all seemed very forced and artificial, like you and Agnes," I said. "Which I don't get…from either of you."

She frowned. "That's just the way women are sometimes," she muttered.

"And Brian? What's the situation? Are you leaving, staying? Did you sign a pre-nup when you got your big payday after *we* screwed over the geezers?"

She smiled at that. "That was *you*, Buttman."

"Nice try. Well?" I *was* serious.

"That's why I'm here, you jerk. I don't know what to do, and Mikal says it's up to me, which is his way of getting back at me in the nicest way possible. And no, I didn't sign a pre-nup, but I won't lose my money from the sale of the Moonlight Arms—"

"But you might forfeit any gains you made on it, if it's deemed community property, which would be ironic—"

"Yeah, yeah, yeah. How do you know all this?" she pouted.

"I have an excellent moneyman."

"Maybe I'll get more from him?" She finished her coffee.

"That depends on your lawyer. Have you talked to Brian about any of this? And Mikal? Should I talk to him? Find out what he really thinks? Might not be a bad thing to know before you do something you'll regret, not that you've ever done that before." I finished my coffee.

"You're just mad because I didn't want to marry you!"

That made me smile. "Maybe."

"So, you'll help me?"

I looked into her pleading eyes. "I can't be the only friend you have."

"No," she said, reaching for my hand. "But I know you care about me, and I need that right now."

"Uh-huh."

She smiled at that.

12

Two o'clock came and went.

OB didn't show.

Joanie had spent the previous hour regaling me about how what she thought being married would be like wasn't, at least for her, and how she missed singing, and how being here with Mikal gave her something to look forward to. I listened and tried my best not to be the jerk I generally was. I wanted to ask, over and over, "Well, what did you think was going to happen?"

We talked till three, or I should say she talked.

Joanie hugged me before she left. "Thanks. It was good to talk, yeah?"

"Yeah," I said, my mind elsewhere.

I assumed OB to be Orestra Blakely, but now I wasn't so sure.

It was in this haze that Anna tapped me on the shoulder. Standing with her was her new man, Jerome. He held out his hand.

I stood and shook it. "Jerome," I said, stating the obvious. "Anna."

"What brings you here?" she asked. I didn't normally stop by on Wednesdays.

"Joanie needed to talk."

"Oh..." A sly grin came to my wife's daughter.

"Anyway," I said, mostly to move the conversation away from OB not showing up and Joanie's, and by extension Mikal's, problems with love and life. "How would you two like to come over for dinner? You can meet Agnes, Anna's mother, and my delightful wife."

"I'd like that," Jerome said, smiling.

Anna rolled her eyes. "Maybe this weekend."

"Big house or little house?" I wondered how much Jerome had been told about me and Agnes.

"We'll see. If I can get Barron and Gerta to come, maybe the big house is better," she said.

"Then we're set." I saw Mikal out of the corner of my eye. "I'd love to stay and chat, but other pressing affairs need my attention."

"Then we won't keep you." Anna noticed Mikal, too.

"It was nice to see you, Monk." Jerome again shook my hand, and they left.

I knocked on the door of Mikal's office and sat down in the chair by his desk. For once, I didn't get the big "Monk" greeting. I assumed Joanie had forewarned him. He was, for him, oddly subdued, even where any talk of Joanie was concerned. We talked of it a little as we first started this venture at the Manifesto. It was Mr. Jones' pipedream to begin with, but with Judith's money, and Mikal's experience and connections, it came to fruition, and through Mikal's particular brand of managing, combining laid-back LA groove with remarkable organization, it ran like a Swiss clock.

I did not want to lose him.

"What?" He must have noticed I was smiling.

"Just thinking..."

"Of?"

I sat back and stared at my hands. "It's embarrassing to admit to now, but for a while I didn't care for you much, and all of it based on my feelings of inferiority mixed with unrequited love for our dear Joanie."

He smiled. "Yeah, I picked up on that. And now?"

"Now I'd rather have you than Joanie, even though that's just the exhaust trails of a plane long gone. You know she was here, yes?" He nodded. "And as I expected, she wanted to talk, to explain things in her own convoluted way. Not that anything was settled, because it never is with her—"

Mikal laughed at that.

"Anyway..."

The room went quiet, with both of us in our own Joanie-land filled traumas.

"What are you going to do?" I asked. No need for me to dwell on the past. Mikal shrugged, but his eyes betrayed him. They were clouded with tears he did not want to let fall. "I know you still love her." He nodded and looked away. "She also said you've left it up to her as a way to, as she said, get back at her in the nicest way possible."

He laughed, which caused the tears to roll down his cheeks. I handed him a tissue. "Yeah." Mikal Thorvaldsen wiped his eyes. "I don't like this," he said, the smile gone. "I've always had a cardinal rule about married women: You stay away. It's just better for everyone involved. No matter how good they look or how badly you want to dive in. And I told her I wasn't... But..." he looked up at the ceiling and then his hands.

"But she's a hard habit to break."

He tried to smile at the musical reference. "Yeah. I don't know what I'm going to do, Monk. I miss her more so than I'd like to admit, and I'm doing things that are both beautiful and horrible at the same time. When she's here and we're making music together," he shook his head at that. "It's as if everything in the world is the way it should be. But...then she goes home, and all I feel is the distance and the shame." Another tear rolled down from his eye. "What do you think I should do?"

I thought about it. What *would* you do, Buttman? my smug inner voice asked. "Well, based on how badly I fucked up things with Agnes and Judith, for me, the answer is simple. I told her then, and I told her again today, that I think you two belong together. If you feel the same way, I think you should say so, and tell her that she has to decide; no more fooling around, because the longer you do, the harder it makes everything else. Be honest with her, be brutal if you have to, in the nicest possible way, but don't make yourself sick."

"And if she doesn't want to?"

"You have all of us," I said, spreading my arms out. "We love you and need you, and I won't let you go."

"No?" He seemed genuinely surprised.

"*No.* I hope Joanie comes to her senses, but if I have to choose between the two of you, and I never thought I'd ever say such a thing, it'd be you."

"Thanks, Monk."

"Sure."

We stood up and he walked me to the front door.

"Oh, one last thing," I said, as I noticed Anna and Jerome in a far corner of the dining area. "What do you think of Jerome?" I nodded in their direction.

A knowing grin came to Mikal. "He's a good guy. Of course, I only know him as a sax man."

I left it at that.

Driving home, I thought about interfering, about getting Joanie on the phone, but it went no further than that. This was their headache, not mine. I had plenty on my plate. That made me think of Orestra Blakely. Again, there was plenty on my plate.

I let it go until Jackson Mallory left me a message three days later. *I'd like to talk to you.*

·　·　·　·　·

I met him at the city morgue. A body had been found along the LA river in brush by the Hyperion Bridge. Not far from the body was a card with my name on it. There was no identification on the body. They were running fingerprints and all of that; police business I had no interest in. I wasn't thrilled at having to go, but I said I'd be there.

What was left of Orestra Blakely was presented to me. Her skull had been caved in, obscuring the left side of her head and a good part of her face.

"Are you sure, Mr. Buttman?" Detective Mallory asked.

I pointed to the tattoo on her right wrist, a series of interweaving vines and yellow roses. It looked as if a bracelet had been imprinted on her wrist. I remembered it from her last visit to the office. "Yes."

The body was taken away.

There was a coffee shop just down the road.

It was noon. Mallory asked if I was hungry. I said no.

He smiled at that. "How did you know the deceased?" It was time for questions.

"I didn't actually know her. I met her twice. Both times she came to my office. Private Investigator. The first time, she said she was looking for a woman named Aisha Diamond. The second time, we talked about black transwomen and how people like me could find or hook up with them without it causing ourselves any trouble."

"People like you…" He glanced up from the pad he was writing on.

I nodded. "Rich. White. Privileged."

"She say why?"

"Not directly. I got a text a few days ago from someone I thought was her. Wanted to meet at the Manifesto, but never showed up. I assumed if there was anything else, it would have come up at that meeting. Then you called."

"What's the connection between you and Aisha Diamond?"

"My brother Sterling had a relationship with her. I had an investigator find her when Sterling's wife asked me to." I added that Orestra knew Aisha through a LGBTQ group.

"Anything else come to mind?"

"I know before she transitioned, she was in the Army. That's about it." I watched Mallory put the notebook in his jacket. "What do you know about this, detective?"

"That somebody killed her and dumped her body. As you saw, she died of blunt force trauma to the head. We're still looking into the rest of it. Now that we have a name, it should move quicker." Detective Mallory sat back. "You have an alibi, Mr. Buttman?"

"Babysitting my delightful grandkids," I said.

He thanked me and headed out.

I spent the next hour staring at the half-empty cup in front of me.

·   ·   ·   ·   ·

After some cajoling, Agnes convinced Barron and Gerta to spend the weekend with us, which necessitated using the big house, which morphed the whole weekend into a big family gathering with kids and grandkids galore, which was something I didn't want, but probably needed. It was all precipitated by my casual remark that maybe Anna would bring Jerome over for dinner.

"It'll be fun," Agnes assured me.

"Maybe Anna doesn't want our meeting with the new guy turned into a circus," I said, somewhat facetiously.

"Gonna have to get to it at some point, huh?" She put her hands on her hips and cocked her head.

"That's your rationale?" I did the same to mock her.

"It'll be fun," she repeated, smiling at my feeble attempt to have a say. "You don't want us to get together? Hmmm?"

"No." I lied.

"You don't fool me for a minute, Monk Buttman," she said. "We both know you'll have a great time."

"That's not the issue here," I protested.

"Uh-huh."

Having lost the argument, I got working on the logistics of what we'd be eating for three days. I decided this was something Emily could help me with.

"Take him too," Rebekah said, handing me an ornery Jacob when I arrived at their house to pick up Emily.

"I wanna go too," Zach demanded.

"And me!" Lizzy joined the chorus.

My daughter grinned and handed Jacob's baby bag to me, which I gave to Emily.

"Festivities begin promptly at four, my dear. Don't be late." I had to say something.

"Sure," was my daughter's response.

Grocery shopping with a teenager, two overly stimulated kids, and a whiny baby was everything I imagined it to be. Emily was both bored and irritated by Zach and Lizzy running around. I put her in charge of the kids as they were grabbing and demanding and pouting when Gamps shut down their demands. Jake would only be quiet when I held him. To make matters all the more enjoyable, the store was packed. Somehow, we managed to find what was on the list, and headed for the land of the rich and famous, where there was the foolish idea that they would spend the rest of the day screaming and yelling and playing in the pool.

"There's homework to be finished," I said to a moody Emily, "and quiet time for you two while Mr. Grumpy here takes a nap." Zach started to whine, but I cut him off. "Otherwise, no pool time. Capeesh, little dude?"

"You're a meany, Gamps," he said, frowning with his arms crossed. Like mother, like son.

"Yes, I am," I laughed.

The afternoon agenda having been set, I put Jacob down for his nap while the other three quietly grumbled.

I sat on the couch with the world doing its thing just beyond the sliding glass doors.

* * * * *

It was the kind of day people in LA live for, the kind that people give as a reason to move here, which included me. It was warm and bright with a slight southern breeze that danced around and kept the heat at bay. The pool glistened in the sunlight and the only sounds were the birds flitting from tree to ground to feeder to tree, and an occasional aircraft high above. It wasn't the kind of day to find yourself at the county morgue looking at what was left of a once vibrant person. I had questions that wouldn't go away, and two diametrically opposed pictures of Orestra Blakely in my head. She was in my office as we bantered, and on the morgue table, gray and broken.

How is it that earlier I was standing with Mallory and now I'm here on this beautiful day, in this beautiful house, and feeling completely disconnected? I watched Emily as she mirthlessly worked through her assignments, while Lizzy colored and Zach played a game on his iPad.

Life is unreal.

Agnes, who had been running around with MaryAnn, sauntered in around three. Rebekah and Fidel at five; Barron and Gerta a little after eight. Anna stopped by, sans Jerome, to Agnes' disappointment at nine.

"I just came by to say hi," she said.

"Yeah, Grandma, lighten up." I felt the need to be a weasel.

"Oh, be quiet, Monk," my disapproving wife told me.

We had a late dinner and enjoyed some grownup time after getting the kids to bed. Emily glommed onto Anna as she had Natalya. Barron and Gerta talked about having kids, and Barron hinted he might be ready to move on to civilian life.

"I've been looking at different options," he said to his enquiring mother.

"Maybe Monk can find you something," she helpfully told him. "Right Monk?"

"If Barron has some ideas, I'm sure he'll let me know," I said, nodding to Barron, who nodded to his mother.

"I'm just trying to help," she said defensively. "So, what were you up to today, Sunshine?"

"Getting ready for this little shindig," I said. "That and I went to the morgue." I took a sip of the whiskey I had in my hand.

Agnes, Barron, Gerta, Anna, Emily, Rebekah, and Fidel went quiet.

"What were you doing at the morgue?" my daughter asked.

"What does anyone do at the morgue? I was asked to identify a body." I took another drink. It was nice and smooth.

Agnes went next. "Who was it?"

"Woman named Orestra Blakely," I said. "Remember?"

Her face went blank and then her eyes grew wide. "The Sterling thing! She's part of that, right?"

"Bingo," I said, holding up my glass.

A knowing smile on the face of my beautiful Agnes. It abruptly left when she added in the morgue part. "What happened?"

"Someone crushed in her skull. They found her along the LA river by the Hyperion bridge." I finished the whiskey and suddenly felt very tired.

"When?" someone asked.

"Three or four days ago. Mallory called me because they found my card nearby. There wasn't any identification on the body." I thought about having another drink.

"Was she raped?"

I focused my eyes on Agnes. "I don't know. I didn't ask." I got up and went to the bar.

It was then I thought of the key.

13

It was still in the box Natalya had been given, resting quietly in the library.

I kept it in my hand nearly the entire weekend, through the parade of family, the kids running around, the introduction and interrogation of Jerome, which veered a little too close to parody as Anna bobbed and weaved at her mother, parried questions about what was up between them, and the grumbling later.

"Why is it so hard to tell me?" Agnes asked when we were alone.

"Beats me, my love."

"You're no help, Sunshine," she groused.

"I'll try to be better in the future," I assured her.

"I guess he's ok," she said after a few moments of silence.

"I asked around," I said, the key in my hand, "and the people I talked to told me he was a good egg."

"Good egg? Who talks like that?" She seemed surprised I would use such a phrase, which surprised me.

"I haven't the faintest idea."

She laughed and kissed me. "You're something else."

"I do what I can."

She kissed me some more. "Good egg, huh?"

"Good egg."

•　　•　　•　　•　　•

The return address was a P.O. box in West Hollywood. I looked up the address on my phone and made a note of it.

The last of the weekend ended with a barbeque/pool party before Barron and Gerta had to head back north to San Luis Obispo, or, as it was referred to locally, SLO. Anna and Jerome joined the festivities, which signaled that Jerome was not put off yet by the clan. I was charged with keeping Jacob Austin Montaigne amused. Since he had shown a fondness for Anna, I handed him to her when it was time to cook.

"Practice," I said.

"For what?" She looked around for Jerome, who was talking baseball with Fidel and Barron.

"For whatever." I rubbed my grandson's head for luck and headed for the grill.

Agnes called to me. "Your phone's ringing, Monk."

"I'll get it later."

I should have answered it.

As there were no simmering family problems to deal with—Jerry and Denise, Agnes' parents, couldn't make it, having other plans for the weekend, and Jerome being a "good egg"—the day went as expected, other than the cloudburst that sent us all inside, except for Zach and Emily, who ignored the rain.

Barron and Gerta were sent off with hugs and kisses and promises of visits soon to come. That was followed by the unhappy task of telling Zach and Emily that the weekend was over and it was time to leave this veritable paradise for the more mundane vistas of West Covina. Both took the news poorly and complained vociferously to little avail. Last was Anna and Jerome.

"Thanks for inviting me," Jerome said, taking care to direct this more towards Agnes than me. "I had a wonderful time."

"We hope to see you again," Agnes said.

I nodded in agreement.

It was our turn to leave. I checked the house and grabbed the box the key came in.

·   ·   ·   ·   ·

The first message I checked, after arriving back at our comfy little house, was from Mr. Jones. "We need to talk, Buttman." He didn't reference what.

The second message, sent before Mr. Jones,' was from a number I didn't recognize. "My name is Orinda Blakely. I want to talk to you about Orestra. Please call."

I checked the time. It was nearly ten.

"Yes?" she said, answering on the third ring.

"This is Monk Buttman," I said.

There was only silence at first. "They told me you identified Orestra."

"Yes, that's true."

"I..." More silence. "I hear you own that music place, the Manifesto."

"That's true too."

Her voice cracked. "I...could you meet me there?"

"I can. What time?"

"Maybe on Tuesday. I only work a half-day. Three or so?" It sounded like she was trying not to cry.

"Sure," I said, not knowing why.

She hung up.

I hesitated calling Jones.

"Yeah?" He, too, answered on the third ring.

"You said we needed to talk," I reminded him.

"No," he said, "it's not important. Sorry about that." I could hear him breathing like Orinda Blakely. "Another time, all right."

"Another time."

He hung up.

Orville Riley, aka Mr. Jones, had many admirable traits: He was forthright in his beliefs, honest, more so than most of us; blunt, which he used to shield his emotions, and with me, judgmental and occasionally sarcastic, which I needed from time to time. Rarely, if ever, did he apologize. To me. Mostly because I didn't deserve it. I couldn't remember him saying, in all the time I'd known him, "Sorry about that."

•   •   •   •   •

I called Mallory the next day.

"Why the interest, Mr. Buttman?"

I thought about that. "I don't have a good answer for that except that it bothers me, and yes, I know how that sounds. I also wondered about my card being there. Why leave that when everything else is removed?"

"Does seem a little odd, doesn't it?" he said. "Like a plant?"

"You tell me?"

"I'll hold that card, Mr. Buttman."

"Nice. What did you find that you can tell me?" I was in the backyard staring at the neighbor's tree that shaded me.

"The victim was identified as Oren Winston Blakely from his service records. U.S. Army. Forty-four years old. Licensed detective in the state of California for the last ten years. Lived in West Hollywood. Had a small office there. We believe he became Orestra prior to getting the license, as that was the name registered on the application."

I heard him jostle what sounded like paper as Agnes waved to me from the kitchen.

"Any idea where we can find Aisha Diamond?" he asked.

"No idea."

"Anything else?"

Agnes was bringing me coffee. "No. Thanks." Mallory hung up and I took the cup of coffee. "Thanks."

"Who was that?" Agnes sat down beside me.

"Detective Mallory," I said.

"What'd he want?"

"I called him." The coffee was good.

"About?" Agnes was looking me over, her eyes tracking mine.

"Orestra Blakely. I wanted to know if they'd found out anything," I said. "What are you up to today?"

Agnes continued to stare at me. "I'm taking Emily to the mall. I need to stop at the fabric store and she wants to scope out the local kids. You?"

"An errand or two," I said.

"Uh-huh." I wasn't fooling her for a minute. "Do I need to be concerned here, Buttman?"

"I don't think so," I lied.

Agnes leaned in and kissed me. "Uh-huh."

We finished our coffee enjoying our little patch of suburbia under the sun.

·　　·　　·　　·　　·

The P.O. box was one in a row of them at the Post Office in West Hollywood. Middle right corner. The box the key was assigned to was of medium size, able to hold letters and small packages. Inside was a bulky envelope containing a set of keys and a note with a series of numbers on it and two addresses. Both were within walking distance.

I observed the surveillance camera above the entrance to the post office.

Orestra Blakely's office was on Santa Monica in a small building just behind a store for lease. This was downscale Hollywood, filled with regular people and businesses, although there were acting schools, film institutes, and the like. It was a tan building, single story with a pitched roof, tinted windows, and a small sign just above the street number. Next door was a notary, and next to that a place offering emotional therapy. I looked for cameras among the three buildings. Only the notary had anything that might house one in its oversized exterior lamp.

I approached the door to OB Investigations and checked the keys against the lock. The keys had identifying tabs on them. There were four keys, one marked with an H, one with a W, a third with a D, and the last one with an S. Next to the addresses on the note were four numbers, which I assumed went with any security systems within. The W key fit in the door lock and deadbolt. I thought about entering, but thought better of it. I made like I was trying the door, looked in the door's window, though it was blocked by a curtain, and left.

The second address was on Norton, a few blocks west of the office. An apartment complex, two story, with what looked like eight apartments on each floor. These were older apartments, I assumed from the 60s or 70s, so I didn't expect much security, but I looked all the same. There was nothing by the first floor south-end unit. As at the office, the key marked H fit and turned the lock on apartment *108*. Again, I thought better of entering. The window to the living room had the curtains drawn, but was of a sheer enough fabric that I could make out a couch and chair, a table, two lamps, and the kitchen at the other end.

I turned to leave and found a middle-aged woman with dark brown hair and a frown on her face staring at me. She had on a faded blue Dodgers tee-shirt and white stretch pants.

"You own this place?" she asked, accusingly.

That made me smile. "No. I was simply verifying an address."

She tightened her eyes and cocked her head. "You looking for O?"

"No. Just the address," I said.

She continued to look me up and down. I assumed it was the suit. I had on a light colored houndstooth sportscoat, gray shirt and slacks, with a white tie. I thought it went well with my graying light brown hair. "You know O?" Another question.

"I've met her, yes," I said. "Have you seen her lately?"

She shook her head. "No, I haven't seen her for a while… That why you're here, mister?"

"Yes. I was supposed to meet her, but she never showed."

The woman smiled. "I didn't think you were her type, but..."

I smiled back. "Who is anyone's type?"

"My name's Aileen," she said, extending her hand. "You?"

"Monk." I said, taking hers. I got the impression if I wasn't Orestra's type, I might be Aileen's.

Aileen moved in closer, looking side to side. "Cops were around here a couple of days ago. Sent a bunch a people through her place. That's why I thought you might be the owner. Maybe she skipped or something, but..."

"But?"

Aileen shrugged. "She didn't strike me as the type, you know?"

"I think I do." I noticed she had deep blue eyes with thick eyelashes, no doubt applied. "Cops talk to you?"

"I'm not fond of cops, so I stayed quiet. You know?" Her eyes darkened.

"Yeah." I leaned in a little. "If you don't mind my asking Aileen, what was O's type?"

"O like girls," she said.

"Thanks. It was nice to meet you," I said.

"Me too, Monk." She still had my hand in hers. "You got a number?" I nodded. "Maybe, if you're interested, I could let you know if I see O, or I hear something."

"I would be." I handed her a card.

A grin came to her as she read the card. Probably the name. "See you, Monk."

"Bye." Whether I saw her again seemed unlikely, but... I shook my head at that. LA is a dangerous town when it comes to women and fools like me.

The next stop was my office. It wasn't far away. My chief of staff was busy doing something important, whether I knew it or not. I sat in one of the chairs by her desk. She smiled and continued doing whatever it was she was doing. After five minutes, she knew I was up to no good.

"Yes, Mr. Monk?"

I put the box that had held the key on her desk. "You said a woman dropped this by."

"Yes."

"Do you remember what she looked like?"

Natalya rubbed her chin. "Black woman," she said. "Well dressed. Why?"

"Do you remember seeing her before? Here perhaps?"

"I didn't get a good look at her." She picked up the box. "I was putting the reports on your desk, and I heard a knock. When I came in here, I saw the box and caught a glimpse of her going out the door. I didn't see her face."

"You sure it was a woman?"

"I think so," she said. "Is something wrong?"

"Probably." I took out the set of keys and the note from my coat pocket. "The key was to a post office box in West Hollywood. In it was an envelope with these keys. They open the office and apartment of a woman who was murdered last week. She stopped by to see me a few days before she was killed. I wondered if she dropped off that box." I handed the keys and note to Natalya.

"You think she knew she'd be killed?"

I didn't want to consider that. "Maybe. It would explain a few things."

She handed the keys and note back to me. "Maybe you should tell the police."

"Yeah." I rolled the keys between my fingers.

"You remember your meeting tomorrow with Isaac and the people from the Lemoye Foundation?" She knew I didn't.

"I do now," I said, rising out of my chair. "I'll put it on my calendar."

"Do you look at your calendar, Mr. Monk?" my chief of staff asked, judging me.

"There's always a first time," I said.

At my desk, I looked for the number of the company managing our building. It was one of Dunkle's. Argot Building Services. Our building's overseer was a taciturn woman named Heidi Bronski, who Xavier liked because she was willing to call him out when he was acting like an ass, which was most of time.

That, and, as he would say, "She gets the job done and the tenants seem to like her."

"Yes, Mr. Buttman, how may I help you?" Ms. Bronski had a practiced professional voice that radiated conceit.

"I'd like to talk to security. A woman dropped off a package here last week without announcing herself, and left before we could speak to her. So, I'd like to know if security has her on their camera feed." I tried to speak as professionally as I could.

"I'll pass this along to Mr. Gambol, Mr. Buttman. Is there anything else?"

"No," I assured her.

"Good day then."

Five minutes later, Mr. Gambol called. I reiterated the request, gave him the date and time, and he promised to look into it and get back to me as soon as possible.

Since I was here, and had an important meeting the next day, I did the prudent thing and took a nap on the big and exceedingly comfortable couch in my office. Mr. Gambol's efficiency, or that of his people, only allowed me twenty minutes of relaxation.

"I'll send it in an encrypted email, Mr. Buttman," he said.

That arrived thirty seconds after he hung up. I clicked on the email and the link. There she was, walking into the building, up the elevator, down the hall, and into our offices before walking out. The high definition of the video made the face quite clear.

It was Aisha Diamond.

14

The next day was another day on the job. Most meetings I was subjected to were conducted on Tuesdays and Thursdays. They were also the days that Emily went with me so she could assist Natalya. She was also taking her fashion cues from Natalya, which at times generated consternation in both Agnes and Rebekah. When asked, I was of no help.

"I think she looks fine," I said.

"Why do I bother," Agnes would say, and I would shrug.

Today, her dress was more conservative. A knee-length skirt of varying purple hues that matched the highlights around her eyes, another trait of Natalya's she was mimicking, and a white top that wasn't too tight.

"Let's go, Mr. Monk," Emily commanded.

Outside the building we were met by Ronnie, a homeless man I'd befriended after the foundation moved here from the house in the hills. Carson Macklgrew, my money man, insisted we have a proper place of business. Ronnie and I had an agreement: I palmed him a few bucks when I came in, and he wouldn't make a nuisance of himself, though that was more the building management's take than mine. I considered Ronnie eccentric and harmless.

"Hey Monk." He liked to greet me in the parking garage.

"Ronnie." I put some twenties in his hand. "Keeping busy?"

Ronnie couldn't sit still. Liked to be on the move. Didn't believe in being indoors; being confined. He was a veteran of the Iraq war and had been injured when his convoy hit a series of IEDs. He ended up with a metal plate in his head.

"Always got things to do, Monk," he said in his staccato style of speaking. "Got a group I'm watching in the morning and another in the afternoon." People watching was his idea of fun. That's how I met him. I noticed him watching me one afternoon.

"Anything interesting?" I motioned to Emily that she could go in without me. I don't think she was comfortable around Ronnie.

"Always interesting," he said as we watched Emily go inside.

Standing by the entry door, the building's security man, Benny, had his eye on us.

"Are you staying on good terms with Benny?" I asked.

"Oh, yeah, oh, yeah," Ronnie nodded. "Doing good, no trouble," he said.

"Want to do me a favor?" I took a couple more twenties out of my pocket.

He looked up and down the street, which he did often. "Like what maybe?"

"Keep an eye out for anyone watching the building," I said.

"Like who?" His eyes darted between me and Benny.

"Black woman. About my height in heels. Dresses sharp." I watched his eyes. "Trans." They widened at that.

He looked over at Benny. "Can't sit here, you know, can't sit here—"

"I'm not asking you to get in trouble. Just in your usual moving around. If you see something, let me know, ok?"

"Got it, Monk." He put the twenties in his pocket. "Thanks again." He spun around and headed down an alley.

Benny was giving me the eye as I came through the door. Beyle "Benny" Abdullahi was a Somali who had moved to LA as a kid when his mother fled the war there. He was tall, slender, had high cheekbones and an easy laugh, but was as tough as he was lean.

"Keeping Ronnie in good money, Mr. Monk?" Benny disapproved of my generosity. Having had to scrap and adjust every day of his life, he was less understanding of people like Ronnie, especially since the foundation was there to help and Ronnie was resistant to that.

"I know, I know. I'll try to be better. Besides, I gave Ronnie a job to do," I said.

"And?" Benny crossed his arms. I asked him on a number of occasions to cut Ronnie some slack, so long as he didn't bug the other tenants.

"I asked him to keep an eye out for a black transwoman watching our fair building."

"Like the one here last week?" He smiled at that.

"Which one?" I smiled back. "There were two but..."

"But?"

My smile faded. "One was murdered, and I think the other had or knows something about it. Just being careful," I said.

"Police know?" His smile was gone, too.

"Yeah. Whether they care is a different matter. Take care, Benny."

"Always, Mr. Monk." He grinned at that. Natalya's moniker for me was getting around.

Emily and Natalya were already setting up for the meeting soon to be enjoined by a reluctant yours truly. I tried to take interest, and every now and again I did, but mostly it was pro forma for me. The final decisions were made by the power troika of Macklgrew, Constantinescu, and Bohrman. Isaac had done well in little more than a year with the foundation, had his own office, title, and a decent salary.

I sat in the conference room in my august chair at the head of the large mahogany table that could seat twenty. Emily brought me a cup of coffee and the folder on the Lemoye Foundation. Theirs was a smaller nonprofit, focused on brain injuries and recovery, and they desired to partner with us.

Isaac showed up a half-hour prior to the start of the meeting, as did Carson Macklgrew. We shook hands and went over the proposal, as Natalya and Emily greeted the two men and one woman who were here to see us.

It was a straight up plea for money, and our using what lobbying prowess we had together to further our joint goal of helping veterans, especially those falling through the cracks at the VA. They struck me as earnest and serious, and I was grateful they were willing to do this work.

They were assured we'd get back to them with our answer in a few days.

Carson Macklgrew, as usual, cautioned restraint. "We can't fund everyone who comes in here with a proposal, no matter how well intended."

"True, but," Isaac countered, "they're a plus when it comes to selling our story to legislators. They like joint efforts and groups pooling their resources. It makes good copy. And they're not asking for a lot of money."

The Air Force veteran Macklgrew turned to me. "Well, Monk?"

"I'll swing with Isaac on this one. It's only for one year—"

"Plus, options," Macklgrew added.

"But we control the yes or no," I said, which was my way of ok-ing the deal.

Carson shook his head. "I know, it's only money."

I laughed, knowing how hard it was for him to even state that out loud.

There were more monetary interests to discuss, which was followed by my taking everyone to lunch. Afterwards Isaac, Natalya, and Emily returned to the foundation, Mr. Macklgrew to his office, while I headed to the Manifesto and Orinda Blakely.

•   •   •   •   •

I was fiddling with the keys from the P.O. box when she approached the table I was sitting at. She had the same strong jawline and probing eyes as Orestra, appeared to be a little shorter, and had her reddish hair fashioned in long braids. She was shaking.

I stood up and extended my hand. "Ms. Blakely." She held it briefly and sat down. "What can I do for you?"

"How well did you know Orestra?" Her eyes were looking at mine.

"Not well. I meet her twice and I believe we were to meet here a week ago, but she never showed. Have the police contacted you?"

She lowered her head. "Yeah, but…" Tears were running down her cheeks. I pulled a package of tissues out of the breast pocket of my jacket and handed them to her. "I assume you knew that O was…"

"Trans?"

"Yeah." She wiped her eyes. "We don't talk about O," she said. "My father won't let us, won't…" she wadded and unwadded the wet tissue in her hands. "He didn't even acknowledge what the police said. He just hung up."

"How did you find out about me, then?"

"I called the police, and they said that a man named Monk Buttman identified the body. I asked a family friend if he could help me find you after I couldn't find anything online."

"And this friend?" I had an idea. Finding me took work. I'd asked Bernie to scrub me from the Internet and only those good at searching could.

"Orville Riley," she said.

I nodded. "Did Mr. Riley tell you that he knows me?"

She seemed surprised. "No. He only said he'd heard of you. You know him?"

"Yes. Though I think of him more as Mr. Jones. He and I have had a few adventures together. He was the driving force that convinced me to support this place." I waved my hand around the room.

Pluto, who was over by the barista's cart, came to our table. "Can I get you something, Mr. Monk?"

"Cup a joe," I said. "Would you like something, Ms. Blakely?"

"Could I have some green tea, please?" she said.

"Absolutely," the loquacious Pluto replied.

"Thanks dude," I said. We both smiled at that. He left us. "Do you know who O left her estate to?" Orinda Blakely shook her head no. "What would you like me to do?"

"I don't know, I don't understand." She wiped her eyes again though they were dry.

"Did you talk to her recently, or should I ask if you talked at all?"

Orinda shifted in her chair. Pluto came over with our drinks.

"Enjoy," he said with his usual brio. If he noticed the sadness in Orinda's eyes, he didn't show it.

We played with our drinks. I thought of my friend, Orville Riley. I knew of his dislike, disdain, for trans-people, and of gender fluidity. God made men and women, and we were what we were, he would tell me on the rare occasions when it would come up. That made me think of Dahlia Leonard; that Dahlia woman, as Mr. Jones would say.

"I did talk with O," she said, pulling me back to the moment at hand. "The last time was a couple of weeks ago. Everything seemed ok. She was doing good, even said there was a job she was working on that might be more important than she first thought, but she didn't tell me what."

"What kind of jobs did O do?"

"She mostly helped LGBTQ clients...they trusted her. I don't really know too much. I had to be careful..." She looked directly at me. "I don't know why now. What good did it do?"

"I'm sorry," I said, wanting to say something more.

"I should go. I don't know why I came here." She pushed the tea away and stood.

I walked with her to the front door. "Do you mind if I look into this, Ms. Blakely?"

Orinda Blakely focused her eyes on mine. "Why would you do that?"

"Because I think Orestra would have wanted me to," I said.

"Then I don't mind," she said. "But that's just me. My father, if he finds out, will. He's never forgiven O for breaking his heart."

I watched her walk away.

I returned to my office at the foundation. My chief of staff and her minion ignored me beyond saying hello. That was fine with me. I had my own things to do. I understood now Mr. Jones' enigmatic response when I called. At some point, I expected him at my door. I'd deal with that then. First, I'd call Bernie, and maybe Art Devaney, though I didn't know how he would help; the problem wasn't with Orestra's, or I should say Oren's, service. This was all post transition. Then I'd go see Dahlia Leonard. Maybe she knew something, heard something, however unlikely. It was possible she didn't have any idea who Orestra Blakely was.

Bernie was in better spirits these days. The events concerning my recent adventure into the land of conspiracy had allowed him to relax somewhat. Bernie, more than I, was worried about the possibility that tech elites and their ilk were planning to reorganize the world in their own Promethean image, to do away with so much pointless human intrigue, and replace it with their own. I was more sanguine, having survived Sobeski's attempt to kill me and Agnes in Michigan the year before.

The world never stops spinning.

"I'd like you to look someone up for me, if you would," I told him. "Person named Orestra Blakely. Transwoman. Was murdered last week. She was known as Oren Winston Blakely before transitioning. Served in the Army. Licensed private dick." I thought that was cute. An inside joke to those who knew me.

"Interesting. I assume you'll explain why later," he said.

"Probably." Nothing more needed to be said.

Next was Dahlia Leonard.

I looked up the number for the outreach center I remembered her running when I was looking for Desiree Marshan, her cohort in criminal stupidity. But that was years ago, and having survived that, and coming into more money than I'd ever need, I always gave money to the LGBTQ outreach center in West Hollywood. I hadn't seen or spoken to Ms. Leonard since I left her at her friend's apartment that terrible day.

"This is Dahlia Leonard," she answered. Still there.

"This is Monk Buttman, Ms. Leonard. I don't know if you remember me..."

Silence. Then, "I remember you, Mr. Buttman. To what do I owe the privilege?"

I smiled at the frost in her voice. "A woman named Orestra Blakely. Did you know her?"

The frost lessened. "Did? What do you mean?"

"I'm sorry, but she was murdered a week ago," I said.

"Oh, my god!"

I gave her a moment. "If you don't mind, I'd like to talk to you about her."

"Why?" She had the same question everyone had.

"Because I believe Ms. Blakely would want me to." I had the same answer.

Her reluctance echoed through the phone. "When?"

"Twenty minutes," I said.

"All right, Mr. Buttman."

•　　•　　•　　•　　•

It was as if no time had passed, except that Mr. Jones wasn't with me. The woman at the counter eyed me with suspicion, as did the three other people there. I tried to be gracious, given that I didn't fit in. The building, the waiting area, the décor, all of it, was as it was the day Mr. Jones and I came by to talk to that Dahlia woman. I was smiling and shaking my head as Ms. Leonard came out.

"Did I miss something?" she asked.

"Just a memory," I said.

She looked much the same, though there were wisps of gray in her blond hair, and more lines on her face around her eyes and mouth. I followed her into her office. As she watched me, I remember those eyes from before, probing, unsure, and fearful. Murder does that, I suppose.

Ms. Leonard took a pencil off the desk. It had bite marks on it. "What do you want, Mr. Buttman?"

"How well did you know Orestra Blakely and a woman named Aisha Diamond?"

"Aisha? What's she got to do with this?"

"I don't know exactly. I know Orestra was looking for her, but I got the impression there was more to it."

She began tapping the desk with the eraser side of the pencil. "How does someone like you even know Orestra or Aisha? You didn't strike me as someone who was into transwomen."

"In that regard, you're correct, but my brother is. His wife found out about him and Aisha, and because of my nefarious past, it was assumed I'd know what to do." I sighed at that. "Anyway, somehow Orestra found out about that and came to see me. Said she was looking for Aisha. We were supposed to meet again, but she never showed. A few days later, the cops called."

"That doesn't explain why I should talk to you?" She put the pencil in her mouth.

I sat back. "Let's just say you owe me."

15

Dahlia Leonard waivered at that. I didn't like playing the debt card, but it was true. Jones and I got her out of South Laguna after she'd witnessed the killers descend on Todd Boyer's beach bungalow and murder her accomplices. We could have left her, but I couldn't do it, even though she'd had me beaten up. And while I gave money to the center through Sunshine Holding LLC, I saw no reason to interfere in her life.

"Is this how you do things, Mr. Buttman?" She was back to tapping the pencil.

"Spare me the umbrage, Ms. Leonard. I'm not seeking any confidences, just some information. Maybe I can help." I leaned forward. "Do you know what Ms. Blakely did for a living?"

"She was a private dick," she smirked. "A real one."

I laughed at that. "Very nice. Was she well known in the LGBTQ community?"

"How well, I don't know. Her specialty was finding missing family members, though that's just a nice way of saying she found trans people for families looking for their own. I know Orestra was trusted in our community."

"Meaning?" Orinda used the same term: Trust.

"Meaning if she thought these families had ulterior motives, she played it coy," Dahlia said.

"Ulterior motives like changing them back?"

"Something like that." The pencil was back in her mouth.

"And Aisha?"

"I really don't know much about her. She'd show at some of our get-togethers every once in a while, but she was never a regular. I know she's tight with some other girls. They were together a lot, but I haven't seen them in a while either."

"Did you ever see Orestra and Aisha together?"

"It's possible, but I don't remember any particular instance." She put the pencil down. "My turn. Why the interest? What do you care? Noblesse oblige? Here to be the straight white moral savior for some wayward black girls? Get them back to playing their stereotypical roles so you feel better?"

"Nothing quite so grand. I liked her. It's as simple as that. Besides, she wanted to take advantage of my obvious privilege," I said. "Being a straight white moral savior gets you into places that wouldn't welcome a transgendered black woman."

"What do you mean?" Dahlia picked up the pencil, became self-conscious, and put it back down.

"Let's say I *do* have a thing for black transwomen, but am loathe to hit the streets or social media. Maybe I worry about appearances. Certainly, there must be more discrete channels for such opportunities? That's what we were going to talk about at our meeting. The one she didn't get to. I think she found or stumbled onto something much more sinister than just where Aisha had run off to. That's why I'm asking. Maybe I can help, even if I come off as a moralizing white savior." I grinned at that.

"What do you want from me?"

"Ask around. Everyone, no matter who they are, gets lonely, looks for love. Why wouldn't they? And if they think it's safe?" I sat back. "I don't live so isolated a life that I don't know there are people easily preyed upon and easily forgotten or thrown away. And, believe it or not, I know what it's like to be looked down on, even if it's not to the same degree." I got up.

Dahlia Leonard stood. "I'll think about it."

I handed her my card. "If you do."

She walked me to the waiting room. "Maybe you should talk to your brother for the information you want."

"Don't worry, I will," I assured her. "But he only knows his side of it. I doubt he knows much of it from yours. Good day, Ms. Leonard."

"Mr. Buttman."

I returned to the office to pick up Emily for the exciting drive across town. Emily was sitting quietly in my office. Natalya was at her desk, staring blankly at her computer.

"Everything ok?" I asked, looking between the two of them from the doorway of my office.

"Everything is ok, Mr. Monk," Natalya said, in a soft voice I didn't recognize.

Emily got up and joined me. I opened the door to the hallway. Emily looked at Natalya, who continued to stare blankly at nothing in particular.

"Bye," Emily said.

Natalya tried to smile and failed.

•　　•　　•　　•　　•

Emily was fidgeting in her seat. "Do you know a lot about Natalya?"

We were stuck in the usual bale of early evening traffic that stretched as far as the eye could see.

I turned to Emily. "Why do you ask?"

"I asked her if she had many boyfriends growing up, and she..." Emily was staring out the window at a tall, rumbling Ford 4X4 pickup.

"She what?"

"She started crying, but didn't say anything and then went to the bathroom. I thought I said something wrong, and I tried to apologize, but she said she wanted to be alone, so I went in your office and worked on some of my assignments. I didn't mean anything. I was just... curious." Emily looked down at her hands. "Natalya's very pretty, and I thought she'd had lots of boyfriends, you know?"

"I know." For a foolish moment, I considered blurting out what I knew of Natalya's life, but smartly kept my mouth shut. It wasn't my place to say anything about Big Mike Kovalenko, or sex traffickers, or old men who thought nothing of fucking terrified teenagers because they could. It hurt just to think about it. I thought of mentioning Serge, but that would only lead to his grandfather, Big Mike.

"Natalya seems so in control and confident, you know, and I was surprised. I..." She went back to watching the other cars with us in the slow-moving parking lot. "I don't want her to be mad at me, Mr. Sunshine."

I put my hand on hers. "It's not you, Em. And while I do know a little about Natalya's past, I think it's best if I let her tell you when she's ready. I found that's the way she prefers it. She hasn't had the easiest life, though you wouldn't know that just by meeting her. She's very reserved in some ways. Don't take it personal. She was the same way with me at first, and sometimes still is," I said.

"Ok." Emily wiped at her eyes with the back of her hand, smudging her eyeliner. Tears started streaming down her face.

"Come on, it'll be all right." I put my arm on her shoulder while trying to keep an eye on the car in front of me. The last thing the situation needed was me smacking into someone.

Emily, her face in her hands, couldn't stop the tears. I saw no reason to press the issue. I knew her well enough that, like Natalya, she'd let me know when she was ready to talk more. If nothing else, fighting with Rebekah when she was young taught me that yelling, arguing, demanding, and cajoling didn't work. And I had an ace up my sleeve; actually two: Agnes and Rebekah. If Emily needed to talk, and I wasn't the answer, they were available.

I held tight to that as Emily cried and the traffic began to break up.

By the time we cruised into the driveway, she'd composed herself. I asked if she wanted to talk anymore. She said, "No."

Rebekah handed me Jake as we walked in the door. She noticed Emily's streaked eyes, gave me the face, and put her arm around Emily.

"We'll be on the couch," I helpfully said. "And it's not about me."

I don't think my daughter believed me. While sitting with Mr. Grumpypants, I texted Agnes that I was at Rebekah's.

What did you do Buttman?

I looked at Jake. He'd fallen asleep. *Nothing,* I texted.

Do I need to come over?

Only if you're bored.

How did people survive without these things? I put the phone in my pocket and closed my eyes. I figured I had ten minutes, tops. I was off by five, but did enjoy the fifteen minutes of quiet.

When I opened my eyes, Agnes was standing next to me, smiling. "What?"

"Nothing," she said. "It's just that you look so peaceful."

"Is that good or bad?" I was suspicious.

"You tell me?" She leaned down and kissed me.

"Emily is upset and talking to Becks. That's all I know. Honest. So, I'm on Jake patrol."

"I believe you," she said in that wonderful way of hers that intimated she didn't.

"Hey, every once in a while, I'm actually an innocent bystander," I grumbled.

Agnes laughed. "I said I believed you."

"Uh-huh. They're in Em's room." I pointed down the hall.

Agnes kept laughing as she walked away.

The talk went on for a while, to the point where it was obvious I'd have to change and feed my grandson. He smiled at me as I passed this along to him.

"I'm your favorite, huh," I said, nuzzling his neck. He made a nasally sound, which I took as a yes.

Fidel, Lizzy, and Zach returned from the park and joined me in the kitchen as I was heating Jacob's bottle. Fidel smiled and held out his hands. I handed Jacob to him. Jacob fussed for a moment before settling in. I took the bottle, swished around the formula in it, tested the temp on my wrist before giving it to Fidel.

"Is everybody hungry?" I asked, knowing the answer.

"Pizza!" Zach shouted.

"Me too," Lizzy added.

I turned to Fidel. "What do you think, Dad?" I tried hard not to be too much of an irritant to him and Rebekah over how they wanted their kids to eat. Enough of that happened when we were all at the big house.

Zach and Lizzy gave their father the pleading, big-eyed look they thought might persuade him. Fidel was not moved by, nor did he like, shouting and wailing, and Zach and Lizzy knew this. It was the quickest way to a sure-fire "No!"

Fidel smiled and said, "We had pizza two days ago. We should see what mom wants."

Zach and Lizzy frowned and wandered off towards their rooms. Or to pester one another. Fidel and I sat down at the built-in table in the kitchen. I watched as he fed his son. It was nice to see Jacob warming to one of his parents, though he was always easier for Fidel.

"Should I ask what's going on?" Fidel looked up momentarily. Jacob was fussing with the nipple, which meant he was nearly finished.

"Agnes and Becks are talking with Emily. She asked Natalya about having boyfriends and that upset Natalya, which upset Emily. There's probably more to it, but she chose not to confide in me." Fidel nodded, as he put the bib across his shoulder to burb Jake. "How's the biz?"

"Busy," he said. "But busy is good; better than not being busy and hustling for jobs. That got old quick, but you can't let your guard down. People and production companies come and go. Gotta stay in touch."

Jake belched, and a portion of dinner dribbled onto the bib.

Fidel wiped his mouth and removed the bib. He looked tired. His eyes were grayer than usual and showed more bloodlines. "Had to shuffle a couple of crews; clashes with directors, secondary directors at that." He shook his head. "Sometimes I wish I was just a tech again..." His eyes went unfocused for a moment.

"Yeah, sometimes it's better to be a nobody," I said, smiling.

"Yeah," he smiled back. "Anything new on your end with the foundation or at the Manifesto?"

I shrugged. "Depends on what you find interesting. The foundation is doing just fine in the capable hands of Natalya and Isaac. Of course, they have to make sure the numbers work for Mr. Macklgrew, who does not abide thievery."

"Isn't that expensive? That oversight?" he rubbed the top of Jake's head.

"It is and worth every penny," I said. "I don't begrudge Carson Macklgrew his fee. He knows his stuff inside and out. The Manifesto, thankfully, is not a money pit and is ably run by Mikal, who is foolishly, perhaps, running around with Joanie." Fidel raised his eyebrows at that. "I know, I know, but they won't listen to me. All in all, I've been very fortunate to have competent people around me, otherwise I might be on the street."

"Sounds like the life," he said.

I reached for the keys in my pocket. "That it does. Now I just have to figure out what to do about this Orestra thing and my life will be as bland as any."

"What's this Orestra thing?" Before I could answer, Fidel raised his finger. "The woman from the morgue..."

"The woman from the morgue," I said. "I don't remember if I mentioned she was a private dick looking for a woman my brother Sterling knew." Fidel shook his head. "Anyway, to make things interesting, the woman Orestra was looking for left me a package with the keys to O's home and business...a day before they believe she was murdered. Got all that?" I wondered if I did.

Fidel tapped the table with his finger as he thought about it. "What do you think this other woman is up to?"

As I started to answer, we were interrupted by the rumblings coming from down the hall.

"I don't know, but—"

There was a loud commotion before Lizzy shouted, "Stop that, Zach!"

After which was heard, "Zachary, get in your chair!"

"Mom!" Zach protested.

"Now!"

"But I didn't *do* anything," he continued.

"Uh-huh."

Fidel rose. "Maybe I should help out," he said, handing Jake to me.

Agnes and Emily came into the kitchen just as Fidel walked out, and joined me at the table.

"Feeling any better, Em?" There was wailing down the hall, but that was being ably handled.

Emily looked at Agnes before saying, "No."

Rebekah had dinner planned, and after dealing with her arguing offspring, commenced to its production. As we were not in the original plans, Agnes and I left the family unit to its devices with the dour Emily in tow.

"What are we eating, Mr. Sunshine" Agnes asked, an unctuous grin on her face.

"Pizza," I said. No sense in arguing. We called in our order and headed home.

Twenty minutes later, the door rang.

It was our old friend, *Agent* Nakatomi, looking dapper as usual in a blue suit and reflector sunglasses.

The pizza guy fell in behind him.

I let them both in, paid the pizza guy, informed Agnes we had a guest, and led the agent into the kitchen. Agnes smirked at our visitor. Emily didn't know what to think. Neither did I. *Agent* Nakatomi had originally presented himself as being a member of the Secret Service, but that turned out to be incorrect.

He worked for Delton Manaforte.

Doing what, I wasn't exactly sure. Art Devaney confirmed my suspicions after Bernie told me of Nakatomi's connection to Manaforte. It was a clever ruse. Manaforte used *Agent* Nakatomi to keep tabs on us during the Ashley Carmichael business and, as it made sense that the Secret Service might know of Carmichael's book and its subtle implication that change in any social construct might include assassination, used that as his angle.

I directed him to a chair.

"What's brings you to our door, *Agent* Nakatomi?" Agnes asked.

"Hungry?" was my question.

He smiled at Agnes, took a long look at Emily, who returned the favor, and said, "Yes."

16

I poured the adults a glass of red wine. Emily asked for a cherry coke, something that was forbidden to her on the farm. Red wine she'd had. The farm was more European in its attitude towards wine when it came to who could drink it, so she was allowed a small glass at important dinners.

I handed Erik Nakatomi a plate with a couple of slices on it. "Do you wish to discuss whatever you're here to discuss with our young ward present?"

"No, I don't think that would be prudent," he said.

Emily, her eyes wide and darting between us, got up and went to the table and chairs in the backyard. Agnes, knowing her as I did, wanted very much to stay, but instead furrowed her brows, frowned at Nakatomi and me, and left to join Emily.

"I expect to be kept in the loop, you two," she said as she left.

I lifted my glass to her.

"Let me guess," I said, after Agnes was out of range. "Our dear friend Mr. Sobeski continues to be a pest from beyond the grave."

Nakatomi took a sip of his wine. "Is that what you think?"

"What else? It's been long enough that it can't be the threat of my going to the media. Not these days, anyway. And as Mr. Manaforte has gone missing, as it were, certainly from what little media exposure he had before, it probably has something to do with the rumblings from Sobeski's other employers over his mysterious disappearance." I took a sip of mine. "Besides, if someone wanted me bumped off, there's been ample opportunity over the last year. *I* haven't gone into hiding."

"You believe Delton Manaforte is in hiding?"

"Maybe sequestered in an undisclosed location is more accurate, but yes, I do. I asked around, and the people I know who have dealings with him and his businesses shared that he was not conducting his affairs in person, but through his subordinates." I watched my guest half-heartedly gnaw at his pizza. "That, and I've been asked about Mr. Sobeski recently, by people I should have no connection with. That tends to heighten any radar I might possess."

"Did this person give you a name, Mr. Buttman?"

"Fairfax," I said. I saw no reason to be coy. "Your turn, Mr. Nakatomi."

He finished his slice and wiped his mouth. "I can say that this does involve Mr. Sobeski and his other associates. It might have been unwise to handle him as we did, but that is neither here nor there. I was asked to stop by to find out if you'd been contacted, and as you've admitted that, there's no reason for me to take up anymore of your valuable time."

Mr. Nakatomi finished his glass of wine.

"And Mr. Manaforte?" I finished mine.

"I'll pass on your concerns," he said with a faint smile.

He stood up, and I escorted him to the door. I stood just inside the house, watching the street as he left. At the end of the block, a dark sedan pulled out from behind a truck and eased past. Two men were in it. Neither looked my way.

"We need more pizza, Sunshine," my dear wife bellowed.

I combined the contents of the two boxes into one, refilled my glass, and joined them under the thin veil of LA smog filtering the laconic California sun above it.

"Bout time," Agnes said, as I handed her the box. "I thought I'd have to get up!"

"Well, we can't have that, can we?" I winked at Emily, who smiled. "Feeling better, Em?"

"Yeah."

"Excellent," I said, plopping down in the chair next to her.

"What did *Agent* Nakatomi want?" Agnes looked up between mouthfuls. Where pizza was involved, manners took a backseat.

"We can dispense with agent, I think he's done with that," I said, before taking in my own mouthful.

"And?"

I raised a finger so I could finish chewing. "He, like others, was inquiring as to the ill-fated gentleman we ran into last year at the lake." I chose not to infer in any way our participation in killing Sobeski back in Michigan in front of Emily. Fortunately, Agnes caught my drift.

"Really?" She glanced at Emily, who was in her own world.

"Maybe later," I said. "And you, Em, care to share?"

Emily rolled her eyes. "No." She took a bite as I waited. "It's just that... I don't feel like I belong anywhere, that's all. And I thought if I asked Natalya about her life, I could, you know, maybe find my place. Instead, I made her angry."

Agnes patted Emily's hand.

"I know you don't believe me, but Natalya's not angry with you," I said. "I think if you ask her about feeling lost or out of place, you'll see that the two of you have a lot in common. For whatever reason, the boyfriend question caught her off guard."

Emily stared into my eyes. "Did you ever feel like you didn't belong, Mr. Monk?"

I looked at Agnes, who smiled and shook her head. "Only for the first forty years," I admitted. "After that, it was smooth sailing."

Agnes groaned.

"What?"

"Nothing," she said. The smile still on her beautiful face.

I sat back, trying to remember my life. "It's true that after my mother left the farm, I never felt really at home there. I don't know what I would have done if the whole thing with James and Miguel hadn't happened, but I can't see me staying. Well, maybe." I smiled to myself. "I didn't do a whole lot of thinking in those days. Probably where my habit of riding along life's waves started. I know I was an irritant to my father, and some of that was me being a jerk—"

"Cause you're certainly not one now," Agnes laughed.

"May I finish?" I tried not to laugh myself.

"This isn't about you, Mr. Monk!" Agnes put her glass to her lips, but couldn't stop laughing.

"Maybe you've had too much to drink," I said.

"Nice try, Buttman."

Time for me to roll my eyes. "Sorry, Em. What do you think?"

Emily waited for us to calm down before speaking. "I don't want mom to be mad at me, and I like everyone at the farm...it's not that. I just don't feel like it's where I belong, and I like being here, but I only know you guys..."

"And we're old," I added.

Agnes acted offended. "Speak for yourself, Buttman."

"My apologies." I meant to say more, but good fortune caused my phone to ring. It was Natalya. "Yes?"

"I'm sorry for how I acted, Mr. Monk," she said, almost in a hushed tone. "I didn't mean to make Emily upset. Is she mad at me?"

"No, it's the other way around," I said. "Would you like to talk to her?"

"Please."

I handed Emily the phone. "It's Natalya."

Emily listened, nodded, said "Yes," and "ok," before handing me the phone.

"Things better?" I asked.

"Uh-huh." Emily stared at me; her head tilted. "Did you call her?"

"No," I said.

"Thanks, Mr. Monk."

Agnes peered over her glass at me. I shrugged. We returned our focus to the pizza and wine...and cherry coke.

.   .   .   .   .

Agnes was pulling on my chest hairs as we lay in bed. "What did *Mr.* Nakatomi want?"

"He was curious if we'd heard anything about Sobeski; people asking, besides him," I said. "I think they overplayed their hand on that, but, as he said, that's neither here nor there. Whatever the issue, it seems that Sobeski's other employers were not duly notified or something."

"Do we need to worry about this?"

I liked that she added me to her possible worries. "I don't know if we need to worry, but perhaps we need to be vigilant. I noticed two guys in a car following Nakatomi after he left. That can't be good."

"Hmmm." She shifted against me, making herself more comfortable. "Thanks for helping Emily. She was really upset about this."

"I didn't do anything, beautiful. That was Natalya. But I agree, it was very helpful."

She shifted again. "Do we need to worry about Emily?"

I kissed her forehead. "Yes."

• • • • •

Sobeski was still on Agnes' mind as I poured her coffee the next morning. Emily was doing her homework at the table outside, deciding to get that onerous chore out of the way.

"You ever say anything to anybody about what happened at the house in Michigan?" she asked. Her years working for a reputed gangster were filtering through.

"Nope. We didn't even tell Bernie, but I assumed he already knew. As far as it goes, it's you, me, and Josef. He informed Manaforte. Other than that, the only thing anybody else knows is that the dear departed Aaron Alan Sobeski has disappeared," I said. "And I think it's his continuing absence that is bothering people."

"So, these people are asking and not getting the answers they want," she mused.

"And they're getting agitated. I don't think that works in our favor." I took a sip of coffee. It was still too hot.

"And since Nakatomi works for Manaforte..." Agnes raised her eyebrows and tipped her head.

"Based on our conversation, he knows too," I said. "The question now is who else knows, can connect us to Sobeski, and what their intentions are. The wild card is Josef, whether he's said anything to anybody." I put my cup down. "Maybe we should ask for a little help on this. I already asked Bernie to look into Orestra Blakely. I could ask about Sobeski. Maybe Art would be a better source—"

"Maybe both," Agnes said.

"Ok, we start there."

"And Emily?" We both turned to look at Emily, who we assumed was working, but she was, in fact, staring at us from the table outside.

"Yes," I said, "what to do about Emily." I'd already gone around once with Calista on this subject and had no desire for another. "What do you think?" Time to put this on Agnes.

"That you're desperate to dump it in my lap," she said.

I hid behind my cup. "You brought it up."

"Uh-huh. Not terribly helpful, Buttman." I shrugged. Agnes waved Emily in. "Might as well see what's on her mind—"

"We know what's on her mind," I said.

"No interrupting," Agnes grumped.

I feigned indignance. "You interrupted me...twice!"

"It's always about you, isn't it, Sunshine?"

"It works best that way," I said, stating the obvious.

Agnes shook her head in mock disdain. We both smiled at that. If nothing else, Agnes and I had gotten good at amusing one another.

Emily came in and sat in the chair next to Agnes. With the morning light streaming in the kitchen, we stared at each other as if there was an easy answer no one was willing to state out loud. Emily wanted to stay in LA. Her mother wanted her to return and be happy at the farm. The happy part was the bugaboo. Emily wasn't happy on the farm. Whether she was happy here seemed pre-ordained, but the previous day had shown that wasn't completely true.

But nobody believed that anyway.

"What's the plan, Em?" It's important to ask, even if you know the answer.

She slumped into her chair. "I don't know. I feel like I should talk with mom, but that never goes anywhere, and..." She looked at me. "We tried having you talk to her—"

"Yeah, that didn't get us anywhere either. In fact, it made it worse," I said.

Agnes laughed. "You certainly have a way with women, Buttman."

I couldn't help but laugh, too. "It's a gift." Emily wasn't amused. "Sorry."

"So, there's nothing but going back and being miserable?" she whined.

"Worked for me," I said.

"Buttman!"

I might have felt bad if Agnes wasn't laughing while trying to be indignant. "What?"

Emily continued to be unamused. "This is serious, Mr. Monk."

The "Mr. Monk" tripped whatever wires still functioned in my head. I snapped my fingers. "The problem here is we're stuck in a rut, going in circles, staring at the same shoes!"

"English, Buttman," my laughing wife chided.

Emily seemed to understand. She sat up; her face visibly brightened. "Like we need to ask someone else, someone other than any of us, like..." She smiled. "Natalya."

"Like Natalya. She might have some angles we haven't thought of. Plus, even if she doesn't, she's got a kind of haughty moxie that might throw your mother off." I raised my cup of lukewarm coffee. "Can't hurt to try, and if it all falls apart, there's always me to blame."

Agnes raised her cup. "Yeah, blaming you never get old, Sunshine."

Emily raised her cup. I watched her expression shift from gloom to light to nefarious as her smile changed and her eyes betrayed the mirth behind them. It also caused me to clampdown on getting too far afield on this. Emily was still a minor and her mother's responsibility.

"All right, we'll start with whether Natalya has any ideas, but remember, your mother is unlikely to just turn you loose, and there's your education and all that," I said, expecting a frown from Emily.

Instead, she shrugged. "We'll see."

17

"Interested in doing some snooping, beautiful?"

We'd walked Emily to Rebekah's house, and her fate with three boisterous kids, and were heading back home.

"Snooping on who?" she asked.

"A dead woman," I said.

"Your Orestra Blakely?"

"Yep." I pulled the keys out of my pocket. "I did a little recon earlier, so I know where, but I didn't go in. These keys go to her house and office, and Aisha Diamond made sure I had the means to get into trouble. If I don't check it out soon, whoever owns the properties might empty them out and get new renters."

"You have the addresses, right?"

"What about them?"

She shook her head at my befuddlement. "Why don't we find out who owns them first?" She tapped the side of her head with her finger. "The renter might be the owner."

"I hadn't considered that."

"So, it seems," she said.

Agnes had her own network of informants from her days with Johnny D. Johnny liked to know who he was dealing with and Agnes was often tasked with getting the rudimentary info, which included what properties they might own or be a party to. Property is almost always valuable, certainly anywhere in the greater Los Angeles basin. And as money was the business Johnny D was known for, he wanted to know if any collateral was part of the deal, and if anyone was lying to him.

Once home, Agnes got to it.

It turns out, Orestra Blakely was a bit of a player in real estate. She owned the small building that housed her office and the apartment complex where she lived. The next question was who might benefit from this property—I assumed her family—and had her will been entered into probate. According to the clerk for the City and County of Los Angeles, nothing had been entered into the court record concerning the properties or on behalf of the estate of Ms. Blakely. Apparently, outside of the police and her family, no one was aware or concerned that Orestra Blakely was dead.

Keys in pocket, we headed to West Hollywood.

We pulled into the apartment complex first. I wondered if Aileen was watching. No one was in view along the walkways and open stairs on either side of the building. And no one approached us as we got out of the car or walked to the apartment.

I opened the door, checked the security system; it was off, and we went in. Nothing appeared out of place. If the cops had gone through it, it wasn't with heavy hands. O's apartment wasn't a big place, maybe a little more than a thousand square feet, with two bedrooms and a bath. The kitchen was tucked into the far corner of the apartment facing the living room, which featured two large plate-glass windows. The inner curtains were drawn, lending a hazy filtered light to the room. The furniture was fairly new and in good shape, as was the apartment in general. Agnes went through the drawers in Orestra's bedroom. The other bedroom was used for storage. Going through the two rooms, I didn't find anything of interest to anyone outside of her family. It was mostly pictures and journals.

The kitchen was much the same, with nothing other than food that was slowly spoiling in the refrigerator. Based on all the pots and pans and utensils lining the shelves, Orestra liked to cook.

"Anything?" I asked, as Agnes joined me in the kitchen.

"Nothing worth writing home about," she said. "Except maybe this." She handed me a legal envelope.

"Where was this?"

"Underwear drawer."

In it were hand-written letters. Love letters. I looked through them before handing them back to Agnes. "What do you think?"

She read through a few of them. "Odd. No names on them, just sweetheart and lover."

"Written by a man or woman?" I thought man.

"Man," she said. "Seems kinda needy." She looked at me and smiled.

I shrugged. "It's genetic." I pulled out the keys. I assumed the one marked *D* was to the desk at the office. The one marked *S* a safe. "Think there might be a safe in here somewhere?"

"Seems unlikely," she said, echoing my thoughts. "One last sweep?"

"Can't hurt."

It was in the empty bedroom closet under a pile of boxes and a carpet square. In it was the history of Orestra Blakely before and after. School records. Army records. Medical records. Money, about ten grand, and legal documents relating to a marriage, a divorce, and the properties she owned. As suspected, the key marked *S* opened it.

So much for home.

I didn't see Aileen on the way out.

Agnes put her hand in mine as we walked to our next stop.

The building where Ms. Blakely conducted her business had two rooms: an office and a bathroom. Like the apartment, the security system was off.

The office and bathroom were strictly commercial, nothing fancy or frivolous, but like the apartment, the furniture was fairly new and in good shape. Aside from the desk, there were three chairs, one for the desk and two for clients. On the wall behind the desk were the business licenses.

The key marked *D* opened the desk.

The desk was oak and metal. There were locked lower drawers on both sides that opened once the key was turned in the center lock. There was a file cabinet behind the desk that the key also unlocked. This was where Orestra kept the expected: Work files on behalf of her clients. A cursory look indicated the files in the cabinet were closed cases and those in the desk were the ones she was working on.

Aisha's file was in the large drawer on the left side of the desk. There were pictures of her, notes, one of which had my name on it, and a brochure from a conversion therapy center. The name Terrance Stanton was circled on the brochure. He was the director of the center, as well as the pastor of a place called Sunlight Ministries in Pasadena. There were lots of smiling faces in the brochure, including one of Jesus, which made me smile.

Jesus the corporate man. Moses would be so proud.

None of the other cases seemed important enough to require my meddling in them as they were contracts for missing women, most of whom were black and transgendered. Orestra's holstered 9mm automatic was in the large drawer on the right, along with a couple of mace canisters and a truncheon.

"That explains that," I said.

"Explains what?" Agnes was sitting in one of the chairs opposite the desk, having returned from scoping out the bathroom.

"Whether she was armed when she left that night...or day, I suppose. I forgot to ask Mallory when they thought she was killed, but it'd been three days," I said. "Seems odd that she wouldn't be armed."

"That assumes she wasn't expecting trouble. Maybe she was meeting a friend or a client." Agnes pointed to the laptop on the desk. "Check that," she said.

I opened it and turned it on. As expected, it was passcode protected. I pulled out the sheet that was with the keys. It had two four-digit numbers, and one gobbledygook phrase. I typed in the gobbledygook and the laptop came to life.

"Ms. Diamond was thorough; I'll give her that." I opened the calendar and scrolled to the date on which Orestra was murdered. I shook my head. Figures.

Agnes noticed. "Well?"

"Aisha Diamond, it says. Seven that night, Atwater Village, by the Hyperion bridge."

"She killed Orestra Blakely?"

I continued looking through the calendar. "If she did, why leave the package with the key to the P.O. box, with the keys and information on O?"

"O?" Agnes asked.

"That's what her sister called her, and that's probably what she was called all her life. Orestra's birth name was Oren."

"Where'd you meet her sister?"

I realized I hadn't let Agnes in on a lot of this. "The other day, at the Manifesto. She called after she heard from the police. I'm pretty sure Oren and Orville grew up in the same neighborhood and were in the Army together."

Agnes let out a long "Oh." She, too, knew of Mr. Riley's antipathy towards the transgendered. I handed her the brochure and watched as she thumbed through it.

"He's that guy in the news," she said after handing it back.

"The news?"

"Yeah, that whole conversion therapy thing." Agnes didn't share my disdain for TV news and was more informed on certain subjects that got the tittering classes excited.

"I thought they outlawed that?"

"Banned is how they like to say it, but as this shows," she pointed to the brochure, "it's still got its advocates like Terry Stanton. He's got all the answers, you know." Agnes had a deep dislike for people who believed they had all the answers wrapped up in a pretty little bow.

"I imagine he does, beautiful." I tapped on the brochure. "How do you think Aisha Diamond fits into this? The brochure's in here for a reason."

"Maybe she tried it or someone tried to force it on her," she said.

"Could be. Could be a lot of things. It's obvious we're being used here—"

"What's this we stuff, Sunshine?"

"All right, *I'm* being used here, but why?" I kept tapping the brochure. "Ms. Blakely was looking for Aisha, had an appointment to meet her, and was killed around the time they were to meet."

"You think," Agnes said. "You don't know."

"True." I put the brochure back in the folder, which I returned to the drawer. "Still, if Aisha was setting her up, why lead us to what appears to be incriminating evidence? Doesn't make sense."

"Why was O looking for Aisha?" Agnes asked.

"I don't know." That made me think of what Orestra had asked of me. "No, that's not right, there's more to this. O wanted me to be a front for her, a beard. Something, I think," I winked at Agnes, "about how Sterling and Aisha got together, places that cater to straight white rich guys. She also said something about people like her disappearing."

Agnes laughed. "Sounds right up your alley, Buttman."

I sighed. "Yeah, it kinda does, doesn't it?"

"Maybe we need to be asking Sterling about this," she said.

"Yes, though I doubt Sterling would confess to anything with you there, even if he was willing to say anything to me, which is a big if." I got up. "We should probably get going."

"Probably." She got up from the chair.

I turned off and closed the laptop.

No one seemed particularly alarmed at our coming out of the office, but then no one seemed particularly concerned with our going in.

Agnes put on her sunglasses. "Think the cops are watching?"

"I would hope so," I said, putting on mine.

• • • • •

The next stop was Bernie's to see what he'd dug up.

He was, as always, smiling. I was good for that. I don't know what exactly his denizens of digital discovery were up to normally, only that he found my entreaties amusing.

"Ah, my favorite amateur detectives," he said as he hugged us.

"Got to kill the time somehow," I said.

"It's either that or baby-sitting," Agnes added.

Bernie held the door open and followed as we went into his office. We took our accustomed seats. He took a folder off his desk and handed it to Agnes. I feigned indignance.

"Anything interesting?" I asked, as Agnes flipped through the pages.

"What's the rush, Grandpa?" she asked.

"Very nice," I said.

Bernie sat back in his chair, content to watch the bickering Buttmans. "If you're looking for something salacious, I'm afraid you're going to be disappointed," he said. "Outside of changing from man to woman, Ms. Blakely's life was standard fare informationally. What's the connection, Monk?"

"Initially, she was looking for a woman named Aisha Diamond, another transgendered woman my brother Sterling was having an affair with. Later, she intimated she was interested in having me help her with some detective work—"

"Shocking, right?" Agnes snarked.

"May I?" I said.

"Sure, sure," she said, grinning.

"Helping how?" Bernie asked. His grin was much like my wife's.

"All the world's an oyster for a guy like me," I said. "She wanted to take advantage of that. Men like Sterling—"

"Or men like you." Agnes looked up from the file. The grin still plastered across her face.

"Are you done?"

Agnes shrugged.

I let out an exaggerated sigh. "Men, particularly rich white men, who prefer a more, what's a good word here, discreet means of meeting the objects of their desire, far from the maddening glare of family and friends."

Bernie nodded. His grin had softened as he took this in. "Do you know how Sterling met Aisha Diamond?"

"No, that was next on the list. I know he comes down to LA periodically for business. I thought I'd hit him up about it on his next trip down. He'd be away from his wife and maybe a little more willing to talk. If not, well, we have to get Emily back up to the farm in a couple of weeks. I could do it then." Wouldn't that make for a fun trip? Hit up Sterling about his infidelities and Calista about giving up her daughter.

Good times.

Agnes handed me the folder. "I don't suppose you've had any dealings with these kinds of discreet dating services?" she asked Bernie. "I mean professionally, of course."

Bernie laughed. "Of course. On occasion that might come up, but it's generally peripheral to other interests. Would you like me to look? Specifically, if I'm understanding this correctly, those that specialize in transgendered women?"

"Yes," she said.

"Should I ask why you're interested in this, outside of any connection to your brother?" he asked. "Sounds like something better left in the hands of the police. Might simply be a domestic situation, or a wrong place at the wrong time kind of incident. Unfortunately, that happens sometimes to transgendered people."

"Might be. But Ms. Blakely was supposed to meet with Ms. Diamond the day she was killed. And Ms. Diamond appears to be leading us on." I pulled the keys and note out of my pocket. "Agnes and I were doing a little amateur sleuthing before we came here, checking out Ms. Blakely's office and home. The keys were given to me through Ms. Diamond."

Bernie looked over the keys and note. "How?"

"She left the package at my office. I checked with security and identified her off the surveillance tape. The package she left at the office led me to a P.O. box where there was an envelope with those in it. If she wanted me to have them, why didn't she just give them to me? She'd been to the office before to give me a message for Sterling. Why the subterfuge?"

"What was the message for Sterling?" Bernie asked.

"That she'd be ok," I said.

"That certainly adds an edge to it," he said. "I'll look into Ms. Diamond. Anything else?"

I looked at Agnes. "Sobeski."

Bernie's face tightened. "Sobeski?"

"I've been asked twice about him in the last week. Mr. Nakatomi stopped by yesterday, and a man named Fairfax—"

"Fairfax?" Bernie seemed genuinely surprised.

"Fairfax," I assured him.

"Fairfax," he said again.

"Know him?" I asked.

"Yes, but that was many years ago. What did he say?" Bernie handed me the keys and note.

"Sobeski's disappearance has rattled some cages and people want to know what happened to him. I played dumb. Should we be worried?" I put the keys in my pocket.

Bernie shook his head. "No, that's not his side of the business. He's an analyst for lack of a better term. He collects and organizes disparate information. It's rare for him to contact people directly. That's a field agent's work."

I stood up. "Should I call you if I hear from him again?"

The wheels were spinning in Bernie Shoor's head. "Yeah, let me know."

Agnes got up. We left Bernie to his thoughts.

18

The next stop was work. I might as well call it that, since it ate up more and more of my time.

"Oh, poor baby has the terrible job of handing out millions," Agnes said, pursing her lips and waving her hand as though queen for a day.

"I know, right?"

"Life's tough, my dear." She smiled and patted my leg.

That it is.

A devious plan occurred to me on the drive over. Enlist one brother to deceive and trap the other. I knew Sterling would have no interest in talking to me about Aisha; he was already ambivalent about talking to me in general. I didn't quite know why, other than the usual bugaboos all us sons of Moses had. He was more amenable towards Isaac and therefore more willing to be duped by his younger brother than his older. Made perfect sense.

Isaac was in the office, as was Natalya, who acted surprised to see us. I was never sure if she was or not.

"Is Emily ok?" she asked.

"I think so," I said. "And you?"

Natalya Constantinescu straightened her back and said, "Yes."

We were back to what passed for normal.

I sat on the corner of her desk, which is what bosses do. Agnes sat in one of the chairs.

"No doubt you know that Emily would like to stay in our fair city, while her mother would like her to stay on the farm. I've already tried to help, and we all know what a fiasco that turned out to be." I smiled at my chief-of-staff. "Since you're something of a wily character, maybe you have some ideas about where we can go with this," I said.

Natalya rolled her eyes, looked at Agnes, who shrugged, then sighed. "It's not good to be a liar, Mr. Monk, especially to someone's mother."

"I'm not asking you to lie, just whether or not you have any helpful ideas."

"Just be honest," she said.

"We tried that," I said, "didn't work. And Emily's gone down the road of the angry, insolent daughter who won't listen. But you know all this." I assumed Emily had filled in Natalya about life with mother.

Natalya stared at me and rubbed her chin as a grin lightened her pretty face. "Why don't we have her kidnapped? Fake, of course, and then you come to the rescue and her mother will be so thankful that she'll do anything you ask."

I stupidly said, "Seriously?" which caused Agnes to burst out laughing.

Natalya joined her in the frivolity. "It works on the TV, Mr. Monk," she said, once her laughter subsided.

The laughter brought Isaac out of his office. "What am I missing?" he asked.

"We're going to fake kidnapping Emily—" I looked at Natalya. "I've got that right, don't I?" Natalya, who was still smiling, nodded. "And then, I come in and save the day so she won't have to go home to her mother and life on the farm. What do you think?"

Isaac looked between the three of us. "That I should go back to my office and wait for the police."

I clapped my hands together. "Excellent. Now that we've solved Emily's problem, it's time to turn our attentions to our dear brother, Sterling. I need you to find out if he's going to be in LA soon. If so, invite him to dinner, nice cozy little Italian restaurant, make him feel at ease and then...I come in and spoil the fun."

"Is this more serious than the kidnapping bit?" he asked.

"It is. I need to talk to him, and I'd prefer to do it when he least expects it," I said.

He looked at Agnes and Natalya. "Is this what we talked about?"

"It is, dear," Agnes answered.

"Do I have to be a part of it?" he said, still looking at Agnes.

"Only if you want to be. Otherwise, you can react however you like," I said.

"I'll give him a call," he said, and got out his phone.

Natalya took the opportunity to push me off her desk, which made Agnes laugh again. Isaac stared at the ceiling as his phone rang Sterling. Sterling answered, and Isaac made his pitch.

"Thursday? Let me look," he said.

I nodded that Thursday worked.

"Eight? See you then." Isaac ended the call. "All set. *The Sugerfish*, down on Sunset."

I turned to Agnes. "Put that on my calendar, will ya, Hon?"

"I'm not your secretary, Mr. Monk," she answered.

I turned to my chief-of-staff. "How about you?"

She held out her hand. I gave her my phone, which she held in front of my face so it would open, and added the date to the calendar. Setting the phone down, she said, "I have work to do, Mr. Monk. Bye," and waved me off.

"Thanks," I said.

Isaac and Agnes followed me into my resplendent office.

Isaac spoke first. "Should I ask?"

"Sterling's girlfriend and how he met her. The irony is that his girlfriend seems to be dropping clues rather than just talking to us," I said.

"Makes you wonder, doesn't it?" Agnes reached into the cooler for a bottle of water.

"What do you mean?" Isaac asked, as she handed him a bottle.

"I mean about Sterling," she said. "Whether he's a part of this, or whether she's playing him, either as a dupe or for revenge."

"Revenge?"

I smiled at Isaac's surprise. "He was supposed to dump her, remember? Felicia was adamant about that. So, either he has, which might be a problem if he made promises he never meant to keep—"

"To either of them," Agnes added.

I grabbed my own bottle of water—Agnes grinned at that. "To either of them," I agreed. "Or, he's still seeing Aisha, which is probably more dangerous, and which means he might be tied up in more than simple infidelity."

"When is infidelity simple, Monk?" Agnes snorted.

I smiled and took a drink. "Just a turn of phrase, my love."

Isaac, disinterested in our cloying remarks, pressed on. "Is that what you're trying to find out? What he's up to?"

"Yes and no," I said. "I also want to know how and where they met. If it was spontaneous, surreptitious, or planned."

Isaac smiled at that. "What do you think?"

"Yeah Monk?" Agnes was smiling too.

"Maybe all three," I said. "Are you in?"

"We'll see." He took a long drink of water. "Do you have time to talk some shop?"

"Sure, what's up?" It's important to stay engaged.

"Jon had an interesting conversation the other day," he began, "and I wouldn't bring it up except he was asked about us, by a guy he knows is working for Russian interests, and it had more to do with you two," he pointed to me and Agnes, "than the foundation. He thought that was odd because Agnes has no association with it, but her name came up."

"Did he say what they were asking about?" I asked.

"How you met, who the two of you used to work for, things like that. Of course, Jon doesn't know much about your history, so he had no answers, but told the guy he could find out." Isaac reached into his shirt pocket and took out a business card, which he handed to me.

The card was for a consulting firm, Dominik and Associates, with offices in DC, New York, San Francisco, and LA. The name on the card was Boris Tsarnaev, which struck me as an alias.

"Interesting," I said before I handed it to Agnes.

Agnes looked it over and gave it back.

I wrote Bernie on it. "What do you make of it?" I asked Isaac.

"I don't know. On the one hand, because you're not widely known and have gone to some length to…obscure who you are, people do ask about you, or more specifically, who is funding our operation, so the questions are expected. But asking about your personal life, and having Agnes' name come up without being referred to first, is something new. I've never been asked about Agnes when I've been out," he said. "Probably because her name is nowhere to be found in our brochures, questionnaires, or on our website."

"Were any other names asked about?" It was Agnes' turn.

"He didn't say, so I assume not."

"I'll have this Tsarnaev checked out," I said. "And we should keep our ears open for anymore of this."

"Maybe we should ask Natalya if she's had anyone asking questions like this?" Agnes asked.

Isaac got up and waved Natalya into the office.

"Yes?" she said.

"Have there been any Russians asking about us lately?" I thought she might find that funny. Instead, the color ran out of her face.

"No. Why… Did you hear something?"

"Isaac did," I said. "A guy named Boris Tsarnaev was asking Jontaveus about me and Agnes. Ever heard of him?"

She shook her head. "Should I worry?" That was self-evident from the way her shoulders suddenly slumped and her eyes widened when I said the word *Russians*.

"No, but if you hear something, let me know," I said.

"I will," she said and returned to her desk.

Agnes was the first to say it out loud. "I know that look," she said. "I've seen it on many faces when I worked for Johnny."

"Yeah, the last time she had that look was when I asked her about her vacation." I rubbed my chin, thinking. "I should ask Josef if he knows." Josef was very protective of Natalya, and I know she had him in her confidences more so than mine. I turned back to Isaac. "Anything else?"

Sadly, there was, but it was mostly more courting by parties interested in our money.

"Lump it into Thursday," I said. "That way, I'll be close for our get together with Sterling."

"Will do." Isaac went back to his office.

Agnes tapped the desk with her finger. "What are you thinking over there, Mr. Monk?"

Evidently, I wasn't paying attention. "That I should go back to being a nobody."

Agnes laughed. "Nice try, but you're stuck in the here and now, not some phony-assed good time in the past."

"Phony-assed?"

"Yeah, phony-assed. You've got it good, Buttman, and you know it."

I got up and turned to the panoramic view of the city behind me. "Yeah, it's looking like my schtick is wearing thin. Might be time for something new," I said.

"I'll say."

I faked a frown. "Duly noted."

"You brought it up," she said.

"I don't think so," I huffed.

"We should get going if you're going to be like that." She got up. "I'll be in the restroom. See if you can get anything out of Natalya."

"Someone's getting kinda bossy here," I huffed again.

She crossed her arms, tightened her eyes, and said, "Get used to it!"

"Yes, dear."

I waited for her to head past Natalya to the bathroom. Natalya looked at me as I stood by the door. One big plus to being around smart women is you don't have to wait long for them to know something is up.

"Yes, Mr. Monk?"

"I know something's bothering you. We all noticed your reaction to my using the word Russians. Then there was Emily asking about boyfriends—"

She stiffened. "I'm ok—"

"*And* I know you can be stubborn about it." I put my hand on her shoulder. "I also know better than trying to make you tell me, but I know something is wrong. I can help."

Tears rolled down her cheeks. "I'm ok, Mr. Monk." She looked away as Agnes strolled in.

I joined Agnes by the door. "Anytime," I said.

Natalya stared at her computer as we left.

"No luck?" Agnes asked as we rode down in the elevator.

"Nope."

"Any ideas?"

"Like I said, start with Josef." I handed the car keys to her. "You drive."

I pulled out my phone and called Mr. Jones.

"Yeah?"

"I need to talk to Josef. And I might need his services," I said.

Silence.

"Hello?"

"Josef isn't here right now. He's on a leave of absence," Jones said.

"When?"

"I don't know, couple of months..."

Don't know? Jones always knew where his people were. His was a business that catered to people who might have needs 24/7. Like me. "What about Anton? He still work for you?"

"Yeah. Just a second..." I could hear shuffling on his side of the call. "When?"

"Thursday. Noon. Here at my office."

"All right."

"Great. Take—"

"I need to talk to you," he said.

"About what?" Though I had an idea.

"You know what," he said before hanging up.

Agnes, ever the efficient eavesdropper, smiled as we got to the car. "We can add Orville to the list?"

"Yeah. Maybe you should call Coretta."

"Maybe," she said as she opened the door for me. "Is it his Orestra thing?"

"Probably." I was sure it was.

Agnes started the car, and I watched as she navigated the parking garage's three levels. It was as we got to the gate that Ronnie started waving. I didn't see him at first. It was Agnes, smacking me on the arm.

"What?"

"Your homeless guy. Ronnie, right?" she said.

"As far as I know."

Ronnie, ever-vigilant, kept his eye out for Benny. Benny was in the lobby at this time of day. I motioned for him to come to the car.

"Hey, Mr. Monk. Mrs. Monk"

Agnes smiled at that.

As did I. "Hey Ronnie. What's up?"

"Been keeping an eye on things like ya asked," he said. "Haven't seen any trannies though, black or white."

"So, it's been quiet?"

"Sure, sure."

I reached in my pocket for some twenties.

"Course, there was that one guy," he said as I handed him the bills.

"What kinda guy?" Agnes asked.

Ronnie did a bit of a shuffle as he thought about it.

"Russian?" I suggested.

Ronnie shook his head. "Naw." Then he grinned. "Less he's a black Russian."

We left him to his mirth.

19

I called Bernie. His concern for the Russian interest matched mine.

"This isn't good," he said, stating the obvious.

"No, but I'm not surprised. A lot of questions went unasked after we got back from Michigan last summer. Maybe it was all the hoo-ha about the assassination attempt, or whatever it was, but I expected to be in the thick of it because of Manaforte. Instead, it's been all quiet on the western front. Manaforte's disappeared, and who knows what the other people who used Sobeski heard about his disappearance."

"We didn't find much of anything about it after it happened," Bernie said. "I had a number of other things come up, and because it was quiet, I forgot to look back into it. Usually when these types of individuals disappear, it's a local matter, if you know what I mean, and as such, resolved. There's no more chatter, for obvious reasons. So, it is odd for it to start up almost a year later."

"Maybe they were bidding their time," I said.

"Maybe," he answered. "It's also possible that there's been some changes we don't know about that have upset the apple cart."

That's what I needed, upset apples.

"Anything else, Monk?"

"I feel like I'm asking for too much already."

"Are you broke?" he asked, laughing.

"No."

"Then it'll work out."

"That's what I keep being told. Anyway, Natalya's been unusually emotional lately. She, too, seems spooked by Russians asking questions, which made me think of Big Mike. I assumed after he split for Eastern Europe, that was that, but maybe not. Can you—"

"Kovalenko's dead, Monk."

"Dead?" I suddenly saw Big Mike sitting in my old bungalow confessing his deep abiding love for Natalya. "Do you know when?"

"No. Heard a veiled reference to it. Couple of groups he was tied to were asking about him and the source said he was no longer to be seen, which means he's buried somewhere. You want me to look in to it?"

"Yeah," I said. "Anything on Aisha Diamond?"

"Still looking into that. Call me on Friday."

I said I would and hung up.

•   •   •   •   •

Agnes was in her sewing room. Swatches of cloth were laid out on a table and she was slowing moving them around and pinning them together in various patterns. I walked in quietly and watched over her shoulder as she assembled and reassembled the swatches.

"Which ones do you like, Sunshine?"

I pointed to a group set in a Nordic triangle pattern. "Those."

"And the colors?" There were reds, blues, yellows, and whites.

"They're good too," I said.

"Better than those?" She motioned towards subtler versions of the same colors set in a star gazing pattern.

"Yes."

She lightly elbowed me in the ribs. "You're sure?"

"Sure as I'll ever be."

Agnes grabbed another pile of swatches. "What'd Bernie say?"

"Nothing yet on Aisha Diamond and that Big Mike Kovalenko is dead."

She put the swatches down and turned to me. "Dead, huh?"

"That's what he said." I picked up a few pieces of a blue cloth with tiny white crosses on it.

"Does Natalya know he's dead?" she asked.

"I don't know."

"Think that might be what's bothering her?"

"Might be, but I would think she'd be relieved. Wouldn't you?" I handed her the pieces of blue cloth.

"You would think, but sometimes it's more complicated," she said, taking the pieces. "Attachments, even those that are incredibly harmful, are hard to break. I outta know. As much as Big Mike abused her, he also protected her and provided for her. He was a father figure, her first sexual experience, and she had a certain amount of personal freedom. She wasn't locked in a basement, remember?"

"I remember. She was also very young—"

"Still is, Mr. Monk." Agnes set the pieces down.

I nodded. "I asked Bernie to look into it. I hope that's all it is."

"Meaning what?"

"Meaning I get the feeling a lot more is going on here, both with Natalya, and with us. I mean Josef has up and left and he has connections to all of us. I don't like that. Jones... I don't know what's going on there, but he acts as though Josef being gone is no big deal, almost an afterthought, and that doesn't make sense knowing the both of them..." I picked up another piece of cloth, this one yellow with white dots.

Agnes took the cloth. "What?"

I looked into her light blue eyes and pulled her close. I ran my fingers lightly along her cheek and nose, looking for the tiny scars from when her face was reconstructed after Jordan nearly beat her to death. I found them endearingly beautiful.

"All of this has been too easy," I said. "That worries me. There should have been more questions asked by more people. The Secret Service. The FBI. Bernie's bunch. Even Art Devaney. Instead, it was as if it were just another day, just something that happened; no big deal. But we both know it was a big deal, so where is everybody?"

"Working through it," she said, before kissing me.

"Which is leading them back to us." I kissed her back.

"So, we play it smart, Monk Buttman."

"That's right, dollface," said the hard-boiled private dick.

•   •   •   •   •

The next day, the hard-boiled private dick spent the day watching his daughter's children. Zach was racing around the house, making a pest of himself. His sister Lizzy alternately argued with and ignored him. Jacob sat on my lap and watched as his siblings made war and peace with each another. Emily was in the sewing room with Agnes. They were set on getting a quilt done before Emily had to go back and time was running out. This required my keeping the kids out of their hair.

"I'm bored, Gamps," Zach said, after his latest effort to antagonize Lizzy had failed.

I smiled and patted his head, which he didn't care for. "You have my sympathies, little dude,"

"Can I play with my iPad?"

"Sorry, you know the rules."

The iPad, one of those cute little electronic monsters that pulls children and their parents in, was filled with games that Zachary Bohrman Montaigne could not resist. His mother could, and her agreeable husband did not interfere. Zach was allotted two hours a day in the evening, when Rebekah needed a little peace and quiet.

"*Please*, Gamps!"

He stuck out his lower lip and widened his pleading eyes. It was a nice look and occasionally I took pity on him. But I had to choose when to antagonize his mother, and this wasn't one of those times.

"I left it at your house," I told him.

The boy flopped on the floor and wailed, which brought the rest of the house's occupants to the scene of his inconsolable misery. If he thought this staged display of desolation would gain him sympathy, he was sadly disappointed.

"Zachary Montaigne, you stop that this instant!" Agnes told him.

Zachary Montaigne frowned at Agnes Duquesne, but relented in his display of woe and sat up. Still pouting, he mumbled, "It's not fair. Lizzy had her turn already."

"Yes," I said, "Lizzy in the morning; you in the evening. If you weren't such a rabble-rouser, you wouldn't be in this predicament, but you are, so how about going to the park?"

He nodded, while still frowning.

I turned to his sister, who was hiding behind Agnes. "Do you want to go, Lizzy?" Lizzy shook her head no. "Then it's us dudes." I pointed to the door. "Let's go Mr. Grumpy-pants."

"I'm not Mr. Grumpy-pants, Gamps," he said in a huff.

"Ladies," I said to Agnes, Emily, and a grinning Lizzy, "we'll be back."

The park was two blocks to the south just as the street curves and eases towards the cluster of stores by the highway. The park was spread out over four acres, with a play area and jungle-gyms on one side, a ball field/soccer field combination on the other, and a grassy area with trees here and there to run around on in the middle. A handful of moms and kids were there when we arrived. As a known commodity in the neighborhood, the moms smiled at us, took turns checking out Jacob, and returned to their conversations. As a general rule, I was not a part of their group and had no quarrel with that. I found if they wanted to include me, they would.

Zach raced to the slide and jostled with the other kids for a turn. Jacob fell asleep next to me. Unlike me, he found the chatter, yelling, and ear-piercing screams to be relaxing. I was deeply envious.

Fairfax, wearing a Dodgers cap, sat down next to me.

With him was a black Labrador that sat quietly at his feet. "Phone," he said.

I took out my phone and turned it off. "They know we're here—"

"But they don't need to hear the content of our conversation. They already have all the information they need as concerns your voice and face. You do use the facial recognition feature, don't you?" he smiled as I nodded. "Are you surprised to see me, Mr. Buttman?"

"Not at all," I said. "I get all kinds of government and quasi-government people stopping by. I'm very popular." I put the phone back in my pocket. "What brings you back my way?"

"The same."

"Interesting how one person can cause so much anxiety." I watched Zach run around the slide with another boy.

"How so?"

"You tell me? I have all kinds of guesses, and as you're stalking me—"

"I prefer watching over," he said. "But we both know you're not some innocent caught in a web of intrigue, certainly not where Sobeski is concerned. Whether you know the extent of his dealings or the nature of what he was involved in is, to some degree, immaterial. You're a piece of the puzzle, right or wrong, good or bad."

"So, what is it you want? And who is it you work for? I've already been jobbed by Nakatomi. How do I know you're not just another of Manaforte's artful dodgers?"

He ran his hand along the dog's head. "Yes, I know about that. Mr. Manaforte is very clever, but I'm surprised you didn't have Nakatomi checked out earlier with Mr. Devaney."

"Not having had too many interactions with government men, I took him at his word. Your answers?"

He took a treat out of his pocket. "I don't work for Manaforte, Mr. Buttman. Who I work for is confidential, but I can assure you we are not in law enforcement. Nor do I, or any of my associates, work for any illegal or illicit groups. My concern is overall trends, and whether they are malignant or benign." The Lab took the snack from Fairfax's hand. "The recent attempt on the president's life set off all kinds of flares, flying in many different directions. One of those led me here."

"And Sobeski?"

"He disappeared. Men of his kind do, so it's not surprising, but expectations were such that his disappearance did not conform to the patterns we anticipated."

I chuckled at that. "When *did* you expect him to disappear?"

"On his return to Eastern Europe, where he was supposed to make certain appointments and rendezvous. It was widely known, within intimate circles, that Sobeski had worn out his welcome, that he was making people uncomfortable in his targets and methods. He was long known for his very quiet, very plausible sanctions—"

"Yes, I'd heard about that."

"From Manaforte?"

"Bernie Schoor." I saw no reason not to admit that. I assumed Bernie to be part of Fairfax's intimate circles.

Fairfax nodded. "To continue, rumors have been bandied about concerning Sobeski's disappearance, and your name has been softly mentioned, perhaps as a ruse or diversion, but it makes you a target, nonetheless. Our understanding of Mr. Manaforte's ambitions are such that we believe he's the source of these rumors."

The Lab, sensing no more treats, set his head down on his outstretched front paws.

I was keeping an eye on the rabble-rousing Zach. He and his new buddy were chasing a couple of girls across the playground. Two mothers, I assumed belonging to the chased girls, had taken notice.

So had Fairfax. "Your grandson is arousing interest."

"It's his thing now." I checked my watch for the time. "I appreciate what appears to be your attentive eye, but what exactly do you want from me? I haven't told you anything you don't already know, and like the others, you can watch me from afar, or have operatives take care of that. So, what's the deal?"

"Information, Mr. Buttman, it's my stock in trade, and the more I have, the better I can use it to delineate probabilities and outcomes. It's true that normally others do the legwork and I make sense of the information, but when someone as close as a Secret Service agent attacks the president, alarms go off, and proceeding as normal can be problematic. You're not a complimentary link in what we know about Sobeski's dealing with Mr. Manaforte. Whether that was by design or happenstance, or as misdirection, it is now a material part of the puzzle."

He stood up and stretched his shoulders. The Lab, knowing it was time to go, rose to its feet.

"I would like you to tell me what happened to Sobeski," he said.

"What makes you think I know?"

He smiled at that. "Because you've admitted as much." He looked over at the cars parked along the street. "It might be advisable for you to be a little less conspicuous for the time being."

"Like Xavier Dunkle?"

"Yes," he said. "When you're ready, Mr. Buttman." He adjusted his Dodgers cap and walked away.

I picked up Jacob, who awoke, and called out to Zach. He ignored me. "Let's go or no iPad time," I shouted.

He groaned and flopped to the ground. The kid he was with watched, unsure of what to do. I hitched my thumb towards the street. Zach got up slowly and glumly trudged my way. "It's not fair," he whined.

"I'm pretty sure we covered that earlier," I said.

The girls were in the sewing room making good use of their time. Without us rabble-rousers making a fuss, the quilt was proceeding nicely. Jacob and I made a point of being impressed by their handiwork. Zach, bored, at least kept his mouth shut while he pressed his forehead against my thigh.

"How was the park, Mr. Grumpy-pants?" Agnes asked.

"Fine," he admitted.

"He and some other kid were chasing girls around the slide," I said.

Agnes laughed. "At least he's consistent."

"So I've been told." I rubbed Zach's head.

Fairfax noted that too.

20

Mr. Jones was waiting.

He was sitting with Anton and an older man I didn't know, but who bore a striking resemblance to Orestra Blakely.

Pluto, taking orders, smiled, and nodded when I said, "Coffee."

Jones' eyes were lifeless and gray, bags sagged below them. For the first time that I could remember, he looked uncomfortable in the black outfit that defined his métier. Anton, clothed in a dark suit; his face, as impassive as always, let his bright, blue eyes do the work of keeping tabs on not only us, but the others milling about the food court. The older man sat stiff with his eyes focused on some point across the room. His countenance clashed with his clothing, that worn by a relaxed man: tan slacks and a dark Hawaiian shirt with low cut tan socks and dark brown loafers. I had on a light herringbone jacket, blue slacks, a white shirt, and a blue tie, which I thought made me look quite sharp.

"Mind if I start?" I asked.

Jones looked up at me. "What?"

"What happened with Josef?" I watched Anton's eyes as I said this. They jumped in my direction.

"He took a leave of absence," Jones said.

"When?"

Jones shrugged. "A few months ago. He went on a trip to Thailand, someplace like that, and hasn't been back."

Anton's eyes tightened at Thailand.

I asked him, "Was this the same trip Natalya took?"

Anton nodded. He was never big on talking. Everything had to be pulled out.

"Do you know where he is?"

It was Anton's turn to shrug. "Back home," he said. Back to Russia.

I knew that wasn't good. Josef had mentioned many times his desire to never return to the place of his birth. I had more questions, but Jones had his own problems, and I could pester Anton later.

Jones put his hand on Anton's sleeve. "Give us a few minutes, man."

Anton nodded, got up, and found a nice spot twenty feet away where he could watch the room.

"I don't want you messing with my daughter," the old man said.

I looked at Jones. "Your daughter Orinda?"

"This is Mr. Jordan Blakely, Monk," Jones said. "Orinda is his youngest daughter."

"I have no interest in messing with your daughter, Mr. Blakely. I only met her once. She asked to talk to me about Orestra Blakely. We did, and that was that," I said.

Mr. Blakely tightened up more at the mention of Orestra's name. "I don't recognize that name, sir," he said.

"Yes, I understand that." I looked at Jones, who was looking at his hands.

Pluto arrived with our coffees. He was cheerful as always, but even he noticed the tension and smartly said nothing beyond, "Enjoy."

More tense moments passed as we fiddled with our drinks. Jones was visibly sweating, air-conditioning be damned. Mr. Blakely put the cup to his lips, but didn't take a sip. I watched the two of them. The coffee could wait. Besides, it was still too hot for my cat's tongue.

"I have the feeling there are some things you'd like to say to me, Mr. Blakely. Maybe we should skip the formalities and press on," I said.

He set the cup down and regarded me as many older black men do, just another fucking white guy to deal with. He had my sympathies. There were many times I didn't want to deal with me either, but I at least wasn't stupid enough to think I knew anything where racism was a daily corrosive part of your life.

"As far as I'm concerned, Mr. Buttman, my son died ten years ago. After that..." His shoulders fell into his chest and his eyes became shiny and wet. He closed them for a minute while he straightened his back. "After that, I had no use for what he became."

"I'm not interested in judging you—"

"Don't lie to me, son. I don't care for hypocrites." He took in a deep breath. "I came to say my piece in this matter, that's all."

I put my hands around my cup of coffee. "My apologies."

He pulled out his wallet and removed three pictures. The first was of a small boy with bright eyes and a big smile. It was easy to see Orestra in that face. The next picture was Oren in his tracksuit, his smile just as bright, holding up a winning medal. The last was of Oren Blakely in his Army blues. Standing next to him, and as resplendent, was Orville Riley.

"I want you to know how much I loved my son, and how much I miss him." He picked up the first picture. "He was my only son. I already have three daughters. I didn't want another. I wanted my son." Picking up the second, he handed the first to me. Tears were streaming down his face. "Look how beautiful he was. My pride and joy. I love my daughters, Mr. Buttman. I want that understood, but I won't deny how much Oren meant to me. Remember how fast he was, Orv?"

Orville took the picture. Tears were running down his face. "Oh, yeah. Fastest kid in school. Every year, O took first place. Won two state titles."

A sad smile came to Jordan Blakely. "He was good at every sport he played. I never felt so proud as when I'd be in the stands watching him out there, making the rest of those boys look like chumps."

I picked up the third picture, marveling at how young they were. I glanced up at Orville as he wiped his eyes.

"My son served with distinction, Mr. Buttman. Served this country with pride and with honor," he said.

"I would never deny that, Mr. Blakely. If he was anything like Orville, I know his service was a source of great pride." I handed him the picture.

He set it with the others. "I know what people say, that I'm hard-hearted, that I...that I drove him away. I won't argue that." Jordan Blakely wiped his eyes and looked at me. "But you can't just take away those years, or pretend they didn't exist because all of a sudden you decide you're someone else. It makes a joke out of me and everyone who loved him. I won't be the butt of someone's joke. And don't tell me that I got to understand. I don't have to understand. I don't have to accept that which I feel is wrong and against the laws of God."

I wasn't going to argue about God.

He put the pictures back in his wallet and let his eyes wander around the food court. "Orv tells me you helped get this place going for him."

I eyed Orv, who shrugged. I also noticed Mikal standing just outside his office. I waved him over. "That I did. Would you be interested in seeing the spaces we have here, Mr. Blakely?"

"I'd like that," he said.

"Mikal," I said, "this is Mr. Jordan Blakely, a friend of our esteemed Mr. Jones. Would you be kind enough to give him the tour? Orv and I have a few things to discuss, and then we'll catch up."

Mikal Thorvaldsen was all smiles. "Sure, Monk. Mr. Blakely."

Mr. Blakely slowly got up and he and Mikal headed towards the performance center. I turned to the esteemed Mr. Jones.

"You look terrible, my friend, and that disturbs me," I said.

"Disturbs you how?" he asked, sounding annoyed.

I took a sip of my coffee. It was lukewarm, just how I liked it. "Because I'm supposed to be the fuckup in this relationship. You're supposed to be the rock on which us lesser men get through our storms."

I expected something more from him than simply, "Yeah."

I put the coffee down. "This is about O, isn't it? She contacted you, didn't she?"

He flinched each time I said, *she*. "What makes you think that?" he said.

"I'm a lot of things, but I'm not stupid—mostly. And I've known you long enough to have figured a few things out, and from my meetings with her, I felt the same way about O. You two grew up together. You were close, very close. Close enough that when Oren became Orestra, it put you in a terrible bind. And I know from our conversations that you are ambivalent, at best, about the transgendered."

He shifted in his chair, staring at his cup of cold coffee. "What's your point?"

"O asked for your help, yes?"

He put the cup down and let out a long, sorrowful sigh as his body shook. It hurt just to watch.

"O asked for my help," I said. "But somebody killed her before I could."

"Yeah?" he said in a whisper.

"Yeah." I ran my finger along the rim of my cup. "I'd like to know if you two talked about it."

Orville Riley took a deep breath and sat back in his chair. He looked at me before turning towards the faux food trucks and the people ordering lunch. "O called, but I wasn't ready. He… O said it was important, otherwise he…wouldn't have bothered me. He wanted to meet, but I blew him off. And now…" The tears returned.

"Now, O is gone." I handed him a napkin.

"Yeah."

Pluto came over, for once subdued and quiet. "Are you hungry, Mr. Monk?" he said at last.

I tried not to laugh, but it was just too hard not to. Orville shook his head. "Have you eaten today, Orv?"

Orv shook his head. "Not hungry," he said, still in a whisper.

"You gotta eat, man." I looked up at the anxious Pluto. "A couple of Anna's specialty burgers, dude."

"You got it," he said, and hustled off.

Once Pluto was gone, Jones looked at me. "Why the interest?"

"Like I said, O asked me to help. I liked her and I feel I owe her that."

Mr. Jones' eyes tightened. "What do you mean, liked her?"

I shook my head. "Nothing like that. I liked her for the same reason I like you. She struck me as a good person. The world needs people like that."

Orville turned away and nodded.

Mikal and Mr. Blakely returned, and I ordered burgers for them. The next hour we talked of music and avoided the gloom and anger from earlier and any talk of the murder of Orestra Blakely.

·   ·   ·   ·   ·

Still having O's keys with me, and as it was on the way, I stopped at her office. Anton waited outside. I went through the stack of files she had organized and put them into a valise I kept in the car. I'd gotten it for foolish sentimental reasons because I thought it went with my clothes, and like my clothes, was a relic of the 50s and 60s when men routinely carried such things with them. I wandered around the office for no good reason other than to see if anyone else might have been here, though I could only imagine one.

The next stop was my office. Natalya smiled as I said, "Hello." Anton kept her company while I went through the files.

They were all black transwomen, between the ages of twenty-five and thirty-five. All had gone missing. The dates went back four years. There were five of them in total. All had come to LA from somewhere else.

It was time to call Jackson Mallory.

But first, I had some questions for my chief-of-staff and bodyguard. It was almost comical as they both looked up at me at the same time. Anton started to get up, but I motioned for him to stay seated.

"What's going on with Josef?" I asked.

Anton maintained his stone face while his eyes focused on Natalya.

Natalya's focused on her computer. "What do you mean, Mr. Monk?"

"I mean, I wanted to talk to him and learned that suddenly he takes off to the one place he told me, time, and time again, he wouldn't return to. That's what I mean. And," I stared at Natalya, "apparently, it was when you went on vacation to Thailand. What's up?"

"Maybe something came up," she said, still not looking at me.

I turned to my bodyguard. "Anton?"

He kept his eyes on Natalya. She slid lower, as if to hide from him. "A family matter," he said.

I checked my fingernails. "I thought all his family was in the states now."

He shrugged. "So did I, but who knows?"

"And Big Mike? I heard he's dead." Neither moved. Silence. I shook my head. "I'm going to find out."

"Why?" Natalya asked her computer. "If he's dead, he's dead."

"I won't argue that," I said. "But people, Russian people, are asking questions, about me, about this organization. You take Josef to Thailand and he doesn't come back. I think he's tied into this too. He's hiding, isn't he?" Again, neither moved. "I know the both of you well enough to know that you're not being open with me. I don't know why, but I've got a bad feeling this is not going away. I think the two of you know that, too."

We sat in silence, save for the occasional tapping of computer keys.

I went back to my office.

Mallory answered on the third ring. "Yes, Mr. Buttman?"

"Got some time to talk?"

"I can meet you in a couple of hours. Where are you?" I was certain he was smiling.

"I'm in my office. Close enough?"

"Close enough," he said.

I turned around and stared out the window. It had been a hazy day with high clouds, but now darker clouds, thick and angry, were cruising in from the Pacific. Drops of rain started pelting the glass. It was as if God or nature was sending me a sign. We hadn't had any rain in months, and fires were burning to the north. Another bad sign. This easy life was making me sick. Too many people I knew were sad or angry or off doing stupid, thoughtless things.

I laughed at that.

Who was I to talk? How many stupid, thoughtless things had I done over the last six years, and that wasn't counting the previous thirty. And yet, I was technically doing great. I should feel great. Most of the time, I did. The kids kept me grounded and kept me from looking too hard at my misadventures. And I let them, but that was a mistake. People don't forget. People like Big Mike Kovalenko and Delton Manaforte and every crook and every business and every scheme they were playing. There were all the other players I didn't know, didn't want to know, but they wanted to know me.

Then there was Orestra Blakely and Aisha Diamond.

What were they doing, and why should I care?

21

Detective Jackson Mallory was late, but not too late, maybe twenty minutes. I was right; he was smiling. He gave Natalya and Anton a smirk as I waved him in. With him was a woman who I assumed was also a detective. She was tall, nearly six feet, wearing a dark blue suit.

He closed the door behind him.

"Feeling a little closed in, Mr. Buttman." He had a nice smile.

I returned the favor. "Depends on the subject matter."

"This is Detective Gallegos," he informed me. "She's handling the Blakely case. That's why you called, correct?"

"It is," I said. "I wanted to know if you've made any progress in the case."

"Have you?" he asked.

"I only know what I've heard. Please sit down."

The three of us found a chair. Time for business.

Detective Gallegos had sharp brown eyes that were just a shade lighter than the color of her hair, which was pulled back. I watched as she took me in. "You were seen entering both the home and business of the deceased," she said.

I noted the glimmer in Mallory's eyes as she spoke. "Are you watching me or the home and business of the deceased?" I asked.

She ignored my question. "Do you have permission?"

"Of a kind," I said. "I spoke to one of the sisters and she was ok with it. Blakely's father wants nothing to do with any of it. As far as he's concerned, Orestra Blakely died ten years ago when she transitioned. And as far as I could find, no will's been entered for probate. So, who knows if there even is a will." I looked at the two detectives facing me. "Given the nature of the crime, I assumed you'd been through those places already, so my taking a look wasn't going to interfere with the investigation."

Mallory continued smiling but said nothing.

The non-smiling detective continued her questions. "Have you heard from Aisha Diamond, Mr. Buttman?"

"Not a word."

"Has your brother been in contact with Ms. Diamond?" she asked.

I smiled at Mallory. "If he has, it hasn't been communicated to me. But then we're not terribly close."

"And in your conversations with Ms. Blakely before she died, did she mention your brother and his relationship to Aisha Diamond?"

"She did," I said.

"And you're aware Ms. Blakely was to meet Ms. Diamond on the night she was killed?"

"I came to understand that, yes." I was picturing Sterling as he and Aisha burst into the apartment in Berkeley. "You think my brother is tied into this?"

"We're setting up a time to talk to Mr. Bohrman," Mallory said.

"Is there anything else?" I felt the need to end our talk.

"Is there anything you think we need to know?" asked Mallory.

"Nothing I haven't already confessed to." I smiled at that.

Detective Gallegos rose and handed me a card. I put it in my pocket and escorted the detectives to the front door. Anton and Natalya looked on, but said nothing.

"What are you up to, Mr. Buttman?" Detective Gallegos asked as Mallory opened the front door.

I shrugged. "If I knew that, you wouldn't be here. I'll keep in touch."

I closed the door after the detectives. Natalya and Anton continued staring at me. I shook my head. "You two aren't the only people giving me a headache." I returned to my office.

I called Agnes to see if I'd told her that Isaac and I were having dinner with Sterling.

"Yes, you told me, lover," she said, laughing. "I worry about you, Monk. You seem so all over the place sometimes."

"Sometimes? There are days when I don't even know which house I'm waking up in," I said.

"Then don't have more than one," she countered. "Is this the meeting where you're going to confront Sterling?"

I hesitated. "Yeah."

Agnes continued laughing. "I'm sure it will go exceedingly well."

"That's why I'm making Isaac tag along. I don't know if Sterling knows I'll be there. Should be fun."

"I look forward to hearing all about it."

I'll bet. "Me too. Bye, beautiful."

"Bye, Sunshine."

•   •   •   •   •

Our meeting with Sterling was at a downtown steakhouse. Isaac met me at the office and Sterling met us at the restaurant. He was not happy to see me, but life isn't always one big happy moment after another.

"What, no hug?" I asked as he sat there.

Reluctantly, he rose and gave me and Isaac a hug. We're still the sons of Moses Bohrman, the man of many hugs.

"Why are you here?" Sterling asked.

"You know why," I answered," but to say it out loud, you blew me off when I was up north, and I need to talk to you about Aisha."

"I'm not going to talk about that," he said, his face darkening.

"It's me or the cops, and probably both, because murder draws in the light to the dark little recesses of our lives." I motioned that we sit down. "Are you still seeing her?"

"I said I wasn't going to see her anymore."

The server came by and we had Sterling order the wine. He was, after all, the expert.

"Why the interest?" he asked after the server had left.

Smiling, I said, "I told you, murder. And your girlfriend is a part of it. Maybe a big part, but who knows? Have you seen her lately?"

"I told Felicia, I wouldn't." Another non-answer.

Isaac had his own questions. "Can I ask where you met her? Aisha, that's her name, isn't it?"

Sterling looked at me. "Why should I tell you guys anything? So you can have a laugh at my expense?"

I shook my head. Sterling was always something of an odd duck to me. He tried to ingratiate himself early on, but I was reluctant, mainly because I wasn't sure I was going to be around much, but Agnes and her love of the farm took care of that. I did what I could to be nice and to be interested in the wine business, but I only cared so much, and he took it personally. Then, with all the drama of Jacob's death, and Moses falling apart because of it, Sterling drifted away, becoming more and more remote. I thought it ironic that I understood him better when he became more like me. The other thing, the thing only referenced to in off-hand language, mostly by his mother and father, was Sterling's interest in the unspoken, the alluded to, which turned out to be his desire for transgendered women.

Aisha.

"Nobody's going to laugh at you," Isaac assured him. "Better us than the cops—"

"And the cops are going to ask anyway," I said. "It's not a bad thing for us to know because they're going to ask us as well. That's how they work. If it seems less of a secret, then it doesn't look as bad. Besides, we're not asking for every gory detail, and believe it or not, we care about you far more than the fuzz, and we can help far more than the fuzz ever will."

Sterling pushed himself as far back into the booth as he could, his head down. "I met her through an agency that arranges these kinds of things." He looked up at us. "I don't expect you to understand, but I've always been... Anyway, I did a little research online and found out about this place, so I called. That's how I met her."

"Can I ask the name of this place?"

His eyes held fast to mine. "Why?"

"Because I'd like to talk to them. Find out if they knew a woman named Orestra Blakely," I said.

"Who's she?" he asked.

I kept my eyes on his. "The woman who was killed in Aisha's place. Didn't she tell you? They were supposed to meet. Ms. Blakely had it on her calendar to meet Aisha Diamond. Only instead, someone beat her brains in."

Sterling looked away. "I don't know anything about that."

I wasn't convinced.

"Where is this place where you met?" Isaac's next question.

"In Hollywood, off Sunset. A person named Flavius runs it. They call it, Here We Gather for Love."

"That's quite a name," Isaac told him.

Sterling leaned towards him. "You probably think it's a joke, that we're all a bunch of perverts, that—"

"I'm not saying that, Sterling." Isaac shot back.

"Guys…" Big brother to the rescue. I smiled to myself at that. I was anything but.

"Sorry," Sterling said as he leaned back.

Our wine arrived, and we ordered our dinner. We sipped the wine before taking a healthier drink. It was very good, but then it wasn't Sterling's judgment in wines that concerned me.

"You know the cops are asking to see you?" I said, as I put my glass down.

After a quiet moment, he said, "I agreed to see them tomorrow." He again looked at both of us, his eyes searching for something. I assumed sympathy. "What should I say?"

"Did you kill Orestra Blakely?" I asked.

I expected him to get mad, but he shook his head and in a low voice said, "No."

"Then tell them the truth," Isaac told him.

"So everyone can know, huh?" Poor pitiful Sterling.

It was Isaac's turn to shake his head. "Sorry, bro, but this isn't a secret. Everybody knows, or thinks they do. We just don't feel like asking a lot of uncomfortable questions." And, as if anticipating Sterling's comeback, he continued. "Maybe we don't understand, and maybe it's because we're not used to the idea, or can't get our heads around it, as Moses would say. But mostly it's because it's new to everybody; a lot of this is. But we do love and care about you, and Felicia, and the kids. And no matter how genuine your feelings for Aisha are, a lot of people aren't going to understand."

"But if it was just another woman, it'd be ok, right?" He looked at me as he asked this.

"Maybe. But from my experience, I didn't find that to be true," I said.

Sterling slumped back and stared down at his hands. "I'm trying guys, I am," he said, as he picked at them. "It's been hard. I love Felicia, I do, but... Aisha's important to me."

Isaac picked up his glass and took a drink. "You're going to have to choose, bro."

A nod was Sterling's answer.

Dinner came and we ate mostly in silence. A few questions were asked about the farm, the foundation, wine, and Moses. But they were only here and there.

No one had any interest in dessert.

As I was paying the bill, I was the rich one after all, Sterling cleared his throat. "I heard about a place that helps; counsels people like me. It's down here in LA. I was wondering if you'd come along with me...as support."

I looked at Isaac, who merely raised his eyebrows. "If you'd like us to be there..."

"I would," he said.

"Where is this place?" Isaac asked.

"Pasadena," Sterling told him. "It's run through a church called Sunlight Ministries and a man named Terrance Stanton."

"All right. Let us know when, and we'll take it from there," I said.

We gathered our thoughts and belongings and headed for the door. I almost made it before a voice called out to me. I turned to see MaryAnn in a booth with a distinguished older man.

"I'll see you guys later," I said to Isaac and Sterling.

They nodded and headed out.

"Have a seat, Monk," MaryAnn told me.

"Only for a moment. I don't like to intrude," I said, with a smile, as I scooted in beside her.

The man looked to be in his late fifties, early sixties, with a trim mustache and graying hair that had a dash of its original auburn at the temples. He, like me, had a on a well-tailored suit, his being navy blue with pinstripes. That continued my smile.

"Don," MaryAnn began, "this is Monk, Agnes' husband. Monk, this is Don."

"How do you do?" he said. "MaryAnn has told me about some of your adventures."

"I imagine she has," I said. "Have you two known each other long?"

"About six months," MaryAnn answered.

"That's sounds serious."

"I like to think it is," Don said with a smile.

I watched as MaryAnn processed that. She didn't seem to mind.

"That's good news," I said. "Perhaps the four of us should get together. I have the perfect place for it, a rambling old house up in Beverly Hills."

Don smiled at that. "Yes, I've heard, though it's my understanding that it's quite the showplace."

"I'm curious what else you've heard about it," I said, while looking over at MaryAnn. I tried not to picture her as I remembered from our last time together.

MaryAnn simply smiled. "A good story is a good story, Monk."

"Can't argue with that." I stood up. "Much as I enjoy being the third wheel on a date, I think I'll leave you two to the rest of your evening. Besides, I promised Agnes I'd be right home."

Don stood up and offered his hand. "It was nice meeting you and I look forward to meeting Agnes."

"As do I. Goodnight."

I left them to the strains of muted voices and piped in music.

22

Agnes was over at the Montaigne's, enjoying a little family time with our boisterous grandchildren. I found this out when I arrived at our dark and empty house. Minutes later, I was greeted by Zach and Lizzy slamming into me as I opened their front door. I smiled at their frazzled mother.

"Let me guess, there was cake," I said.

Rebekah handed the fussy Jacob to me. "Here."

The fussy Jacob stared at me.

"What?" I asked him.

Instead of answering, he simply put his head to my chest and closed his eyes.

"It's not normal," his mother muttered.

"What in life is," I said, enjoying the moment.

I sat on the couch, as I often seemed to do when I came over, cradling my now sleepy grandson. Agnes sat next to me as Zach and Lizzy raced around the house. Rebekah sat in the chair across from us. Fidel was off on assignment, doing his thing in the filming of some Hollywood masterpiece I'd probably avoid. I'd wearied of big box office spectacles. They seemed to be nothing more than live action cartoons that were driven more and more by computer generated imagery and little story.

Agnes turned to me. "How was—"

"I want to go to the big pool, Gamps!" Zach demanded, interrupting Agnes.

I frowned at Zach. "What did we say about interrupting people, little dude?"

Zach put on his best sheepish expression and big-eyed Agnes. "Sorry." Having figured that was enough, he pulled on my slacks. "Can we, Gamps?"

I rolled my eyes. "We'll see," I answered, knowing that wasn't what he wanted to hear. "Where's Emily?"

"She's out with Natalya. They went to the movies and I assume the mall," Rebekah said.

I ran my fingers along Jacob's downy hair. "Sounds exciting."

"It is to a sixteen-year-old," Agnes reminded me.

I nodded as if I did anything remotely like that when I was sixteen. No, when I was sixteen, I was knocking up my girlfriend, Lisa, who became Astral, and then Lilith. Good times.

Agnes tried again. "So, how was your evening, Monk?"

"Interesting," I said.

I got an elbow to the ribs, but in the nicest way. "Do tell."

"I'd love to, but seeing as we're in mixed company, it'll save it for later." I winked, as it seemed appropriate. "I did see MaryAnn there…"

"And?"

"And I got to meet Don. Have you met Don, beautiful?"

"No, not yet. What did you think?" Agnes was playing with her hair, looking at nothing in particular.

"Seemed nice enough," I said. Zach tugged again on my pants. "Should we plan a weekend retreat at the house in the hills, or let Zach stew in his juices?"

"I say let him stew," Rebekah answered, much to Zach's consternation. A deep frown found his otherwise cherubic face.

"Maybe if he's good for the rest of the week," I offered.

"I can be good," he whined.

"We'll see," his mother said.

"That'll have to do for now, little dude." My assurance did little to improve his disposition.

Rebekah got up and announced, "It's bedtime, you two." To which Zach came perilously close to bellowing, "NO!" Frowning at his mother, he marched off to his room. Lizzy followed her grumpy brother down the hall.

Kisses and hugs were doled out, as were goodnights, and I handed the sleeping Jacob back to his mother. I wished her all the best. I don't think she believed me.

Back home, I relayed what Sterling had said and what was supposed to be the plan going forward.

"Do you think he's still seeing her?" Agnes asked.

"He said he wasn't, but I wouldn't be surprised."

"Then why go see this Terrance Stanton? Why not just say you're taking care of it or it'll be over when she kicks me to the curb?" She smiled at that.

I tried not to. Instead, I said, "We'll find out."

She didn't ask about MaryAnn or Don.

· · · · ·

The next morning, after making coffee and pouring myself a cup, I pulled out the laptop to see what I could find on Terrance Stanton and Sunlight Ministries. There was plenty. Paster Terry ran one of those mega-churches where thousands of worshipers gathered to hear the good word. The church itself had the look of a mid-sized sports arena, concrete and steel, with a large granite cross rising between and above two sets of stained-glass windows on either side. Very majestic. The brick exterior was decorated with smaller crosses and large colorful images of Jesus and Pastor Terry rather than those of athletes. To me, it lacked the charm I found in the traditional architecture of the church. There were no steeples, no nave. No great flying buttresses found in cathedrals meant to serve as many as Sunlight Ministries, but then our small church in Virginia didn't have them either. It struck me as very business-like. If you took away the cross, it would be indistinguishable from any other business corridor in the area.

Inside was a daycare and a school, along with clubs and classes in the evening for adults and teens. There were plans for a university of love and faith. Also featured were videos of Pastor Terry's sermons. Another section had his hand-written notes; guides for everyday living. He was, as most of them were, energetic, positive, and infused with self-confidence and belief. He made it sound so easy to come in from the dark and believe.

I was reminded, though not in a positive way, of Lucian DeBerry, the murdered preacher in Oklahoma.

Under Missions, a variety of services were listed for those struggling with the vicissitudes of a secular modern life, including gender dysphoria, which the church titled: *What are a Man and Woman in God's Great Plan, and Finding Fulfilment and Happiness in How God Made You?* In it, the church offered counseling for those struggling with identity. There was also counseling on sex addiction, pornography, and how to achieve a satisfying God-driven sex life.

Probably didn't include threesomes.

Agnes came in to the kitchen, poured herself a cup of coffee, and sat down at the table. I looked her way and passed along a wan smile. She returned the favor.

On to the next exciting search.

Whoever this Flavius was, and whatever Here We Gather for Love was, though I knew or suspected, wasn't stated in the single page on its website. Matchmaking for those falling outside of society's binary sexual mores was all it implied. There was a single contact point, which assured the individual interested that it was both confidential and encrypted.

Agnes continued watching, as if something previously unknown might reveal itself.

"What?" I asked, as I closed the laptop.

"Just wondering what you're up to. You rarely use the computer." She smiled at my disdain for the vicissitudes of modern secular life.

"Checking out Pastor Terry and his Sunlight Ministries is all. Oh, and someone named Flavius who runs something called Here We Gather for Love," I said.

Agnes raised her eyebrows. "Here We Gather for Love? What's that?"

"It's where Sterling went to find forbidden love. Apparently, they connect the lovelorn who wants something other than what you can find on other dating or matchmaking services." I put the laptop away.

"Maybe we should check it out, Mr. Sunshine?" she laughed at that.

I did not.

She continued watching; her smile gone, drinking her coffee as I poured myself a second cup and sat down. She peered over the rim of her cup.

"You're not happy with me, are you?"

"Why would I be unhappy with you?"

"Don," she said.

"He seems like a perfectly decent guy, but what do I know? Maybe he's one of those jerks you mentioned concerning MaryAnn." I peered over my cup.

Agnes frowned. "It's not like that."

"No?"

"No," she said. "It's…"

"It's none of my business," I said.

Agnes opened her mouth to say something, but my miserable phone cut her off.

Isaac.

"Sterling set up a time this afternoon to talk at this Sunlight Ministries place." I smiled at his tone of voice when saying, Sunlight Ministries. We didn't talk much about religion, but I knew he did not hold it in high regard. "Are you sure you need me to go?"

I laughed. "Right back at you, bro."

"Fine," he groaned, "but you have to go, too."

"Where do you want to meet? Office?" I didn't want to leave the house.

"Sure. I've got some things I need to go over with you before I head out tomorrow. Sterling said he'd meet us there at three."

It was my turn to groan. "Does one-thirty give us enough time?"

"Sure. See you then."

Agnes continued to peer at me over the rim of her cup.

.　　.　　.　　.　　.

The campus of Sunlight Ministries was everything you'd expect it to be. Bucolic in its landscaped splendor, busy, as smiling folks came and went, and filled with a purposeful vibe. Neither Isaac nor Sterling shared in the purposeful vibe. Isaac was less than enthusiastic and Sterling glum. It was up to one Monk Buttman, or perhaps William Bohrman, as I once called myself, to take it in and enjoy the beatific vibe. Almost made me miss going to church.

A pleasant young woman named Vanessa greeted us.

"We're here to see Pastor Terry," I said. From the website, I learned this was how he preferred to be addressed. I gave Vanessa our names. She passed this on through an intercom to someone named Vern, who literally bounced into the waiting room to greet us.

"Gentlemen, my name is Vern Norlin. I'm one of Pastor Terry's assistants. Unfortunately, he's running a little late, so he asked me to greet you, and, if you'd like, give you a tour of our campus."

I looked at the sourpuss and grump next to me and said, "We'd love to, Vern. Lead the way."

Vern, filled with a zeal the rest of us couldn't match, led us across the campus, enthusing about this and that, from the large chapel where Pastor Terry gave his moving and heartfelt sermons—it had seating for five-thousand, with a grand stage, lighting, and a sound system that could match any auditorium of equal size in the greater Los Angeles basin—to the classrooms where school was taught during the week. The school's rooms and halls were decorated with encouraging bible verses and images of Jesus looking upon us in all his resplendent glory. Some I recognized; some were new, but they were always the same, the Jesus passed down to us from the European churches, which made me think of Max von Sydow, our great Swedish Jesus.

"Are any of you gentlemen practicing Christians?" Norlin asked.

I smiled, knowing I was probably it. "I was part of a small Baptist church for many years when I lived in rural Virginia," I said. "Churches of this size are new to me, Vern."

"I imagine so," he said, a glint in his eye. "I, myself, am from Kentucky, so I know how that is. And yes, to be a member of a congregation of the size of Sunlight Ministries takes some getting used to, but I think the size works to our advantage because we have so many people from different backgrounds and races. It gives you a greater sense of the world and all the different people in it. It certainly makes our potluck dinners much more interesting."

I nodded. "Must be quite a spread."

Sterling and Isaac nodded as well, but had little to add. Neither, to my knowledge, had set foot in a church, save for Sterling when he got married in the church Felicia grew up in. Vern started to ask my two brothers if they'd given any thought to turning their life over to Jesus, when his phone buzzed and alerted us that Pastor Terry was waiting. The bros may have thought they'd dodged a bullet, Isaac certainly, but I had no doubt that Pastor Terry would bring it up.

Vern led us back to Vanessa, who led us in to see Pastor Terry.

He was waiting by the door, wearing what was his standard form of dress. A brightly colored Hawaiian shirt; today's being orange and yellow, off-white slacks, and brown loafers. He stood about five-ten, had blue eyes, sandy blond hair that was nicely trimmed, and, as this was southern California, a rather immaculate tan. In any other circumstance I'd take him as a refined surfer dude, and, as I liked to think that, freed from his earthly bonds, Jesus was off surfing the cosmos, apt.

Like Vern, Pastor Terry greeted us with an enthusiastic smile. Introductions were made, with Sterling being singled out as the one seeking help and guidance, in the nicest way, of course.

"Please sit down, gentlemen," our host directed, gesturing at seats and a couch on one side of the room. The three of us sat on the couch, while Pastor Terry sat in a chair next to the couch near Sterling.

It was a large space, no doubt expected for someone atop so large a congregation, numbering around thirty-thousand locals, and many beyond if the website's numbers were to be believed. It was flooded with sunlight that shone through stained-glass atop large clear windows, which illuminated the many awards and accolades vested upon Pastor Terry. Photos of him with prominent members of faith and politicians of various stripes covered one wall, while another was covered in artwork created by the kids here at the school. By the desk, in front of the large windows, was a large bible on a reading stand. I smiled at that. Judith had one very similar to it in the library with its own stand.

"It's a very beautiful book, Monk," she said when I called her on it; her being less than devotedly religious. "Don't you have one, seeing as you spent so many years in the church?"

"Sadly, it didn't make the trip back to California," I said. I assumed that Astral had donated it to the church, notes and all.

"Then save the sermonizing," she said, rather pointedly. This from a woman who liked to romp around the house naked.

"Yes, dear."

Pastor Terry pulled me back into the conversation. "And what do you do, Monk?"

"Our foundation provides services to veterans in need," Isaac said.

"Yes, that's right. But we're here as moral support to Sterling in his moment of need." As I said this, I wondered why we were seeing Pastor Terry himself rather than a counselor? I assumed they employed them, but then again, Pastor Davis at my old church ended up handling much of these kinds of problems on his own. But in a church this size? No, I thought; they had to have their own, with their own religious predisposition.

Pastor Terry nodded. "I understand. The support of family is of great importance to us here at Sunlight Ministries. I, myself, rely very heavily on the support of my wife, Jeanine. She has given me great strength for many years." He set his eyes on Sterling. Sterling did the same to Pastor Terry before dropping his, but for an odd moment, it seemed as though he were sizing the pastor up. "It's my understanding that you seek our help in overcoming your desire for those who no longer accept how God has made them."

"Yes," Sterling said in a low voice. "I don't like what this is doing to me, and to my family, I..."

The office was suddenly very quiet.

Pastor Terry turned to the light streaming through the windows. "These are difficult times, gentlemen. Unfortunately, we have allowed our rather crass society to accept all things, no matter how incongruent to God's design, and by doing so, allowing them to corrupt us." He looked across at the three of us. "I don't say that to be harsh or unloving, only that we must confront this eroding of the pillars of God's work, that we must face the evil that sometimes is taken for progress as a kind of warped individualism. To love, we must reconcile with what should be, for the good of all, not just for the good of the moment, or for what we're fooled into believing will satisfy an unnatural hunger, for that inevitably leads to the destruction of everything we love and cherish."

"I know, it's just that... I love her, too."

Pastor Terry put his hand on Sterling's. "There is unselfish love, and there is selfish love. There is the love that brings great joy, and that which, as you've obviously come to understand, tears at the soul. I don't want you to think that this person you love is bad, only misguided. Our mission is to help you see that, so that you may offer to help them. You're not the first man I've helped through these kinds of ordeals. Our program is designed to free you of the desires that have led you to this low point, and we hope that it also leads you to accept Jesus Christ as your lord and savior."

"I'd like that, too," Sterling whispered.

"Then let us say a prayer for Sterling, thanking the Lord, and that his coming to us will help us help him in his hour of need."

We bowed our heads.

There was more praying and promises made. I gave myself a friendly pat on the back for keeping my big mouth shut. Isaac and I, for the most part, said little, other than to confirm our willingness to help Sterling stick to the road of salvation that would, in the end, repair his damaged soul. Sterling, for his part, promised to stay in contact; he had to return north that evening, but did set up a schedule for additional consultations. After thanking Pastor Terry, and his escorting us to the door, I noticed a brochure like the one I found in one of Orestra's case files.

"Ever heard of a woman named Orestra Blakely?" I asked.

"Not that I can remember," he said.

"Aisha Diamond?"

Pastor Terry shook his head, but the color in his blue eyes darkened. "Is it important?"

"Probably not. Thanks again."

"I need a drink," Isaac said after we sent Sterling on his way.

23

We found a martini bar not far from his apartment, which was not far from the office. He ordered an exotic drink called a Hangovertini. Not feeling particularly adventurous, I ordered whiskey.

"Two fingers," I said to the barkeep, who rolled her eyes. To my younger bro, "Shouldn't you have a hangover first?"

Isaac rubbed his forehead. "I have a headache. Isn't that close enough?"

"You weren't energized by the pastor's good news?" For some reason, I felt like needling Isaac. Maybe it was my playing nice with Pastor Terry Stanton.

"No."

The barkeep set our drinks in front of us. "Thanks," I said, setting a credit card on the bar.

Isaac took a drink of his Hangovertini. "Were *you* energized to go back and reclaim your faith, *Sunshine*?"

I laughed at that. "We'd first have to debate how much is left to reclaim or how much was there to begin with. It was what it was. That's the nature of it."

Isaac shook his head. "All that does is make me more sympathetic to Agnes and her having to deal with your evasions."

"Agnes loves it."

"Uh-huh." Isaac took a bigger drink. "Do you think it'll have any effect on Sterling?"

"I don't know. I got a weird vibe from Sterling as we were listening to Pastor Terry's spiel; that there was something else going on, but I can't imagine what it would be. I do know that you have to buy into all of it: Jesus, the church, the theology, otherwise it doesn't hold, and sooner or later you either leave, or live the life of a fraud."

"Like you?" Isaac smiled at that.

I took a sip of whiskey. "Like me."

We finished our drinks, contemplated another, decided against it. I paid the bill and sent Isaac home. He was off to Dallas in the morning.

Agnes and Emily were in the kitchen, both hunched over the laptop, looking at quilt patterns. I grabbed a bottle of water and sat across from them. Both mumbled hello, or what sounded like it. Occasionally they'd look up at me, or spin the laptop around and ask me what I thought of a particular pattern.

"I like it," "it's very nice," "that'd be fun," were my usual rejoinders.

"How'd it go?" Agnes asked.

"It was interesting," I said, not sure how much to say in front of Emily.

"Is this about Sterling?" Emily's turn. I looked at Agnes, who looked at me. "I heard he and Felicia were having problems."

"Who told you that?" I asked.

"Mom and Andrea were talking," she said. "*Maybe* I wasn't supposed to be listening, but you know…"

Agnes frowned. "Sounds like something Mr. Sunshine would say."

I feigned outrage. "I know, right?" I leaned towards them. "I heard that guy's a jerk."

Agnes rolled her eyes. "And then some. Is there any news?"

"He agreed to continue counseling, but beyond that, I don't know. We'll see. Anything here I need to be enlightened about?"

"I'm going with you to work tomorrow, Mr. Monk," Emily said, as if I didn't know that, "so don't forget." As if I would.

Well, maybe.

•   •   •   •   •

Ronnie waved me over as we were heading into the building from the garage. Benny crossed his arms and shook his head, but didn't say anything.

Emily stood behind me. "Is it ok to talk to that guy? Natalya says you have to be careful with street people."

"It's ok. I know Ronnie, he's harmless."

Emily crossed her arms. "Uh-huh." Now I had two of them judging me.

"Off you go." I point to the door and the other person judging me. "I'll be there in a minute." I wandered over to Ronnie, who had tucked himself just inside the entrance to the building's adjacent parking garage. "What's up?"

Ronnie scanned the street, his hands fidgeting, and crouched deeper into the nook behind the concrete column. "Seen these two guys for a couple of days now come and go. Morning and afternoon. Seems like they're seeing who's working when."

I was surprised by his skittishness. "Any idea who they might be?"

"Russians," he said.

"Not our black Russian?"

He smiled at that. "Nope. Real Russians. Know 'em a mile away and heard 'em talk. But I saw our black Russian. He's careful. Hard to see. Knows the garages; knows how to stay outta sight."

"How many times have you seen these Russians?"

"Three times over the last week. We need to worry, Mr. Monk?" His eyes were darting between me and the street.

"Maybe. I'll let Benny know." I took five twenties out of my pocket. "Thanks."

"Should I keep watching?"

"Yes," I said, "for both." I left him where he crouched.

Benny listened patiently as I told him what Ronnie had passed on, nodding every now and then. "I'll keep my eyes open."

Natalya and Emily were sorting mail. They looked up for a moment, noticed it was me, and went back to the mail. I sat at my fancy desk and let my mind wander. I pulled Orestra's files from the valise I had locked in my desk, turning them over, looking for anything that might connect them. In one was the Sunlight Ministries brochure. The ministry was mentioned in multiple files. In three others, the name Flavius appeared. For whatever reason, I remembered O's journals at her apartment, and wondered if there was anything in them, whether it was just personal stuff or something else. The clock and calendar on my business laptop, something I rarely used, told me I had nothing till one in the afternoon. I had time.

"I'll be back shortly. I have an errand to run," I told my chief-of-staff.

"Ok, Mr. Monk," Natalya said, not looking up. Emily was in Isaac's office shuffling papers.

"You'll be alright?"

Natalya looked up at me, her left eyebrow raised. "Of course."

"Of course," I mumbled to myself as I left.

It was a short drive to O's apartment. The inside was as it was the last time I'd been there with Agnes. The food in the fridge wasn't getting any better. Why, I was concerned I don't know, but I found the trash can and spare liners under the sink, and emptied the fridge of that which was expired, decaying, and inedible. The dumpster was on O's side of the complex, so it was a short haul. I had to be careful not to get any on my rather nice suit. Having finished that, and feeling like I'd accomplished something, I collected O's journals and the love letters from the drawer, stuffing them into the valise. Aileen caught me as I was leaving.

"Howdy, Monk."

"Aileen. How are you?" She was standing just inside her door. It appeared she'd had her hair done recently; the ends were trimmed and the highlights refreshed. She was wearing form-fitting pants and a Lakers jersey.

"I'm ok." She looked me up and down. "You look nice."

"Thanks."

She looked at the valise. "What brings you here?"

"Business. It turns out O owned the place, and I've offered to keep it going till whoever owns it next gets going." Sounded plausible.

"Yeah, I miss O." Aileen smiled as she turned her eyes to O's apartment. "We had some good times, and I wondered if she had a stake in this place." Her attention, and a smile, returned to me. "Got a minute, Monk?"

I smiled back. "What're you thinking?"

"I dunno. Might be nice to have some company." She cocked her head towards her place.

I thought about it. "How about lunch? There's a café down the block." Seemed safer.

"Your treat?"

"My treat."

Aileen, still smiling, hooked her arm in mine. "Sure."

It was a small place, specializing in tapas. Aileen had been there before and knew what she wanted, besides me. I noted the half-smile as she took in my wedding ring.

"Happy?"

"For the most part," I said.

"I was for a while." The half-smile faded. She confessed to being forty-three, divorced, and working a series of contractor jobs, mostly online. "It pays the bills." Her cheeks dimpled when she smiled, and she had a breezy kind of personality, so long as you weren't an authority figure. She liked to talk, or maybe hadn't had too many opportunities lately to talk. I let her ramble. It was nice to hear about someone else's problems for a change. I asked about Orestra Blakely. "Easy to get along with. You could drop in for a laugh, or a drink, or...just to talk." She picked up her margarita, stared at it. "It broke my heart about O. I really liked her, you know? She was fun, easy to talk to, but real, know what I mean?"

"I think so. I liked her, too, though I didn't know her well."

"Yeah. You wouldn't know it by how she acted, but the whole thing with her family hurt her pretty bad. We had some good cries together. I guess that's life for ya." I nodded. "What's your story, Monk?"

"Grew up on a commune, was a teenaged punk, then ran off to Virginia where I was an unhappy farmer. Came back to LA after my first wife left me. Was a nobody for a while, and now I'm a figurehead at a philanthropic organization that helps veterans. The usual," I said.

She took a bite from one of her plates. "Doesn't sound too usual to me."

"I guess you had to be there." I took a bite of mine, goat cheese and tomato.

Aileen focused her blue eyes on me. "You dress nice. Don't really see that anymore." I assumed it was the tequila talking.

"Yeah," I laughed. "It's a lot of work." I tried not to focus on her blue eyes. "Not that I'm changing the subject, but how did paying the rent work?"

"Bill pay. Company called Brentwood Property Management. Guess that's how O worked it." Aileen reached across the table and took my hand. "Probably can't talk you into spending the afternoon with me, can I?"

"Not that I don't think you're an attractive woman, but probably not. I've got plenty to deal with as it is," I said, slowly withdrawing my hand.

"Other women?"

"Just life."

We finished lunch while she talked about nothing in particular. I walked her back to her apartment. She smiled before closing her door. "If you change your mind, I won't mind."

Sometimes you're tempted to say you'll think about it, but I simply said, "Goodbye."

In the car, an odd thought occurred to me, as odd thoughts do when you're thinking of something else. *Russians.* Mr. Jones answered on the third ring.

"What?"

"Anton available?"

"Can be. Important?" He didn't sound overly down, which I took as a good sign.

"Ghost of Big Mike Kovalenko," I said.

"Big Mike? What's he got to do with it?"

"Big Mike is dead. Two months ago, in Thailand, if I'm putting the pieces together. Josef and Natalya might be tied up in it. Anyway, Isaac said people have been asking questions about me and the organization; people you wouldn't normally associate with the Jacob

Bohrman Veterans Service Foundation. Like Russians. And they've been seen coming around the building."

"I'll send him over. Do I need to worry?"

"I wouldn't have it any other way," I assured him.

"Same old Buttman," he laughed.

•   •   •   •   •

Nothing was out of the ordinary upon my return. Didn't see anyone outside of the building or in the parking garage. Natalya and Emily were being terribly productive, as I assumed they wished me to be.

"I put some contracts on your desk, Mr. Monk," my chief-of-staff informed me.

"I'll get right to it," I said. "Anton should be here in a little bit."

"Anton? Why?" She seemed genuinely surprised.

"I'm a worrier."

She cocked her head and frowned. "Is this about Josef?"

I cocked my head. "I don't know. You tell me."

"I have work to do, Mr. Monk," she said, returning to her computer, "and so do you."

"Yeah, yeah, yeah."

Back at my desk, not wanting to do anything, I unloaded the valise and set the journals and letters on the credenza behind me. That led me to look out the window at the city and the Pacific in the distance. Minds wander, as they say.

I didn't hear him enter, only what sounded like a door opening.

It was then I heard Emily scream.

24

He hit me as I came out of my office, hard enough that all I saw were stars, and stumbled to the floor. He then shoved me into the wall. Somewhere I heard more screaming, and felt him pulling me into the corridor by the lapels of my jacket, where he let me fall. Through fogged eyes, I could see Natalya, barely; my head still spinning, struggling to get free of the man before he slapped her and knocked her to the ground. He got close to me, shouting something in Russian, and waving a gun.

"We're taking your pretty young pussy, motherfucker," he said in a thick accent, pointing to Natalya. "Then we'll—"

Out of the blue, Benny hit him on the side of the head. The gun went flying. The punk looked up just as Benny struck again. This time he fell to the floor, his eyes rolled up in his head. Natalya grabbed the gun and would probably have killed the guy had Benny not calmy taken it from her.

"We should call the police, Mr. Monk," he said.

"Yeah," was all that came out of me.

The fuzz showed up quick this being a pricier part of town. Anton arrived about the same time, pulling another woozy looking guy with him. "Driver," he said, when asked by the fuzz. They didn't ask why the guy was woozy, never mind the fat bloody lip.

"I know him," Anton said later. "Knew he was trouble. Asked a few questions he didn't like, pulled him out. Figured he wasn't alone." He smiled at Benny and the other punk, who was slumped against the wall, his face bloody and his hands cuffed behind his back.

Even Jones showed up, a scowl on his face for yours truly.

"Now do you understand why I worry, Buttman?"

"No need to shout. My head hurts enough already." I ran my fingers along the side of my head and the fast-growing welt on it.

Medics had arrived and were checking me and Natalya out. Natalya waved them off. She was cradling Emily, who was still shaking. I, on the other hand, having learned my lesson when the Falcon was smashed, let them do their thing.

"Doesn't look too bad," a medic named Matt said. He asked me a lot of questions: name, rank, serial number; took my blood pressure and pulse, checked my eyes, the usual. That made me think of Aileen, which made me smile. "Take some ibuprofen or acetaminophen for the headache. If you start feeling dizzy, vision gets blurry, I highly recommend you head to the emergency room, concussions can kill."

"Will do," I said, knowing Jones, and no doubt Agnes, who I'm sure Jones called, would be on my ass about it. Other than the two Russians, as Anton said the driver was, the rest of us were taken to the conference room to make statements to the fuzz.

Emily had calmed down. I watched Natalya take charge of moving us around the room while still keeping Emily close. The woman continually surprised me. I was certain she'd fall apart. She probably thought the same of me. Instead, she was as cool as the other side of the pillow, a phrase I used to hear when Jones came over to the big house to watch his beloved Clippers. After an hour, the fuzz left us to our shakes and sour heads.

Jones sat across from me, tapping the table with his fingers. Anton sat to his left, Benny to his right. Natalya and Emily sat to my right.

"What are we going to do here, Monk?" the man in black asked.

"My thoughts exactly," I said. "If nothing else, and given everything that's come up, we're going to have to up the security, at least till we find out what this is all about, though I have an idea." I looked at Natalya as I said this.

She looked at Anton, who shrugged. "Probably what happened to Big Mike."

I looked at Emily. "You ok? Still want to live down here?"

She frowned and held on to Natalya's arm. "I'm ok, ok?"

"Ok," I said.

Jones sat back and stared at me and Natalya. "What do we need to know here? About Big Mike?"

I gestured to Natalya, who gave me the evil eye. "He started bothering me about six months ago. I guess someone followed me and found out where I lived because the notes he sent were addressed to me at my apartment. I ignored them, threw them away. I'd get one every couple of days. I asked Josef what to do. He said he'd ask around."

"Did you know about this?" I asked Anton.

"I knew," he said. Just as I knew that he and Josef had taken it upon themselves to keep an eye out for Natalya. She was their soft spot.

"Josef found out that Big Mike was hiding in Romania, and that there were people in Russia who wanted to talk to him, people he didn't want to talk to," she continued. "He said they could take care of Big Mike if I was willing to help. If I was willing to meet him."

A picture was forming in my sore head. "Lure him out into the open, so to speak. This was in Thailand?"

Natalya nodded. "Yes. Josef set it up."

Anton frowned when she said this.

"You didn't agree?"

Anton shook his head. "No."

"What was the deal?" Jones asked.

"I would agree to meet him in Thailand. They would take it from there. So, I opened his letters and…" Her face darkened as her hands balled into fists. "It was the same terrible shit he said before. It made me sick. It took everything I had to say I'd meet him, but I told myself it would just be this one time. Josef took care of the rest. We flew to Thailand. Bangkok. The Hilton; Big Mike liked the Hiltons. They grabbed him there. I don't know what they did to him. I don't care. Josef said it was finished, but that he had to go home and fix some things. I went to Sidney for a few weeks and came back. There were no more notes."

I shook my head. More bad thoughts filling it. "How bad are Josef's money problems?"

"Bad," Anton said. "Real bad. He owed a lot. Made some bad choices."

"Then why didn't he come to me? I got more money than I'll ever need. Why get sucked into this shit with Manaforte and gangsters—"

"He was embarrassed. He didn't want you to think poorly of him."

"Fuck!" I slammed my hand on the table, then realized Emily was listening and Jones was frowning. "Sorry, Em."

"I've heard the word before, Mr. Monk. I'm not a baby," she harrumphed.

Anton smiled at that.

"What?" I asked.

"They're tough," he said, "like babushka. Never fuck with babushka. Bad business."

"Of that I have no doubt," I said, "but we still have to deal with this. Do you have time to watch over our babushkas here?"

Natalya scowled at me. "I'm not old like some babushka, Mr. Monk!"

"My apologies."

"I'm good," Anton said. "We'll work it out, Natalya and me. You keep eye on Em when I'm not here, yes?"

"Yes. And I'll see what Bernie's dug up. Good times."

"They always are with you, Sunshine." Mr. Jones, stating the obvious.

We went our separate ways. Jones left with Anton and Natalya. Benny still had two more hours left on his shift. He walked Emily and me to my car.

"Did Ronnie see the two Russians?" I asked.

"Ronnie did good. Ran up when he saw the one get out of the car and the other drive into the garage. I was with housekeeping when he found me. That's when I came up. Maybe Ronnie's not so bad," he said.

That made me smile.

Emily was quiet on the drive back to West Covina. I saw no reason to add to the delight of an evening drive across LA. Agnes was waiting in the kitchen. Emily ran and gave her a big hug, but didn't cry or whine, just held on for a while. Agnes frowned at the darkening welt on the side of my head.

"So, how was your day, my love?" I felt it was important to ask.

"You're something else, Buttman." At least she smiled.

. . . . .

I had no interest in cooking, so we went out. Place called Chester's Steakhouse. Emily was still quiet, and Agnes spent more time than usual staring at me.

"How's your head, Sunshine?"

"Sore. The bastard hit me pretty good." I touched the bulging bruise. "Good thing my neck's better, eh?"

"Yeah."

"I assume Orville called and gave you the gory details," I said as I looked over the menu.

"He did," as she did the same. "What are we going to do here, Monk?"

"Decide what to eat. I'm thinking a nice sirloin and a baked potato. Maybe even dessert. You?"

Agnes shook her head. "Why do I even bother?"

"Gives you a reason to get up." I smiled as she rolled her eyes. Emily groaned, but didn't say anything. "If you mean our circumstances, Anton's keeping an eye on Natalya, and Em's with us. I'll hit up Bernie tomorrow. Plus, I have some of Orestra's journals to go over. Maybe check out this Flavius character."

"Seriously? With what just happened, you're still fooling around with that?"

Our server interrupted our happy banter and took our order. Agnes continued to frown at me.

"Sterling's mess won't go away either," I said. "That's just the way it is. Maybe you can tell me what the deal is with Don and MaryAnn if you don't want to dig into all this other stuff?"

Her frown deepened. "You said you weren't angry about that."

"I lied." I took a nice long drink of my expensive beer. "You lied."

"It's not like that," she huffed.

"Then what's it like?" I noticed that we had Emily's attention, which Agnes picked up on.

"We'll talk about this later." It was her turn to take a nice long drink of her T&T.

Dinner and the rest of the evening went quietly into that good night, with each of us upset about something different.

·   ·   ·   ·   ·

I got up early for no particular reason other than my mind wouldn't turn off. Emily found me in the kitchen, nursing my second cup of coffee.

"Would you like a cup?" I asked.

She crinkled her nose. "You know I don't like coffee, Mr. Sunshine."

"Sorry. Hungry?"

She sat down. "Shouldn't we wait for Agnes?"

"No." I picked up my cup and tipped it towards her.

"Are you mad at Agnes?"

I thought about it as I took a drink. "Yeah."

Emily nodded. "Want me to talk to her for you?"

That made me smile. "We'll see. Maybe you should go wake her. I expect the kids any minute now," I said.

Sure enough, the Montaigne brood was over five minutes later. Rebekah handed the grump to me as Zach and Lizzy sat in their chairs. "Hungry?" I asked.

Rebekah frowned at her dear old dad. "I'll make breakfast if you get little dude number two to sleep."

Little dude number two ignored his mother as I laughed. "Sure."

The rumpled woman of the house sauntered in as the kids yelled her name in unison. She stared at me and little dude number two. "It's not normal. And you two," she pointed at little dude number one and his sister, "no yelling till I've had my coffee."

"Yes, Grandma Agnes," the two said, smiles on their cherubic little faces. Agnes glared at me.

"I had nothing to do with it," I said, which, amazingly, was true.

"Why don't I believe that?" Agnes groused as she took a cup out of the cupboard.

"Personal issues," I said. I was going to ask Jacob his opinion, but he'd fallen asleep.

Rebekah stared at the sleeping Jacob. "It's not normal." I shrugged. "How's your head?" She carefully touched the lovely black and blue knot just above my right ear.

I touched it as well. "I woke up. How bad could it be?"

"Not funny, Dad." She sighed and returned to the task at hand and the two squirming kids waiting to be fed.

The calls started after breakfast, after Emily and Rebekah hauled the two kids bouncing off the walls to the park. Agnes was working on making herself presentable, her term, for the day. The first was from Bernie.

"Heard you had some visitors yesterday."

"I heard that, too. Couple of Russian punks, probably aligned with the late Big Mike Kovalenko," I said.

I was on the couch with Jacob on my lap. Agnes wandered in after pouring herself a second cup of coffee. She sat down next to me. I passed along what Natalya had confessed to. Bernie took it in with an occasional, "Uh-huh."

"What have you heard about that?"

"Straight up hit. He was found in his hotel room, shot in the face. Word was that he absconded not only with his money, but with some of his associates. That never goes down well. Still nothing on Aisha Diamond. It's pretty obvious at this stage that she isn't using that name on anything official. Her apartment in Berkeley was under your brother's name. We'll need to find her birth name." Agnes was listening in. She'd moved in closer and was running her hand along the side of my pants. "Monk, you think there might be more to this?"

"What do you mean?"

Agnes rolled her eyes. "He means Sobeski, Sunshine."

"Well, since Josef had his hands in both, it's certainly possible."

"Ever heard of a man named Zosima?" Bernie asked.

"Johnny mentioned him once," Agnes said. "He's big time in the Russian mafia."

"Among other things, yes. He's also a mover and shaker, behind the scenes, in the Russian government. It's believed he's the one pushing to find out what happened to Sobeski. He's also tight with Manaforte, among others, including Marsyas Durant. He's also associated, discreetly, with Dominik and Associates."

"Then I'll just march up there and ask what's what," I said, trying to be glib.

"I'd hold off on that." Bernie wasn't. "Dominik and Associates are an influential lobbying group with lots of friends in Washington. We have to be very careful with people like that. Too much at stake. If his people are behind this, then they know of your connection to both Sobeski and Big Mike, and that Natalya Constantinescu would make an excellent pawn."

Lovely. "Any ideas?"

"Let me think about it. Call Art, see what he thinks."

"I'll do that."

"Keep in touch, Monk. Bye Agnes."

"Goodbye," Agnes said, ending our call.

The second one was from Detective Gallegos.

25

Detective Gallegos called five minutes after we finished our call with Bernie, as Agnes was trying to cozy up to her recalcitrant husband.

"I'd like to talk to you, Mr. Buttman. will you be at your office?" she asked.

"I hadn't planned on coming in today, Detective. Can this wait till tomorrow? I'll be in then. Otherwise, it means you'll have to take a delightful trip to West Covina."

"I could have you come downtown for an interview," she said. I admired the deadpan in her voice, smooth and steady.

"You could, but I'd have my lawyers whine, and it'd take longer that way than just waiting until tomorrow. What's your preference?"

"Tomorrow at ten sharp, Mr. Buttman?"

"Tomorrow at ten, Detective." I looked at the sleeping Jacob. "Looks like I have an appointment tomorrow."

Agnes snuggled in closer, but that was interrupted by the gang bursting through the door.

"I'm first," Zach shouted, as he ran to the spare bedroom, no doubt going for his swimsuit. Lizzy was right behind in hot pursuit. Rebekah dragged her sorry butt in last, already worn out by her two eldest children. She plopped down on the couch next to Agnes.

"Should we draw straws?" I asked.

"Shut up, Dad!"

"Wow, someone's a little peevish. Apparently, your recent walk in the park isn't paying off as you thought it would. Maybe I should hand off your latest to you?" I gestured to the sleeping Jacob.

Rebekah pinched her eyes at the old man. "Can't you just be nice for a few minutes and watch the kids?"

"I'll watch them," Agnes said, pulling herself away. "Not much action here, anyway."

My daughter's face went from perturbed to inquisitive as Agnes left. "You and Agnes having problems?"

"Why would you think that?" I said, smiling.

"Cuz I know you, that's why."

"Uh-huh."

Her two boisterous children raced out of the bedroom, through the living room and kitchen, and out into the backyard. Agnes followed at a leisurely pace. I got up and followed her. I assumed Rebekah wanted the opportunity to catch a quick nap.

As I stood at the kitchen door, I realized Emily was missing.

"Where's Emily?" I asked Rebekah.

Rebekah stretched out on the couch. "She wanted to take a walk."

I handed her Jacob. "You know what happened yesterday, right?"

"Oh…"

"I'll be back."

·   ·   ·   ·   ·

She was still at the park. At the far end, staring into space. She didn't see me till I was right in front of her.

"Mind if I join you?" She shrugged, so I sat down. "What's on your mind?" though I had a fair idea.

"Natalya." Emily rubbed her hands together, still staring at the few people populating the park. "I was thinking about yesterday, what she said about this Big Mike person…" She looked at me, searching my face, focusing in on the bruise. "It's bad, isn't it? What he did to her."

"It's bad."

"She told me not to worry, that it would be ok. She said she'd be strong for both of us. I didn't know what that meant, but now that I think about it, I feel like I should be strong for her." Emily took my hand. "He raped her, didn't he?"

"Yes. Did she say anything to you about it?"

Emily turned her attention to our hands. "She said it wasn't important anymore. She said sometimes bad things happen, but that you can't let it destroy you."

"Did you believe her?"

"I want to." I put my arms around her and she settled in next to me. "She thinks the world of you, Mr. Monk." Emily wiped her eyes. "I'm not supposed to tell you that, but I don't think she'd mind."

"Probably not." I pictured Natalya, her arms crossed, as she shook her head at my supposed incompetence. Made me smile. "Have you changed your mind about wanting to live down here?"

"Nope."

"Well then, we should get back before the kids wear out Agnes and Rebekah," I said, letting her go.

Emily got up and stared in the direction of the house. "Yeah, they're a handful."

"Like your brothers and sisters?" I smiled at that.

Emily frowned. "Don't push your luck, Mr. Monk!" Natalya would be so proud.

•　　•　　•　　•　　•

Art Devaney was, as usual, delighted to hear from me. I was sitting in the kitchen; too much noise outside with the kids splashing around in the pool. Emily had gone out to help Agnes. Rebekah had retreated to the bedroom with Jacob.

"What great intrigue are you up to now, Mr. Buttman? I'm assuming nothing to do with the president. There's already enough going on about that."

"Not directly, Art, but I'm getting the feeling that, no matter how much I'd like to think not, I'm far more involved than I'd like to be."

"Do tell?" I knew he had a grin on his smarmy face from ear to ear.

"It has to do with characters named Sobeski, Zosima, and Fairfax. Some, or all of whom, are connected to Delton Manaforte. Then there's the intrigue surrounding the assassination, if you want to call it that, of Big Mike Kovalenko in Bangkok that Natalya got sucked into by Josef Rostikov, a security guy I employed from time to time. Once worked for Big Mike. How's that for starters?"

"Not bad," he said.

"Oh, and I'm looking into the murder of a trans private detective who was killed when she was supposed to be meeting my brother's trans lover. Possible mistaken identity killing, but that led me to other missing black transwomen and, naturally, back to religion and free love. Questions?" I knew that would get him going.

"It's never boring when it comes to Monk Buttman," he said with a laugh. "Some of the names I know, and I should be surprised by Fairfax wading into this, but maybe not. Zosima I've heard of, but only in passing. I know he's a formidable figure in Russia, mostly in the underworld, but with ties to the Kremlin. I'll ask around. Don't know if I can help with the local stuff. That's more Bernie's area of expertise—"

"What if these missing black women were being trafficked, maybe by a person named Flavius? Think the Russians might be involved?" I was throwing out whatever popped into my head, which still hurt.

"If they are, it's local. Not too many black transwomen in eastern Europe." I could hear him shuffling papers. "I'll ask around. As for Sobeski, rumor has it that he's been put out to pasture permanently, if you know what I mean…"

"I know what you mean. But I think there's more to Sobeski than his simply being a problem for a few gangsters. And if he is out to pasture, why the questions?"

"Why indeed? Any ideas?"

"Who knows, maybe a secret cache of documents exposing his former employers."

"Sounds like something out of a crime novel," Art chuckled.

"You never know. Also, a lobbying group, Dominik and Associates, was asking questions about me and Agnes, which is odd, since Agnes has no role in the foundation's dealings."

Silence. "Where'd you hear that?"

"Isaac said that a guy named…let me look…" I rummaged around in my pockets looking for the card Isaac had given me. "Boris Tsarnaev's the name. He was asking Jontaveus Montgomery. I'm sure you've heard of him."

"I've heard of the both of them," he said. "Maybe your joke about a secret cache of documents isn't so farfetched. Tsarnaev represents a lot of interesting characters."

"Should I be concerned?" A question I regretted the minute it came out of my mouth.

"You never know."

"Well, whatever you can do, Art, I'd appreciate it," I said.

"There's a lot here, Monk. Maybe I should ask for a retainer?" he laughed.

"Fortunately, I have a few bucks to my name." A few plus a few more. "If you do, let me know."

"That I will. I'll be in touch."

"Thanks, Art." I started to end the call—

"Monk…"

"Yeah?"

"I know I tend to be a little playful in our dealings, but these are some problematic names you've given me. They aren't part-timers or low-end types. Be careful," he said. "Seriously."

"Thanks."

I stared at the phone after ending the call. An old familiar knot was forming in my stomach. I absentmindedly tapped the table as Agnes walked into the kitchen. It took a minute for me to realize she was staring at me.

"That good?" she asked.

"Even better," I answered.

"Should I be worried?" I laughed at that. "What?" She put her hands on her hips and tilted her head. "Don't play games with me, Monk."

"Yes, dear."

"Is it?"

I thought of Art. "Is it what?"

Agnes frowned and rolled her eyes. "If it wasn't for that big bruise on your head, I'd smack you. Is it bad?"

"It's bad." Why lie?

The gang, tired from playing in the pool, congregated at the sliding door while Emily collected the towels to dry them off.

"We're hungry, Gamps!" Zach bellowed.

"I'm shocked," I said. "I didn't think you'd be hungry till dinnertime. How about some bugs and dirt?"

"No!" shouted Lizzy, who was becoming more like her demanding brother every day.

I eyed the grinning Agnes. "What's on the menu, beautiful?"

"It's a mac and cheese day, Sunshine."

"Isn't it always," I muttered.

So informed, I went about my task. Soon they were at the table, waiting anxiously for their midday grub. Agnes called to Rebekah to see if she was interested; she was and entered the kitchen just as I was setting out bowls and dishing up their cheesy favorite.

"Here you go," she said, handing me Jacob as the rest of her brood chowed down.

"When do *I* get a break?" I whined.

Emily and the kids ignored me, while Agnes and Rebekah smirked. Classy. I was about to say something pithy when the doorbell rang. They all looked at me.

"Need to get the door, Sunshine," Agnes thoughtfully told me between mouthfuls of goop.

"Thanks."

I opened the door to find Erik Nakatomi smiling at me and Jacob. "Have a moment, Mr. Buttman?"

Excellent question.

26

"If you're selling something, I'm not interested," I said. "I have enough on my hands already."

The former secret service agent smiled at me. "So, I see. Fortunately, I'm not selling at the moment. I'm here on behalf of Mr. Manaforte."

"I assume you're always acting on behalf of Mr. Manaforte. Come in. Don't mind the baby. He knows how to keep quiet, if you know what I mean." I stepped aside as Nakatomi entered the house.

Agnes stuck her head around the corner. "*Agent* Nakatomi!"

Nakatomi nodded at Agnes.

"She's having a hard time dealing with that," I said, smiling at my suspicious wife.

"Misrepresentation is misrepresentation, Sunshine," she answered, before returning to the family scarfing down mac and cheese.

"My apologies—"

"No apologies, Buttman!" she bellowed.

"So, what brings you to my home?" I asked after we waited for any other comments from the peanut gallery in the kitchen.

"Mr. Manaforte is interested in setting up a meeting with you," he said, looking towards the kitchen. "Maybe it would be better if we step outside for a moment. Without the baby and your phone."

"Sure." I put the phone on the coffee table and wandered into the kitchen. Rebekah frowned as I handed her Jacob. "Man talk," I said.

Agnes frowned as well. "Oh, brother."

I shrugged. Outside, I scanned the street for any vehicles or people I didn't recognize. Didn't see any. Nakatomi noticed me checking things out.

"Are you being watched?" he asked.

"I was thinking more if you were, but you never know. Have a seat." I pointed to the two patio chairs on the front porch. "Should I ask why you didn't just call? Or is the fact that my phone is elsewhere the answer to my question?"

"It is," he said, settling into his seat. "Mr. Manaforte decided it would be best if I came in person."

"I see. So, when does he want to meet?"

"Next week, on his yacht."

"In or outside of US waters?" I asked, having a sense of where this was going.

Nakatomi arched his eyebrows for a moment. "Either is possible. Fortunately, that's outside of my responsibilities. A week from tomorrow?"

I thought about it. "Sure."

Nakatomi rose. "I'll let Mr. Manaforte know. I'll set the arrangements and will contact you early next week, most likely on Monday. Good day, Mr. Buttman."

"Mr. Nakatomi." I got up and walked him to his car. We both scanned the street.

"It's quiet today," I said.

He smiled and got in his car. I stood by the mailbox as he drove off. A car I didn't know drove by a minute later with tinted windows. A big black Ford SUV. Seemed appropriate. I returned to the clan to finish my lunch.

·   ·   ·   ·   ·

"Well?" Agnes was eyeing me as I was enjoying the afternoon sun, resting comfortably in my chaise lounge chair. Rebekah had reluctantly taken her kids back home. Emily went along to help.

"Well, what?"

Agnes smacked me, which I might have deserved, but made me laugh. "You *know* what! *Agent* Nakatomi and what he wanted."

"Oh, that. Manaforte is setting up a meeting with the five families where I'll be assassinated. Pretty straight forward stuff," I said. "You know."

Agnes rolled her eyes. "Unfortunately, I do. Seriously."

I sat up. "Manaforte wants to meet on his yacht next week."

"Is it a nice yacht? I mean, if you're going to be assassinated, might as well go out in style, right?" She had a rather delightful smirk on her beautiful face.

"Oh, absolutely," I agreed. "I have just the suit."

"Jokes aside, what's the deal?"

"I'm assuming Sobeski," I said. "Fortunately, I have a week for Bernie and Art to find out a few things before I—"

"What's this 'I' stuff? I'm not invited?" she huffed.

I smiled at her being peeved over this. "What? You want to be assassinated, too?"

"We're in this together, Buttman. Don't forget that." She crossed her arms, so I'd get the point.

"Yes, dear. I'll make sure I find out if you're invited."

Agnes leaned over me. "Insist, Monk."

"Yes, dear."

The remainder of the afternoon and evening were thankfully non-eventful. Emily stayed the night at the Montaigne's. The night was filled with dreams of black Russians and transwomen.

Morning brought the joys of a new workday and fun filled times with Detective Gallegos and God knows what else. Reports, as usual. I tried to remember if Isaac would be there, couldn't, and thought of Emily, bound and determined to go regardless of the attack two days earlier. I heard the front door open, and she wandered in as I was pouring my morning cup of joe.

"Want some?"

She curled her nose. "We talked about this, Mr. Monk!" Business as usual.

"Then maybe some orange juice. Hungry?"

"I ate with the kids. Isn't it time to go?"

I smiled at her determination to get to it. "Probably. I'll let the queen know we're off."

The queen had no interest in staying home alone given recent events.

"We'll be late," Emily whined.

"I don't take that long," Agnes whined back.

I said nothing and enjoyed my coffee.

•   •   •   •   •

Ronnie was waiting at the entrance to the garage, tucked in the corner, as was his wont. "No Russians today," he said, "but our black friend's been hanging around."

"Is he there now?"

"Ain't seen him today."

"Let Bennie know if you do." I handed him a few bills.

"Will do. Thanks, Mr. Monk."

I shrugged as Agnes and Emily shook their collective heads.

Natalya was busy as usual. Outwardly, no different. She smiled at me and Agnes before handing Emily a stack of papers; her work for the day. I didn't see Anton. "He has things to do, Mr. Monk. He'll be back."

"And Isaac?"

"He'll be back from Dallas tomorrow. Do I need to call him?"

"No." I started for my office. "Oh, Detective Gallegos will be here at ten to talk to me."

Natalya looked up. "Is this about the other day?"

"No, I think it's about the two black transwomen. Remember them?" You never know, a lot's been going on.

Natalya tightened her eyes. "Should I be concerned, Mr. Monk?"

I noticed Agnes and Emily looking, too. "I wouldn't have it any other way."

Agnes followed me into my office. "What's the plan then, Mr. Monk?"

I sat down and grinned at my wife. "I'm a by the seat of my pants guy, babe. I take life as it comes. I thought you'd figured that out by now?"

She sat down and crossed her arms. "You would think. But seriously…"

I picked up the journals and letters on the credenza that I'd taken from Orestra's apartment and handed the letters to Agnes. "Seriously, we'll start with these."

"What do I do with these?"

"You read them," I said. She frowned at that. "Hey, you wanted to come to work today."

"Maybe I should go over the reports you hate to read?"

"Don't worry, there'll be time for that, too." I pointed to the letters. "Get to it."

"You're a jerk, Buttman!"

"It's all a part of God's great plan, my love," I said.

I don't think she believed me.

I opened the first journal. It, as I suspected, covered Orestra's transition from Oren. Her writing was clear and concise, in a kind of block printing. No cursive. All capitals. In it, she noted that her therapist thought it would be good for her to collect her thoughts and beliefs, write down her struggles with her faith and family.

O wasn't so sure.

I don't know if I want to do this, all this writing. I'm tired of thinking about it, were the first lines written. *I know who I am. I know what I want to do.*

"Monk?" I looked up at Agnes. "These are love letters. Did you know that?"

"I thought you told me that when we first went to her apartment?" I answered.

"Did I?"

"Or maybe I did. It's not important," I said, waiting…

"Not important? These are…" Agnes' face went blank. "Well, they're personal," she said, after finding the words.

"Aren't all love letters personal, my love?"

Agnes sighed. "Why do I bother?"

"Sure seems to come up a lot," I said, returning to the journals.

The first few pages were either declarative or "What I did today" narratives. The dutiful minimum required by the teacher of the recalcitrant student. But after a while, the journal became more contemplative, both inward and outward looking, as she began the process of wearing what she wanted, going where she wanted, and slowly opening up to others. As I read, I found myself being drawn in to Orestra's storytelling, hearing her voice. The more she wrote, the more writerly it became. And she was good at it. I could see and hear her saying these very things to me, reminding me of our talks.

She attended more of her therapist's group sessions. Sought out and introduced herself to others in the transgender community. Felt at home. Felt at peace. *Finally*, she wrote. That left Oren's family and friends, particularly a man named Orville Riley. She and Orville had grown up together, gone to school together, joined the Army together. They were brothers through and through. Orestra wrestled with this more than anything else. Of her father, she knew that would go nowhere. *He'll never understand.* She would still try, promised herself she would, hedged and put it off again and again, until the painful day when he said exactly what she knew he would.

They were through.

He couldn't bear to look at me. Wouldn't even let Orinda into the room. Threw me out. It hurt more than I could stand. Still hurts. His other sisters, Maybelle and Doris, named for their great-grandmothers, he told separately. They were just as shocked, they said, but they knew Oren better, knew his secrets. They didn't cut Orestra out of their lives, but were distant. Formal. *It is what it is* she wrote time and time again. Orinda was more receptive, but very careful not to let her father find out. She stilled lived with him. Took care of him.

That left Orville Riley.

There was a long letter tucked into the journal addressed to him. I couldn't bring myself to read it. I set it aside. Throughout the rest of the journals, Orestra chastised herself for not giving the letter to Orville. They had tried to talk; Orville having heard the news from Jordan Blakely, but it was too hard for the both of them. *If I give him time, I believe he'll come to understand,* she wrote. I don't know if she thought that was true. There were no more entries concerning Orville Riley. The first journal ended with her declarations.

I knew at seventeen I was a woman. Knew it through and through, but I continued to play the part of Oren because he meant so much to my father. And I played the part well, whether in sports, or the Army, or when we set up our security business. But I was never truly Oren. Always Orestra. Always in my heart. I would look at Oren in the mirror and wonder how long will you be here? How long must I play this part? Why can't I be Orestra? The person I truly am? Thirty years is long enough, is too long. I don't want them to be angry, but I don't want to be angry either. I want them to understand, but even if they won't, even if...even if they let me go, I will be alright. No, I will be better because I will be who I am!

I am Orestra Blakely.

I will always be Orestra Blakely.

I closed the journal just as Natalya knocked on the door.

"Detective Gallegos is here," she said.

27

"Come in, Detective. This is my wife, Agnes."

Agnes stood. "Detective."

Detective Gallegos gave Agnes the once over. "Is your wife going to be a part of our conversation?"

I looked at Agnes.

Agnes eyed the detective. "Yes, she is."

"And that answers that." I gestured to the chair next to Agnes. "What's on your mind, Detective?"

"I don't know that anything is on my mind, Mr. Buttman. Mostly, I was wondering what I should think of you."

I smiled at that. "Me?"

"You," she said officiously, as I assumed she would be. "You have quite a reputation in the department, from Captain Goncalves on down to Lt. Descartes and Detective Mallory, who thoughtfully had me assigned to the investigation into Orestra Blakely's murder. He gave me a look at his unofficial file on you and told me that, if nothing else, you have connections that might be of use to me, even if it means having to deal with you—" Agnes burst out laughing at that. "Something funny, Ms. Buttman?" Now it was my turn to laugh.

"No," Agnes stammered, trying to regain some sense of decorum; we were, after all, talking, I think, about a murder investigation. "It's just that I'm very familiar with Detective Mallory's, um, interactions with Mr. Buttman here."

"Yes," I said, "*Ms.* Buttman is correct, and to a degree Mallory, that I am an acquired taste. But you're not here for laughs or my unfortunate interactions with the LAPD."

The detective straightened her back against the chair. "I'm here to see if you're still involving yourself in this, and, much as I don't care for that, what, if anything, you've found that may help us."

"May I first ask if you've talked with my brother, Sterling?"

"Not yet. We were scheduled to talk to him two days ago, but his lawyer informed us that he wouldn't be available, and could we move it to next week. Would you know anything about that?"

I sat back and half-smiled. Figures, I thought. "No, I had nothing to do with that. In fact, I told him it was better to play ball as, he assured me, he has nothing to do with this."

"Do you believe that, Mr. Buttman?" Gallegos asked.

"Do you, Monk?" Agnes tilted her head just so.

"For now, I have to assume he had nothing to do with Ms. Blakely's murder. Whether there's more, that depends on if he's still seeing Aisha Diamond."

The detective took out her phone. "Do you think he is?"

"It's possible, though, like I said, he's assured me that he no longer is." I watched as Gallegos noted this in her phone. "May I ask if you're looking into other homicides that might be linked to Orestra Blakely?"

"Why do you ask?" the detective answered.

"I could say curiosity, which is true, but if you did indeed go through Ms. Blakely's files, you know she was looking into several missing persons cases. She asked me to help her, said I was the type she needed to make certain inquiries."

"What type would that be, Mr. Buttman?"

"Rich, white, straight, and possibly interested," I answered.

Agnes frowned at that. "And just what were you going to do, Buttman?"

I shrugged. "Never got that far." I waited for Gallegos to look up from her phone. "Ever heard of a person named Flavius, Detective?"

"I have. What have you heard?"

"That he runs a service that matches individuals who might be looking for relationships of a particular kind, but outside of pickup joints or apps. Discretion being a part of the service, as it always is for people like me, I suppose." I grinned at Agnes. "Right, my love?"

"Nice try, Sunshine," she answered with a grin of her own.

"Not he, Mr. Buttman, they," the detective said. After noting our blank stares, she added, "Flavius uses the pronouns, they and them."

"Good to know," I said.

The detective had more questions. "Are you planning on meeting with Flavius?"

"I might. Depends on what I hear from my sources."

She returned to her phone. "Are these the ones referenced in Detective Mallory's files?"

"If those references are correct, then yes," I said.

Detective Gallegos put her phone away and looked directly at me. "You asked if I was looking into other cases like Ms. Blakely's. The answer is yes. As you may know, there have been a series of murders within the LGBQT community, particularly among black transwomen, and the department is feeling a lot of pressure because of it. That has been handed off to me. And while I dislike the idea of having someone like you being a part of this, and by that, I mean someone outside of proper police authority, I recognize that there are limits on our time and resources. And as Detective Mallory has somewhat vouched for you, I'm willing to remain open to what you might find. Does that answer your question, Mr. Buttman?"

"It does," I said.

"If you continue to pursue this, I will continue to persist in checking in on your activities. Consequently, it might be in your best interest to keep me informed." The detective tightened her eyes. "Agreed."

"I have your card, Detective. I'll be in touch."

Detective Gallegos rose and turned to Agnes, who rose. "Ms. Buttman," she said, after which she left us.

"Well, *Ms.* Buttman, what do you think?" Agnes had been unusually quiet during the detective's time with us.

Agnes sat back down. "I don't know and don't call me *Ms. Buttman!*"

I laughed. "Yes, dear. Then perhaps we should finish up with these journals and letters."

•   •   •   •   •

The remaining journals had less to do with Orestra herself than with the transgender community and the people she found herself being and working with. As her business grew and she became accepted as someone who could be trusted to be both helpful and understanding, she noted certain troubling patterns that years in the security and sleuthing biz had taught her. *People are people*, she noted, *whatever their outlook or where they are in society, they all long to love and be loved, to find acceptance, often in another person's arms.* That wasn't so easy for transpeople. Orestra noted her own issues with it, and her attempts at relationships. I smiled when Aileen was mentioned. *She was interested, curious, she said. And we had some good times, but I knew it wasn't serious, but a warm body and kind words go a long way when you're lonely. I guess we both were.*

Made me think of Agnes and MaryAnn.

There were also mentions of violence. Rape. Assault. Sex trafficking. All circulating in the trans community. *Some days I can't do this. It's too much. Pain, anger. I want to do something, something that will make a difference, but days like this...I don't feel it. All I feel is a deep sorrow and helplessness.*

I put the journal aside for a moment and turned to the window and stared at the blue water sparkling in the distance.

The last journal continued O's unease that someone was preying on a particular kind of black transwoman. *Maybe that's not the right way to say it*, she wrote. *Aside from love, people like to be taken care of and are willing to believe whether in the end it's good for them or not.* There were three of them she was searching for. All were missing. All about the same age. All from similar backgrounds, with similar stories from worried family or friends. And all transgendered. LaToya was from rural Texas, Samantha from just outside of Vegas, and Janisha from a small town in Tennessee. Word was they had found a service to help them.

All had, at one point or another, cycled through Sunlight Ministries.

Coincidence?

The last entry was about a woman she'd met named Aisha Diamond, who knew the three missing women, who wanted help exposing what Diamond said was a coverup by a dangerous man, but there were no details, just a plan to meet.

I closed the journal, and absentmindedly picked up the letter to Orville, and tapped the end on the desk. Agnes was finishing up the last of the letters. She set them aside before saying, "Geez."

"What?"

"Guy's a complete whiner," she said, passing them to me.

I unfolded the one on top. "In what way?" Just to ask.

"He can't decide if his *love* is real, or maybe it's just lust, or maybe the *Lord* is trying him; nonsense like that." She rolled her eyes for effect. "Meanwhile, he begs the person he's writing to keep the faith and bear with him—"

"Sounds familiar," I said.

Agnes snorted. "Simon was bad, but not this bad. Geez."

"I looked at the writing. Cursive. I open Orville's letter just to check. Block printing. "The letters aren't from Orestra, but I didn't think they would be."

"Wouldn't they be to her?"

"Ordinarily you'd think yes, and maybe we're supposed to believe that, or maybe they were given to O, but O wasn't the object of desire," I said.

Agnes leaned in. "How do you know that?"

"Aileen told me O was into women," I answered.

"Who's Aileen?" she asked, crossing her arms.

"Just a woman I met. They had a thing for a while. Aileen lives next door to O's apartment. Which reminds me, I was going to look into O's business holdings." I put Orville's letter back in its envelope. "I wonder if our elusive friend Aisha had something to do with these letters. Maybe they belong to one of the missing women," I mused, mostly to myself.

Agnes sat back. "Maybe Detective Gallegos is right about you nosing in." I noticed the smile on my beloved face.

"No doubt, but, as she also said, I have access to time and resources that she doesn't. Can't hurt to look." I touched the bruised side of my head just so she knew the irony wasn't lost on me. Natalya came in with a stack of papers. I pointed to Agnes. "She's the curious one." Natalya shrugged and placed the papers in front of the frowning Agnes. "Remember, you said you wanted to."

Her frown deepened. "You're a jerk."

"Yeah, that sounds about right."

I picked up the phone to call Ms. Lagenfelder. She was, as usual, delighted to hear from me.

"Yes, Mr. Buttman?"

I wondered how far she was from being made a partner? Idle thought. "I'd like you to have someone look into the business holdings of Orestra Blakely. Owns at least two buildings that are managed by a company called Brentwood Property management." I spelled out the name for her.

"Just information?"

"Yeah. Also, can they look to see if Ms. Blakely has a will on file?"

"We'll find out. Anything else?" I wondered if she was smiling or shaking her head.

"That'll do for now," I said.

"Heard you had a little excitement the other day." Now I was sure she was smiling.

"I heard that, too. No worries." Agnes looked over at me when I said that. My turn to smile.

"Be careful," was my lawyer's advice.

"Where's the fun in that?" I asked.

"Goodbye, Mr. Buttman."

"Ms. Lagenfelder."

.   .   .   .   .

I sent Bernie a text asking if he could find anything on Flavius, and as I thought about it, Pastor Terry. He said he'd check. Anton wandered in.

"Got a minute?"

"Always," I said. I noticed he was not happy. "Josef?"

"Yeah."

"Money?" Agnes asked, not bothering to look up. "How much?"

"Too much," he said. "A hundred grand."

"That's a lot. Him or family?" I gestured it was ok for Anton to sit. After a moment, he reluctantly found a chair.

"Brother-in-law," he said.

"Legit?" Agnes asked. She'd put aside the papers; this was more interesting.

"Some," he said. Anton, like Josef, was a man of few words.

"But that left him open to being played, and they put the screws to Josef's wife," Agnes added, now in her private dick element.

"Yeah. That's why he did the job for Manaforte." Anton shook his head. "Don't trust that guy."

"Why not?" My turn.

"I asked around, you know? Friends, guys in the business. Said he was dealing with the Russian syndicates—"

"Zosima?" I asked.

His faced darkened. "Is possible. He's a top guy, knows everybody." Anton sat back and let out a long sigh.

"Think this guy Zosima will deal?" Agnes asked.

"There's more," Anton said. He looked at me and Agnes.

"His work with us last year," I said. He nodded. "That explains, maybe, the interest of Dominik and Associates in you and me, Detective Duquesne." I smiled at Agnes.

"Always the bright boy, Sunshine," she answered, smiling back. "So, what's the plan?"

I turned to Anton. "Know of anyone we can ask, discreetly, about this?"

"Marsyas Durant," he said.

28

I wasn't surprised. I don't think Agnes was either.

"Maybe you should have asked Ms. Lagenfelder about that," she said.

I shook my head. "I think it might be above her paygrade for now. I'll have to enquire personally of Mr. Durant."

"I think we both should." Her smile had not abated. "After all, we were both there."

"True," I said. "That leaves the question of whether any of this had to do with Big Mike, or if that was used as a way to get rid of a problem, Big Mike, while pissing off his people and having them come after us."

"Maybe just money," Anton added. "Guys got to work."

"That they do." I noticed Natalya and Emily just outside the door. "Come in. We have some things to work out." Both came in and stood behind Anton. "I have to get you home next weekend," I said to Emily, whose scowl indicated she didn't want to go. "And I might have Isaac come with us. Are you planning on staying close to Natalya, Anton, or do you have other things to do?"

"Family obligations," he said.

"Then maybe we close up shop for a week." I smiled at Natalya. "Perhaps we find out if Xavier has time to take you on a vacation to one of his family's expensive properties. I know he has protection. What do you think?"

Natalya simply said, "We'll see."

"Good. Let me know when you know, otherwise you may have to join us up on the farm—"

"I'm not a baby, Mr. Monk!" she pouted.

"I never said you were. But until we get a better handle on what's going on, we need to follow Mr. Jones' directive and be careful."

"You said you wanted to go to New York," Emily said. "Ask him to take you there."

Natalya frowned at our unhelpfully organizing her time. "We'll see," was all she'd agree to.

"Good enough. I'll break the news to Mr. Bohrman," I said. "Now, back to work." It's important to show who's boss.

·　　·　　·　　·　　·

I left a message on Marsyas Durant's private line asking if he could find a moment to discuss a personal matter with me and Agnes. That it might be important. Ashley Carmichael's book, *The Court Jester*, was still stashed in a secure location within Aeschylus and Associates. Now that time had passed, I assumed it was just a relic collecting dust.

Maybe not.

Isaac was just as enthusiastic as Natalya when I called to tell him he needed to go north with us. "I got my own life, you know?"

"I thought that, too, but the pull of family…"

"Not funny, bro. How do you know I don't have plans of my own?" Such moral outrage.

"You have this weekend for all that. If she's special, bring her along. Might as well have her find out about us sooner rather than later cause we're not going to change," I said.

"Why is this so important?" he whined.

It was my turn to play up the moral outrage. "Because we just had our moment of family catharsis and we don't want dear ol' dad to think we were stringing him along. But more importantly, we need to check in on Sterling. I think he's far more involved with his girlfriend and with one, or maybe four, murders than he's letting on. Do you want to lay that on Moses? And Meri?"

"I should have stayed in Africa," he groaned.

"Right there with you, bro. See you Friday?" That boss thing again.

"Yeah, yeah, yeah."

"And bring donuts," I commanded.

"Don't push it, Sunshine," he said.

I laughed as he hung up.

My beloved smirked at my joviality. She was across the table dutifully going through the foundation's reports, as well as fiduciary statements from the dear Mr. Carson Macklgrew. "You should be doing this." She passed a stack of reports my way.

I shrugged. "It's just money."

"Just money," she echoed. "You're the luckiest man on the planet, Mr. Monk, and not just because you have me to keep you happy." She slid her chair over and closed the door. "Speaking of which, you haven't seemed too interested lately. Should I be worried?"

"Depends on what you mean by worried." I was idly thumbing through the reports. Looked like I'd be rich for the next few centuries.

"Monk! Is—" A knocked interrupted her and Emily came in. "Monk and I are having a talk, Em—"

"It can wait a moment," I said. Agnes glared at me. Must be the reports. "What's on your mind, Emily?" Though I was pretty sure what.

"It's about what happened," she said.

"And whether we should bring it up when we get back to the farm?" I asked.

She tightened her eyes and pinched her lips. "Mom would freak out and I'd never be allowed to come back here again. You know how she is." Emily leaned in so I'd get the point.

"Probably..."

"And since nobody was seriously hurt, I don't see why we have to bring it up." She had crossed her arms by this point. So had Agnes, but probably for different reasons.

"What about my bruise?" I pointed to my head.

Agnes chimed in, "Tell them you fell off your bike. Isn't that the excuse you used before, Buttman?"

"Sounds familiar, and who knows, in ten days the bruise will have faded. So, I suppose, for now, there's no need to say anything."

"Anything else, Em?" Agnes was itching to get on with her *talk*.

Emily looked at the two of us, slowly caught Agnes' drift, and said, "No, that's all." She smiled and headed back to the small room where she worked on the boring stuff Natalya gave her.

Agnes waited for me to say something, which I chose not to do. She didn't care for that, but recognized that I wasn't terribly interesting in talking. She slouched back into her chair. "There's no reason...well, maybe a little, but it's not like you think."

"Ok." I went back to my reports.

Agnes crossed her legs, waiting for more. "Monk?"

"Yes?" I pretended to be engaged with the report I was reviewing.

"I'm sorry if maybe we weren't totally upfront with what was going on...I mean with MaryAnn and Don. But MaryAnn has her reasons, and I promised to let her explain when she was ready. Ok?" It was kind of cute that she was trying to make it seem like a simple misunderstanding.

It probably was.

But it bugged me, and I didn't know why. "Well," I said, after turning another page of the report, "I guess we'll wait and see what MaryAnn has to say. Ok?"

"Ok."

I handed back the reports. "Time to head home."

•   •   •   •   •

Because Emily only had a week left, and because danger was afoot, Agnes and Emily suggested that the big house would be the best secure location in which to hide out. I found it amusing that it was suggested rather than demanded. Little dude number one immediately joined the lobbying when Agnes brought it up.

He grabbed my leg. "Please, please, please, Gamps." Lizzy grabbed the other leg, but simply looked up with big doleful eyes.

Rebekah, sitting at the kitchen table, holding little dude number two, who for once was being nice to his mother, shook her head at Zach. "I don't know, you haven't been listening lately—"

"I'll be good," he pleaded.

"Me, too," Lizzy added, though she was usually well-behaved.

Emily, who was standing behind Rebekah, made her thoughts plain. "Since I might not be back for a while, I think it's only fair, Mr. Monk." Her inner Natalya was coming out.

"Maybe Fidel will object?" I said, knowing better.

Rebekah rolled her eyes. "If that's all you have, Dad, give it up."

I gave it up.

In preparation, I boxed up the food to take with us as Rebekah and Emily got the brood packed and ready to go. Agnes sat at the table, watching. Durant's personal assistant called and said he could see us the following Tuesday. I thanked her and passed it along to my sulking life partner.

"You should be nice to me, Monk," she whined.

"I'm always nice to you, and you can survive a short break."

"You don't know that!"

I thought that funny.

"You're a jerk, Buttman," she pouted. Fortunately, I was only a jerk for a moment. Anna called. "Yeah?" was followed by "Sure, we'll be at Monk's fancy place," and "Bye."

"Am I still a jerk?" It's important to stay on top of these things.

"Huh?"

"The call?"

"Oh, Anna wants to bring her new boyfriend over." The amazement still on her face. "That's ok, right?"

It was cute that she'd ask. I said, "No."

"Ha, ha. We should get going, Mr. Smart Guy." With that, she rose from her chair and pointed to the door.

"Yes, dear."

Along with us, the miasma that was the population of LA was on the road going God knows where; they can't all have fancy places in

Beverly Hills! Zach was riding with us, a moment of freedom from his overly oppressive mother. Or so he liked to think. He was preoccupied with a silly game on his iPad. Oddly, he didn't find being trapped on the LA freeway system to be a pleasurable experience, and decided to use his daily allotted iPad time while on the drive to Gamp's fancy place and its fancy pool. Agnes flip-flopped from being annoyed with me over my perceived inattention to her carnal desires and how serious Anna's new guy was.

"What's this Jerome do again? I mean beside the band thing."

"Patent lawyer," I said.

"Do they make good money?"

"Sure, why not," I said. As if I knew.

She slumped into her seat. "It's like pulling teeth with you sometimes."

"Oh, I don't think it's like that at all." I looked at my grandson in the rearview mirror. "Is it, Zach?"

He didn't even bother to look up.

At the big house, Agnes had Rebekah to bounce worries off of.

I put the food away and moseyed out to the sunshine and the two kids splashing in the pool. Rebekah had handed Jacob to me. He didn't seem to mind. Emily, in full LA mode, was wearing her new bikini and sunglasses while sunbathing. How quickly it sucks them all in. Jacob and I sat close, but not too close to the preoccupied teenager. Jacob watched his siblings before lolling off to sleep. I put him in the shaded playpen.

As often happens when there's nothing important to do on a fine early evening, my mind began to wander. It tended to be at these times that questions I should have asked at another time and place came to me. For reasons unknown, outside of someday giving it to him, I had taken Orestra's letter to Orville with me, and now a thought occurred to me that didn't while I was going through O's journals and Agnes through the love letters.

The two of them looked my way as I walked in and interrupted their talk. Both frowned at me, which made me smile.

"*What*?" was my beloved's question.

"*Yeah*, Dad?"

I chose to ignore my haughty daughter. "I know there were no names in the letters, but were there any references to work, or an occupation? A job, anything like that?"

Agnes' frown disappeared into curiosity as she went over the letters in her head. "Now that you mentioned it, he did reference the church a lot; that was one of the reasons he was so wishy-washy about whether he loved her or not. Whether it was a sin; whether he was going against God's wishes, stuff like that. At the end, he pleaded with her to come with him to therapy. Maybe to change her back or something. Think it's important?"

"I do."

Agnes' eyes widened. "Wait. Didn't you tell me...that place, sorry church, where you went with Sterling—"

"Sunlight Ministries," I said.

"Yeah, maybe that's the place, though in the letter it doesn't say, only that it's where he's found his people and they could be her people, too." She seemed quite pleased with her deductive reasoning.

Rebekah had her own thoughts on the matter. "Is this why you're not sleeping with your wife, *Dad*?"

"*Yeah*, Sunshine!" Agnes was back to petulant.

I merely shrugged and gestured towards the pool. "Sorry, I have kids to watch."

29

Anna and Jerome arrived a little after seven. Agnes, as she had since Anna informed her that she and Jerome were on their way, vacillated between wanting answers and acting nonchalant. Rebekah, weirdly, was right there with her, which nicely kept me out of it. I had kid duty. Emily was intrigued, but not to the degree Agnes and Rebekah were. She was trying mightily not to dwell on having to go back home. Fidel was at work.

Jerome was, I suppose, the epitome of his generation. A series of contrasts. He was quiet, but opinionated; strait-laced in his work as a patent lawyer, yet a hipster sax man when out and about. He had tattoos along his arms, sleeves as they say, but kept his face and neck clean. He was a little taller than Anna, around my height, and thin. Like many men his age, he wore his dark hair in a big wedge on top with the sides cut close. Seemed decent enough. I asked Mikal about him after Anna said she and Jerome were an item.

"Haven't heard anything that might worry me," he said.

When I relayed this to Agnes, she was nonplussed. "We'll see. Assuming they stay together."

So far, they were.

Pleasantries were exchanged, and, much as she wanted to not seem overly inquisitive, Agnes couldn't help herself and peppered Jerome with all kinds of questions she hadn't asked the first time around. Some, concerning work and music, he answered; some, concerning his family and his intentions, though Agnes and her co-inquisitor, Rebekah, shied away from that term directly, he sidestepped. Jones would be so proud.

"I first got a degree in mechanical engineering," he said. "After doing that for a while, a friend asked me if I'd help him with a patent application, and after that I was hooked. I got my patent license, and that's what I do."

"Big law firm?" I asked.

"In the beginning, but I got tired of being on call 24/7, and found a smaller firm that just did patent law. They're not as go-go-go, so it gives me time for other things like keeping up with my music." He was also an arranger and orchestrator for the groups he was in.

"How many are you in?" Agnes asked.

"Three at the moment," he said.

"Wow. Seems like that would eat up a lot of your time," Agnes continued. I noticed Anna grimaced at the question, no doubt thinking her mother was concerned he wasn't paying enough attention to her.

Jerome smiled and looked at Anna. "Probably. But it gives me plenty of time to see Anna, since most of our rehearsals and gigs are at the Manifesto." Well played.

"See," I said to the inquisitors.

"When's dinner, Sunshine?" was my wife's response.

"Yeah, Dad?" was my daughter's.

"When Fidel gets here," was mine.

Fortunately, Fidel arrived by seven, and I ushered everyone to the dining room for their evening meal. Anna and Jerome made a point of peppering Fidel about the movie business as a way of blunting Agnes and Rebekah's peppering them about their future together. As usual, Fidel took it all in stride.

It gave me the opportunity to let my mind wander back to the love letters. That only darkened my mood.

At the end of the evening, there was dessert by the pool, and more promises to get together again, either here or at the Manifesto, or out in West Covina, or at Anna's condo. Something. We said our goodnights, and once the door had closed, Agnes, Rebekah, and a somewhat reluctant Emily, returned to the living room to replay the evening's events and decide if this Jerome guy was still a good fit for Anna. Fidel and I decamped for the pool and a cold beer.

"What'd you think?" I had to ask in case Agnes asked.

"Seemed ok to me," he said. "You?"

"The same."

He took a drink before tipping his bottle in my direction. "Then our work is done."

I laughed at that.

A half-hour later, the working stiff wandered off to bed. Agnes came over while I had my eyes closed. I opened one eye and turned her way.

"MaryAnn invited us to have dinner with her and Don on Thursday at her place," she said.

I closed my eye. "Fine with me."

"You sure?" I was surprised at her uncertainty.

"Sure," I lied.

She sat down beside me. "What do you think of Jerome?"

I sat up. "Well, Fidel and I had a long talk about the guy, discussing the pros and cons, this and that, and basically we decided that he's an ok Joe."

"Really?"

"Absolutely."

"Uh-huh. How much have you had to drink?"

I smiled at that. "Apparently not enough."

She ran her hand along the top of my leg. "I don't suppose you'd like to come to bed with me?"

I put my hand on hers. "I'll be there in a minute."

She stood and stared at me, her eyes looking into mine. "Ok."

I closed my eyes and stayed by the pool a while longer.

•   •   •   •   •

Morning brought out the gang for breakfast. Other than Agnes, everyone was hungry. I made sure Fidel got fed before he headed out for another long day on the job. Agnes watched as I handed the plates to the kids and their mother, who was watching Agnes. Rebekah frowned at me, to which I shrugged. Emily came in last, holding Jacob. Zach and Lizzy argued over syrup and who had the bigger pancakes. I took Jake from Emily so she could eat. The arguing continued until Rebekah told them to stop or there'd be no pool time. Both took heed. After breakfast, Agnes and the kids went about their chores while Emily returned to her room.

"What's going on with you and Agnes?" Rebekah asked, as I let Jake play with my finger.

I moved the finger he was holding to his nose. "Why do you ask?"

"Pretty obvious, don't you think?"

I tapped Jake's nose, causing him to laugh. "I try not to…"

"Dad…"

"There's nothing going on," I said, annoyed at the questions.

"So, I hear."

Jake and I looked at the concerned woman across from us. "Hey, I'm not a machine, alright? Everyone goes through down periods. It's not an indictment of Agnes, or our relationship, or any of that. I don't hassle you about Fidel, do I?" I was surprised at how angry I was.

Agnes and Emily came out of their rooms. "Something wrong?" Emily asked.

"No," I said.

Rebekah tilted her head and stared at me. "I just asked if everything was alright."

Agnes just stood there. Emily might have wanted to say something, but Zach and Lizzy, already in their swimsuits, grabbed her hands and dragged her out to the pool. Rebekah took Jake and followed them.

Agnes came over and sat on a stool. "What's wrong, Monk?"

I tried to think. "I don't know. Something…"

"If it's the Mary—"

"No, it's not that." Why would it be that? I came around the kitchen island and gave her a hug. "It'll pass." I kissed her. "Just need a quiet day."

•   •   •   •   •

For once, I got what I asked for.

The weekend, on the other hand, was busy with trips to the beach and the Manifesto. A lot was going on there. One of Jerome's bands played, followed by Joanie singing with Mikal's quartet. She sounded wonderful. The band was great; they were in their element. I didn't see Brian, tried not to care; they knew what they were doing. Natalya and her friends came and picked up Emily for a girl's night out. Sunday was spent by the pool. Pizza, naturally, for dinner. I kept an eye on Jake and stayed out of the way. Isaac came by with a woman named Celeste. Pretty. Chatty. Loved the place. Joined the others in the pool.

"Anything serious?" I asked, as I would be asked.

He smiled and shrugged before jumping in the pool. "We'll see," was all he said.

I relayed this to any and all concerned.

"Should I tell Meri?" was Emily's concern. My turn to smile and shrug.

The weekend came to a close with a call from Art. He was, for the most part, his ebullient self. He laughed when I asked how big was the bill for his services. "Oh, we'll work that out at the end, or should I just be put on a retainer?"

"Either," I said. "What's the good word?"

"Surface-wise, nothing to see here. But there has been a lot of scuttlebutt at the cooler concerning Mr. Manaforte, his relationship to the president, and to a number of high placed Russian oligarchs, including Zosima. If there's anything there, it's being held tight. No one wants to talk right now. As for Sobeski, the churn over his disappearance has quieted, either because nothing has come up or it's being suppressed by the Russians. That's probably the connection with Dominik and Associates, since they know of your connection to Manaforte."

"And maybe the attack?" I was curious.

"Maybe. It would explain Fairfax's interest. Election's not far off, and, as you might expect, DC is spending most of its time on that," he said. "As to the other, I'm going to need a little more. A name perhaps. Flavius isn't enough."

"I'll see what I can do." Maybe Bernie's found something.

"Monk…"

"Yes?"

"You didn't mention that you'd been attacked yourself. Are you taking precautions? If it involves the Russians…"

"I didn't want you to worry," I said.

He laughed at that. "With you, that might be a full-time job. How's Agnes?"

"She's good."

"Glad to hear it."

"Oh, I'm meeting with Manaforte this week." Thought I'd mention it.

"Interesting." I could sense the wheels turning. "He's been out of circulation these last six months. Wide eyes, my friend. Do take care. If you hear anything, let me know."

"It's on his yacht."

Silence. Then a chuckle. "I assume you know how to swim?" were his parting words.

30

Nakatomi called Monday morning. "I'll meet you at your office Thursday morning, ten. We'll leave from there. Questions? Comments?"

"My wife will be joining us," I said.

The line was quiet. "Of course. Good day."

Agnes was playing with Jacob on the couch. "We'll be thrown overboard on Thursday," I told her. "Dress appropriately."

"I have just the outfit," she said.

The next exciting call was from Xavier Dunkle II. "What are you up to, Monk?"

"Why, whatever do you mean?" I asked.

"Natalya wants me to take her to New York. That's what I mean." He seemed rather put out.

"And?"

"And I want to know what's up?"

I liked that he was peeved. I missed the old Xavier. "Did she mention that we were attacked last week by Russian thugs tied to Big Mike?"

His voice softened. "No."

"Well, we were. Anyway, I have to take Emily home this weekend, and Anton, who's keeping an eye on Natalya, has family commitments, so Emily suggested that Natalya hang out with you since you have a security detail. You still do, right?"

"Yeah…"

"And Natalya has always talked about going to New York, yes?"

"Yeah…"

"*And* if I remember correctly," I continued, "your family has properties in and around the city, right?"

"Yeah…"

"You still like Natalya, right?" I was enjoying this.

"I do…it's just…"

"Just what?" I waited for him to dream up some excuse. "It's a big opportunity. Be together. See the sights. Buy her a few nice things. Get out, enjoy life. Are you actually busy next week?" I asked, somewhat pointedly.

"Well, not really…"

"Then what?" I wondered if he was enjoying this.

He must have picked up on that. "Yeah…" His voice grew stronger. "Yeah. Why not? My Aunt Clarissa has a travel agent she raves about… Why not?"

"Anything else?"

"No…and thanks." Finally, he was chipper.

"Don't thank me, thank Emily. She suggested it." I then thought of something else that might amuse him. "Oh, and I'll be seeing our friend on his yacht Thursday."

He laughed. "Hope you can swim."

Two for two.

•　　•　　•　　•　　•

The next day was a workday. As I was set to meet with Marsyas Durant, Agnes decided to tag along. For Emily, it was her second to last day at the office.

"Sure I can't stay for the rest of the summer?" she pleaded.

"Nice try," I said, "but you also have to visit your father in a couple of weeks."

"I can stay here and fly out of LAX," she offered.

"We both know the answer to that. And no, you can't run off to New York with Natalya either. I'm sure Xavier has big plans and your mother wouldn't go for that, even if they did."

She glared at me, which made Agnes laugh. "You're a real jerk, Mr. Monk!"

"Unfortunately, someone has to be. To the car, ladies." I pointed to the garage.

Rebekah, lounging by the pool, waved, and wished us the best.

Isaac was in no better mood about our impending trip. "Why do I have to go? You can bug Sterling a lot better than I can."

"Nice try," I said.

"Bring Celeste," Agnes chimed in. "She was fun."

That got a smile out of the family playboy. "Maybe next time. Meanwhile, we can go over my trip to Dallas."

"I don't want to go over all these stupid reports." I put on my best pout.

"Nice try," they said.

Our meeting with Durant was at one. Natalya had a tasty lunch brought in before we had to leave. I asked about her impending trip. She played it coy, but was clearly more excited than Emily, Isaac, or me about ours. Agnes poo-poohed our gloom, but then she had a weird affinity for the farm.

Durant's assistant met us in the lobby and took us up to his palatial office. He welcomed us with his usual smile. "Monk, Agnes, to what do I owe the pleasure of this meeting you requested?" As if he had no idea.

"Well," I said, "to be honest, your name came up concerning a man we know who is having financial difficulties in his native Russia. Not that that's unusual or important to you. What is important is that he was with us on our trip last year to Michigan, and our aborted meeting with Mr. Manaforte and his confederates. The man's name is Josef Rostikov. He once worked for Big Mike Kovalenko, who I learned was assassinated in Thailand, and in which Josef had a hand. He nominally worked for Mr. Jones' security outfit, but also did work for Mr. Manaforte just prior to our trip. Is that confusing enough to start?"

He smiled and said, "I'm with you so far."

I went on, "After Thailand, he headed back to Russia to deal with family matters involving his wife's brother, who apparently has money issues with the wrong types there; I'm assuming gangsters, and hasn't returned. I think there might be more involved in this besides money—"

"That involves you two?" he looked towards Agnes.

"With Manaforte in the picture, anything's possible," she said. "We'll be seeing him Thursday on his yacht. Isn't that right, Sunshine?"

"We are, and a number of people hope that I know how to swim."

Durant laughed at that. "Then perhaps it's to your benefit that I ended my trip to Europe a week early. Assuming there's anything I can do."

I nodded. "An associate of Mr. Rostikov asked around. That's how we know he's in trouble. But if it's just money, once again assuming it isn't more than the hundred-thousand quoted to me, then I could take care of it on my own. But—"

"But the intimation is it'll take more than money. Connections, say." Durant sat back and tapped the armrest of his chair with his finger. "Did he say who?"

"He didn't say directly. I mentioned a name who he admitted was a very connected individual in all realms of Russian life. His name is known to many in U.S. Intelligence. That's where I first heard it, in reference to Manaforte and an assassin named Aaron Alan Sobeski. A man named Zosima. Your name came up as someone who might have the connections with this individual to intercede on Josef's behalf." I leaned forward in my chair. "So, we're here to ask what you think?"

"And what do you think, Agnes?" Durant didn't bother to look her way this time.

Agnes gave it some thought. "It depends. Johnny always said it's best to wait unless you're certain. Guys will always show their hand at some point. They have to, otherwise nothing happens that's going to be beneficial to all the parties concerned. But that means someone has to be on top of it. My worry is that no one is, that some powerful people are rummaging around in the dark, knocking over this and that to see what happens."

Durant kept tapping. "Anything else?"

It was apparent to me that he probably knew already. "We've suddenly become very interesting to many people. A man named Fairfax wants to know about Sobeski. Boris Tsarnaev from Dominik and Associates has been asking about me and Agnes through our foundation representatives; asking questions that have nothing to do with aiding veterans. Then there's Manaforte, who suddenly wants to talk to us after many months of being incommunicado. But mostly we're here to see if you might be able to help us get Mr. Rostikov and his family out of Russia."

Durant took a pen from his desk and made a few notes on his desk pad. "I have met the man Zosima, though I know him by his given name." He looked at the two of us. "We're talking about a very powerful and influential man, so we have to be certain that we're not wasting his time with what he would consider a triviality. And I'm sorry to say this, but most likely, he would consider Mr. Rostikov's problems trivial. That doesn't mean he can't help, only that we have to have the right inducement. I know some people through whom I can inquire about Mr. Rostikov. If this is just a matter of monies owed, are you willing to make the payment?"

"Within reason," I said.

"Fair enough." It was then a sly smile came to Marsyas Durant, which he directed at Agnes. "Since you're going to meet with Delton Manaforte, let's hold off on any other actions till you know what's on his mind. Presumably, your being here allows me to be in the loop as well. Agreed?"

"I think that's to our mutual benefit," Agnes answered.

"We have to head up north this weekend to the farm, but we'll keep you informed." It was my turn.

"Then I have something for you." From a safe hidden behind a cabinet door behind him, he produced a phone. "Please use this to contact me."

With a big smile, Agnes said, "Sweet."

Durant rose. Our allotted time was up. "I look forward to hearing from you."

Agnes tapped her brow with her left index finger. The hard-boiled private dick was ready to roll.

* * * * *

"How much do you think he knows?" I asked as we were driving back to the office. We had to pick up Emily before heading to my fancy place.

"Plenty," she said with evident glee.

It was a good thing I was driving.

Emily was quiet on the drive to the house. Her time here in decadent LA was fast coming to a close. "We looked at places to see in New York," was all she would say they did in our absence. Once home, she joined the gang out by the pool. Little dude number one was in his timeout chair. A deep frown on his face.

"I told him to stop splashing me and he chose to ignore that," his mother informed us.

"It's not fair! Lizzy was splashing, too!" he whined.

Rebekah's frown mirrored her son's. "Yes, but Lizzy listens, and you don't!"

Ah, domestic bliss.

I foolishly grabbed a beer and the love letters, wanting to read them for myself. Maybe there was something Agnes didn't catch, and with our impending trip, including a delightful get together with Sterling, I wanted to know as much as I could.

They were just as Agnes described them: alternatingly lovelorn and manipulative. He whined about his desires and how she was the answer to them, but maybe not as God desired for them. It was there, as he went on and on about struggling with his desires, that I found the two words that interested me the most.

Our Ministry.

The last stop for the day was at the computer. I looked up the number to Flavius' place of business—I assumed it wasn't a free service—to arrange a meeting. The voice at the other end had an interesting lilt to it as it ended each sentence.

"What is it I can do for you?" the voice asked.

"It's my understanding that you match individuals with certain desires in a way that is discreet," I said.

"Do you have a personal reference? I hate to ask, but we like to have a sense of the people we serve, and we find that personal references from people we know and trust are much better than some impersonal search. Don't you agree?"

"Yes, I do." I gave the voice my name and Sterling's as my reference. A promise was made to call back soon. Soon was half-an-hour.

"Would tomorrow afternoon be a possibility, William?" they asked.

"That would be fine," I said.

William. Ask the right people and it's still my name.

31

Agnes raised her eyebrows when I told her of my meeting the next day at Here We Gather for Love. "Am I going?"

"Maybe next time," I said.

To assuage her fears, I went to bed early with her and made sure she got to do all her favorite things. "I'm still concerned that something is off with you," she said, as I poured her coffee the next morning, "but I had a good time last night. Thanks."

"My pleasure."

Everyone was up and bouncing around. It was beach day. Even Fidel was going, taking a rare vacation day.

Bernie called as I was changing Jake. Perfect timing. "What's up?"

"Got some information on the individual Flavius," he said. "Like you, he's had quite an interesting life, though as I understand it, Flavius uses they/them/their pronouns."

"I heard that, too. From the LAPD." Having finished with Jake, I focused on the phone rather than the family running around in the surf.

Bernie continued. "Was born in '62 with the name Berkley Fellows. His parents became well known from the late 60s through the early 80s in certain Hollywood circles as enablers and procurers of any and all drugs and pharmaceuticals that were popular, and probably still are, in the LA artistic community. Were also alleged to have facilitated certain sexual liaisons between underaged girls and prominent actors. Both parents were arrested and convicted of drug charges in 1985 after a series of well-publicized ODs. Berkley was not charged, but was said to have been a part of the police investigation. After that, he dropped out of sight before reemerging in the late 90s as Flavius. Has a matchmaking business that is very low key and out of the mainstream, catering to gender fluid and non-binary identifying individuals. But I assume you already knew that."

"True. Heard it from Sterling. That's how I got drawn into this mess." Agnes came and sat down beside me, taking Jake into her arms. "On the other side of things, we have a meeting tomorrow with Manaforte on his yacht. Are you going to joke about swimming?"

"Naw," Bernie laughed, "they'll tie weights to you and throw you overboard once they're further out. Seriously though, let me know if something comes out of it. Maybe it's just a social call."

"Maybe," I said. "I'll stay in touch."

The next call came as everyone was gearing up for lunch. I'd packed sandwiches and fruit, with Rebekah and Emily in charge of handing the food out.

It was Flavius. "I thought it might be more to your liking if you come by this evening. I'm having a party with friends. Bring your wife. Nine-ish?"

I looked at Agnes, a grin coming to me. "We'll be there."

"Should be interesting, *William*."

"Should be. Till then." I noticed the others staring at me. "Agnes and I have a party to attend this evening. That's all."

"I can't wait to hear about it," Rebekah said. She had her own grin going.

"I think you already have enough going on."

All that produced in my daughter was a shrug.

●   ●   ●   ●   ●

Flavius owned a pre-war Spanish colonial revival in Whitley Heights, an old Hollywood part of town off Cahuenga Pass. The driveway was filled with cars, as was the street. Music drifted down the drive, insinuating itself in the carefree vibe of the neighborhood. Trees and shrubs adorned the front of the house and the winding walk obscuring the door. The house, as well as the neighborhood, appeared as if it were out of a 1930s movie reel that featured famous actors and where they lived, only this one was in color. I half-expected to see a porcelain statue of a colored lawn jockey waiting to greet us. It may have had one once, but that was a no-no these days. Instead, we were greeted by the houseboy, or its present approximation, a fair-haired creature named Jess, dressed in a bowtie, white waistcoat, no shirt, and black shorts.

"Please come in."

I was wearing a vintage off-white dinner jacket with black slacks and a turquoise tie. Agnes, deeply uncomfortable about what to wear, had on a simmering blue dress, knee-length, with silver open-toed pumps. I expected us to look terribly out of place. Surprisingly, not so much. There were guests with a modern sensibility; expensive jeans and tees, but there were others in drag, vintage clothes, or sporting ethic dress. Some were hypermasculine, others hyper feminine, still others androgynous. This included our host.

Flavius was heavyset, five-six with short silver hair, silver eye shadow, wearing a bright blue Chinese Cheongsam suit. They had bright blue eyes and the habit of running them along the contours of the people they was speaking to. "You must be William?"

I waited for Agnes to make a comment, but she only smiled. "I am, though I'm also known as Monk."

Flavius echoed Agnes' smile. "So, I've heard. No doubt you've heard things about me."

"Some. This is my wife, Agnes."

"Welcome Agnes. My partner is by the pool. Her name is Gisele."

Gisele came over to greet us. She was the approximate size of Flavius, wearing a tailored sharkskin suit and a black tie that matched her short black hair. If she was younger than Flavius, it wasn't by much. She smiled as she looked us over. "Straight out of one of my mother's fashion magazines."

"I have a penchant for that time," I said.

"And fancy words," added Agnes.

From there we were shown the house in all its hundred-year-old glory. Artwork abounded, making getting around the house and guests a challenge. "We probably have too much, but art is addictive," Gisele told us.

As people came and went, Flavius introduced us. We got a few odd looks, but for the most part, everyone was personable. I wasn't surprised, as most were the age of our hosts.

"You have quite a lovely home here," I said.

"Yes, I fell in love with the place as a kid. Fortune allowed me to buy it some years ago. I hear you have quite a home yourselves."

"That we do," I said.

With introductions out of the way, our hosts wandered off. We mingled, listening to the various conversations. Agnes made sure to note we were philanthropists when asked what it was we did. The food was good, as was the booze. An hour later, our host returned.

"My dear." Flavius bowed slightly towards Agnes. "Would you be offended if I were to take our William here for a short private talk?"

Agnes turned to me. "Yes, but I'll allow it this one time."

Flavius nodded at that. "Then I'll promise to be brief. Till we return, I hope you'll continue mingling with our guests."

Agnes watched as Flavius led me to a study down the home's main hall.

We sat down on two purple velvet chairs. Flavius' demeanor became more formal. "What is it you want from me, Mr. Buttman? or do you prefer William?"

"Only in Virginia. But I'm not particular," I said. "What I'm looking for are answers."

"Concerning?"

"Recently, I met a private detective, a black transwoman, looking for my brother's lover, another black transwoman. She was, I came to find out, looking into what happened to several missing black transwomen. Unfortunately, someone murdered her not long after we met. In her notes, I came across your name. My brother also owned up to having met Aisha, his lover, through your business. I'll add that

Ms. Blakely, the detective, wanted me to be a beard for her. Here I believe, though she didn't mention you directly. But having considered that, and a few other things I came across along the way, I figured it might be better to skip the nonsense."

"Then why not use the name you use now?"

"Because you might have thought it a joke or a put on," I said.

"I see." Flavius said. After a moment, they asked, "Tell me, what is it you know about me?"

What to say. "I know you have this business, of which I know little. I also know something of your history, or I should say, that of your parents. Beyond that…"

Flavius ran their fingers along the armrest of the chair. "And why should I say anything to you?"

"Why not? I'm not the police. I'm not even a proper detective. Mostly I'm doing this on behalf of my family, out of their concern for my brother."

"You come from a wealthy, important family, *William*?"

"Hardly. I come from freaks who settled on a commune up north near Ukiah. My wealth comes from a previous relationship with a rich woman, who thought it'd be fun to give me her money after she died. Before that I was a nobody, and before that a farmer in Virginia named *William*." I smiled at that.

"Interesting," they said. "I, too, come from that particular world, though through a different lens. Would you like to hear my story, or should we get back to Agnes and my guests?"

"I'd love to hear it. And I'm sure Agnes is having the time of her life."

That got a smile out of my host. "You might bear watching, Monk. Anyway, my little story begins with my parents, who were beatniks before they were hippies, and before they had me and my sister. Our early days were spent running around from one place to another, mostly here in LA, but we spent time in San Francisco, too. It was pretty heavy." Flavius smiled at that. "I got to hang out with just about every important musician and band of that time. And as you may have heard, my parents liked to provide these important people with drugs. Also, girls, sometimes boys…it was all very groovy, you know. I got to meet Charlie Manson and his family once. One of the many stops we made for those we took care of. I remember they were all filthy. And strange…"

"Sounds like the perfect childhood." I remembered Moses' admonition that there was a lot of darkness during the summer of love.

"If only. And for a time, it was all very hip if you don't mind certain eccentricities. Quite a few, if I remember correctly. And people were very experimental sexually in those days; I got to see that firsthand, too. You wouldn't believe what some of those big-time actors were into. Shocking!" They laughed at that. "Still, I'll confess to loving most of it. I've been queer from day one. All the kinds of queer you can think of, whether it was orientation, dress, sex, you name it…or just being odd. Something very other than Dick and Jane."

"You didn't miss anything," I said. "We just knocked up our girlfriends and ended up farmers in Virginia."

"Dick and Jane on a commune? I don't believe it. Anyway, where were we…ah, yes, my mother, Hope. Great name for an enabler, don't you think? Had a doctor friend to take care of those kinds of problems, be it adoption in Mexico or an abortion. But that has nothing to do with where I am now…" Flavius stared at their hands before winking at me. "Of course, that's a lie. It had everything to do with what I do these days. I was already non-binary when Teddy and Hope were locked up. They didn't miss me, and I didn't miss them." They ran their fingers along the edge of the desk. "My sister never forgave them for offering her up to all those creepy Hollywood types who were into young girls."

"Where's she?"

"Complete opposite. Straight as a line. Lives in Dallas, of all places. But she tells me she's happy," they said. "But you're not here for any of that. You want to know about missing black transwomen and whether I had anything to do with it, correct?"

"For the most part. But to be honest, I'm mostly curious. I've had very little interaction with people who don't identify with the gender they were born with. Some of that was the inward nature of the commune, some of it the religious conservatism of my rural community in Virginia. It wasn't till I came here that I found myself living among individuals, such as yourself, who don't identify as traditional men and women. And even then, not much," I said.

"Ah, but your brother has more diverse interests and desires, and that led you here."

"Yes."

Flavius sighed. "It's quite simple, really. People are people, and, whatever their path, all, at some point, desire to be loved or held or cared for. But outside of, as you say, traditional men and women, whatever that is, it can be hard, and often dangerous, to find someone. So, having been a part of this community all my life, I felt I could provide a certain service." They ran their fingers along the seam of the Cheongsam suit. "I do my best to make sure no harm comes to any of the parties that utilize my service. And I try to be very discreet and very discerning in the people I help get together. But there are always bad actors, I'm afraid." Flavius looked at me. "I understand the perception that's out there about me and my service, and why your detective friend thought she might use you. But I can assure you that I had nothing to do with or know anything about those poor girls who disappeared, or your detective friend who was killed."

"I didn't think you did, only that, like me, you got caught up in this." I rose, as did Flavius. "One more thing, if you don't mind?" Flavius raised their eyebrow. "Ever heard of Pastor Terry or the Sunlight Ministries?"

Flavius rolled their eyes. "If only I could say I hadn't. Is your brother now in their evil clutches?" I nodded. "Yes, I've had a few go arounds with our dear *Pastor* Terry. He's tried, on repeated occasions, to save me, though from what..." They started towards the door. "You know, like many of his kind, he's a reformed sex addict. Have you met him?"

I smiled and said, "Yes."

"And his always sunny assistant?"

I had to think. An image of Vern filtered in. "Yes, I have." Another thought came to me. "What about Aisha Diamond?"

"I know her well. I hope your brother does." They smiled at that. "She can be a lot of fun, but she, too, likes to ask a lot of questions, and when she gets angry, well...it's best if you watch your back." We stood in the doorway. "I know you're programed to fear me and my kind, but..." Flavius looked me up and down. "I'm probably the least of your worries, *Mr. Buttman.*"

32

The party went well into the night. Sadly, Agnes and I only made it to one in the morning. We had more fun on the calendar later that day and had to go. Flavius and Gisele bid us farewell with a wave from the pool. I was thankful for the short drive.

"Boy, are we out of touch," Agnes said as she got out of the car.

I tried to feign outrage. "We? You, I can see that. But me?"

"Nice try, Buttman," was what I got in return.

"What part makes us out of touch, my love?" We were in the process of getting ready for bed.

"I don't understand any of it," she said. "And yes, I know how that makes me sound, and I'm not being judgmental—"

"No?"

"No!" she held her towel in her hands as if to snap me. "Are you going to listen, or do I have to use this?"

I laughed. "My apologies. Please continue."

Agnes snapped me anyway. "Happy?" I shrugged. "As I was saying, people can do what they like. It's not that. I just don't get it is all. And I don't mean that disparagingly. I just don't understand."

I picked up my toothbrush. "That's the beauty of it. You don't have to. It's when you try to force people to be what they aren't that problems arise. Like with Simon."

Agnes frowned at that. "Maybe. What about Sterling?"

"Maybe the same thing. Being dishonest with yourself."

Agnes got ready to snap me again. "What about you, Sunshine?"

I acted as if deep in thought. "I'm ok with the way I am."

"Good answer," she said, before snapping me again.

I just laughed.

Later, as I lay in bed, staring at nothing but the darkness of the room, I found I had no interest in Manaforte, Flavius, Pastor Terry; any of it. I wanted to be free of it. All of it. That included Sterling and his problems. He was a grown man; he could worm his way out of it without my help.

. . . . .

Didn't matter.

Nakatomi called promptly at nine with our instructions. "I'll be there to pick you up at your offices at eleven. Please be ready."

"Where exactly is Mr. Manaforte's yacht? I don't know that I want to be out in the open seas or beyond U.S. territorial waters." My late-night machinations were catching up to me along with everyone's mordant jokes about knowing how to swim.

"Mr. Manaforte's yacht is moored in Santa Monica Bay, off Marina del Rey. Safely in U.S. waters, Mr. Buttman," he said, the humor evident in his voice.

"Eleven then, Mr. Nakatomi."

Agnes, who had stumbled through the living room, sat at the kitchen island waiting to be served her morning coffee. "Well?"

"Eleven, at the offices of the Jacob Bohrman Veterans Service Foundation. So, no dawdling," I said, handing Agnes her coffee.

"I'm not the dawdler, Sunshine," she huffed.

"Nice try." I placed her breakfast of eggs and bacon before her. "Now chop-chop."

Agnes smiled and said, "Yeah, yeah."

Natalya was not happy that she was not included in our little soiree with Delton Manaforte. She had used her few meetings with the man to pepper him with questions on the nature of business. Something she felt I was not doing enough of. I didn't care.

"It's important to know these things, Mr. Monk." This was often said in a condescending manner. I still didn't care.

"I'll fill you in when we get back if any important matters of business are discussed," I said. She frowned at that, but held her tongue. Anton looked up from his phone for a moment, but likewise has no comment. "Don't forget that tomorrow is Emily's last day. I hope you have something fun planned." I waited for her grave disapproval and didn't have to wait long.

"I'm well aware of that, Mr. Monk! Thank you."

Agnes shook her head. Nakatomi had arrived, and it was time to go.

•   •   •   •   •

Manaforte's yacht gleamed in the distance. The hull was a brilliant blue, while the various decks were a shimmering white. A helicopter perched upon the bow. The drive from the office was short, Marina del Rey being close to downtown, relatively speaking, and the yacht not far from the dock where we caught the motorboat, a miniature version of the yacht, mimicking its color scheme, that ferried us to the gleaming ship. Manaforte was standing in the tender garage, as I later learned it was called, where the motorboat was stored. Three crew members and another man were standing with him.

"Agnes, Monk, good of you to join us," he said, as we got out of the motorboat.

"Always a pleasure," Agnes answered, eyeing the man next to Manaforte.

"This is another of my guests," he replied. "Boris Tsarnaev."

Tsarnaev stepped forward, offering his hand. "Mr. Buttman."

"I heard you were making inquiries, Mr. Tsarnaev. Perhaps I can answer a few." That produced a crooked smile from Agnes.

Tsarnaev, noting Agnes' crooked smile, said, "I think that would be beneficial."

"Boris arrived just before you," Manaforte said, "and I was going to give him a tour of my expensive toy. Would you care to join us?"

"We'd be delighted," I answered. Better his money than mine.

The hundred-million-dollar-plus yacht did not disappoint. God only knows how many square feet it contained, but there was enough room for Manaforte, who had his own private deck; six staterooms for guests; salons and decks aft on each level; grand living rooms and dining areas, as well as a gym, spa, diving platform, and sauna. Then there were the mechanical spaces, the galleys, and the crew quarters. All of it was well-appointed, with the finest materials and design. A resplendent sun deck sat above the bridge deck, which was where we ended the tour.

Lunch was ready.

"Quite the place," I said. "Puts my little Chris-Craft to shame."

"Come now, Monk, surely you have your own yacht. Maybe not as ostentatious, but then there are others that put this one to shame." Manaforte laughed at that.

I sighed. "Sorry, I'm simply a paltry multi-millionaire."

"Oh, brother," was Agnes' comment. "I don't suppose I could get a drink on this barge, could I?" That elicited a number of smiles as a crew member came to satisfy Agnes' demand.

With LA to the east, sweltering in its noonday smog, and lunch finished, we got down to the business at hand.

"What is it you'd like to know, Boris?" I'd been instructed earlier to be less formal.

Boris Tsarnaev had a square Slavic face with small blue eyes set above a thin nose and a closely trimmed heavy beard. He stood about five-eight, was fit, and appeared light on his feet. During our walk around, he offered compliments to Manaforte or any obliging crew member. To the captain, he gave a slight bow. He struck me as deeply sneaky. But given the world he inhabited, perhaps that wasn't a bad trait to have.

"It's simple curiosity mostly," he said. "I heard of your philanthropy's interests through a friend of your brother's. Thought I'd find out more. Never hurts to know people and what they do."

"I agree." It sounded nice.

"Perhaps, if you have a moment, I could stop by and discuss it."

"I have a window of opportunity tomorrow afternoon," I said to Agnes' groan and Manaforte's smile. I pulled a card from my pocket. "I'll let Natalya know to expect your call."

"Excellent." Tsarnaev handed me his as he stood. "I understand that Mr. Manaforte would like some private time with the two of you. I'll confess that I'm a little early, so I'll leave you and take advantage of the salon on the lower deck."

We rose to see him off.

With Tsarnaev gone, Manaforte led us to his private deck and *its* salon.

"What is it that you wanted to see us about?" Agnes asked, sipping her T&T.

He nodded towards the lower deck. "Our Russian friends."

"I assume you heard about our recent encounter with some of Big Mike's old chums," I said.

"Yes, I heard. All the more reason to be mindful." He wandered towards the tall glass doors separating the salon from the deck aft.

"Mindful of what?" Agnes looked at me, then Manaforte. "Our good friend, the late great Aaron Alan Sobeski? I would think that by now, whatever story you concocted has made the rounds." She took another sip of her drink. "Not going quite as planned?" Agnes grinned at that.

Manaforte did not. "Unfortunately, questions remain, and as the presence of Mr. Tsarnaev shows, our Russian friends are continuing to ask, and..." He turned to face us. "Adding a little pressure of their own."

"The little visit to our office? Odd way to go about it, or was Big Mike tied in with Sobeski?" Agnes was on a roll.

"It's possible. Mr. Kovalenko had many friends and enemies," he said. "Are you aware of your assistant's involvement in Mr. Kovalenko's death?"

I nodded. "I'm also aware of that playing into the disappearance of Mr. Rostikov and his current money woes."

"As am I." Manaforte walked back into the salon and sat on the couch across from us. "It seems apparent that the Russians have pieced a few things together, maybe on their own, possibly through Mr. Rostikov, and are looking for either conformation or contradiction of the word on the street—"

"Which is?" Agnes again.

"That Sobeski and his accomplices met their end in an ill-fated attempt to kill a number of conspirators in Detroit," he answered. "To confuse matters, there were two more boat explosions on Lake Michigan around the same time that your Chris-Craft went up. These were on the Illinois side where Sobeski was last communicated with. Our assumption is that the Russians are, in their own inimical way, trying to verify that."

"Then I'm assuming that this little get together is to keep us on the same page, minus the fact that we were supposed to be collateral damage in that affair." It was my turn.

"We've covered that part of it, and your...ability to leverage the situation to your benefit. For now, it *is* to our mutual advantage to stay on the same page concerning what happened to Sobeski until I can find the best time and opportunity to resolve the matter." Manaforte tapped the arm of the couch. "You've, no doubt, upped your security and, no doubt, consulted your friends in the intelligence gathering business. So have I. Then there's this business with the president, but fortunately, outside of your brother, that isn't of any concern to you."

"The Russians might think otherwise," Agnes quipped.

"True, but the Russians are troublemakers more than anything else in that regard, using our own internal problems to their advantage." Manaforte rose. "Are we in agreement?"

I looked at Agnes before getting up. "We are." Agnes raised an eyebrow, but didn't comment.

"Good. Mr. Nakatomi will continue to be our liaison. Unfortunately, I have other matters to attend to, so I have to bid you goodbye."

He walked us back to the tender garage and our liaison. The boat ride and the drive to our offices were quiet. Natalya and Anton were unconcerned outside of any business news for Natalya. I had to inform her there was none. She frowned at that.

"Sorry." I turned to them before going into my office. "Oh, a Mr. Boris Tsarnaev might be stopping by tomorrow afternoon." I watched as the two of them looked at each other.

"Ok, Mr. Monk."

Agnes hadn't lingered at Natalya's desk. She was already ensconced on the couch in my office. A drink in her hand, her second, and we hadn't even made it to MaryAnn's and our get together with her and Don. I perched myself on the end of my desk.

"What's on your mind, Dollface?"

"Manaforte," she said.

I was pretty sure there was more, but I'd wait for that tonight. "Don't think he's got it all worked out?"

She took a long drink, gave me a half-smile, and said, "I think this is turning into what Johnny would call a class-A clusterfuck."

Couldn't argue with that.

33

MaryAnn had a nice little house in Alhambra that she bought after her divorce from her first, and, to date, only husband. I'd been there a couple of times, the last being one of our threesomes. That cluttered my thoughts as we got closer, driving from the office. Agnes didn't say much. Odd, since where other people's relationships were concerned, she typically had a lot of questions and opinions; her daughter being a prime example. I expected her to be quite talky about Don, but she was mostly monosyllabic in her responses, so I let the questions go.

"You alright?" I asked as we pulled into the driveway.

"I don't understand the question." At least she was smiling.

The house was a typical 70s ranch, brown and white with red brick, set back from the street; a style that was in demand, and one that realtors constantly asked if she was interested in selling. "Where would I go?" was her response when asked.

She and Don were there to greet us with wine in hand. I took mine and watched the scene play out. I knew that Agnes knew more than she would admit to, and I, and possibly Don, were the chumps in this morality play. I didn't mind. I thought maybe I should, but with Sterling on the horizon, given we were taking Emily home on Saturday, and Tsarnaev's visit tomorrow, whatever was going on here was none of my business outside of how it might affect my sex life.

I tried not to go down that road.

Dinner was fried chicken, mashed potatoes, and green beans. Dessert was apple pie. During dinner, the conversation turned to what Don did for a living.

"I have a consulting business, though it's just me and I don't have too much going on…" That caused him to smile. "Which I don't mind.

I worked way too much when I was younger, never thinking about how fast the years would fly by. When Boeing shut down the plant, I finally looked up and realized it hadn't been the best use of my time. I had two kids I barely knew, and a wife who promptly divorced me. I thought it was the end," he grinned and reached for MaryAnn's hand. "Now I have someone to be with who makes me laugh and likes to live."

Don had come to California from Texas, he said. First when he was in the Navy, and then when he went to UCLA, where he studied aeronautical engineering. Worked for McDonnell-Douglas, then Boeing after the two companies merged. Married out of college. Had the prototypical Southern California lifestyle that he never really got to enjoy.

"On the plus side, I'm not broke," he said, growing quiet for a moment. "What I miss most is not getting to know the kids when I had the chance." Both had moved out of state. One to St. Louis, the other to Vietnam. "Shows you how times change; my father fought over there."

There was more talk of how Agnes and MaryAnn met, and how I entered the picture, which precipitated my long torturous tale of woe.

"Oh, stop," my beloved wife groaned, "you've got it good."

"I never said I didn't."

Don laughed at that. "It's certainly more interesting than mine. But I'm making up for that now." More mush from the lovebirds. On the plus side, as Don intimated, it appeared to be genuine. It was a nice evening, and there were assurances all around that we'd get together soon, most likely at my fancy place.

"Works for me," I said.

We didn't stay late. There was a lot going on the next day. We were tired, and had to get Emily for her last runaround with Natalya, before it was off to West Covina and the less fancy place.

On the drive home, Agnes posed the question: "Well?"

"A total jackass," I said. "I think MaryAnn is making a big mistake. I'm sure he's a notorious playboy."

"Seriously?"

"Seriously what?" I waited for the smack.

Didn't take long. "Can you just be nice for a change?"

"I'm always nice," I said in the most annoying way possible. Agnes slumped in her seat. Evidently, I'd touched a nerve. "Alright, I'll confess he's a nice guy and they seem very fond of one another. My concern is it appears our recent sexual interludes overlap with how long they've been together, and whether I should be worried. Should I?"

Agnes only shrugged. "MaryAnn will explain."

"Uh-huh. Are you concerned?"

Another shrug.

•　　•　　•　　•　　•

Emily was not keen on the fact that her LA adventure was coming to a close. "I don't want to go back," she pouted.

"Out of our control," I said.

She didn't care for that. "I think you're a coward, Mr. Sunshine."

Which made me laugh. "I think that, too, but it doesn't change the situation, so try not to let it infuse the day with glummery."

"That's not even a word," she said, still pouting.

She was more excited to see Natalya and Isaac, who was also hoping to get out of a trip up north.

"You two are worse than me," I lied. "You're going and that's the way it is. If I have to suffer, so does everybody else. Besides, it's going to be a fun day. No reason to dwell on tomorrow till tomorrow comes."

"I still think you're a coward," Emily huffed. Natalya and Isaac smiled, but were bright enough not to laugh. Anton merely looked aside.

Xavier was picking Natalya up at five that afternoon. She had a big lunch scheduled to celebrate Emily's modest contributions to the foundation, and as a reason to take us all to a fancy restaurant on my tab. Anton planned to take off when Xavier arrived with *his* goons. Isaac mumbled something about a meeting. There was work to do.

I thought about calling Bernie, but decided to wait till I had my little talk with Tsarnaev. Orestra's files were in the drawer, as I absentmindedly looked for something to do before lunch. I pulled them out and went through them again. That's when Pastor Terry's assistant, Vern, called.

"We're concerned about Sterling," he said. "He was scheduled to come in both last week and this, and each time he hasn't been able to make it. Have you talked with him recently, Monk?"

"No... No, this is the first I've heard of it." I wondered what the weasel was up to. "I have to go up north this weekend. If you'd like, I can see if he'll talk to me."

"That would be wonderful, Monk. It's important that your brother knows that he's in our thoughts and prayers. Jesus be blessed," he said, ending the call.

Isaac wandered in. "Problems?"

I wondered if Vern had called him. "Sterling has missed his appointments with Sunlight Ministries."

"Interesting," he said, sitting down.

"Interesting?"

Isaac raised his eyebrows and pinched his lips. "I was surprised he even went there. That he's not going back doesn't surprise me in the least. He's never liked having to face his problems or mistakes head on."

I sat back. "You think it was a dodge?"

"Don't you?"

"I don't know. A part of me wants to think he's caught up in something he isn't ready for, but..." I waited to see if Isaac was following my inference.

"But," he said, after a moment, "what if he knows exactly what he's into, and is playing us?"

"That's why I'm dragging you along. Plus, you need to see your mother."

He rolled his eyes at that. "I saw her last month. You haven't seen your mother since you got married."

I brushed the thought away with my hand. "That's different. My mother doesn't like me."

"Uh-huh. Do we have any plan here?"

"Plans, shmans. As long as he doesn't take off, he has to, at least, talk to us. Whether anything he says is true, or of use, we'll see."

"You're the boss," he shrugged.

I laughed at that. "Just don't tell Ms. Constantinescu."

Isaac turned his head to the door and Ms. Constantinescu beyond. "You think Xavier has a chance?"

"As long as they both have a good time, I don't care. Whether they'll ever be lovers or more, I have no idea." I tried to picture them together. Couldn't quite; let it go. I had other things to deal with.

Detective Gallegos, as it turned out. "Got a minute, Mr. Buttman?" Isaac and I looked at the detective standing in the doorway with Natalya behind her.

"Sure. Do you need to talk to Mr. Bohrman here?" I pointed at Isaac for no reason.

"No," she said. Isaac took that with a smile and walked out, joining Natalya and Emily looking in. Detective Gallegos closed the door.

"Anything new?" seemed like the thing to ask.

"You?"

I looked at the files. "I know that all of them are connected in some way to Flavius and his matchmaking service, and some to Sunlight Ministries. I had my talk with Flavius the other night. Invited me and Agnes to a party. Made it all seem pretty strait-laced, if you'll pardon the pun. Just a place for those on the periphery of society to find love and companionship." I tapped on the files. "Ms. Blakely, in these, noted that was true for some, while financial opportunity or stability was of interest to others. When I talked to Pastor Terry. When Isaac...Mr. Bohrman and I accompanied Sterling to Sunlight Ministries, Pastor Terry didn't recall the names I gave him. Did you talk with Sterling?"

"Briefly." She pulled the notebook from her jacket pocket. "He said he didn't know anything beyond knowing Aisha Diamond, and that he was no longer seeing her and had no idea where she was."

"Did you believe him?"

"Do you?" she asked.

"Off the record?" The detective nodded. "Not particularly." I continued to stare at Orestra's files. "I have to take Emily home this weekend and plan on seeing my brother. I have a few questions—"

"Concerning?"

"Concerning his lack of interest in the counselling he set up at Sunlight Ministries. Apparently, he's missed his last two appointments. Maybe he's just embarrassed. Maybe he thinks it's no longer necessary. I wanted to ask face to face with Isaac there," I said. "And on your end?"

"The three missing women in Ms. Blakely's file have been identified through the morgue's Doe files. All three were murdered. Two strangled. One beaten to death. They had been stripped, and their personal information removed to complicate their identification." She put the notebook away. "No one claimed the bodies."

"Probably because no one knew," I said.

"Or," she stood up. "No one cared. When will you be back in LA?"

"Tuesday or Wednesday."

"I'll be in touch." She pointed to the files. "Mind if I take these?"

"No." I handed them to her, got up, and walked her to the door. Natalya, Emily, Isaac, and Anton were standing by Natalya's desk.

"Time for lunch, Mr. Monk," my chief of staff informed me once the detective was out of earshot.

It's always something!

·　　·　　·　　·　　·

Lunch was at a pricey restaurant that Natalya assured me was worth the cost. "Don't you want Emily to experience the finest Los Angeles has to offer, Mr. Monk?"

"No," I whined.

"Cheap and a coward," Emily huffed, which caused Isaac to burst out laughing.

I shook my finger at him. "You're supposed to be on my side, dude."

That only made him laugh harder, which got a smile out of Natalya and Anton. "You're lucky Agnes isn't here," he said.

"Don't worry," Emily added, "she'll hear about the cowardly cheapskate."

"I love you, too, Emily." What else was there to say?

The rest of lunch was surprisingly light and enjoyable, minus the bill.

$$\cdot \quad \cdot \quad \cdot \quad \cdot \quad \cdot$$

Boris Tsarnaev was waiting when we returned.

34

I introduced him to my merry band. He knew Isaac.

"Good to see you again, Mr. Bohrman," he said.

"Mr. Tsarnaev."

Next were my chief of staff and her bodyguard. "This is Natalya Constantinescu and Anton Nerzhin." Then, "This is Emily. She's helping us out this summer." I saw no reason to say anything more about Emily and where she fit in.

"It's a pleasure to meet you all. And a fellow compatriot." He bowed slightly to Anton, who returned the favor. Natalya did not, but kept her eyes glued to the lobbyist.

I motioned towards my office. "This way." The others watched till the door was closed. "Would you care for something to drink? I have water, soda…a fine Kentucky bourbon?"

"I can't say no to your fine whiskies in this country," he answered. I took care of the drinks as he made himself comfortable on the couch. "I half expected your wife to be a part of our talk."

"Unfortunately, Agnes has other business to attend to," I said as I handed him his glass. "I'll pass on anything you think is relevant when I see her." My turn to get comfortable behind my desk. "What's on your mind, Mr. Tsarnaev?"

"Boris, please."

"Boris."

Boris Tsarnaev savored a drink of the whiskey. "What do you know about me, Monk?"

My turn to savor the whiskey. "That you're a lobbyist in DC for Dominik and Associates; that you represent both the Russian government and important, and influential, members of Russian business."

"Very true."

"Which brings up why you would have any interest in me, outside of my relationship with Delton Manaforte."

He took another drink. "You believe that's why I'm here?"

"Why else? I'm not rich enough, or particularly important. And while I believe in the efforts of our foundation, I don't see how that would be of any interest to the people you represent, apart from some mischievous PR." Tsarnaev nodded. "There's also the nature of your questions to Mr. Bohrman about me and my wife, which have little to do with the foundation. So, perhaps it would be best to save the flattery and oblique references for another day, or a more public gathering, and get to the point. It'll save us both some of our precious time."

Tsarnaev smiled and set his glass down. "Again true."

"Who are you here for?" seemed a good thing to know.

"I'll save that for the moment, since it's possible there's no genuine connection between you and your wife and the people I represent."

"And the connection?"

"An individual named Aaron Alan Sobeski. A former member of your CIA. Do you know him?" Tsarnaev picked up his glass.

I took a drink of mine. "Why do you ask? Or better yet, what do you believe is my connection to Sobeski?"

"We know he was operating in this country and was last contacted, just prior to his disappearance, on his way to a home on the western shores of Lake Michigan. You have a home there, do you not?"

"I do." I saw no reason to lie.

"We also know that he was in communication with Mr. Manaforte, as you were at the same time."

"True."

"Since that time, he has not been heard from. We know that there were several boating accidents on the lake, and an inference has been made that he was killed in one of these accidents." Tsarnaev, who had been looking at his glass, looked over at me. "It has come to our attention that one of the boating accidents involved your boat."

"True again. It was stolen from my dock. An old Chris-Craft. The Coast Guard informed me that debris from it had been found on the lake."

Tsarnaev finished the whiskey in his glass. "I think it is unlikely that this is all coincidence. Don't you agree?"

I finished mine. "Depends. What did Mr. Manaforte have to say? Or are you waiting till you get a little something out of me before you press him on the matter? I'm assuming that you are involved in this to...how shall we say it, to minimize any *American observation* of your people getting together with, say, Manaforte, given what's going on in Washington over the attack on the president."

He smiled at that. "Yes, because of the incident at the White House, we have been...cautious in our inquiries. And, as you have surmised, we have been holding our cards, as they say, in regards to Mr. Manaforte. His has both great friends, and dare I say it, great enemies in my country."

"So, I understand. Do your people believe Sobeski is dead?"

"It would appear that way," he said.

"But..."

Tsarnaev repositioned himself in his chair. "What do you know about Sobeski, Monk?"

I thought about what to share. "I know he once worked for the government. I, too, was told the CIA. That he was hard to control or did not follow protocol, something, and was let go. In recent years, he has been doing work for what we in the west would call eastern European criminal syndicates. I heard he was quite good at misdirection in his sanctions, terminations, murders. It was also intimated to me that he was becoming problematic to his employers there, and if he should disappear, that wasn't such a bad thing. That's what I know. In answer to your earlier question, I did not *know* him. Would you care for a little more whiskey?"

He held his thumb and forefinger close. "Just a touch."

I poured a small amount into his glass and mine. "What do you want, Boris?"

"Answers," he said. "If Sobeski is indeed dead, we want some sort of proof, either physically, or the *trusted* word from someone who was there."

"And in return?"

Tsarnaev drained the glass of whiskey. "You tell me."

"What do you know of a man named Josef Rostikov?" I asked.

"You tell me."

"He's in Russia, attempting to resolve a monetary issue his brother-in-law precipitated. I want him allowed to return to the United States. I'm willing, within reason, to make restitution on what is owed. My understanding is it's a hundred thousand dollars. That, however, may be a fiction, as I think you already know." He nodded at that. "I have two final questions. One, do you represent Manaforte's great friends, or his great enemies? And two, do you know a man who goes by the name Zosima?" I finished my whiskey.

"Good, good," he said, rising. I followed suit. "We have our parameters."

"And the answer to my questions?"

"The first answer lies in the fact that we did not have any personal connection to the attack that you and your Ms. Constantinescu were victim to recently. That doesn't mean we do not know those behind it. Or the reasons." He opened my office door just a little. "As for the name Zosima, I know it, and the man behind it. For now, we'll leave it at that." He pulled a card from his pocket. "This tit-for-tat I'll relay it to my people."

"Good," I said, moving out from behind my desk. He waited for me to draw close. "You believe I have the answers?"

"We know you do." He did not smile.

Natalya and Anton watched as I let Tsarnaev out the front door. When he was out of range, I asked, "What do you two think about our visitor?"

"He knows a lot of dangerous people," Anton answered. Natalya didn't say anything. Emily, standing by the door to the other office, was quiet as well.

"True, but if we want to get Josef out of purgatory, we're going to have to deal with dangerous people."

The two of them didn't appear particularly enthusiastic about my answer.

•   •   •   •   •

Xavier Dunkle II arrived a little before five. Two stout men of Anton's size stood not far from him. He was well dressed, not quite the suit and tie I favored, but wearing an elegant gold shirt with tan slacks that were properly tailored. He'd even had his hair done. His hard work in the gym and his diet had paid dividends, as he was now slim, rather than the roly-poly he was when I first met him running errands for Link Deal. Natalya had her bags by her desk. She was quite excited, rather than the cool reserve she often presented to our dear Xavier.

"Looks like someone is ready to have themselves a wonderful time," I said to Xavier.

A big grin covered his face. "That's the plan."

Emily's face did not hide the disappointment that she was not going with them to the glamour of New York City.

"You have the glamour of the farm," I said.

She glared at me. "Mr. Monk?"

"Yes," I answered.

"Shut up!"

Natalya tried, somewhat, to no avail, to assure Emily that it was no big deal, which none of us believed. Emily's gloom deepened as we saw the merry pair off.

Anton quickly followed, taking his leave of us. "We're going to Disney World."

I shook my head. "Why? Disneyland is here in town?"

He shrugged. "I only go where I'm told."

"Sounds familiar," I said to myself.

We armed and locked up the foundation's offices and headed for our cars. "Tomorrow morning, nine-ish, Mr. Bohrman."

"Yeah, yeah, yeah," Isaac said. His gloom mirroring Emily's.

"You two," I said to Emily, who was ignoring me.

Ronnie flagged me down as I was getting ready to steer the car out of the parking garage. I hadn't seen him since before the attack. Bennie's admonitions that I shouldn't be enabling Ronnie's homelessness were sounding in my head. That was amplified when I noticed the bruises on his face. "What happened to you?"

He waved me off. "Ain't nothing. Disagreement is all. Don't worry about me."

"You live on the street, Ronnie. I'm going to worry. You sure we can't find you a home?" he laughed at that. "So, what's up?"

"I saw our black Russian earlier. Hadn't been around lately. Thought maybe he'd moved on."

"Really?" I took a bunch of twenties from my wallet. "No regular Russians or their confederates?"

"Nope. It's been quiet," he said, as I handed him the money.

"You shouldn't be doing that, Mr. Sunshine," Emily admonished as we drove off.

"Yeah, yeah, yeah," was all I could think of.

35

Agnes was waiting in the backyard with Emily, a glass of wine in her hand. "MaryAnn would like to talk to you. Is that ok?"

I was surprised she asked. Usually, I wasn't given the choice. "When? Here?"

"She wants to know if you can go over there."

I didn't want to go. "I don't know. There's a lot to do be—"

"Everything's ready, and I ordered pizza for dinner. We'll save you some, won't we, Em?"

"I promise nothing," the still grumpy teen said. Agnes laughed at that.

I didn't like this. "What if I don't want to go?"

She reached for my hand. "Please, Monk."

She knew I was easy prey to her taking my hand. "Only if there *is* pizza when I get back," I whined.

"I promise, even if Em won't," she said.

She let go, and I was on my way, having just gotten home and off the road.

MaryAnn was waiting when I arrived at her house. As I expected, Agnes had alerted her to my coming over. "Come in. Can I get you a drink?" Her eyes, which liked to dance in my presence, were quiet and searching.

"Sure. What did you want to talk to me about?" though any idiot would know.

"Me and Don," she said, handing me a glass of wine. She directed me to the couch and sat next to me, which heightened my anxiety.

"What about you and Don?"

She smiled. "Agnes is right, you're something of a pain in the ass to talk to."

I took a drink of the chardonnay. "You like me being a pain in the ass. Isn't that what we need to talk about?"

"I spose." She put her hand on my knee. "I...I didn't say anything about Don because...because I know one of your rules, as you like to say, is you don't like sleeping with someone else's woman."

"Sounds familiar." Sleeping with Agnes and Judith at the same time was proof of what could go wrong, never mind Monika, and none were technically with anyone else at the time.

MaryAnn took a drink of her wine. "I think that's probably a smart move, but there are reasons why this situation is a little different, and that's what I want to talk to you about."

"Does Don know about this? Our getting together?"

MaryAnn twirled the wine in her glass. "No, not directly..."

"Then what does he know?"

"The same thing you and Agnes know, that I like sex...a lot." She looked at me and moved her hand from my knee to hers before turning away. "Unfortunately, sex is a struggle for Don. He likes it, but not like I do. It's just not as important to him. Plus, there are, well, he has certain issues that make sex more problematic." She patted my face. "Not everyone can get it up like you."

"Then the obvious question is, why are you with him if sex is a struggle?"

She sighed and sat back on the couch. "Because there's more to life than sex. And yes, coming from me, that says a lot. But I really like Don. I mean, I really like him. He's the first man I've met in a long time that I really enjoy being with. And I've looked, Monk, really looked. Finding a decent sex partner, or as one of them once said, a sex buddy, isn't that hard, but someone you genuinely want to spend time with, to go places with, well, that's been much harder. That's why I was so happy for Agnes when she found you. It was clear right away between you two." MaryAnn returned her hand to my leg, running her fingers along the crease in my slacks, producing a very unwanted erection, which she ran her finger across, causing me to flinch. "Sorry."

She moved her hand to her lap. "I know the noble thing is to be true to Don and all that, and a part of me wants to, but I like our get-togethers." She looked at me. "I won't lie; I really like the sex. It fills a void that's missing with me and Don. I know that makes me sound terribly selfish and unkind to Don, and it's not like I'm not going to tell him...well, maybe."

I took her hand in mine. "But maybe not, because telling him might only make him walk away."

"Yes." She rested her head on my shoulder. I could feel the tears as they fell on my jacket. "Are you mad at me? Agnes is worried you're upset about this..."

"A little," I said. It bothered me more than a little. "For now, I don't know. On the plus side, I have all kinds of distractions to deal with..."

"I've heard. Normally, I'd invite the two of you over." She wiped her eyes. "I guess that's no longer an option."

"Probably not. I should get going. Do you want to join us? Agnes ordered pizza?"

She shook her head. "It'll just get me into trouble." She leaned in and kissed me, drawing her lips tight to mine. They were soft and salty. She pressed herself against me. My stupid cock wanted badly to fuck her. I felt like an immense heel. She must have noticed, even as her hand caressed my erection. "You better go," she said, after ending the kiss.

"Yeah."

She got me to the door.

Agnes and Emily were in the backyard, strangely, or maybe not, with the Montaigne clan, enjoying pizza and the cool evening air. Rebekah glanced over just long enough to see who it was. "Well, look who the cat dragged in."

"I love you, too." Smartly, Agnes had ordered enough pizza that I was not robbed of the opportunity to sublimate my sexual desire with food. "Are you heading north, too, or just availing yourselves of free pizza?"

Rebekah turned to Fidel, who shrugged. "Sure, why not?"

•　　•　　•　　•　　•

Nine-ish was more like ten-ish. "What? Like they won't be there?" Isaac's desire to visit the place of his birth had not improved.

"We've got a timetable, dude, a tight, precise timetable," I told him.

My brother was not impressed. "Agnes is right, you're a jerk."

"Yeah!" Emily adding her two cents.

Rebekah and her bunch had already left. Agnes was waiting by the door, unconcerned.

"Come on. Come on. Come on, there's doin's a transpirin," I said.

"Yeah, yeah, yeah," was the chorus from Isaac and Emily.

The drive was a quiet affair. Isaac slept. I assumed a late night; Emily pouted. The good times were over, and Agnes stared at the road ahead. She didn't ask about my talk with MaryAnn; not after pizza, not before bed, or as we were getting ready to go the next morning. And, as it wasn't the kind of conversation to have in front of Emily, or Isaac for that matter, it would have to wait. The Montaignes were graciously waiting for us at the In-N-Out Burger in San Jose, our usual stop for lunch.

Rebekah stood at the entrance with her arms crossed, a frazzled look on her face. "Geez, Dad, it's about time. The kids are starving."

I looked at her kids. They didn't seem particularly famished, though Zach did say, "Come on, Gamps."

I turned to Isaac. "See?"

He pushed me towards the restaurant door. "Yeah, yeah, yeah."

As the others found their own booths, Agnes and I found one in the corner. "Are you ok?" she asked.

"Is this about my talk with MaryAnn?"

She looked around to see if anyone was listening, which reminded me of the last time we talked about sex in a public place, the In-N-Out Burger in Hollywood. "Yeah."

"How long have you known about this?" I asked, just as our number was called.

Agnes stood up and grabbed the receipt from me. "I'll get that."

I wondered if there was anything to say, really say, about this, and whether if what she knew was even important. She returned with the basket, set it down, looked at me, and said, "Want some ketchup?" which was a silly question because she knew I did. After that, there was the matter of consumption. We ate our lunch in relative silence. The ambient noise came from the other customers, my occasionally loud grandson among them.

"Are you mad?" she asked as we were emptying the basket into the trash.

Am I? "I don't know. Actually, yes, but I'm not going to worry about it. There are other problems to deal with. Sterling being front and center."

That must have sparked Agnes' thought process. "Hey, did that Boris guy show up yesterday?"

I gave her a hug. "Yes, he did." The clan was piling into the cars. My grumpy daughter handed me my grumpy grandson, little dude number two.

"Here! Maybe he'll sleep for you." She stomped off as Jacob stared up at me.

I pulled the car fob from my pocket and shook it in the direction of Agnes and Isaac. "Who wants to drive?"

Isaac took the fob. The rest of the drive was Jacob sleeping in my lap, Agnes sleeping next to me in the backseat, and Emily and Isaac commiserating on having to go back to the farm. The best of times.

•　　•　　•　　•　　•

Meredith, Calista, and Andrea were waiting as we arrived. Andrea was cheerful as ever, and Meredith gave her recalcitrant son a big hug.

"Where's Moses?" For some reason, I had to ask.

"He's in the dining room. Sterling and Felicia are here with the kids," she said. "Put your things away and we'll see you there."

The big happy family was here. All the surviving sons and their children, and in my case, their children's children. It had been a while since we'd all been together, not so much from my end, Agnes and Rebekah had dragged us up here at least once a month, and for all his bitching, Isaac had made himself something of a regular, too. It was those closest that had been absent of late. Sterling and Felicia. But they'd been having difficulties, worrying Moses and Meredith, and, of late, me.

"There you are," Moses bellowed. "Come join us." As if we would beg off.

Well, some of us. Zach was already fidgeting. He didn't care for grownup talk. Neither did Lizzy. "We want to see the animals," he whined. Tess, Mary, and Michael, Sterling and Felicia's kids, were just as bored and ready to split the scene.

"Tess, why don't you take them?" Felicia said to their oldest.

Tess gave her mother a withering stare. At thirteen, she had no interest in herding this motley crew. But providence produced Emily, whom Tess looked up to, and knew had been living the good life in LA. "Will you come with us, Em?"

Emily took in the gaggle and said, "Sure."

And off they went.

Isaac sat down and poured those of us not already drinking a glass of wine. Merlot. As I picked up my glass, I watched Sterling and Felicia. I hadn't seen them together since that day in Berkeley. This time, they seemed in better spirits. Both were smiling. Sterling was effusive about the merlot, which was very good, and Felicia about how the kids were doing. The Mackinaws and Andrea joined us. More wine was poured, and the business of grapes and the wines they produced was discussed at length.

In watching, I noticed how old the three of them had become, Brewster, Franco, and Moses, the founders of our commune. Brewster was on his own now, his wife, Murphy, having died the year before from cancer. Franco's wife, Belle; she had changed it years ago from Jody, ran the kitchen, but had passed on most of that responsibility to some of the newer members. Given her interest and involvement, I wondered if Andrea was the titular leader in waiting. It certainly wasn't me.

Rebekah strode in with her perpetual headache in hand, and handed him to me. Jacob immediately calmed down to the wonderment of all.

"I know, I know, it's not normal," I said, to preempt the comments from those around me. Jacob promptly fell asleep. I shrugged. Rebekah shook her head and poured herself a glass of wine. Fidel, also a lover of animals, had joined the kids in the barn.

As the chattering continued, and as I ran my fingers along the edges of Jacob's soft downy head, something caught my eye. It was Felicia's necklace. A thin silver chain with an outlined silver heart was around her neck. Crossing the heart were two hands joined in the middle, holding a deep blue Sapphire.

36

"That's quite a necklace."

We were in line for dinner, which mercifully broke up the business talk until everyone had their plates and returned to their tables. Felicia took the necklace in her fingers, smiling as she did. "It is, isn't it?"

"It's very interesting," I said. "Antique. May I?" She reluctantly allowed me to hold it for a moment. "Very nice."

"Sterling gave it to me," she said, anticipating my next question. "To make amends."

"Things are going better?"

"Yes. He's getting help down in Los Angeles. A church. He said you and Isaac went with him." I imagined he did. Felicia once again held the necklace in her hand.

I smiled. "That's true. I wanted to talk to him about it for a minute."

Her eyes clouded. "Everything is ok, isn't it?"

I handed her a plate. "As far as I know."

"Good," she said. I don't know if she believed it any more than I did. "I want to thank you for helping us. It means a lot to me." She gave me a hug before moving on to the more pedestrian activity of piling on the food.

While there was some business talk at dinner, for the most part it centered more on the ailments of the old, ribbing by those of us younger, but not that much younger, and the kids making noise, and occasionally annoying one another and their parents.

My daughter included. "Zach, don't make me come over there!"

This elicited a deep frown from Zach...and laughs from the rest of us, except Rebekah.

"Dad!"

"What?"

After dinner, smaller groups formed, one being Isaac and Sterling. I watched them for a moment. The last of the sun was fading, and, as I held no important position here on the farm, I took my glass, and the remainder of the bottle of wine, and wandered outside to find a little peace and quiet. That lasted five minutes. Franco and Brewster were looking for me.

"Sunshine, we got a proposition for you," Brewster said, a wine laced smile on his face. We'd been drinking most of the afternoon. Fortunately, dinner kept us from becoming overly inebriated.

"What?" I didn't need any more propositions.

"Now, now," Franco sat next to me. "Hear us out. Not everyone is as financially secure as you are."

"I'm broke," I said, hoping...

They both laughed. "Nice try. Know the place north and east of here?" Franco asked.

I had to think. "The Forester-Gertner Homestead?"

Brewster sat on the other side of me. "The one."

The Forester-Gertner Homestead was a euphemistically named hundred-acre site liberated from the Pomo Nation by settlers following the gold rush. Legend had it that the Foresters went broke in a failed business venture and sold the land to a family named Gertner, who many years later sold it to a Roger Smith in the 1950s. Smith did little with the property and there was always conjecture, locally, as to who the guy was, as he hadn't been seen in years. After a while, there were questions about whether he even existed.

I looked between them. "Let me guess. It's for sale."

Brewster smiled and filled my glass. "It is."

"Well, gosh," I stammered, trying to figure out a way to say no, "I don't know if my acquisition team wants me to buy a decrepit old farm that we used to think was being used to grow illegal drugs—"

"That's just local gossip," Franco assured me. "We could use the land to expand our business, but...getting that kind of loan might be tough. So Moses suggested we approach you."

I imagined Moses whining about my ill-gotten gain. "Let me guess. He said, 'Why don't you hit up Mr. Moneybags? He's loaded,' or something to that effect."

Brewster laughed. "Maybe something like that."

"Would you prefer it fall into the hands of some equity outfit that specializes in land speculation, forcing working people off their property for rich elites?" Franco asked.

I took a sip of wine. "Isn't that right up my alley now that I'm a nefarious oligarch?"

Neither laughed.

"Seriously, you can check it out tomorrow. I'll let the realtor know," Brewster said. "Obviously, we'll work out some kind of repayment plan."

Obviously. "I'll think about it," not wanting to.

"Good." Brew and Franco stood and left me to the next challenge as Isaac and Sterling came over. I motioned to the two seats that just opened up.

"I wanted to explain why I haven't come down for the counselling at the church," Sterling said.

I stared at the last of the wine. "I assumed you changed your mind."

He rubbed his hands together and sat back in his chair. "No...it's just that... I don't know if it's the right thing, that all." He looked at Isaac, who was looking at me. "Anyway, I have business in LA this coming week. I can go then."

"It's up to you," I said.

"You always have us," Isaac assured him.

"Thanks. That's important to me." Sterling sat up.

"It's been a long day," I said. "We can revisit this tomorrow if we want."

Sterling nodded. "Sure."

Isaac raised his eyebrows at me as they got up and left.

Agnes was waiting in our room when I returned. I had no idea what time it was as I finally got my moment of peace after our little talk with Sterling. I thought about sleeping in the bunkhouse, but changed my mind after remembering that Andrea had turned most of it into a print shop.

Agnes was sitting up in the bed, her arms crossed, hiding her breasts. "Are you ok?"

I smiled and undid my tie. "Didn't you ask me that earlier?"

"You didn't answer."

I crossed my arms. "That's because you ran off to get our burgers and then the ketchup."

"I was just being helpful," she said in a pout.

I sat on the bed next to her. "Yes, you were. And now that the day has passed into that good night, you want to know if I'm angry about this thing with MaryAnn and Don? If I'm mad at you for not mentioning it, even though you knew about it, right?"

She put her hand on my leg, exposing herself. "Yes, but in my defense, MaryAnn asked me to wait. She wanted to tell you."

"Uh-huh." I watched as her hand moved up my leg.

"I'd like to make things better," she cooed. "Maybe do that thing you like."

"I like lots of things," I said.

"Whatever you like. I'm willing." She shook her breasts just in case I wasn't getting the message.

I eased in next to her and kissed her. "Don't be angry, but I'm going to take a raincheck on your offer. I'm tired and I've had too much wine and my head hurts. I should have come back sooner, but..." Fucking Sterling. "I'll tell you in the morning."

She tried to smile, and I could see she was worried and disappointed, but I wasn't in the mood, strange as that was to say. Between Sterling and Aisha and MaryAnn and Flavius, and Orestra lying on that morgue table, my libido had taken to the hills.

.   .   .   .   .

Agnes got up early to help in the kitchen. I got up late, hungover, and increasingly ill-humored. It was a good thing I had a diversion in going over to the property the Mackinaws wanted me to buy.

"I'll be back in a while," I told her. She kissed me but didn't say anything.

I stopped by the car and retrieved the 45 automatic I kept in the trunk of the car.

The realtor, a fellow name Marty, met me at the gate, unlocking it. That made me smile. Every teenager in the county knew how to get into this place, including a dimwit named Sunshine who knocked up his girlfriend. I told him I wanted to check it out on my own, that I would lock up.

"It's choice land, Mr. Buttman, won't last long," he said.

I looked around at the dry, sun-parched grass and the rutted road. "Probably not, Marty. That's why I wanted to have a look. Don't worry, I'll be in touch." I waited till he drove off to make my way down the road.

Fairfax was with his dog, sitting on the front porch of the dilapidated farmhouse.

I wasn't surprised to see him. In fact, I had expected him sooner. Maybe it was that I'd left my phone back in our room. No one could listen in unless they were hiding close with a parabolic microphone.

"I was wondering when you'd show up. I was beginning to think you'd lost interest in me. But then nothing has actually been resolved, has it?"

He gave the dog a treat. "The answer to that is no."

I wonder. "I promised to check out the property. We can talk as I look it over. It'll give the dog a chance to run." Something I wanted to do.

Fairfax stood up and joined me. A worn path ran alongside the house to the barn and the fields beyond. The dog trotted around us.

"You said you wanted to know what happened to Aaron Alan, and you're sure I have the answers, correct?"

"It is," he said.

"Alright. Let's set some parameters on this, as you're an analyst. The first concerns what happened to Aaron Alan Sobeski. Is he dead? I know what I know. You know what you know about him based on past experience, which I'm assuming you know through reports and reputation. You weren't, say, his case manager, correct?" I smiled at that.

Fairfax did not. "I did not oversee any sanctions carried out by Sobeski."

"Fair enough. Even though I think there is more at play here, we'll stick, for the moment, to Sobeski." We were past the barn, staring out at the sun-bleached grass. "First, I need a picture of Sobeski. Bernie said there weren't any, but if he worked for the CIA, or whomever, even if it's old, there should be one out there." I looked down at the lab sitting at Fairfax's feet.

"I'll see what I can do," he said. The path twisted through the grass to a stand of trees in the distance. "Are you armed, Mr. Buttman?"

I patted the 45 in my pocket. "Yes. Shall we?" I pointed to the path. He nodded. "Here's what I know."

·   ·   ·   ·   ·

"I'll be in touch, Mr. Buttman," Fairfax said, as I locked the gate.

I stayed back. Marty had picked me up at the farm and I felt like walking back. Too many different questions banging around in my head. The three miles would give me time to think. Between this mess with Sterling, and all the lingering questions about the dearly departed Aaron Alan, I had things to work out.

The weather was kind to the out-of-place town dude walking through the fallow fields in a suit. I stood out everywhere I went. I didn't mind having gotten used to the stares years ago. Men don't wear suits anymore. Outside of a professional subset; lawyers, businessmen, that type, suits were long out of favor. The only thing that might make me stand out more was if I affected a Hip-hop look with my hair in braids.

At least the suits were culturally appropriate.

I didn't see a soul on the walk back. The old gate along the fence dividing the farm property from the Forester-Gertner Homestead still stood. Weirdly, it swung open easily even though it was never used. The Mackinaws were waiting in the courtyard, wine in hand.

"Is there a time when you two aren't drinking?" I asked, as they offered me a glass, this one filled with a Riesling.

"It's good for the soul," Franco answered. "What'd you think?"

"It's perfect. Room for my bunker and my secret plans to force all you bastards out. Then we'll have our great country back again." The Riesling was refreshing. Maybe the answer *was* drinking all the time.

"Then a toast." Brewster raised his glass, which his brother matched. "To ridding the land of us rotten bastards!"

We clinked our glasses just as Moses came into view. Brew handed him a glass. "What am I missing?"

"Sunshine's going to buy the Forester-Gertner Homestead, and drive us bastards out," Franco told him.

Brewster added, "We made a toast."

Moses stared at me, which I returned with a tip of my glass. He drank the wine in his glass, shook his head, and said, "Figures."

37

Dinner brought out the news that I was buying the vacant homestead next door, to which I said I was considering it. That was, for the most part, ignored.

"Can I have your house in Beverly Hills, then?" Emily was still peeved about having to come home. A few people thought that was quite humorous.

"No," I said.

"It'll be good to have room to grow," Moses enthused, imagining more young families joining the commune. And in truth, there had been more inquiries. Oddly, younger generations were either sick of or less than enthralled with capitalism. "Maybe we're not the bane you made us out to be, Sunshine," he said to me.

"I never used the word *bane* to describe this place. Nor have I ever denied its charms. Other than that, I didn't think it was my cup of tea," I said.

"Yet there were all those years farming." His favorite dig.

I wasn't biting. "We sailed that ocean already. As for the homestead, I have a guy who knows a guy and we'll see," which was mostly true. Macklgrew's firm had real estate specialists I could tap.

"When will your guy, who knows a guy, get to this?"

"What's the hurry?" I loved the ball being in my court.

He knew I knew. "We have several families who would like to join us, and we'd like to have an answer for them. Right now, there isn't enough room for all of them. With the added land, we could build an adjacent housing area. All that takes time. That's why. Good enough?"

"What's in it for me? And how do I know you'll behave?" That was probably cruel, but it would give me an idea of where his head was at. It had been a rough couple of years since Jacob's death.

He pressed his forefinger into my chest. "I'm just fine. As for what's in it for *you*, you said this place was important to you, and since you're the nefarious oligarch; yes, I heard about that. You can put a little money in."

I pressed my forefinger into his chest. "We're not talking about a *little* money. It's a large investment. And while I'm not poor, a lot of my ill-gotten gains are tied up in your son's foundation." I smiled. "Are we done with the finger pointing?"

He smiled back. "For the moment."

Meredith and Isaac were standing to the side of us, apparently watching our little tiff. "Are you two done?" she asked.

"Maybe," I answered, to which Moses rolled his eyes.

"Good." She pointed to the serving table. "Dessert is ready."

Isaac added, "Apple pie, if you're interested." Like I wouldn't be.

•   •   •   •   •

Bernie was intrigued, though not entirely sure my bet would pay off after I told him of my talks with Manaforte, Tsarnaev, and Fairfax. "I'd ask Art what he thinks. Whether Fairfax or Manaforte are playing sides, I can't say, though I'd be shocked if Fairfax was. But times have changed and people switch sides."

"Like Nakatomi?"

"Possibly, but again, it might just be the job and the money," he said. "It might also be disenchantment, or he buys into what Manaforte is selling. As for Rostikov, I agree, you'll need something to bargain with to get him out since it's possible he's already told his side of it and it didn't set him free."

I pondered that. "Maybe they just want corroboration."

"Maybe. Or they sell him out to their enemies and let him take the brunt of their reprisals. That's the chance you take."

"Why wouldn't Manaforte protect him? He was working for him."

"The fate of a pawn, remember?"

I did. "Alright, I'll call Art and hope the package arrives. I have one more favor to ask. I want you to hack Pastor Terry Stanton's calendar."

•   •   •   •   •

It was too late to call Art. Save that for the next day. Agnes joined me and my bottle of wine in the courtyard. I filled her in on the day's events as I filled her glass.

"What if he can't find a picture?" she asked. "What if they've scrubbed the archives?" she loved that kind of talk.

"Then we go with what we have and pray it works," I said.

She sat close to me on the bench. "Are you still mad at me?"

"No. If I'm mad at anyone, it's my idiot brother."

"I'm not surprised," she said. "Felicia is hoping like crazy that he's telling the truth. Is he?"

I took her hand. "No."

"What then?"

I stared at the light reflecting off the wineglass. "I think Sterling is digging his grave while being told how clever he is. And all for the sake of a forbidden blowjob."

"Speaking of which..." Her hand was back on my leg.

"Is that all you think about?"

Agnes patted my crotch. "That was what I was taught was all you think about, you men!" I couldn't quite tell if she was offended or just playing with me.

"That's just an old wives' tale," I lied.

"Well? Are you interested?" She had that smile going.

Before I could answer that, out of the corner of my eye, I saw Andrea, who was walking towards us. She, too, had a glass and a bottle. "Is everybody drinking now?" I asked out loud.

She laughed. "It sure seems that way, but mostly it's because we've got you guys here, and with the hope that we might be able to expand. So...why not?"

"At least that way it gets used. We have this really nice house in Michigan that we've only been to once. Don't we, Sunshine?" Agnes tipped her glass my way.

I shook my head. "I heard a rumor to that effect. Evidently, the plan is to methodically corner me such that I have no choice but to buy the homestead whether I want to or not. What's your pitch, Andi?" We were advised that's how she preferred to be addressed going forward. As a former Sunshine, William, et al., I wasn't going to object.

"My pitch is simple. We need the room," she said.

"Fresh blood?" The ugly truth was the triumvirate was now long in the tooth. "Makes sense, and I hear lots of good things about how you're jumping in and getting things done."

Andi shrugged. "Just doing what I can." She smiled and looked out at the surrounding houses and towards the barn and the pens. "I really like it here. Feel like I'm doing something meaningful, something that isn't just about me. If I can pitch in, help out...isn't that kind of the whole idea?"

I thought of Moses and his many sermons. "Sounds vaguely familiar."

Agnes groaned, which made Andi laugh. "Moses does go on a little, doesn't he? I don't mind. For the first time in my life, I'm happy. I love my life, Calista, Em, and now baby Jasper is here. I want to see the farm succeed. I want to continue what your father and the Mackinaws started."

"I think that's wonderful." Probably better her than me. "As for the Forester-Gertner Homestead, the best thing you can do is have a detailed plan; expenses, revenue, housing costs, any money you can put down. Something I can give to Mr. Macklgrew. That's what impresses him. Otherwise, he'll see it as me wasting money on some foolish family venture, like the Manifesto." I was proud of myself for channeling my moneyman.

"The Manifesto's doing great, Monk," Agnes said.

"No, the Manifesto is breaking even because I'm not, though I shouldn't mention this out loud, a Scrooge that nickels and dimes the help. The homestead doesn't have to be a profit center, but it can't be a money pit. Sorry."

Andi nodded. "I expect that. As a matter of fact, I have some numbers ready. I'll get them to you before you go." That reminded me of Theresa and her flower shop and how she had all her numbers lined up. "The other thing I wanted to talk to you about was Emily."

I looked at Agnes. "I didn't promise anything to Emily. In fact, I said no—"

Andi noted my unease. "Yes, she mentioned that."

I took a drink of wine. All this talking was leaving me parched. "So, what about Emily?"

Andi looked around. "For now, this is between us, ok?"

I looked at Agnes, who smiled and shrugged. I knew when she did that the fix was in. I nodded.

Andi leaned in. "Calista and me think that it might be in Em's interest to let her dip her toe in the waters of public education."

"Calista thinks that?" She'd given me quite a lot of grief over Emily's long-standing desire to pull a Sunshine and split.

"Calista thinks that," Andi said.

"I'm shocked."

"You and me both," she said.

The thought of Emily living with us began to sink in. I narrowed my eyes at Agnes. "Beverly Hills or West Covina?"

"West Covina," Agnes said, like it was no big deal.

"What if we have guests and need a room?" I was clutching at straws.

Agnes was having none of it. "That's what your fancy place is for."

"Uh-huh. And when are you going to spring this on our put-upon teenager? And Calista is actually ok with this?" I still didn't believe it.

"That's what she tells me. As for Em, we'll have to work out a few things, like her coming home for the summer, and her time with her father. We had a long talk about it while Em was gone. I know Calista would prefer that Emily stay here, but she also knows how much Em wants to be out in the world. She's getting older and she should have a say. It doesn't mean it's forever, and maybe she'll find she doesn't like going to a regular high school."

I wondered about that, but having underestimated Emily before…

Andi sipped her wine. "We'll tell after she gets back from Philly."

"Did Em say anything about her time in LA?" Agnes was curious.

Andi pursed her lips for a moment. "She did. She said she really liked working at the foundation, that she'd found a mentor. Natalya's her name, isn't it?"

"Yes, she's been very kind to Em," I said.

"She also said there was an incident, and that it was pretty scary, but said if she was strong enough to get through that, she could get through whatever LA threw at her." Andi looked at me. "I didn't ask for specifics."

"It's true," I said. "Some people came looking for Natalya and made trouble. Em handled it far better than I thought she would. I expected her to want to come right home. Instead, she blew me off." I smiled at that. "Whether she can survive the politics of high school, I don't know. I never went. But she has Agnes here, who, as I understand it, is an old hand in such matters."

"Nice try, Buttman."

"I do what I can." I held up my glass. "A toast. To Emily."

"To Emily," they said in unison.

38

Art called me!

"I hear you've got a few ideas," he said.

"I always have a few ideas. The question is whether they're nonsense or not." Might as well be honest. "And as usual, I have a lot on my plate."

"A far cry from the nobody you once yearned to be," he laughed.

"Yes..." I had visions of my previous life slacking in my bungalow or at the beach. "But, as they say, life goes on. What have you heard?"

"Our Russian friends' interest in Sobeski, and the attack on the president. Close?"

"Yes. Boris Tsarnaev intimated concern that they'd be blamed for instigating the attack. I don't know if they are or are not involved. And I wouldn't be surprised if Manaforte is purposefully drawing them in through the Sobeski business. Sobeski had ties to both U.S. intelligence and the Russian mobs."

"True, and I'm sure it's being looked into, but the idea that the Russians would personally target the president is a big deal. It would be an act of war. And while they like to delve into all manner of mischief, I don't see them knowingly crossing that line," he said.

"What about unknowingly?"

"Anything's possible," he agreed. "If outside agencies are seeking to put the blame for the attack on the Russians, I can't see them sitting still on this. It would explain Tsarnaev's charm offensive here in DC. It would also explain the quiet surrounding the investigation. Tight lips and all that. And Sobeski? Where would he fit in? Word is he's dead."

"He wouldn't. So why the continued interest? That's why I think something's not right here. That's my concern. Why would the Russians care about a dead guy? A dead American assassin. To do what? Get revenge?" I was thinking out loud.

So was Art. "What you're looking for then, is whether there are activities, unexplained activities, that ordinarily might be connected to Sobeski?"

"Yes. Is someone acting in his name in order to muddy the waters?"

"I'll ask around. I know a few gossips who might find that intriguing. Anything else?"

"No, that ought to be enough," I said. "Thanks for calling, Art."

"I'll be in touch."

I was ready to go home.

·   ·   ·   ·   ·

Unfortunately, I'd have to wait. The kids wanted another day to live the farming life. Isaac was as bored as I was, and, as I was, somewhat willing to lend a hand. One of the new families joining was moving in, so we helped with that. Sterling as well. If nothing else, it gave me an opportunity to watch him. Normally, that made me feel a little queasy, spying on my own, but this was different.

This was murder.

"The necklace was a nice touch," I said, as we carried a couch in.

Sterling nodded and smiled. "Yeah, I found it at an antique shop in Napa. Kind of a touristy place. It's been...hard lately—"

"These things are."

He ignored my interruption. "But I think we're getting there."

"Have you said anything to the kids?" Isaac asked. We were standing by the moving van waiting for another couple to bring out a pair of lamps.

Sterling seemed caught off guard by the question, having to take a moment before answering. "They know we've been...struggling. I haven't said much. I think Felicia has just letting them know we're working it out. I don't want them to worry."

Better to have Moses, Meredith, and Felicia worry, I thought to myself. Like the kids wouldn't know, anyway. "You have to be careful. Kids are pretty perceptive. More so than you might think. But if they see the two of you together, and you're happy, they'll be ok."

I watched as he pondered this. "I think so too," he said. "Like I said, we'll get there."

Isaac and I looked at each other. The question was where.

The rest of the day came and went with the usual rhythms of the farm; the adults doing their thing, while the older kids corralled the younger ones. Zach dragged me to the barn to see the lambs; there were thirteen. There were also a dozen calves in the field with their mothers.

"See!" he shouted.

And, as if I hadn't already been advised at how wonderful having the Forester-Gertner Homestead would be, dinner included more plaintives from a fresh slew of people, including Agnes.

"Meri showed me," she explained." Seems perfect, don't you think?"

"I try not to," I muttered. Oh, to be a broke-assed nobody.

"We can afford it, Sunshine," she assured me. "I've seen your bank statements."

"Uh-huh."

"And I need you to see to my needs," she said. "Soon!"

I took a drink of a fine chardonnay. As always, there was plenty of wine. "We'll have to see what Macklgrew thinks."

"You're a jerk, Buttman!"

"So, I've heard," I shrugged.

The next day we headed home, after a slew of goodbyes, and hugs, and a last pitch for the homestead, as if I hadn't gotten the message already. Sterling promised to stop by; I had Isaac remind him just in case he was leery of my asking. Emily was in full grump mode, and no doubt assumed our smiles and attempts to cheer her up were merely more nails in her coffin of rural doom.

"It'll all work out," I told her.

She glared at me. "You're a coward, Mr. Monk."

"I love you, too."

They all stood there and waved, including Felicia, wearing her new antique necklace.

.   .   .   .   .

The drive home allowed more mental wandering. As had become custom, I drove us to San Jose and lunch, followed by Jacob duty for the long haul to West Covina. Bernie had sent a text saying he had what I asked for. I promised to call when I got home.

Sterling, in his "It'll all work out" talk, convinced me that he and Aisha were up to something, and she was probably playing his stupid ass. For the most part, I hadn't wanted to consider that she had killed Orestra. But maybe that was foolish thinking. Solidarity among a persecuted group didn't mean they were all in lockstep supporting one another. Bad blood exists everywhere, whether in a family, group, or institution. Who's to say that something bad hadn't happened between Aisha and the other three missing black women Orestra was looking for? Maybe that led her to Flavius and Sunlight Ministries, and back to Aisha.

Maybe.

Flavius had intimated that Pastor Terry was no saint. A former sex addict, he said. Pastor Terry? Another man who, through his own fall from grace, found god. Just as Lucian DeBerry had. His hand-written...

The letters. Love letters.

The letters were in my desk. I thought about heading to the office, but it was late, and after a long drive, everyone was tired. Sitting at the kitchen table, it occurred to me I could pull up the laptop, go through his hand-written notes posted on the ministry's website.

Agnes sat across the table from me, her fingers drumming along its edge. She was not a happy-camper. Isaac had headed home the minute we got back to my less fancy place.

"You coming in tomorrow?" he asked, as he got in his car.

Technically, we were closed for the week. "Yes," I said. "I have things to do, and Detective Gallegos might want to see me."

"Sounds like a good time. See you then."

On the laptop I read the pastor's notes, paeans to a troubled life made whole by the bright presence of our lord almighty. Terrance Stanton was careful to couch his words where his sexual addictions were concerned, but admitted to craving the lustful life, one that threatened his family and marriage, even his well-being. All of it written in his own peculiar handwriting. Cursive.

"I'd like you to look at this," I said to Agnes, turning the laptop in her direction.

She snorted. "Why do I need to read this stuff?"

"Humor me," I said.

"Only if you fuck me," she countered.

I crossed my arms. "It's like that, is it?"

Agnes crossed her arms. "It's like that."

That made me smile. "Alright. But first you have to look at the writing. Remember the love letters?" Agnes nodded, her eyes growing wider. "Think it's the same writer?"

Her curiosity piqued; she drew closer to the screen. "Could be," she said, after a minute of reading. "Some of the same whininess." Agnes looked over the screen at me. "He and who?"

"Aisha," I said.

"Sterling's babe?"

I laughed at that. "Yeah, Sterling's babe."

Agnes closed the laptop and unbuttoned her blouse. "It's time, Buttman."

I feigned ignorance. "Time?"

She shook her finger. "To pleasure me. Let's go!"

I did as I was told.

• • • • •

Detective Gallegos did indeed want to see me. I told her I'd be at my office.

The letters were where I left them, in the fancy credenza that matched the desk and the coffee tables Natalya said I needed to look the part of a wealthy philanthropist. On my desk laptop, I compared them to the notes on the Sunlight Ministries website. I didn't hear the two Russians come in. They made their presence known by sauntering into my office.

"Where's Natalya?"

They were the big stocky types you'd associate with gangsters. Neither was particularly well-dressed; one wearing an ill-fitted suit, too small, and the other in what was a Russian riff on Hip-hop style; low slung pants, a black tee shirt, and oversized sneakers.

I sat back. "She not here."

The one in the suit leaned over the desk. "Where is she?"

I pulled the 45 from my pocket and pointed it at his head. The tough stood back. "Who are you, and who do you represent? Can't be Big Mike, he's dead."

"Our business is with Natalya," he said.

"To do what? Kidnap her? Kill her?"

The gangster smiled. "Just talk."

I smiled back. "Let me guess? You want to know who set up Big Mike? Well, gentlemen, she didn't have anything to do with that. Natalya went because Big Mike asked her to. She just wanted him to leave her alone, to get him off her back. Your quarrel isn't with her."

"Maybe we decide for ourself," he said.

"And maybe you don't. Anything else?" As I said this, providence, in the guise of Detective Gallegos, walked in.

"Are we having a problem here?" she asked.

"No, these two were looking for Natalya Constantinescu for the purposes of discussion. I personally don't believe that given what happened here recently, but who knows? Would the two of you like to talk it over with the detective?" Detective Gallegos produced her badge. The goon in the ill-fitted suit shook his head. "You didn't say who you're working for?"

The goon produced a thin smile. "You already know."

I put the 45 on the desk. "Then have a good day, gentlemen."

We watched them leave, aided by Isaac, having just arrived, who held the door for them.

"Should I ask?" he said.

"Just more of the usual," I answered.

It was going to be that kind of day.

39

"Have a seat, Detective."

Isaac, still watching, asked, "Do you need me to be a part of this?"

"No," I said. "You can close the door."

Detective Gallegos sat down once the door was closed. "Any news, Mr. Buttman?"

I smiled at the formality. "I don't suppose I can get you to call me Monk?"

"No," she said.

"Probably for the best. Anything new on your end?" I asked.

The detective nodded towards the door. "Perhaps I should ask about those two who just left, but then I was forewarned about you, remember?"

"All in a day in the life. Do you remember Big Mike Kovalenko?" I took the detective's sly smile as a yes. "Natalya was the object of his sexual obsession. He's dead, you know. Killed in Bangkok. Maybe it had something to do with that."

"Did you have something to do with that, Mr. Buttman?" A wider smile.

"Nope," I said, "not my thing. So, what's new?"

The notebook came out. "Did you speak with your brother?"

"Yep. He hemmed and hawed and promised he'd be in town this week. Said everything was proceeding nicely in his efforts to put all this unpleasantness behind him." I watched as Gallegos noted that. "I know there's more going on, that he's thinking I'm simply going through the motions because his mother asked me to. There are other things—"

"Such as?"

It occurred to me that I hadn't given the detective the whole story. "Do you know where I got the keys for Ms. Blakely's home and office?" I didn't wait for an answer. "Aisha Diamond. You know it was her that Ms. Blakely was supposed to meet the night she was murdered?"

"Yes," the Detective said.

"Were you a part of the search through Ms. Blakely's effects?"

"No," she answered. "I came in after that."

I passed the letters to her. "I found these at Ms. Blakely's home. Since I knew the police had been there and had not taken them, I assumed they, you, did not deem them important. But they are. And maybe they weren't there when the apartment was first searched." Gallegos picked up one of the letters. "I believe they were written by Terrance Stanton to Aisha Diamond, and it's possible that Ms. Diamond planted them in Ms. Blakely's home after the police were there for her own purposes."

Detective Gallegos looked over the letters. "What makes you think these came from Terrance Stanton? They're unsigned."

I turned my laptop towards her. "Compare them to these hand-written notes on the church's website supposedly written by Stanton." I waited as the detective did. After a few minutes, she looked over at me. "They're very similar, aren't they?"

"They are," she said, setting the letter down. I took the letter back. "Those might be evidence, Mr. Buttman."

"Yes," I said, "they might be. Tell you what, I'll give you this one, while I hold the others. That way, you have at least one in case something happens to these." I passed a letter back to her.

"And what do you think will happen to those?" she asked.

I sat back. "I expect them to be used as blackmail."

Detective Gallegos folded the letter and put it in her pocket. "And your brother and Ms. Diamond?"

That made me smile. "Yes, what of my brother and his lover? I think he's either being played, or is up to his neck in this...he and Aisha. You think that, too, don't you, Detective?"

Her turn to sit back. "I do."

"You didn't say what was new on your end?"

The detective stood. "Having determined their identities, we've confirmed certain relational connections between the victims and both Here We Gather for Love and Sunlight Ministries. Beyond that, I don't have anything new."

I got up. "If you did, would you share that?"

"I don't know," she said.

I walked her to the door.

Isaac came in after the detective had left. "Should I ask?"

I laughed. "That's my question."

"What's that mean?" He seemed genuinely surprised.

"Sit." He stood for a moment before sitting. "What's Sterling up to? And before you blow this off, be aware that I saw the two of you talking, and I know more than Sterling thinks I do." I pulled two glasses from the credenza.

"Maybe it was just the stuff we usually talk about; the farm, Moses, the things we've talked about for years," he said, believing it about as much as I did.

"In any other situation, I wouldn't say anything for those very reasons." I pulled out the bottle of whiskey. "And I'm not saying *you're* up to anything, but I know that Sterling is. And because this involves four murders and his girlfriend, who he is still seeing...did he admit that?" I poured two fingers into the glasses and handed one to him.

"It's a little early for that, isn't it?"

"It's long past early, my friend. Did he?"

He took a drink. "Yeah."

I took a drink as well. "Has he tried to make you understand that this isn't what you think it is? That he knows what he's doing. That I don't know what I'm talking about. That I don't know him and what he's going through, but you..." I set my glass down... "his brother, who grew up with him and knows him, you would understand."

Isaac took another drink. "Yeah."

"Do you believe what he told you?"

Isaac stared at his glass before looking up at me. "No." He set his glass on the desk. "I'm not exactly a babe in the woods when it comes to playing people; that's probably why I like this job. But even I have a sense of what I can pull off and what's going to blow up in my face—"

"But Sterling?"

"He says they've got it all worked out."

"Did he say what?"

Isaac shook his head. "Not directly. But he did say that the people who screwed Aisha over were going to pay, and he was going to help her."

I picked up the glass, thought about downing it all in one gulp before placing it back on the desk. "I don't suppose he mentioned whether Aisha killed Orestra Blakely because she figured out what was going on?"

"What is going on?" he asked.

"Blackmail and murder," I said.

•   •   •   •   •

I waited for the calls, knowing I'd be a part of it. I gave Isaac the basic facts about Aisha and her relationships with Stanton and Flavius. It was the stuff of bad B-movies, I thought, but this was Hollywood, so why was I surprised? The call I didn't expect was from Mr. Jones.

"Got some time?" he asked.

"Always," I said.

"Manifesto? Tomorrow noon?"

I assured him I'd be there. I didn't ask what he wanted to talk about.

That was answered by Ms. Lagenfelder. "We have the information on Ms. Blakely's estate, Mr. Buttman. While there is no will on record, the estate is in good shape as far as its legal documents are concerned."

I said I'd pick them up the next day.

I didn't like waiting around, but I knew there'd be more. A text to Orinda Blakely, letting her know I had Orestra's journals and papers for her, killed a couple of minutes. I stood at the window, watching the world go by on the streets below. It was strange being in the office by myself. Natalya was still in New York with Xavier, Isaac had his own work to do; a planned trip to the national convention of The American Legion, and Emily was fuming up north, getting ready to travel to Philly to spend time with her father's family. That made me think of the time she snuck down to Virginia. Staring at the people below, I half-expected the Russian goons to come back, maybe work me over. Instead, I was greeted by a UPS guy with a package.

Fairfax had come through.

In the bland folder was a picture of an unsmiling young man and a file report on his methods. Aaron Alan Sobeski was what I thought he'd be. Very careful. I locked the folder in the desk with the love letters.

Benny was at his desk in the lobby. "Do you know if Ronnie's around?" I asked.

"Ronnie runs around this time of day," he said. "Might be around, might not. Want me to look?"

"No, I'll check myself."

"Maybe I should go with you. Keep an eye out for our Russian visitors from earlier." Fortunately, he was serious.

"Couldn't hurt."

Ronnie packed light. He wasn't one of those folks you'd see pushing a grocery cart. Didn't have a car. The Army taught him how to stay lean and while he had his favorite spots around this part of town; he kept moving, less he be given the proverbial bum's rush. I knew he had a corner in the garage he liked to use. It was secluded and afforded a view of his surroundings in case anyone was coming up on him. It was also why the tenants tolerated his being in the garage; he didn't leave a mess.

Most of the time.

He was a bloody mess. He'd been hit more than once, and dragged a fair distance from where he was attacked. On the plus side, he was still breathing. The fire department and the police arrived within ten minutes. I went to where I knew he liked to sleep, and gathered up his pack and bag, all he possessed in this world. I asked Benny to store the bag and pack. He reluctantly returned to his desk. I followed the ambulance to the ER. The woman at the admitting desk seemed surprised that a guy in a nice suit would have any interest in a beaten homeless man. The police had a few questions, but it all felt very pro forma. In the waiting room, I called Durant on the burner phone he gave me. Asked if it was possible to set up a meeting with Zosima.

"Anything's possible, but probably unlikely," he said.

Exactly. Who, after all, was I? "Tell his people it's about Sobeski. Better yet, can you run this through Mr. Tsarnaev? Tell him I'm ready to talk in exchange for the release of Josef Rostikov and his family. He knows what it's about."

"Will you tell me what it's about?"

Will I? "I will, but not over the phone. I have to swing by tomorrow to pick up some documents. Will you have any time, then?"

"Till then," he said.

I let Agnes know what was going on, and that I might be home late. "Should I be worried?"

"No more than usual," I said.

The doctor came out after an hour. Ronnie had been run through the X-ray machine and the CT-Scan. "Mr. Delmar has a nasty cut and a concussion, but, fortunately, there were no fractures. We'll need to monitor him for a day. At that point, he'll probably be released."

I thanked the doctor. Ronnie was lying on the stretcher, doped up, but he seemed reasonably coherent. We had a few minutes before he'd be taken to his room for the night.

A wan smile crossed his face. "I messed up, Monk."

"How so?"

"Got too close. Thought I'd act like they were homeless, too. Spooked 'em though. Next thing I know I'm here." He put his hand to the bandage on his head. "How long?"

"If it all goes well tomorrow."

He looked around the room and squinted. "Too bright. Maybe a day. Just a day."

"Just a day," I repeated. "Our black Russian?"

"Yeah," he said, as the transport team arrived. "My stuff?"

"We have it. You can pick it up when you get out tomorrow."

He reached out for my hand. "Thanks, Monk." We shook hands before they wheeled him off.

40

The call I had been waiting for came after I returned to the office. Flavius.

"I hear you have something I might find interesting," they said. "Love letters."

"Who told you that?" Never hurts to ask.

"Little bird."

"Did the little bird say anything else? Who the letters were from? Who they were to?" I asked.

"Why our dear concerned friend, Pastor Terry," Flavius purred.

"And why, if I have any love letters written by Terrance Stanton, would I give them to you?"

"We both know why," they said.

Do we? "Maybe we start with one," I said.

"I'm home all day." I imagine so.

Isaac came into the office after I ended the call. "I heard Ronnie got jumped."

"I heard that, too. I also heard from Flavius…"

"What'd he, I mean they, want?"

"The means to blackmail Pastor Terry," I said. "Be sure to let Sterling know if he asks."

Isaac sat down. "And you think he will?"

I watched Isaac process that. "I wouldn't be surprised."

"Maybe I should stick around, skip the Legion conference," he said.

"No, that's ok. We've still got foundation business to deal with."

"You're sure?"

I admired his concern. "I'm sure."

"Alright." He stood. "I'll be back Sunday night."

I walked him to the lobby of the building, Benny mindful at his desk. I was ready to head home. As I was walking to my car, Don stopped me. My mind was elsewhere, and it took me a minute to put two and two together.

"Got a minute?" he asked.

Theme of the day. "There's a bar just around the corner," I said. "We can talk there." He nodded, and we made our way to the bar and a booth at the far end. "What's on your mind?"

"MaryAnn," he answered.

"I figured that. Anything in particular?" I ordered a rum and coke from the tattooed bartender; Don ordered a pilsner.

"May I speak freely?"

I considered saying no. "Sure."

The bartender set down the drinks. I took in a generous portion of the highball. Don did the same with his beer. "I want you to know that my feelings for MaryAnn are genuine," he started, "and I've come to really enjoy being with her. And as Agnes is good friends with MaryAnn, and I know how women like to confide in each other, I know it's possible that certain aspects of our relationship have been brought up."

I should have said no. "Every relationship has issues, Don. If Agnes has shared anything, it was more about how things are going between the two of you, how she feels about you, stuff like that."

"I appreciate that. And I appreciate your reluctance to repeat what you've heard, but I know that MaryAnn has shared certain aspects of our...of the physical aspects of our relationship. I know that her needs and desires do not match mine, and I know that this can be what causes relationships to end." He took a handful of peanuts from the basket in front of us. "I don't want that."

I watched as he played with his glass. "How does that—"

"I want MaryAnn to be happy. I want her to feel she's enjoying life..." He finished his beer. "What I want to say is that I'm ok with how she is conducting her affairs. Strange as it may sound, it doesn't really bother me. She's been very careful not to hurt my feelings, and she's been discreet." He smiled at that and ordered another pilsner. "I'm not interested in the particulars, only that she's happy and we have our time together."

"Have you told her that?" I finished my drink.

"I have."

"Then why tell me?"

Don waved to the bartender to bring me another. "Because I don't want you and Agnes to worry." The bartender brought our drinks over. Don raised his. "Do we have an understanding, Monk?"

I raised mine. "I believe we do."

"Life is too short." He turned to the large screen TV across from us. "You like baseball, Monk?" The East Coast games were coming on. The Red Sox versus the Yankees.

"Yes, I do."

"Red Sox fan?"

"Not particularly," I said. "I tend to root for teams who have never won a championship, so I root for the Rays."

Don smiled and shook his head. "It's your money."

·   ·   ·   ·   ·

Agnes was waiting. The sun had long since faded in the west, and the house was dark, save for the porch light and the light in the kitchen above the stove. I found her in the backyard, nursing a glass of wine. Having had four drinks over the course of the evening, I saw no reason to have more. Instead, I poured myself a glass of iced tea. Agnes noticed as I sat down next to her.

"Hungry?" I asked.

"Fortunately, the kids took pity on me and let me eat dinner with them," she said.

"You are indeed fortunate."

"And you, Sunshine? What have you been up to this fine day?"

"Me?" I knew she was making fun of me.

"You!"

"I was at a bar near the office watching baseball with Don. And since we were hungry, we had dinner too." Wait for it...

"And you didn't have time to call?"

"Yeah, I probably did, but we got into a gentlemanly argument over the Red Sox and Yankees and lost track of time. Sorry." I leaned in and kissed her.

"So, what else did you and Don talk about?"

"Well, if I understood the gist of it, he's ok with our pleasuring MaryAnn so long as we continue to be discreet and not horn in on his time with her. But you already knew that, didn't you?"

Agnes shrugged and said, "Maybe."

"Uh-huh." I stretched out my legs. "It was really just to let me know, since I was the one who was uncomfortable with the idea of fucking another guy's squeeze."

"Is that all we are to you?" she huffed.

I shrugged. "Mostly."

Agnes rolled her eyes. "What else did you do today? The office is closed, right?" I nodded. "I can't see you sitting in an empty office all day."

"Well, Isaac was there for a while. Detective Gallegos stopped by, as did a couple of Russian goons. Ronnie got beat up; had to go to the ER. Flavius called saying he knew about the love letters and wanted them to, I assume, blackmail Pastor Terry. Then I ran into Don, who was told I'd be there, I assume by you, and I already told you what we talked about." I took a deep theatrical breath. "And that's been my day so far."

"What did Detective Gallegos want?"

"An update."

"And the goons?"

"They wanted to talk to Natalya."

"Just talk?"

"Just talk is what they told me," I said.

"Who beat up Ronnie? Another homeless guy?"

"Nope. It was our black Russian, and I think a confederate."

"Really? And how did Flavius know about the love letters?"

"Aisha," I said. "She's driving all of this. I saw Isaac talking with Sterling at the farm, and he admitted that Sterling told him he is still seeing her and helping her get revenge on her former lover. At least that's what I think. Oh, and I talked to Marsyas Durant about setting up a meeting with this Zosima to get Josef out of Russia."

She tapped her wineglass against my glass of tea. "You have been busy."

"Oh, and I'm meeting Jones at the Manifesto tomorrow."

She was finally surprised. "Why?"

"Orestra Blakely," I said.

•   •   •   •   •

Agnes was up before me. "Up and at 'em, Buttman! Places to go; people to see!"

"Have fun," I said, as I pulled the covers over my head.

"Nice try." She pulled the covers back off me. "And I'm hungry."

I shook my head. "You're always hungry."

She grinned and crossed her arms. "And it's your job to see I don't get fat eating crap!"

Having gotten up, dressed, and having fed my in-detective-mode wife, I was hustled into the 68 Dodge Dart that Bernie had to fix after the fiasco in the desert with the now dead goons on the motorbikes. The first stop was the foundation, followed by Aeschylus and Associates.

As we were waiting on the elevator, I thought out loud, "I wonder if they have good divorce attorneys here?"

Agnes elbowed me in the ribs. "Give it up, Sunshine. It ain't gonna happen."

Ms. Lagenfelder greeted us and handed me the documents detailing Ms. Blakely's estate. "Is the expectation that we will be handling this?"

"I don't know," I said. "I'll let you know if we do."

"Then I'll let Mr. Durant know you're here," she said.

Agnes gave me the queer eye, "Why are we seeing Mr. Durant, Monk?"

"I told you, remember? To confess," I said. "Both of us."

Durant greeted us, and after we sat down and were given cups of excellent coffee, I told him of our adventures with Aaron Alan Sobeski at our estate along the shores of lake Michigan. He listened intently, and didn't seem particularly disturbed about our killing our would-be killers. I detailed Manaforte's part in it, at least the part I knew, and the subsequent interest of intelligence agents and Russian oligarchs. Agnes added her two-cent with her usual hard-boiled private dick tude.

Durant sat back, working our story over.

"There's more," I said. I set out the folder Fairfax had given me. Durant opened it and examined the picture and report. "That's my bargaining chip."

"A picture and report on a dead man?" Agnes asked.

I gave her the picture. After a minute, she gave it back. "Understand now?"

She took my hand. "This is some serious shit, Sunshine."

Durant smiled at that. "Then the parameters have changed."

"Have you spoken to Mr. Tsarnaev?" I asked.

"This morning," he said.

"And did he, in confidence, explain why the Russians are so concerned?"

"Concerned about what?" Agnes asked.

"That they're being pulled into a situation that might, in certain quarters, be construed as an act of war," I said. "That they were a part of the attack on the president."

"And that Aaron Alan Sobeski, a former U.S. intelligence operative, known to be working for the Russian mafia, was part of it," Durant added.

"But how can that be? Aaron Alan Sobeski is dead. His neck broken in a fall and his body obliterated when the boat he was put in exploded." I finished my coffee. "Think they'll go for it?" I asked Durant.

"I think they would like to hear it from the horse's mouth. I'll have to pass some of this on to Tsarnaev. He'll need it if he's to persuade Mr. Dimitriev of our terms." He looked at the two of us. "You're both to be at this meeting if it can be arranged?"

"Yes," I said.

"And are you aware that it won't be held in the U.S. or any of its territories? Most likely off the coast of Mexico. You're comfortable with that?"

"Are you going to be there?" Agnes asked Durant.

"I think it's only appropriate," he said with a smile.

41

Mr. Jones was waiting for us at the Manifesto. I expected that. Orinda Blakely was with him, along with her sisters, Maybelle and Doris. That was more of a surprise, but not totally unexpected. They rose as we approached the table. I set the envelope and the journals on the table. Anna and the irrepressible Pluto came over with lunch.

"I asked what was new," Jones said. "It sounded good, so..." he spread out his hands.

We sat down to lunch.

Orville introduced Orestra's sisters to Agnes, and we made small talk about this and that, mostly focusing on the Manifesto, while we ate our lunch. When we were done, Agnes picked up the plates as an excuse to talk to her daughter. As she left, I gestured towards the envelope.

"These are all the legal documents associated with Orestra's estate. I didn't know if you had them. My apologies if you do."

"No need to apologize, Mr. Buttman," Maybelle said. "We appreciate the effort, but from this point, we can take care of things."

"I assumed as much." I set the keys on the table that Aisha had taken and passed on to me. "These are yours as well."

"Where did you get these?" Doris asked.

"Indirectly from a woman named Aisha Diamond. How she got them, I don't know. But I do know she's involved in O's death." I pulled Orville's letter from my pocket. "I also came across this. It's addressed to you." I handed it to him.

He looked at the letter and then at me. "Did you read this?" That made me smile, to which he said, "What?"

"Marsyas Durant asked me the same thing after I came across a letter Judith had written to him. My answer's the same. I read only so far as to determine who it was addressed to. In this case, Orv was at the top. That's all I needed to know. I didn't read it."

The three sisters looked at the letter in Orville's hand. Maybelle tapped Orinda's arm, and the three of them got up from their chairs. "Thanks again for this, Mr. Buttman." She put her hand on Orville's shoulder. I watched as they picked up Orestra's journals, the envelope, and left. Orville continued to stare at the letter. Agnes returned to the table with three frothy drinks.

"Here," she said, setting them down, "they're supposed to keep us young." Jones glanced at his. "How are you doing, Orv?"

"I don't know," he said, turning the letter over in his hands. "Did you read O's journals?"

I took a sip of the frothy drink. It was awful. "I did. I wanted to see if there was anything in there about what she was doing before she was killed."

"And?" He looked up.

"She was working on the disappearance of three black transwomen, who I subsequently learned from Detective Gallegos were murdered. Aisha Diamond knew them, too. They were supposed to meet the night O was killed."

Agnes grimaced after taking a drink. "They?"

"Aisha and O," I said.

Jones sniffed his drink. "You think this Aisha killed O?"

"I don't know. Maybe. Or she was the target and sent O in her place. Since then, Aisha has gone missing. I know my idiot brother is involved, though he's denied that to me," I said.

"Is that a hunch, Sunshine?" Agnes being cute.

"No, dollface, he admitted it to Isaac, remember? Told him that he's helping Aisha get revenge on her former lover. Pastor Terry."

Mr. Jones looked at us, his eyes wide, unbelieving. "The Sunlight Ministries pastor?"

"Surprised?"

"Yeah," he said. "Goddamn."

Agnes pushed her drink away. "You know him?"

Jones nodded. "Met him at a conference through the church." He shook his head. "Ain't anybody straight-up anymore?"

"It's a big world," I said, "good and bad. Speaking of which, I'm working on a deal to get Josef and his family out of Russia."

Jones tried to smile at that. "I heard that…"

"Anton?"

"Yeah." He put the letter in his pocket. "You need me to be there?"

"Shouldn't. We'll have Marsyas Durant with us," I said.

"We?" He trained his eyes on Agnes.

"Yep, I'm going to the party too," Agnes admitted.

"And Marsyas Durant…" Jones got up. "Well, I got to get back to work. I'll be in touch. Normally, I'd say take care, but with you two…" He smiled, sighed, and was out the door.

Anna came over, noted the frothy drinks were unconsumed, and laughed at our sour expressions. "Not to your liking?"

"Sorry, but they're terrible," Agnes said.

"To each their own," she said, the big grin still there as she went back to work.

•　　•　　•　　•　　•

"Interesting," was Bernie's comment when I updated him on all the plans afoot. He was less concerned with Aisha Diamond and Sterling than with the circling drain of Aaron Alan Sobeski. I let Bernie go through the folder Fairfax had sent. I wondered if Fairfax would show before any meeting was set up. "You think it was wise to let Durant in on all of this?"

"Would you be able to set up a meeting with this Zosima, though Durant used the name Dimitriev?" I asked.

"Piotr Dimitriev, known in certain circles as Zosima. A name he acquired after the Soviet Union broke up. No, I wouldn't be able to set up any meetings with him, and if you asked me who could, I'd probably recommend Durant." He smiled at that. "My concern is how safe any of this is, and once the information on what happened to Sobeski gets out, what that might mean for your well-being."

Agnes leaned in. "Meaning?"

"It's highly likely, given Fairfax's involvement, that there are individuals way up the intelligence chain who are aware of this, even in a deep background position. And if what you're intimating is true, it's possible that you may need to be sequestered or…to some, eliminated."

"Try number two, eh?" Agnes, the private dick, was on the job.

"Exactly."

"Any advice?" It was my turn.

"Have a credible exit plan for this meeting. And let me, Art, Mr. Jones, know when and where the meeting's going to be," he said. "Oh," he reached for a folder on his desk. "Here are Terrance Stanton's meeting schedules going back four years. That's when they upgraded the church's scheduling program."

"Thanks."

The private dick chimed in, "What do you expect to find in there, Buttman?"

"The answer to the question of who killed who," I said.

·   ·   ·   ·   ·

"Are you going to tell me?" Agnes asked on the drive home.

"First, let's see if there's anything there," I answered, pointing to the folder Bernie had given us.

I put in a call to Detective Gallegos, asking for the dates when the three women Orestra was looking for were killed. "What do you want with that?" she said.

"I'll let you know if I find anything," I said. "Don't want to waste your time if it's nothing." The second call I made was to Flavius. "I'll have the letter for you in two days."

"I'll expect you to be true to your word, Monk," they said.

"I imagine so."

The question now was when I'd hear from Pastor Terry. Part of the answer came in the form of Sterling Bohrman. A text. *I'm here in LA. Will you go with me to the church?*

A chump is always a chump; both of us.

Sure, I texted back.

The beauty of bureaucracy is in the prosaic, scheduling being among the most mundane. Here or there at this place and time; who came calling. And the beauty of our digital revolution? No more working through the scribblings of overworked secretaries and underlings. All in easily readable black and white, or in the case of modern scheduling programs, color coordinated blocks. The schedule and notes Bernie gave me showed that Pastor Terry took a personal interest in those struggling with gender identity. LaToya Richards, Samantha Bisharin, and Janisha Champlain, the three missing and now murdered women, had all been given a moment of Pastor Terry's time.

All three disappeared shortly after their meeting.

"Here's is your answer," I said to Agnes.

"It's a good thing Sterling isn't seeing his girlfriend like he said, isn't it?" Agnes snarked.

"Yes, it is," I agreed.

I sent the information along to Detective Gallegos. She wanted to know how I knew this. "Little bird," I said, recommending she have the schedules subjected to a warrant.

"I'll take it into consideration," she said. "And this meeting you and your brother are attending?"

"I'll let you know."

The meeting was at four in the afternoon. In the meantime, I had Jacob patrol. His cranky mother had work to do, and Zach and Lizzy demanded pool time.

"You need to be nicer to your mother," I told him. Jacob simply grinned and cooed as I held him. Agnes, who was in the seat beside me, watching this, shook her head. "I know, I know, it isn't normal."

How was any of this normal?

·   ·   ·   ·   ·

Sterling was waiting in the church's extensive parking lot. "Thanks for doing this."

I thought about slapping his stupid ass. "Sure."

I was in a foul mood. I didn't want to leave the kids or my mirthful wife, who decided to make a series of aspersions on what I assumed would be a less that delightful afternoon.

"See if they have a class on improving your love life through prayer," she laughed.

"Nice," I said, as I was leaving. "I believe it starts by embracing the complementarian belief of obeying your husband."

"What?"

My turn to laugh. "Look it up."

Vanessa, the cheery woman at the front desk of Sunlight Ministries, called Vern. As we were waiting, I mentioned the hand-written letters on the website, and how they were a nice personal touch by Pastor Terry.

"Such nice cursive," I said. "You don't see that much anymore, particularly with men."

Vanessa smiled and shook her head. "Oh, Pastor Terry didn't write those."

"I thought they were his letters?"

"They're his, but just between you and me, Pastor Terry's hand-writing isn't very good."

Before I could ask who did, Vern arrived, happy as ever, and led us to our appointment with the therapist. The therapist, a man named Jordan; I thought it best not to mention that he had the same name as my wife's dead abuser, went over how the therapy worked. In the hour we were with him, there was a lot of prayer, and questions, with the requisite answers by Jordan, about the depth of our faith, and how a personal relationship with our Lord and Savior was the means to that end, as well as ending a desire to blow a transwoman. I didn't say that out loud either. Sterling played his part to the hilt, with contrition, and a desire to find his spot on the right side of the Lord.

Given my mood, I said little other than "Amen," at the end of each prayer.

"I think this is going well, Jordan," Sterling said, at the end of the session.

"I think so, too, Sterling. I look forward to seeing you next week," Jordan answered. "God be praised."

"God be praised," Sterling repeated.

I had no comment.

On the way out, Pastor Terry asked if I had a minute...

But only me.

42

I followed him to his office. Sunny, as always. I sat down on a big couch, just out of the sun's reach. Pastor Terry stood in the light, a halo effect rendering him a golden child blessed by the Lord.

"I understand you have some letters that belong to me," he said.

The circle was now complete. "Little bird?"

Sadly, the pastor didn't get the reference. "I don't appreciate the humor, *Mr. Buttman.*"

"And I don't appreciate murder, *Mr. Stanton,* so save the sanctimony for the sermon." My mood was no better now than it had been with Jordan. The pastor smartly held his tongue. "Yes, it's true that I am in possession of a series of unsigned letters, letters written by a conflicted individual to his trans lover. Are you saying they are yours, that you wrote them?"

Pastor Terry's bravado faded. "I didn't say that."

My anger did not. "Then how can they possibly belong to you?"

Ironically, the sun was suddenly obscured by a passing cloud, rendering the god-like pastor human. "The letters...belong to a member of our church family. If you've read them, you know how conflicted this individual was. These are personal issues, Monk, that should be...dealt with outside the harsh light of our current media circus environment. I apologize for the manner of my speaking to you. It's only through a desire to protect this individual—"

"Four women have been murdered. At least three of them have connections to Sunlight Ministries—"

"And that perennial devil, Berkley Fellows," he said.

To which I answered, "They called themselves Flavius now," but then he knew that already.

"I'm not particularly interested in what he calls himself now. I only know he has made it his business to persecute the church for its standing on his deviancies, and no doubt he, too, is interested in getting those letters." The pastor rubbed his hands together. "I don't want that to happen."

Of that, I was sure. "How would he know who the letters were written by?"

"Your little bird," he answered.

"No, Pastor Terry, *our* little bird. But when I asked you before, you said you didn't know her. But I didn't believe you then any more than I believe you now." I stared at him and realized I wanted to go home very badly. I got up and headed for the door.

"Monk, wait. The letters—"

"What of them?"

"Don't let them…"

I turned to the pastor. "Don't let them what? Follow it through? You don't need to pretend in front of me. I think you're fully aware of the people involved in this…and their motives. The mistake was in killing Orestra Blakely. That pulled me in. The circle, your and Aisha's Diamond's circle, is complete… Almost—"

Pastor Terry stepped toward me. "What do you mean, almost?"

"Time and place," I said. "But you know that, too."

He turned to look up at the beautiful stained glass above him. "People make mistakes, Monk. That shouldn't define them for the rest of their lives."

It was a nice window. Our loving savior, his hands held out to forgive a wayward soul. "I've never doubted that. But then I'm not the one you need to convince. God be praised."

I don't remember if he said anything in reply.

Sterling was waiting by his car. "What did Pastor Terry want?"

That made me smile. "The letters, of course."

"What letters?" Yeah, stick to the script.

"The letters we're delivering to Flavius the day after tomorrow. You know." I patted him on the shoulder. "I sure hope the two of you know what you're doing."

I don't remember if he said anything, either.

.   .   .   .   .

I filled in Agnes once I got home. The kids had been retrieved, so there was no balm for me to use to get the sick taste of this out of my mouth. To add to the weirdness of the day, Agnes made me dinner. A chicken and broccoli stir-fry.

"Just don't expect this to become a regular habit," she said, a sly grin on her face.

I raised my glass of Riesling. "Heaven forfend."

She raised her glass to mine. "That better mean what I think it does, Sunshine."

I shrugged and said, "I promise nothing."

After dinner, I sat out in the backyard, enjoying the drone of the neighbor's TV. The fate of the letters could wait till the next day...

...Which came way too quickly.

.   .   .   .   .

"Why don't we stay at my fancy place, take the kids? It's probably safer there." We were sitting at the kitchen table drinking our coffee. I had things to do.

Agnes shrugged.

Rebekah was happy to get a break, though she thought she'd come, too. "I can work in the library." Her excuse.

With the rabble collected, we made for the fancy place and a day by the pool. Once there, I got organized for what was going to be an interesting following day. I called Macklgrew about the Forester-

Keltner Homestead, expecting him to be unenthusiastic, but he was quite the opposite.

"Land is almost always an excellent investment outside of desert scrub in the middle of nowhere. We'll get it going," he said. Great, more stuff to take care of.

Sterling was next. I invited him over for dinner. He reluctantly agreed.

As the kids splashed and yelled, I went through the letters one last time. There were eleven, not counting the one I'd given to Detective Gallegos. The more I read them, the more I found them formulaic; the same pleas repeated over and over, as if a sad sort of interpersonal game. Love itself was expressed only as a last resort; desire was the overriding theme. Want. Need. I put them aside.

The other matter was Sobeski. I reread his file. Also bland. Redundant. Maybe that's why he left. Impulsively, I called Art. He laughed as he answered.

"I was just going to call," he said. "What's up?"

"Curious about the gossip. But also, I was given a file on Aaron Alan. Most of it is routine did this, did that, nothing terribly intriguing other than a comment on a propensity to add his own particular mark on an action as a subtle signature. I assume that's what got him in trouble. True?"

"The opposite," Art answered. "Sobeski left of his own accord. Naturally, there is no official stated reason for his departure, and while he later began working in Eastern Europe, his activities were such that as long as it didn't move into the realm of government sanctioned action, he was monitored, but that was the extent of it. The gossips told me his leaving was more his tiring of the sanctimonious justifications for what he did, but most of that is conjecture. As far as I could find out, no one who knew him here has had any contact with him since he left. He's become a ghost. A name tied to some fairly interesting terminations, but none of it verified. I think that's what's driving this interest."

"Then what? The level of the termination?"

"No," Art chuckled. "The company."

"The Russians?"

"And others. There are aspects of any organization, once it reaches a certain size, that any competent intelligence service can monitor. But some things, like actions, physical actions, can be a problem if the country or location, or business for that matter, is difficult to penetrate. The concern, the fear, is whether Sobeski has turned his knowledge of certain aspects of our operations over. Your file did note that he started out in the Secret Service, did it not?"

I look through the file. "It's not here."

"Who gave you the file?"

"Fairfax."

"And the purpose of your having the file?" Ah, Art's mirthful tone.

"I'm trying to set up a meeting with Piotr Dimitriev. A man I know is stuck in Russia and I'm trying to get him out. I know a few things about Sobeski that the file has corroborated. I was going to use that knowledge as a bargaining chip," I said.

"And your contact, if you're willing to say..."

"Boris Tsarnaev through Marsyas Durant."

"Yes, I can see that," he said. "And it jibes with why I was planning to call—"

"To let me know that it's not a secret?" Time for my mirthful tone.

"Yes. Then you expected that?"

"I'm counting on it," I said. "My proverbial life jacket."

"Let's hope so. Keep in touch...and be very careful, Monk."

I promised I would.

Evening came along with Sterling for dinner. I made lasagna. Sterling brought the wine. We made small talk, which was mostly on the entertainment business, once Fidel showed up. After dinner, we sat by the pool watching the sun take its leisurely stroll to the west. The adults were tired, enjoying the rare moment of quiet after the kids had conked out.

"You're always welcome to stay here," I said.

"No, it's ok," he said. "I already have a room paid for. Business."

I told Sterling I'd pick him up at one the next day. He took that as his cue to head out. I walked him to the door. "Till then," I said, watching his expression.

"Till then," he said, watching mine.

. . . . .

Morning came quickly. Agnes wanted to go along, but I said no. "Someone has to watch the kids."

She stood there; her arm crossed. "Nice try, Buttman."

"I'll think of a better excuse when I get back," I said, after I kissed her.

"Uh-huh."

Sterling was waiting outside his hotel. He said nothing as he got in. It wasn't far to Flavius' house. The neighborhood was quiet, save for a squawking bird flying between two trees. There was no response when I knocked. No one to answer the door like the last time. I knew we were expected. I opened the door and called out their name. Nothing. Sterling trailed behind me as I wandered through the house. We found Flavius and Pastor Terry in the study. Flavius was in his chair behind the desk, face contorted and blue. His eyes rolled up in his head, and a nasty red welt cut into his neck. I put my fingers to his throat. No pulse.

Sterling stood there; the color gone from his face. His wide eyes were moving between the strangled Flavius and the subdued Pastor Terry sitting in one of the purple velvet chairs.

"Stay here," I told him. "I'll be right back."

Gisele was by the pool, her head crushed in. Blood pooled around it, a crimson halo. I sent a text to Gallegos.

The rest of the house was empty.

When I returned to the study, Pastor Terry was still in the velvet chair, his head down. Sterling was by the window, his hands clutching at the garrote around his neck. Vern was behind him.

Smiling.

43

"I need those letters, Monk," the pastor whispered.

I shook my head. "What the three of you need is a good defense attorney." To Vern, I said, "Let him go."

Vern Norlin kept smiling. The garrote was just tight enough to put the fear of God in Sterling, but I could see he was still able to breathe. "The letters, Mr. Buttman. We want the letters."

"Which one of you did Aisha call?" I asked.

"The letters or I'll kill your brother." He tugged at the garrote, a thick black wire, causing Sterling to flinch.

"You're not going to kill anyone. Who did she call?" I took out my phone.

Norlin tugged at the garrote again. "Put the phone down."

"Who?" I asked again.

"She called me," Pastor Terry admitted. "She said Fellows would have the letters."

"I imagined she did. Probably enjoyed the thought of the two of you fighting over those odious paeans to love." I took the letters out of my pocket and set them on the desk. "Now they'll probably be evidence in a murder trial."

"Put the phone down and give Pastor Terry those letters!" Norlin demanded.

"Give him the letters, Monk. Please," Sterling croaked.

"To do what?" I sent Gallegos another text. "No one's leaving here. The three of you are responsible for six murders. And how many of those women were you fucking, the three of you?"

"They weren't women," Vern sneered. "They were men pretending to be women, violating God's laws." He looked at Pastor Terry, who looked away. "I have God's will as my guide. I am his servant."

"Ah, yes, murder in the name of the Lord. The self-appointed right to do whatever you think is in God's interest, whether God commands it or not," I said. "I've heard it over and over again from zealots like you. God as the justification of your bigotry. Pathetic."

"They were no longer God's children—"

"Vern!" The pastor rose. "You shouldn't say that."

Vern Norlin's face tightened. "God knows my true heart and will forgive me."

"You three are something else. Two self-loathing cocksuckers and a sociopath." Norlin pulled the garrote tight. Sterling struggled to breathe. I pulled the 45 from my pocket and pointed it at Vern's head. "Let him go."

"Vern please," Pastor Terry cried, "stop this!"

Vern laughed, pulling the garrote tighter. "God will not let you stop me! You don't have—"

A 45-caliber automatic makes a fearful noise in a closed room. It's a big nasty gun. The back of Norlin's head blew off before he could finish his smart-assed remark. The two of them fell to the floor, Sterling desperately trying to loosen the garrote still in the clenched fists of the dead zealot. I set the 45 on the desk and helped Sterling free himself. Out of the corner of my eye, I saw Pastor Terry try to leave.

"Stick around, Mr. Stanton."

"I'm going to—" The vomit spewed out from between his fingers. He, too, fell to the floor, crying. There were sirens in the distance. I sat down in the other purple velvet chair, waiting as two grown men cried and two others were dead.

I didn't have to wait long.

There was a pounding on the front door. I got up and let the police in. Detective Gallegos arrived not long after. Soon, the street was lined with police cars, fire trucks, and aid cars. Everything in front of the house was cordoned off.

I was thirsty. As it was on the way, I grabbed a bottle of water from the fridge. "I don't think they'll mind."

The detective didn't see the humor in that.

We were directed outside as the police went about their work. There were a lot of questions about who killed who, and why we were here. The next stop was police headquarters for statements. Mallory was there. Humored, no doubt, by another of my escapades. I called Ms. Lagenfelder to let her know, and to have her let Agnes know. I expected to be here a while.

Stanton corroborated my statement as to how and why I ended up shooting Vern Norlin, but was hesitant to say more. Probably for the best. As for Sterling's interrogation, I asked if I could be there. This was turned down, so while Gallegos talked with Sterling, I traded pleasantries with Jackson Mallory.

"Who killed Orestra Blakely?" he asked. Might as well get to the heart of it.

"I'd ask Aisha Diamond. Have you picked her up yet? I gave Detective Gallegos an idea of where to find her." Mallory shrugged. "I assume it was either her or Vern Norlin. I don't know all the ins and outs with Aisha and Stanton, or Sterling, or where Norlin fits in, whether he was involved sexually, or just doing God's work. Pastor Terry would know. But at this point, he's probably clammed up. My personal opinion is that Aisha played both sides because she believed they both played her, and she wanted some kind of payback. Maybe she was hoping for a little blackmail of her own. I'm sure she was watching Stanton and Flavius, and she had my idiot brother by his..." I think Mallory got my drift.

A uniformed officer came into the room and whispered something to Mallory. Mallory nodded, and the officer left. "Ms. Diamond was just picked up."

"And her disguise?" I had an idea.

A thin smile came to the detective. "Aisha Diamond was dressed in men's clothing."

"Where?"

"Across from your building," he said. "How'd you know?"

"A little bird and an observant homeless man named Ronnie Delmar, who noticed our black Russian," was my answer. "I'm pretty sure Aisha's the one who assaulted Ronnie."

Mallory made a note on the pad of paper he had with him. "Why would she attack Ronnie?"

"Ronnie told me he got too close."

Detective Gallegos came in. "We're going to release you and your brother, Mr. Buttman. That doesn't mean you're free and clear, understand?"

I got up. "I do. And maybe I should expect a visit in the next few days?"

"That's up to you," she said. "Don't leave town without informing us."

I smiled at that. "I might have an important meeting with a Russian oligarch off the coast of Mexico. If I do, I'll pass it along."

Mallory rolled his eyes and waved me off.

I grabbed Sterling in the lobby. He had the foolish idea he had lucked out. "Let's go."

He tried to pull away. "I'm going home!"

"After our talk, lover-boy." I hustled him to a waiting cab. My car had been impounded. Fortunately, the foundation wasn't too far of a ride. Once inside my office, I pointed to a chair. "Sit down."

He rubbed the red welts on his neck. "You can't keep me here!"

"I can always send you back to the fuzz," I said, reaching for the whiskey.

"They let me go," he whined.

"Uh-huh. And when I tell them about the necklace, your stupid ass is going to be on the line in a murder investigation, if it isn't already." I pulled out a glass. "Want any?" He nodded. I grabbed another glass.

"Where'd you get the necklace you gave Felicia? And don't tell me some antique shop in Napa." I handed him his glass of whiskey.

Staring at the glass, he said, "Aisha."

"And where'd she get it?" I drank mine.

"I don't know."

I threw my glass at him. Unfortunately, I missed. He just sat there; a sad, wounded look on his face. "I'm going to let you in on one of your girlfriend's little secrets. The last time I saw that necklace, it was around Orestra Blakely's neck. I asked her about it. It was her grandmother's. So how did Aisha get her hands on it? Are you connecting the dots here, Sterling? Are you beginning to understand the gravity of the situation? This put you as an accessory to murder. Unless, of course, you were there helping her bash in Orestra's brains."

He set the glass on the desk and stared at the floor.

"You think it's going to be tough telling Felicia that you lied about continuing to come down here to fuck your sweetheart, but your sweetheart put your stupid ass in a sling with that necklace. Now, where did she get it?"

"I don't know, I don't KNOW!" He was crying.

I didn't care. "Has it occurred to you that maybe part of the plan was for Vern Norlin to kill you, to get you out of the way? Was he supposed to be there?"

More crying.

I had more questions, but suddenly felt very tired. My hands were shaking such that I had to hold them together. After a moment, I handed Sterling the tissues from my desk. "I'll get you a cab."

•   •   •   •   •

I had my head under the water. It felt good. Agnes had questions, as did Rebekah, but I waved them off. "Later. Pool time...and order a pizza."

Because the Dart had been impounded, I had to take another cab ride. I thought about asking Agnes to come get me, but didn't want the questions. After dinner, after a silly Disney movie by the pool, I was ready to talk.

"So, talk," my loving wife chided, pointing her glass of wine at me.

"Flavius and his wife are dead—"

"Yeah, we heard that, Dad." Rebekah sat back. "What else?"

"I killed a man named Vern Norlin because he was strangling Sterling. The fuzz took my 45, too." I leaned in, as the three of them—Fidel having joined us—shocked at being in the presence of a killer, did as well. "Remember the necklace Sterling gave Felicia? The one she was showing off at the farm?" Three nods. "It belonged to Orestra Blakely. Sterling owned up that he got it from Aisha. The problem is, Orestra had it on the night she was killed. So how did Aisha get it? I assume you know where this puts Sterling. So, for now, this is between us, capeesh?" Three more nods.

Agnes finished her glass of wine. "Now the whole story, Sunshine."

•   •   •   •   •

I finished the whole story, took my leave, and went to bed. I spent the night reliving the moment the back of Vern Norlin's head blew off and the strange look on his face as he fell. The serene calmness I felt as I put the gun to his head. Sterling desperately grasping at the cord around his neck; his own special necklace, a gift from his lover. The way his eyes searched for some explanation for his nearly being murdered. It all drifted away into darkness.

I must have gotten some sleep, since the next thing I knew, an impatient grandson was telling me to get up. "I'm hungry, Gamps."

"You have a mother."

"I like your food better," he said, rather emphatically.

"Your mother sent you here, didn't she?" I gave him the stink eye.

He tried to play it straight, but couldn't pull it off, a smile crossing his face. "Yeah."

"Go tell mommy I'll be out when I'm ready," I huffed.

"But we're starving, Gamps!" Lizzy had joined the act.

"Uh-huh." I pointed to the door. "Out. Both of you." They took off laughing.

After dragging my sorry butt out of bed and feeding the rabble, I was mercifully given most of the day off to lie in the sun and pretend that more terrible shit was not on the horizon. In fact, the rest of the day was deeply surreal. Because of that, I hoped for a quiet weekend, but that was quashed by Detective Gallegos and Marsyas Durant.

The detective wanted to meet. Durant wanted to let me know Zosima was interested, and wanted my terms. I agreed to meet the detective downtown. My terms for Zosima were simple: Josef and his family would be allowed to leave Russia and Natalya was to be left alone.

It all seemed pretty straightforward.

44

Saturday morning, I was back at police headquarters, waiting for Detective Gallegos. Other than the necklace, I didn't think there was anything for me to add. The detective had a bit of a smirk on her face when she came for me, something of a change from her usual strictly business approach. "Aisha Diamond would like to speak to you."

"Does she?" Why? "Has she been charged with anything?"

"We haven't charged you with anything yet."

I smiled at that. "Something to look forward to. I'm assuming an inquest. Will you be present when we talk?"

"Yes."

"Then time's a wasting," I said.

Aisha Diamond was brought into one of the nicer interview rooms where Detective Gallegos and I were waiting. There was water and coffee. The coffee was strong and bitter. Apropos, I thought. Aisha, her hair short, was dressed in a shiny blue pantsuit. Light makeup. Evidently, she hadn't been holed up at the county jail. Detective Gallegos sensed my surprise.

"She was given bail."

"Sunlight Ministries?" I asked.

"Through an intermediary," the detective answered.

Aisha smiled at that. "We have things to work out."

I poured myself a cup of joe. "No doubt. Why did you want to talk to me? What's there to say?"

"I wanted to talk to Sterling, but he won't see me."

"Maybe that's because he was nearly strangled and you had a hand in it," I said between sips.

Aisha frowned at that. "He was only there to make sure Flavius got the letters. I didn't think Michael would be there, or that bastard Norlin."

"Who's Michael?" though it seemed obvious.

Aisha sat back, her hands in her lap. She turned her head towards the door. "Michael is what Terrance Stanton called himself when we met him on the beach in Santa Monica. We—"

"We?" the detective asked.

"LaToya, Sam, Janisha, and me. We liked to run around together, have fun. You know?" I nodded. "That's where we met him. We got to talking. He was sweet, kind, and liked to laugh. He bought us lunch. Asked if he could see me again. That's how it started."

My turn. "You didn't know he was a well-known pastor in Pasadena?"

A petulant smile came over Aisha Diamond. "I don't go to church anymore."

I took another sip. The coffee was bad. "Why did you kill Orestra Blakely?"

"Norlin killed her," Aisha said.

I looked hard at her. "But she was supposed to meet you, not Norlin or Pastor Terry. You! That's how you ended up with her necklace. And then you had the gall to give it to Sterling, who stupidly gave it to his wife. Right?"

Aisha's eyes tightened. "It was my necklace! I let Orestra borrow it. I..." she reached for a cup of water, then changed her mind. "I was supposed to meet Michael that night. But I was frightened. LaToya, Sam, and Tanisha had gone missing. I heard that Orestra was looking for them, that she was a detective. So I thought if she was there with me, it would be ok. So, I set it up for her to meet me, but I was late, and when I got there, I saw Norlin standing over her. He didn't see me. I watched as he took her purse and ran off. I...I moved closer and...it was so terrible, but I noticed my necklace and I wanted it back, so, I... I took it." She turned to me. "I don't know why I gave the necklace to Sterling, maybe—"

"Maybe what?" the detective asked.

I answered. "So that maybe, like with Michael and Sunlight Ministries, you'd have yourself a nice little bargaining chip for later. You're very clever. Hiding in plain sight, keeping an eye on us all, though it wasn't very nice of you to assault Ronnie."

"You think you know it all, don't you, Sunshine?" A tight little smile found her thin lips. "What do you know? I know guys like you, like Michael, who have the run of the town." Aisha leaned towards me. "People like you don't disappear. They don't end up in the morgue, unknown and forgotten. Your family doesn't spit on you and kick you out."

"No," I said, "they shipped me off to Virginia."

Aisha leaned back. "Well, I got shipped here." She smiled at that. "I like it here. There are people like *me* here. And if that means I have to protect myself, if I have to find my own—"

"Fools?"

"Call them what you like. We have our connections, our desires. I like Sterling, the sex is good. We like being together," she said. "But Michael. He was different. Not just some goodtime Charlie, who liked to fuck. I thought...but that was a mistake."

I tried one last sip. "That's when you found out about his preaching gig? That's when he took you to his church?"

"We went on our own. I found out about Sunlight Ministries at one of the meetings at the outreach center. A brochure was handed around. I recognized Michael's face. I was stunned. I didn't believe it. So, I got my sisters together, and we went and checked it out. And sure enough, there he was in that great big auditorium preaching about how God was going to save them from the sins of people like me, people who were *subverting* the fabric of America." Aisha smiled to herself. "The same words I heard in my family's church back in Texas before they kicked me out. I meant to confront him there, in his precious church, but I...I couldn't do it."

"That's when the letters started?"

"Yeah, letters. I don't know why. And it turns out he didn't write them! He had that bastard Norlin write them. He lied to him, too! Told him they were to some cis woman he once knew. Then I did something really stupid." Aisha, her eyes red and wet, looked away for a moment. "I...I confronted him with my sisters by my side. Him and that bastard Norlin. He was all kinds of sorry and all that. Promised to make things right. And I thought, maybe... But then Sam disappeared and no one knew where she was. Then Tanisha. Then LaToya. That's when I went to talk to Orestra. She said she'd look into it, found out that they'd been contacted by someone at Sunlight Ministries before they disappeared. Then out of the blue, Michael wanted to talk, so I set up the meeting with Orestra, so she'd be there."

"But you didn't tell her Stanton would be there, did you?" Gallegos asked.

"I wanted to surprise Michael. But it didn't turn out like I thought, so..."

"So, you decide to play Sterling and me." Sterling and me. "Drop hints, like letters planted in Orestra's apartment; directing me to a P.O. box, where I'd find the keys to O's office and home. Right? And Sterling?"

She shrugged. "He was mad at you for telling his wife about us, and he knew you had people who would help; people who wouldn't help me. He said it was exciting. It turned him on."

That made me think of Agnes and Sobeski. "I imagine so."

Detective Gallegos, who had mostly listened, had a few more questions. "So, what was the endgame here? What was supposed to happen at Flavius' house?"

Aisha ran her fingers along the edge of the table. "I met Flavius not long after I got here. Met some interesting people through him. When I heard they'd had their own run-ins with Sunlight, I called to see if they'd like a little leverage. I wanted to put some pressure on Michael. So did Flavius. Use the letters, get a little something out of it." Aisha glared at the detective. "You weren't going to save me from those bastards any more than you saved Sam, or LaToya. I had myself to think about. I didn't think he was stupid enough to bring along that bastard Norlin. That's on Michael."

"Anything else?" I asked.

She looked at me. "I'm sorry about... Ronnie. He startled me, so I hit him and ran."

"Sure." I got up. "And Sterling?"

"He'll get over it," she said. "They always do."

As the detective was walking me out, she had a question for me. "Do you believe her?"

·   ·   ·   ·   ·

The Dart was released on Monday, the same day that Natalya came back from her trip to New York; the same day Isaac returned from the Legion convention; the same day I got word that the meeting with Dimitriev was set. Thursday night. International waters off the coast of Mexico. I let Agnes know.

"How dressy should I be?" she purred.

I rolled my eyes. "You better hope we make it back alive."

"Like they're going to bump off Durant and me," she snarked.

I let Bernie and Art know about the meeting. Whether I'd hear from Fairfax...

The days moved along. There was a concert at the Manifesto with Anna's boyfriend, Jerome. Mikal's trio opened the show with a guest singer named Joanie Whalen. Orville Riley showed up with his wife, Coretta. Whether he read, or would ever read, O's letter, I didn't know or ask. Xavier brought Natalya, who had gone on and on at the office about what a wonderful time she'd had. I missed her more reserved and haughty persona.

"So, it appears it all went well," I said to Xavier.

"We had a nice time," he said, smiling.

Everyone had a nice time. Everybody smiling.

Pastor Terry was in seclusion, shocked, as was the Sunlight Ministries congregation, by the events that unfolded at the house of one Berkey Fellows, known of late, as Flavius. I assumed they were hard at work at how to distance Stanton from his previously close personal aide, who now appeared to be a sociopathic killer. They had time, money, and a whole army of expensive attorneys to work the system and the media. Whether Aisha could work the system was an open question.

.   .   .   .   .

Thursday morning, bright and early, we headed down to A and A. Durant was waiting. A and A had given notice to the LAPD that I'd be out of town, but would return within twenty-four hours. It was time for the three of us to go over our plans for the meeting, though it was, to me, relatively straightforward: In exchange for what I knew about Sobeski, the Russians would free Josef and his family.

A and A's coffee was infinitely better than the LAPD's.

"What's this Dimitriev guy like?" Agnes was slipping into her hard-boiled private dick mode.

"He's a very gregarious individual. Nothing like the image of a stone-faced Soviet," Durant answered.

That jibed with what Anton had told me the day before. "All smiles. It's the other guys around him," he said, as he ran his thumb across his throat.

"And since he agreed to this meeting, he's ready to deal?" Agnes continued.

"Yes. The big question is whether they agree that it's worth the price of Mr. Rostikov and his family." Durant looked my way. "Do you agree, Monk?"

"I think it'll give them a clearer path forward," was my answer.

A limo whisked us to a Private jet at LAX, which flew us to Ensenada. There, we were met by Eric Nakatomi.

"Surprise, surprise," was Agnes response to seeing him.

Nakatomi nodded but didn't speak.

From Ensenada, we boarded a helicopter, which delivered us to another beautiful yacht floating on the surface of the vast Pacific Ocean.

Manaforte and a man I assumed to be Piotr Dimitriev were waiting on the ship's helipad.

45

"Welcome aboard, my friends," he said, offering his hand. "Delton, I believe, you know."

"We do indeed." I took his hand. A nice firm handshake. "I want to thank you for your warm hospitality." I gestured towards Agnes. "This is my wife, who will be joining us."

Dimitriev took Agnes' hand and bowed slightly. "So I am to understand. This way, please."

Much like Manaforte's yacht, Dimitriev's was spacious and bright, with multiple well-designed decks and staterooms. Lunch was on the owner's deck in its sprawling salon. Joining us were Tsarnaev, Josef Rostikov, and his wife, Anya. Their two boys were being watched on a lower deck. Neither seemed particularly upbeat. Neither spoke. Most of the talking was courtesy of our host. He was, as everyone noted, gregarious and outgoing. The menu featured Russian and Eastern European dishes, fine caviars, wines, and, surprisingly, French pastries.

"I have a soft spot for those," he enthused.

"They're very good," I agreed.

In conversation, our host bemoaned the strained relations between Russia and the U.S. "It's too bad that some feel it must be one way or another, but that there's no room for both. We come from different histories, no? Better to have many approaches rather than so few. Don't you agree?" Dimitriev asked.

"Here the question is how much say the people should have," Durant countered.

"True, but as Mr. Manaforte will tell you, the people are not always the best to decide where important matters are concerned. Too easily are they distracted, too easily do their emotions get the best of them." Dimitriev turned to Manaforte. "Yes, Delton?"

"I haven't been shy about my concerns for an educated electorate and the privilege to vote, to have a say," he answered.

And on and on.

Much as I wanted to butt-in, I decided to listen rather than speak. Besides, I was more interested in the food. Agnes was bored to tears, whispering to me, "If we don't get on with this, I'm going to take a bottle of wine and get drunk in a lounge chair out on the deck!"

"Now, now," I whispered back, "they're all decks. You mean the salon," knowing it'd irk her.

"Uh-huh."

Fortunately, lunch did not linger for too long. The table was cleared, and we moved to where the couches and chairs were. Josef's wife left to be with the boys. That left Dimitriev, Manaforte, Tsarnaev, Durant, Josef, Agnes, and me. The good cheer from lunch quickly dissipated into the salt air. Dimitriev motioned to me.

"I think it's time for this business of Mr. Sobeski to be resolved. Mr. Buttman?"

"I agree. I'm tired of being asked about it." For some reason, I felt the need to be on my feet, be able to move. I got up. "I asked for this meeting in order to get Mr. Rostikov out of trouble. Some of that is his doing, some of it is Mr. Manaforte's, some of it is mine. All of it revolves around the disappearance of Aaron Alan Sobeski. Everyone from the government to groups such as yours, Mr. Dimitriev, have been unusually interested in what happened to Sobeski. I get the feeling he's having quite the time with this."

That got me quite a few looks.

I walked over to where Agnes was sitting and stood behind her. "So, what happened? In brief, Sobeski and two thugs accosted me and my wife at our home in Michigan. Ironically, but probably not, it happened on the same day the President of the United States was attacked by one of his Secret Service agents. Mr. Rostikov was with us, but he was working for Sobeski at the behest of Mr. Manaforte. We were to be killed and so was Sobeski, though I assume he wasn't aware of this."

Manaforte nodded when I looked his way.

"Obviously, the three of us survived. At the time, I thought myself quite clever. I had outwitted someone who was presented to me as a top assassin. A man known for his ingenious and nearly undetectable killings."

"What are you saying, Mr. Buttman?" Tsarnaev asked.

"Do you think he's dead?" I asked him.

"They tell me his is," Dimitriev answered.

The big question. "Do you believe them?"

"You tell me," he said.

"Have you met Sobeski, Mr. Dimitriev?"

Dimitriev shifted in his chair. "No."

"Have you, Mr. Manaforte?"

"Yes, I have," Manaforte admitted.

I removed the picture from my pocket and gave it to Manaforte. "Is that him?"

"Yes." He handed it back to me.

I gave it to Josef. "Is this the man we killed?"

He shook his head. "No." He gave the picture back to me.

I handed it to Dimitriev. "You wanted to know what happened to Sobeski. The answer is simple. Nothing. He conned you, either directly, through Manaforte, or through someone else. But the man who presented himself as Sobeski to us, the one we killed and blew to pieces on Lake Michigan, was not the real Sobeski. *He* is still out there." I watched as Dimitriev considered this. "But I think you suspected that. That's why Mr. Rostikov could not leave. Why Ms. Constantinescu was pushed into betraying Kovalenko, but that had the advantage of being two birds with one stone. Big Mike was another headache."

Dimitriev smiled and said, "Perhaps." He handed the picture back.

I put it away. "And this corroborates what Josef, Mr. Rostikov, told you."

"It does."

"And our bargain?" I was ready to leave.

Dimitriev looked at Josef and tapped his finger along the edge of the chair. "Assuming you're willing to cover his debts, I see no reason not to allow it." He rose and approached Josef. "If you like your nose, keep it clean." Josef nodded. "Good." Dimitriev came to me, all smiles now, and put his hands on my shoulders. "I'll confess that I had doubts, Mr. Buttman. But Delton assured me that, while maybe not as clever as Sobeski, you're not to be dismissed too lightly. Have a safe trip back."

I smiled back. "Mr. Dimitriev."

There were minor pleasantries for Agnes and Durant as we were walked back to the helicopter. Josef and his family's meager belongings were put on board. I made sure he and his family got on before I did. Nakatomi, as before, joined us for the flight back to Ensenada, and the private plane that got us back to LA. Little was said. It wasn't until we were on the ground and through customs that Josef broke down, falling to his knees. His wife, also in tears, thanked us again and again.

"No worries," I said.

I promised Durant we'd be by later to talk. I was exhausted.

Anton was there to welcome Josef and his family home when we dropped them off. Time to pass the baton. Soon enough, we were back at my fancy place. I called Bernie and Art. Both were mildly surprised Dimitriev let Josef go.

"There's a certain element of cruelty in the Russian spirit," Bernie said. "A great love for the idea of Russian solidarity, but also a deep level of suspicion from a long history of oppression."

"So I noted. Think it's over?" I was curious what he thought.

"I wish I could say yes," was his answer.

That was Art's answer as well.

•　•　•　•　•

Life, as always, persevered. There was the matter of getting Emily registered for school. She could barely contain herself once the good news was given, but she had to stay on the farm through the rest of the summer, and she had to test out for the school district so they'd know what level of competency she had so far achieved. She didn't care. All that mattered was she was going to live the LA life. Calista wasn't thrilled, but was ready to move on.

Zach, much as I hated to admit it, was becoming more of a pest, more demanding, much like his mother at that age.

"Hearsay," was Rebekah's response when I brought it up.

Lizzy was her usual adorable self, which she took full advantage of, to Zach's continuing disapproval. He was certain she was up to no good, and she probably was, but he could produce no proof.

"Sorry, dude," was my answer to most of his entreaties.

Jacob, after scorning his mother for most of the first year of his life, of late, decided to be more appreciative. I took full credit for it, telling my unbelieving daughter I had been lobbying him to be nice for some time.

"Uh-huh," was all she'd agree to.

The inquest into the death of Vern Norlin was a perfunctory affair as the DA, with input from A and A—money being what it is in this country concerning legal representation—had already decided that I would not be charged. Still, it required testimony from those of us there. Sterling described how he was sure Norlin was going to kill him; Pastor Terry how Norlin was a disturbed individual who misunderstood how God wanted us to deal with those who had fallen from the true path; and I testified that I feared for Sterling's life, and under the stress of the moment blew out Norlin's brains versus clinically shooting him in, say, the knee. The police introduced evidence that pointed to Norlin as being responsible for the deaths of Berkley and Gisele Fellows, which drew media protests because Flavius no longer used that gender identity or name.

Outside of his testimony, as expected, Terrance Stanton withdrew from public life, taking a sabbatical from the pulpit to reassess his actions, and re-devote himself to our Lord and Savior Jesus Christ. The video on the Sunlight Ministries website showed his stone-faced wife diligently standing behind him. Very Russian. Agnes, watching with me, told me not to expect her to do the same should I fall down the rabbit hole as Pastor Terry and Sterling did.

Sterling, now separated from Felicia, made up a story about the necklace being stolen property. He returned the necklace to me, which I returned to Orinda Blakely. They had wondered about it, and were glad to have it back in the family. Aisha was still under investigation. Ronnie refused to press charges, so she was cleared of that. It was whether Norlin had killed Orestra, or if she had.

I don't know if Orville ever read Orestra's letter, but I chose to believe he did. I had a big speech mentally prepared should he ask me about his longtime friend. I asked Orinda about it when I gave her the necklace. She said that, like Jordan Blakely, it was unlikely that Orville would ever talk much about it, if at all.

"He did say he missed her," she said.

And lastly, I bought the Forester-Gertner Homestead.

Whether I'd let the farm use it, I hadn't decided. I did decide it was important to keep Moses a little worked up about something.

46

Fairfax caught up with me as I watched the kids at the park. Rebekah had work to do and needed a break. Emily was off with Natalya, buying clothes for school. Agnes was finishing a quilt and didn't need the distraction of Zach whining about Lizzy. Jacob was asleep in his stroller. Like the last two times, Fairfax had his dog with him. He sat next to me on the bench.

"How long have you known Sobeski?" I asked.

"I brought him into the company. And when he left, I kept tabs on him." He reached in his pocket for a treat. "I understand the meeting with Dimitriev went well."

"Well enough," I said. "My only interest was in getting Josef and his family out of Russia."

He gave the treat to the dog. "I'm curious how you figured out the ruse."

I smiled at that. "I'd like to think I picked up on it right away, but in truth, it only occurred to me after you started asking questions. Like I told Zosima, I thought I was pretty clever in one upping him, but the more I thought about what I was told about him, and the murders leading up to his attempt to kill me and Agnes, I realized it didn't quite smell right—"

"In what way?"

"Well, either he wasn't as good as people said, or he was playing us all for fools. Consider the amateurish deaths of Loran Tasabian and his two henchmen. He hung himself and then somehow untied his hands after he died. And the henchmen's car obviously had its brake lines cut. Yet when my Ford Galaxie was examined by Javier, not only was a crude tracking device found but also a very sophisticated bomb attacked to the gas tank. That was his clever way of giving anyone who knew better a signal. Bernie and Javier knew of his work. That's what clued them in. Then there was all the interest by the Russians. Why would they care? If the guy's dead, he's dead. Move on. There are more guys out there. Obviously, there's more to it, but I don't have any interest in that. It's their problem now." I watched as Zach and his new pal Teo raced around the Jungle Gym. "I have my grandkids to deal with."

"There's always that."

"Besides, if he draws close, I'll know by your presence." I ran my hand along the dog's fur. "He's avoiding you, isn't he?"

Fairfax stood. "Yes." The dog got up when Fairfax raised his hand.

I looked up at him. "The others in your line of work don't think this is over. Do you?"

"I expect we'll find out soon enough. Goodbye."

That was that.

     •   •   •   •   •

I had expected to run into Fairfax. Monika Danalek was another matter. Natalya and Emily had dragged me down to a gallery I didn't want to go to. "You promised, Mr. Monk," Natalya admonished.

It was there I bumped into Monika. She came up behind me, curves and all, her scent filling my senses. "Monk, it's so good to see you. Why don't you buy me lunch?"

I looked over at my disapproving chief of staff. "So long as it's only lunch. I'm pretty sure I've something to do later."

"Only lunch." She smiled at Natalya. "I'll see he gets back in one piece, my dear."

I don't think Natalya was convinced.

Lunch was down the street. Quaint little place. Nuevo Italian. Not a lot of ambient light. A bit pricey.

"Still in love?" she asked.

"Still in love," I said.

She put a finger in her mouth and grinned. "Do you ever think about our brief encounter?"

I smiled back. "Every once in a while."

We ordered our food and drinks between small talk about what she was up to, what I was up to. I might not be into transwomen, but I knew my weakness was a woman like Monika Danalek. She knew it, too. That made me think of two things, both relating to my foolish brother. I no longer considered him an idiot. He simply couldn't say no. That was the first thing; his desire, his lust for Aisha Diamond.

"You're thinking hard, Monk. Of what?"

"Desire," I said, before telling her Sterling's sordid tale.

"My." She said, after I finished. "The things people do." I cocked my head, which she laughed at. "Am I that bad?" Then she said, "It's the desire, isn't it?"

"You tell me?"

She shook her finger at me. "No, your turn."

That was the other thing. "Alright. A few years back, I was walking along Hollywood Boulevard. I don't remember why. I was dressed nice, a beautiful houndstooth jacket; I remember that. And I was at a corner waiting for the light when a couple of young girls approached me. They said I looked nice. I said, thanks. They then said that for five-hundred dollars, one would suck my cock while the other gave me a rim job. They didn't look to be more than sixteen, if that. Didn't look homeless or strung-out. They were cute, pixyish. And I'll admit, for a nanosecond, I was tempted. But they were still teenagers, so I said no." I leaned back in my chair, staring at Monika's fine curves and her inviting mouth. "But I wasn't the only well-dressed older man on Hollywood Boulevard that day. So, I assume they made their five-hundred dollars or more. After all, it's only sex, right?"

"To some," she said. "To some, it's much more."

"No matter how it might fuck up their life?" I asked, smiling.

"They never think of that," she answered.

Lunch was over. As we stood, ready to leave, Monika Danalek pulled me closed and kissed me, then ran her hand along the ferocious hard-on she knew I had. "As long as you think about it."

Thank God, it was only lunch.

·　　·　　·　　·　　·

I was headed back to the office. Agnes texted: *On my way to A and A. Meet you there.* For a moment, I didn't understand. That's right, the FBI. They wanted to talk to us, and we'd agreed to meet them at Aeschylus and Associates with Ms. Lagenfelder present.

Be there soon, I texted back, and put the phone in the pocket of my jacket.

I don't remember the car, only the pops and being knocked to the ground.

Pain radiated through my head and shoulder.

The light began to thin...

Emptying...

Into white.

Read on for a look at the next exciting installment in the Monk Buttman Series:

INTO WHITE

Two more reports.

It was all Detective Jackson Mallory cared about: Two more reports. He stared at the computer screen with no desire to continue. It was hot. The AC was down. Someone said the compressor was shot. It was that kind of day. Three shootings. Three reports. The cursor was blinking at him.

Next to his left hand was a pencil, worn and abused. He'd had it for almost ten years, maybe more. It must be more; it was pre-computer, a reminder of the good old days, when reports were filled out by hand. He could feel his fingers cramp just thinking about it. He took a drink of the warm soda and closed his eyes.

Two more reports.

"No rest for the weary, eh, Jack?"

Mallory opened his eyes to see his old partner, Lt. Louis Descartes, leaning against the doorframe.

"What brings you my way, Lou? Laughs?"

Descartes shook his head. "Still pissed? It's bad for your heart, Jack. No, I was sent here special…" He waited till he had Mallory's full and undivided attention.

Mallory knew the drill. "Alright, what?"

"There's been a shooting in West Hollywood."

"Send Murtagh, I'm slammed."

"Can't. They want you on this," Descartes said. "Captain Goncalves called."

"Goncalves?" Mallory didn't like that; it meant big shots were involved, pressing their thumbs, wanting answers. Quick. "Why? Whose been shot?"

"A man named Buttman," he said.

"Buttman?" Mallory was momentarily confused. "Monk Buttman?"

"How many Buttmans do you know? They want *you* down there, Jack." Descartes waited till Mallory had gotten out of his chair and picked his jacket off the hook by the door. "Take Gallegos with you."

Mallory sighed. "What do you know about this, Lou?"

Louis Descartes took a hankie out of his pocket and wiped the sweat off his brow. "That they want you on this, Jack."

Evidently, the reports could wait.

About the Author

An engineer for 40 years, Mr. Pearce, following open-heart surgery, decided to pursue his muse and write. He is the author of the *Monk Buttman Mystery* series. When not writing, Mr. Pearce is the accomplished recording artist, Mr. Primitive. He and his wife live in Kenmore, Washington.

Thank you so much for reading one of
David William Pearce's novels.

If you enjoyed the experience,
please check out where it all began.

Where Fools Dare to Tread by David William Pearce

It's easy to be a nobody when you've got nothing to lose, but with his life and potential redemption on the line, can Monk be a somebody people will remember?

Note from David William Pearce

Word-of-mouth is crucial for any author to succeed. If you enjoyed *The Object of Our Desire*, please leave a review online—anywhere you are able. Even if it's just a sentence or two. It would make all the difference and would be very much appreciated.

Thanks!
David William Pearce

We hope you enjoyed reading this title from:

www.blackrosewriting.com

Subscribe to our mailing list – *The Rosevine* – and receive **FREE** books, daily
deals, and stay current with news about upcoming
releases and our hottest authors.
Scan the QR code below to sign up.

Already a subscriber? Please accept a sincere thank you for being a fan of
Black Rose Writing authors.

View other Black Rose Writing titles at
www.blackrosewriting.com/books and use promo code
PRINT to receive a **20% discount** when purchasing.

www.ingramcontent.com/pod-product-compliance
Lightning Source LLC
Chambersburg PA
CBHW051438190726
48289CB00001B/236